Anywhen

Beth Duke

ANYWHEN

Copyright © 2024 by Beth Dial Duke

No part of this publication may be reproduced, distributed, or transmitted in any form or by any means, including photocopying, recording, or other electronic or mechanical methods, without the legal permission of the author. The story, names, characters, and incidents portrayed in this book are fictitious. No identification with actual persons or places is intended or should be inferred unless stated otherwise.

ISBN 979-8-218-51719-9

www.bethduke.com

*To my book club women everywhere
You've given me love, laughter, and memories
I'll always treasure.
This one's for you, and I hope it leads to
pineapple upside down cakes and 60s music
and bell bottoms*

and me.

Art decorates walls
music decorates time
books decorate our minds
people decorate our hearts

"The important thing that you've proven to the world
is that a half a million kids – and I call you kids because I have
children that are older than you are – a half million young
people can get together and have three days of fun and music
and have nothing but fun and music, and I – God bless you for
it!"

*Max Yasgur, owner of the dairy farm where
The Woodstock Music and Art Fair was held in 1969*

PART I

1

Unity SE35.86

DECEMBER 9, 2101

As I type this on an antique "laptop" a chittering monkey sits opposite me and watches, occasionally lifting a paw to his mouth and gnawing at it. I have never seen him before and likely won't again.

He is an apparition, an artificial intelligence-generated manifestation of my nervousness.

I am your direct descendant and so is this situation. So, it seems a good way to introduce myself and the world I live in. The work you did at the dawn of artificial intelligence led to this incredible place, well over a century later.

The first known instance of animagenesis (animal genesis) was two years ago in what you'd have known as Coventry, England. A woman slammed the door of her homepod and stalked away from her husband as passersby stared at the Bengal tiger padding along slightly behind her, baring its teeth at those in proximity.

Of course, no one has seen a Bengal tiger in more than fifty years. All of Unity NE521.5 was terrified until the truth was known. They cowered indoors well after the tiger strolled out of sight with the oblivious, furious wife.

Then, people all over Unity started having animals appear, always reflecting their moods. My neighbor, when he became eligible to begin his Reproduction Cycle, was accompanied everywhere by a panting labrador retriever whose penis was exposed like a 20th century lipstick. A lady who lives by the town square walks to the park alongside a sloth; her male companion occasionally appears with a menacing wolf.

I think the monkey is here because I finally decided to sit down and write to you. I'm generating text on paper with this computer and printer my friend Daniel found and persuaded to work.

These days, we all find the animals amusing, if a little embarrassing sometimes. I thought you'd be interested in them as an illustration of how far artificial intelligence has come since the days of your research.

I'm called Baezy (rhymes with daisy). I'm almost thirty-two years old and you are my M5, my great-great-great-grandmother on the maternal side. You're a legend to me for so many reasons, Kelly Jean Adams, especially your experience at Woodstock. Does it surprise you we know all about that? Well, the year I was born was the centennial anniversary of The Woodstock Music and Art Fair, of all things hippie, peace, and flower power. Much of the world went crazy in 2069 with celebrations; there were holos on every town square of many of the original performances, and singer/actors hired to imitate Janis Joplin, Santana, and Joan Baez. (With modern prosthetics, you'd never have known the difference.)

That's where my name comes from: Joan Baez Smith. Baezy for short. My mother wore a beaded headband and bell bottom jeans; she kept a pink flower tucked behind her ear, accenting long, straight purple hair, through her entire pregnancy.

We celebrate every truth your generation realized, and I want you to know we've achieved the world you dreamed of.

You began it all, Grandmother. From crude computers to the society we've achieved through artificial intelligence and human compassion. There is no hunger here. There is no war. The average lifespan is one hundred and fifty years, thanks to our ability to eradicate disease and combat aging at a cellular level. To you, I'd look about seventeen, and I won't even begin my Reproduction Cycle until I'm at least thirty-five or forty.

Our lives hold promise like no generation's before.

My mother (your M+4, gr-gr-granddaughter) was one of the most celebrated mathematicians and physicists of the 21st century. You would be very proud of her. Her name is Anantha and along with your brilliance she has a great beauty; I can even see a bit of you in her, especially her green eyes.

Of course, human work has been supplanted by AI in her field, but Mom's still well-connected at TIP (Time Insertion Protocol). This visit with you at Woodstock is her birthday gift to me, a huge honor as there are many with greater qualifications and privileges who could be traveling instead.

Of all the times I could choose, you and the greatest gathering of love the world has seen are an irresistible combination.

I had my orientation for TIP yesterday; the first thing Faisa (more about her in a minute) told me was that I needed the 1960s language module. I already have that. It's helping me write this journal in terms you'll understand, though I have every intention of talking to you. This is merely a backup in case I don't fully materialize for your perception, especially in the first hours. (You may not be able to see or even hear me when I arrive.) TIP is a new system and there are what you would have called "glitches", though I'll be perfectly safe. And Mom has arranged seventy-two full hours at the festival. I'm confident I'll be as real to you as the friends who accompanied you to Woodstock.

I was told TIP will furnish contemporary clothing, but I have that, too: Mom's pre-pregnancy bell bottom jeans and peasant blouses (and headband!) will travel with me. Faisa says I'll be inserted in the woods near the festival. I must travel naked and my groovy threads (see?!) will be carried in the pouch that accompanies me; it will open upon entry (there's no technology in your time that could release the seal). Best of all, it looks just like a fringed suede handbag! The pouch will also hold this journal, the beacon to locate me for return (it's too big to be implanted like my chip), and a South Dakota "driver's license" for a girl named Sarah Sandoval. Sarah ran away from the Sioux Falls area in 1968. Her name and identity will be mine for the visit, for obvious reasons. In your time, people would think I've "gone ape" if I told them where I'm really from.

And if you're wondering why Sarah, it's simple. Obviously, as a runaway, her presence at Woodstock could be easily explained. More importantly, her faintly Native American features and skin tone resemble my own. The driver's license photo is an uncannily accurate match.

I should explain.

I have never really seen a Black person. I have never seen a White person, or Asian, or Latino person. The G-HOP (Genetic Homogenization & Optimization Project) in 2062 made huge strides in eradicating illness and lengthening lifespans, and it also ensured we are all One.

Like I said, the world you dreamed of.

All the knowledge I need is readily available to me. What you called "school" no longer exists, though I have to admit the idea of being at MIT in 1969 fascinates me. But can you imagine knowing everything about calculus or 20th century history or English literature in seconds? Isn't that cool? And your work made it all possible.

I'm going to stop now because Faisa (Fully Automated Integrated Support Assistant) just delivered my NC (NourishCube: it's perfectly designed for my nutrition and general health at this portion of my life). Our bodies are monitored daily and each cube is custom-formulated and brought to every person in Unity at mealtime (they are incredibly delicious and irresistible). My travel pouch will, of course, contain NCs for a full three-day period; I've been repeatedly warned about their importance during my stay with you. They'll protect me from disease and keep me healthy for my return.

As I mentioned, hunger has been completely eradicated, thanks to NourishCubes. There is no such thing as restaurants or even what you know as "food'—though it is rumored some leaders in Unity secretly meet in buildings and consume plants and animal flesh. It's unthinkable to most of us.

Faisa, by the way, is my roommate as well. She looks like a woman my age, and you probably couldn't tell she's AI-generated. Right now she's reminding me, once more, to consume my NC. Then it will be time for my exercise circuit outdoors. Maybe I'll run past Kaitlyn Connors and, if her sloth is present, I'll shoot by to inspire her.

Oh, and the monkey is gone because I feel much more settled after typing this all out for you. I have to split now (another of your words I have learned). See you soon.

Love,
Baezy

2

Massachusetts Institute of Technology

AUGUST 10, 1969

The room was small; it reminded Kelly of a kindergarten classroom, except surely kids would be afforded windows. Its walls were an unsubtle green probably designed to evoke the outdoors, a sterile, blank, unadorned field devoid of flowers or ornamentation of any kind. Spring before blooms or even buds. The temperature was ever-chilly due to attempts to maintain computer equipment, and, Kelly thought, to keep project workers alert. She regarded her companion, an annoying yet endearing math student from Delaware. Usually, Laura had the courtesy to remain quiet while Kelly scribbled calculations on the chalkboard, but she was a chatterbox that day.

"Please, KJ, please. Can you just stop being a brainiac for one minute and consider something fun?"

"My name is Kelly, Laura, and what I'm doing *is* fun." Kelly erased her latest equation with a sigh.

"Oh, *Kelly Jeannnnnn*," Laura drip-drawled an imitation of Kelly's Alabama accent as she crossed the room, waving a computer card from the box she'd been sorting. "Do not fold, spindle or mutilate my weekend, please. I'm going to this festival with Rodney, Eric, and Jack. Kristin's coming, too. That's three boys and two girls. You have to come. Rodney's already bought six tickets. Eric has the van to take us all. It'll be so much fun!" Laura placed a carnation-pink-manicured finger on Kelly's arm, tracing between her elbow and hand. "You know you want to."

Kelly clamped her mouth into a smirk and shook her head. "I am not a hippie," she said, "I am not a festival person. I'm a mathematician at MIT, developing the future of computers. My research is important; it might even lead to the artificial intelligence McCarthy and Minsky talk about. I don't want to sit in a cow pasture and pretend to like Jimi Hendrix, much less pretend to like Eric. And you know that's why you want me to go with you."

"You don't have to pretend to like Eric. He's crazy about you whether you do or not. And Jimi Hendrix isn't the only musician they'll have. Rodney says John Sebastian will be there." Laura launched into a loud, off-key screech of "Do You Believe In Magic" as she walked away, glancing over her shoulder at Kelly.

Kelly grimaced. "Not tempted. You've given me a great reason to avoid music. Maybe for the rest of my life."

"You don't have to insult my fine vocalization," Laura replied. "And with all due respect, it isn't good for you to spend every waking moment swimming in math." She paused for effect and casually added, "Oh, and there's one other singer I thought you might want to see. Joan Baez."

Kelly's eyebrows shot up. "That's not true. I would have heard."

"It is true, whether you read it in your magazine or not," Laura answered. "You'll miss your precious Joan and who knows what else if you don't go. Why would you pass up the opportunity to see the only person in the world besides yourself you regard as a genius? It's only a weekend, KJ, we'll leave there Sunday. We'll be back on campus in plenty of time for you to impress Dr. Lawton with your computations next Monday. Maybe you'll be the next rocket scientist at NASA. Maybe the first woman astronaut jumping around on the moon. Only, do it after this weekend. Please? Will you just think about it?"

Kelly exhaled, exaggerating the noise so Laura would hush. "I have nothing to wear to a music festival." She swept her hand down the front of her outfit, a sensible white blouse and paisley knee-length skirt with black tights and sturdy air-cushioned Doc Martens to walk across campus. "There will be bugs and heat and all the things I hate. And hot dogs. They'll probably have hot dog stands. I'm sorry. You'll be better off without me. I'm too old to go to a music festival."

Once again, Kelly tried to focus on her calculations.

Laura plopped down on a desk chair with a laugh and swiveled her back to face Kelly. "You're twenty-three, Elderly Spinster Adams. Come on, I'll loan you my yellow daisy sundress. You can wear my pink t-shirt and cutoff shorts—"

"That's another thing," Kelly interrupted. "Where would we even use the bathroom? Change clothes? Sleep?"

"Oh, they'll have all kinds of bathrooms built, and we'll sleep in the van while the boys stay in a tent. They've sold less than two hundred thousand tickets and the farm is huge, acres and acres for us to wander, probably stages on every corner. And I'll pack a bunch of peanut butter and jelly sandwiches so your taste buds won't be offended. Come on, KJ. Do something wild and spontaneous for once. Once in a *lifetime*."

Kelly turned to address Laura's back. "Since you acknowledged I'm a genius, I'll point out you want me along to keep Eric occupied while you sleep in the tent with Rodney and Kristin tries to seduce Jack."

Laura giggled. "Well, I'd appreciate the favor, but..." she hesitated and searched the ceiling for inspiration. "Look, you emerged from the womb crossing t's and dotting i's. You were probably solving equations in your head before you uttered your first word. You're happily following every linear rule your big, mathy brain lays out." Laura shook her hands in the air to accent her exasperation. "All of that's the reason this weekend should be important to you. Try a detour into fun, KJ. One time. Surely you know how beautiful you are, with those…moss-green…eyes and mahogany hair. You look like a model, and you spend all your time in this lab."

Kelly laughed. "Moss green and mahogany? Is that the best you could do?"

"It was extemporaneous. I'll wax more poetic if you give me a while. But please come with us, Kelly. I'll call you by your real name the whole time," Laura said. "I kind of promised Eric I'd persuade you. He doesn't even want gas money if you'll be in the van," Laura added with a bright smile.

"I'm flattered."

"There's one more thing. Rodney would kill me for even mentioning it, but there's another reason we're going."

"Is Rodney finally going to propose to you with Jimi Hendrix screeching in the background?" Kelly returned to her board and didn't offer Laura another look. "How romantic."

"I'm serious, KJ, there's something important about this trip—"

"Tell me later, maybe at dinner, Laura. For now, you have work to do. We're both way behind on this project." Kelly tilted her head and began the equation in a new way, smiling and then gaping at the inspiration she'd just had. If Laura talked any more, she wouldn't hear her, lost in the beautiful symphony of numbers and symbols in front of her.

Kelly barely noted Laura's departure, mumbling "bye" as Laura wished her a good night and said something about going to meet her boyfriend. Her stomach reminded her around 7:15 she hadn't eaten since morning. Kelly sighed and left her board reluctantly, walking through a silent parking lot to her rusted white VW Beetle. She drove past students wandering campus, some of them couples smiling as they strolled and a few solitary figures like herself, heads down as they walked. They all looked twelve years old to Kelly at this point.

Kelly entered her apartment and immediately put a frozen turkey pot pie into the oven, then poured herself a glass of Boone's Farm wine. It reminded her of PawPaw Neely's annual muscadine wine in Alabama, her first sip in MawMaw's kitchen at sixteen the most rebellious thing she'd done in her entire math-prodigy life of competitions and trophies and ultimately, a full scholarship designed to make the world think MIT was accommodating to female students.

She sank into her faded hand-me-down couch, tossing her shoes as she did. The small living room featured gold shag carpeting and a wood veneer coffee table that liked to attack Kelly's big toe in the dark, just like it did in her parents' house in Weaver, Alabama when she was a child. At 9:00 p.m., when it was affordable to use long-distance, she placed her weekly call.

"Hi, Mama," she said into the black plastic receiver, "how are y'all?" She told her mother her friends had invited her to a music festival but she probably wouldn't go.

3

Unity SE35.86

DECEMBER 10, 2101

A Typical Day in the Life of Baezy in 2101: I wake in the sleep chamber of my homepod, which is optimized for both my body temperature and spine. It might surprise you to know we sleep standing up, supported by comfortable braces and pillows. Faisa literally "tucks me in"! I'm always fully rested and alert in the morning; stimulants like the coffee you were so addicted to aren't necessary.

(I've read about insomnia in your time. People should have tried a vertical approach.)

Faisa controls the windows and everything else in my homepod. At 0800 hours she opens shades to reveal the exterior view of my choice; today it's an image of Max Yasgur's Bethel dairy farm in 1969, shortly before Woodstock. I've been studying it for a while, staring at the almost-finished stage and wondering what it'll be like to watch Sly and the Family Stone, Jimi Hendrix, and (of course!) Joan Baez. This will better allow me to locate you, too, though it's not really necessary as my travel pouch will direct me.

Early instances of misguided TIP journeys revealed some travelers didn't actually encounter their person of choice, so post-arrival guidance technology has been implemented. Crude as it might seem, a series of tugs forward, backward, left, and right will take me to you.

(Imagine a handbag that can lead you where you need to go! You can't know this, but it won't be all that long before you'll see small handheld computers guide people to their destinations.)

Back to my typical day: Faisa delivers my NourishCube at 0815. It's then time for me to meet my friends for exercise and social time in the park. I've already mentioned Daniel to you. He's about my age and hasn't begun his Reproduction Cycle, either. There's Coifa and Juleen as well. They're women slightly older than we are, also not yet eligible, though.

If it seems like I'm making a "big deal" out of the Reproduction Cycle, that's because it is. The RC is a huge shift in our lives. Hormone levels are increased, for one thing, and that (obviously) causes body changes. The biggest thing, of course, is meeting our selected mate, falling in love, and beginning new lives together. The RC is a joy we all look forward to.

This "season" I'm in has its own pleasures, however, in both freedom and youth. The science and history etc. learning modules I mentioned are intended for this time of life; they're not generally approved once a child is delivered. My focus then will be infant care, child rearing, and maternal bonding/attachment. My mate and I will live in a larger homepod designed to accommodate us and our child.

About homepods: not much architecture from your time remains. There are some "buildings" to visit and experience as art, but homepods make up almost our entire landscape, along with the town square and park where we exercise. Homepods are in level structures divided into twenty living spaces each; the closest comparison I can make to what you'd know would be concrete or stucco construction. They're connected by corridors we can use to visit others.

Teleportation (we can only do very short distances) or transpod is the usual method, but walking is encouraged for health.

(Cars and other vehicles like you knew are long gone. Transpods accommodate up to four people and traverse both air and ground.)

Since I've talked about the tiger and monkey glitches, I want you to know Faisa can decorate my homepod with butterflies or flowers or any beautiful thing I want. Today, it's bright orange roses climbing a trellis on my dark gray relaxation room wall. Tomorrow I might ask for a litter of kittens. On Sundays when my mother visits, I always have her favorite dark purple irises everywhere.

I use my days to absorb all the knowledge I can and savor my friendships, especially with Daniel, who makes me laugh. Daniel is six and a half feet tall, very slender, with blue eyes so dark they resemble…well, for you, unwashed jeans right out of the package. Like most men in 2101, he's removed all the hair from his head and his scalp is completely covered in artwork that varies all the time. Yesterday he greeted me with freshly painted bright pink and yellow "flower power" daisies and peace signs.

"Do I look 'farmed out'?" he asked me. I didn't even bother to correct him, but he actually did look "far out."

Daniel has a secret, which is he doesn't want to participate in the RC. That will be his choice to make officially when it's time. For now, I keep telling him he should consider it. Imagine not wanting to leave progeny behind!

(Children are our greatest gift to bestow for Unity and for all time.)

Modern exercise would be familiar to you. Running and walking and the many other ways people have derived health and wellbeing from moving their bodies haven't changed. We have climbing equipment and stationary running pods that echo early 21st century "gyms." The main difference is, it's all climate-controlled (including spritzing of water to cool off).

Everything, actually, is climate-controlled. There's no such thing as "weather" in Unity. Our world is maintained at a constant temperature, roughly equivalent to your 68 degrees Fahrenheit. "Storms" are a thing of the past. The "natural disasters" your era faced are all gone. If it rains (remember, we don't grow crops), it's because AI has determined irrigation of our trees and flowers needs to be augmented, supposedly. Some of us think they just send a light, soft rain because it makes everyone happy.

Ours is the most pleasant place to live you could imagine. There's no work in the traditional sense of the word. There is no want, there is no worry. Unity provides all we need and ever will need.

I'm guessing mate selection would make you curious. Unlike generations before, our mates are chosen as invariably perfect matches in temperament, physical attraction, intelligence, natural energy, knowledge/interests and, of course, genetics. The greatest aspect is that we all "fall in love", as you would put it. It's assured during and after the RC.

(I should point out romantic love is unknown until RC.)

Back to my day: after exercise and social time, there's a fresh NourishCube, then we're free to pursue whatever we like in our homepods. Faisa and I usually explore learning modules to consider. My interests are varied, but lately I'm concentrating on 20th century customs and events. (Tomorrow I'm going to learn and practice handwriting! On real paper!)

We rest for an hour, have another exercise circuit, and then it's usually time for an evening NourishCube, depending on how much energy I've expended. Around 1900, there's always some form of entertainment in the park, often holos of the latest entertainers acting out a story. Oh, and we dance. A lot. Music is more popular than ever; much of it still features the instruments of your time. Mostly we listen to AI rearrangements of old 21st century songs, but there are a few Woodstock hits like "I Want To Take You Higher" by Sly and the Family Stone that people grew to love back in 2069 and still ask for in the park. Daniel and I have so much fun dancing to that and it's unbelievable to think I'll experience it in person soon. (He's pretty jealous.)

Around 2300, we return to our sleep chambers after a perfect day. Oh, how I wish I could bring you back with me!

Love,
Baezy

4

Massachusetts Institute of Technology

AUGUST 12, 1969

Avuncular. Grandfatherly. *A bit like a walrus.*

Kelly tilted her head as she sat in front of Dr. Lawton's desk, trying to decide how best to describe him. She watched as he talked on the phone, acting as though she wasn't listening to him drone on at his wife about dinner plans, hiding her irritation at being made to wait after arriving precisely at four o'clock, as requested. He'd waved her in and held up a hand to indicate he'd finish soon. It was now 4:03. As her former professor debated the merits of broccoli versus asparagus, he pushed his coffee cup across the desk toward Kelly with a wink. She automatically jumped up to fetch his refill from the adjacent room, returning as Dr. Lawton told his wife goodbye.

"Miss Adams!" He offered his best smile as he replaced the receiver, the friendly look he'd personally delivered to innumerable calculus students for thirty-five years, whether he was planning to flunk them or not.

Dr. Lawton was not known for his sincerity, or, for that matter, his people skills. "I called you in today to discuss some changes in the department."

Kelly sat up a little straighter, tugging the hem of her knee-length skirt. Dr. Lawton cleared his throat and touched the end of his bristly gray moustache with his forefinger, something he did reflexively whenever he felt uncomfortable. Kelly braced herself.

"First of all, Kelly, your work has been exemplary. I want to thank you and Lisa for all the support you've offered the project this year."

"Laura, her name is Laura," Kelly corrected. "And thank you. We're both grateful to be a part of Project MAC. It's the most exciting research into computers anywhere."

Dr. Lawton nodded his head and mumbled, "Laura. Yes, Laura." He patted his hands on his desk. "Well, you see, our funding for 1970 is going to be increased dramatically, Kelly. DARPA is providing additional millions of dollars per year going forward."

Kelly raised her eyebrows. "The Defense Advanced Research Projects Agency? Then the work we're doing is directly impacting the Vietnam War now?"

Dr. Lawton shook his head. "It's peripheral involvement. Defense sees ways to utilize a 'self-healing' computer network for communications. It's a natural extension of our efforts; it makes sense. I've heard talk they'd like to develop a mechanical elephant to traverse the jungles of Vietnam, but thankfully, that doesn't fall under our remit." He chuckled and leaned back in his chair, legs splayed, resting his elbows. Kelly directed her eyes over his right shoulder instead of taking in his pose. She laughed politely and wondered for the tenth time why she'd been summoned.

"Anyway, so, is all going well for you and Laura? As I mentioned, we're very pleased with your work." Dr. Lawton responded to Kelly's nod with one of his own. "Good. Well, to cut straight to today's topic, this increased funding will accelerate our development timeline. There will be more to do, more to manage. I'll be adding an assistant to oversee Project MAC next month as a result."

Kelly smiled as realization dawned on her. "That's wonderful, Dr. Lawton," she began. "I appreciate—"

Dr. Lawton leaned forward, arms on the desk now, hands clasped, smiling once more. "I know the extra support will be greatly appreciated by you and Lisa and all who work on the project. Next month you'll begin reporting directly to John Rutledge."

Kelly arranged her open mouth with great effort to breathe the word, "Oh."

"Do you have any questions?" Dr. Lawton asked.

"Well yes, I do. How is it that I've been working on this project for two years longer than John, and know it far better than he does, but I'm not going to oversee it?" Kelly shook her head and crossed her arms despite herself. She knew she looked anything but assertive.

"Oh, Kelly, honey." Dr. Lawton rose from his desk chair and walked around to place an unwelcome hand on Kelly's shoulder. "You don't want that kind of responsibility. It's better suited to John."

"Why? Why is it better suited to John? I'm every bit as capable as he is. I've devoted years to Project MAC at the expense of my personal life." Kelly stopped and looked at the fluorescent light above. "I don't have a personal life. It's been the lab almost twelve hours most days."

"Kelly, that's exactly it," Dr. Lawton replied as he re-took his seat. "You're a pretty girl. You're, what, twenty-two? You're going to want to find a husband and start a family soon. Running a project won't allow you to do that—"

"That's not what I want!" Kelly allowed the first bit of anger to flash at her old mentor. "That's not what I want at all. I want to be your assistant. I want that responsibility. I *deserve* that responsibility, Dr. Lawton."

"Oh, sweetheart, you say that now, but in months or a year you'll change your mind. And then where would we be?" Dr. Lawton swiveled his chair to reach a silver-framed photo. "Look at this. Our daughter Michelle is only two years older than you, and she just gave us a beautiful new grandson. Her husband has a great job in Boston. He's an accountant." Dr. Lawton nodded along with the word "accountant" as though Kelly should be impressed. "They have a nice home, and Michelle couldn't be happier as a wife and mother. That's what you want, Kelly, not to spend your life in a computer lab. The hard work you're doing now will make it much easier for those who come after you. You're a valuable resource, Kelly, don't get me wrong—"

"Apparently I do get you wrong, Dr. Lawton. And you get me wrong. My work is superior to any John Rutledge has ever done, and you know it."

"Kelly," Dr. Lawton sighed. "He's a man. No one will take direction from a girl. I mean, from a woman. It's out of the question. Your natural mathematical talent and scientific skill make you irreplaceable in the lab. We'll miss you when you make the inevitable decision to leave. But it's a man's field, and no female will be accepted in a leadership position."

Kelly fumed for a full fifteen seconds before answering. "A man's field. You mean to tell me that what separates you men, a pathetic little dangling—" Kelly paused as Dr. Lawton's eyes widened in shock. "You mean to tell me that the lack of a *pathetic* little dangling *y chromosome* is going to keep me from my rightful place?"

"There's no need to be vulgar or start all that women's lib crap with me, Kelly." Now Dr. Lawton crossed his arms, clearly too ill at ease even for his artificial smile.

"It's not crap, Dr. Lawton. It's the reality of change and it's arriving sooner than you expect. And you know what? I'm going to take Friday and Monday off. I need a break and Laura does, too. We've worked continuously for months. So please make sure to inform John Rutledge I'll meet with him when we return. Maybe. Unless I decide to move to Cal Tech or some other institution where I'll be fully appreciated."

Kelly stood to leave.

"You wouldn't do that, Kelly. You've contributed far too much to simply walk away. But take a few days off at the week's end. Obviously you need to calm down and settle your emotions." Dr. Lawton tapped and then stroked the end of his moustache. Kelly noted his hand was shaking a little.

"You're exactly right, Dr. Lawton. I've contributed far too much," she said.

Kelly closed the office door with enough force to startle the secretary down the hall. She watched Enid pat her ash blonde bouffant nervously and return to typing, then stomped away to tell Laura not only would she go to Woodstock, they could leave early and come back late.

5

Unity SE35.86

I guess you're wondering about my father.

(So am I.)

When my mother and Henry Averell Cavanagh met in 2060, the Genetic Homogenization & Optimization Project hadn't officially begun, though Unity had informally been working toward it for decades. They started living together shortly afterward (Anantha was only nineteen; Henry was thirty-nine). By the time they were ready to have me, they were legally what you'd call "grandfathered in" as a couple. It wasn't required they follow the RC protocol, as they had the blessing of both their geneticists.

If only they'd had the blessing of fate, as well. According to my mother, at the age of forty-eight my father met another nineteen-year-old and formally entered the Reproduction Cycle with her. This took place shortly before my birth. Mom had no legal protection from Unity, as they'd not been in a sanctioned RC relationship.

Such things would never happen now. Mom calls Henry "The Last Middle-Aged Crisis Known to Humanity." She calls him much worse things, too, but that's a lengthy topic for another time.

Henry's homepod with Garralla is located about three hundred miles from here, and he's never shown the slightest interest in meeting me. He and Garralla have a son, Thrune, and they keep to themselves. Mom says it's better that way.

I don't think Thrune has any idea I exist. In this time of G-HOP and carefully planned families, it's an incredible embarrassment to have a half-sibling running around. Having two offspring is highly irresponsible of my father and while what he did wasn't illegal at the time, it's very offensive.

I'm grateful we have an official Reproduction Cycle now and the assurances it grants. No more sons or daughters will grow up missing an anus-faced duplicitous Walking-Penis-of-Immaturity father figure in their lives. (I told you Mom calls him worse things. That's a favorite.)

My generation will never have to deal with these issues.

So far, I've not had to encounter my father, but he's only eighty so it could still happen, especially if Thrune moves to a different sector. I can't think of one nice thing I'd say to him and I hope he spends all his years elsewhere. Mom says if anyone lives to a hundred and seventy, it'll be Henry, just to spite her.

On to more pleasant topics:

I've been fully prepared to join you and leave in only two days! Faisa droned on and on about 20th century diseases and lack of hygiene, reminding me over and over my NourishCubes are vital. There are rules I must follow, all of them to ensure I don't alter future events. No one can know who I am and when I'm from but you, and you won't be able to tell anyone because in 1969, health authorities ("head shrinkers"? Did you really call them that?) would almost certainly diagnose a major psychiatric disorder and confine you for treatment, altering your life course irreparably. I must protect you and all people I encounter from both interference and "unauthorized knowledge." Blah blah blah, as you would say.

"It is vital you locate an opportunity to communicate with your subject in complete privacy. If this is not possible, you must adhere to guidelines and participate as Sarah Sandoval only, with no verbal interaction regarding your true identity and origin."

Like I said before, all this typing on paper is simply a backup plan in case you can't perceive me, or I can't talk to you for whatever reason. I've been assured more than once the journal will be neither necessary nor advisable, as I'd have to guard it from others' view and destroy it before my return to 2101, anyway. Faisa mentioned multiple times that my TIP is unusual in that I'm traveling specifically to meet an ancestor. Most people request insertion into a historical period they find interesting, like medieval times or the Old West or, yes, Woodstock— but they don't have the privilege of relation to an actual attendee. I feel like they're making up the rules for me as they go along.

I eventually requested a brief shutdown of Faisa's vocal process. There's nothing else for her to tell me. I'm a responsible person who can be trusted. (Obviously, that trait came from my mother.)

Later, Faisa presented me with my return beacon, all ceremonious and delighted with herself, because it looks like a 1960s mirror a girl could carry in her purse. It's flower-shaped, bright yellow, and has a little red ladybug on the non-mirror side.

I've never seen myself in a mirror before. I admit to staring at this a long time, putting it down and picking it back up. Our modern version is a 3-D rendering we can look at any time we want. I kind of like this tiny flat reflection! It's a thing of groovy.

Love,
Baezy

(I'd probably better start calling myself Sarah, like my driver's license says. Faisa occasionally practices it on me to see if I'll answer. Oh, and I've decided to add a Sioux language module to my knowledge before I leave, because Sarah grew up on Pine Ridge Reservation in South Dakota. It's highly doubtful I'll encounter anyone fluent in Lakota Sioux, but I could.)

6

August 15, 1969

CAMBRIDGE, MASSACHUSETTS

Kelly regretted her decision to go to Woodstock almost immediately when she was forced to sit next to Eric in the front passenger seat of his VW van, trying to ignore him prattling on about the "microbus" and how he'd bought it last year with no idea he'd be taking it to a music festival but they were lucky he had it, weren't they? And he was so glad Kelly came along because he knew she was a serious person with a, like, heavy job and she was uptight a lot and this festival was going to give her time to relax and it was all going to be a gas and the van would be a great place for them to crash but he and the other guys packed several tents too so there would be plenty of room for everyone and they had lots of food because he was used to camping and knew what to bring and Kelly was welcome to a sandwich right now if she wanted one and...

"Hey, Eric?" she interrupted after five solid minutes. "I'm going for one reason, to see Joan Baez sing. The rest of the time, I'll be working on this." She waved a black notebook in the air. "I can solve equations anywhere. Y'all go off and do your hippie thing and leave me to my research. I don't mean to be rude, but—"

Kelly felt Laura's hand on her shoulder from behind and swiveled to look at her friend, who was shaking her head back and forth until she rested it back on Rodney's shoulder.

"What Kelly means," Laura said, "is that she'll catch up on some work but we'll all have fun together. This trip is about sharing an experience and Kelly will be a part of it and enjoy it with us. She'll forget all about work."

Eric nodded at Laura's eyes in the rear view mirror and turned back to Kelly. "I love it when you say 'y'all', Kelly. Your accent is so cute and sweet. You're a true Southern belle. I always said I'd find myself a Southern belle." He tapped his hands on the steering wheel and stole a glance at her legs in Laura's dark green skort. "That's a nice skirt you're wearing. It matches your eyes."

It was the most uncomfortable garment Kelly had ever encountered. She kept tugging at the shorts part underneath when she thought no one was paying attention. Kelly looked out the window and wondered whether they'd be stopping anywhere she could catch a bus back to Cambridge. Eric was most definitely not attractive to her: tall, skinny, blond, with a rangy patch of beard so light it was almost nonexistent, and completely unctuous. Kelly's one and only real boyfriend, in high school, had been dark-haired and so had the rare few men she'd dated since. She'd long ago decided she had a type and Eric was certainly not it. Plus, probably because he was a part-time disc jockey in Boston, he seemed to need to fill every second of silence with gale-force conversation.

"Do you think we'll be stopping anytime soon?" she asked Eric.

"Well, we're not even out of town yet," Eric answered, "so no. Unless you need a restroom." He shot her a worried glance. "Do you need me to find a ladies' room? I'll be happy to—"

"No," Kelly assured him. "I was just wondering." She picked up her notebook and pretended to stare at it, hoping he'd stop talking. After thirty more minutes, she'd successfully tuned him out and fallen asleep, head resting on the window, lulled by the van's motion and the lullaby of Eric's drone.

She woke two hours later, surrounded by a landscape that reminded her of home. They drove past cow pastures and small houses surrounded by oak trees.

"Where are we?" she asked Laura, but Eric responded.

"Somewhere in Connecticut," he said. "Only two hours to go. We'll stop soon to get some gas. Map says the next town is Hartford. Right, Jack?"

"Right," came the answer from the back of the VW. Kelly had only caught a glimpse of Jack as he'd arrived at the last second, throwing a huge duffel bag and two folded tents into the rear of the van. She longed to change seats with Kristin, a shy, soft-spoken kindergarten aide she knew only through Laura, barely at all. Maybe she could announce sitting in front made her carsick. Maybe Kristin would fall madly in love with Eric if she got to sit with him. Maybe Kelly could emerge from this van in New York with her sanity intact.

She clutched her stomach. "Ugh," she muttered. "I don't feel too great. I think riding up front is giving me motion sickness."

Eric slid his pale blue eyes to hers for a second. "I thought riding in back made people carsick, not up front."

"Yeah, I'm weird," Kelly announced. "I'm sorry, I should've thought of that before I sat up here." She made an exaggerated show of tilting her head back and inhaling deeply.

"Are you gonna be all right? Do we need to pull over?" Eric asked.

"I'll be okay. It won't be that long until we stop in Hartford, right? I'll eat some crackers and I'm sure that will help." Kelly rested her head on the window and continued to count cattle. Sixty-seven. That was useless information but she often found herself unconsciously counting things, even as they raced by a window.

"It'll be about ten minutes," Jack yelled. "Let's stop at the first station we find. I think we all need to stretch our legs. And I'm burning up back here."

Eric glanced at the mirror. "Well, I'm sorry, Jack. I should have brought the air-conditioned limo. Don't be such a downer, man. It's

August. What did you expect? Don't sweat it. Like, literally." Eric smiled at his clever response and nodded at Jack's reflection.

"We're all sweating it, man," Rodney said. "No offense, Eric, not your fault, but it's like an oven in here."

"I have the window down, Ghost," Eric replied. "That's as much air as I can get to you."

"Stop calling him Ghost, Eric," Laura said.

"Hotter than Georgia asphalt," Kelly said, and immediately regretted it.

"You Southern belles and your expressions. I'm writing that one down," Eric told her. "Far out!" He grinned at Kelly. "Are you feeling better yet, foxy lady?"

She rolled her eyes and slid her hand to her stomach as she spotted a HARTFORD 7 MILES sign. *Seventy-eight cattle*, Kelly told herself. Probably ten to eighteen more cows at this rate of speed/encounter until she could jump out, ceremoniously eat some crackers, and somehow talk Kristin into trading seats with her.

As it turned out, Kristin really *did* get carsick from riding in the back. She asked Kelly to switch as they walked into the ladies' room of an Esso station somewhere just outside Hartford.

"I mean, I know Eric wants you up front with him, but I'd really appreciate it. I've been miserable for at least a hundred miles. All Jack's done is complain about the heat, and thinking about it just makes my stomach worse."

Kelly said, "I'll do even better than that. I'll go inside and buy us both some crackers and a Coke. The combination will settle your stomach. Go ahead and take my seat while Eric's talking someone's ear off in the gas station. He won't be able to do a thing about it."

As soon as Eric saw Kristin seated next to him, he inserted an 8-track tape of Iron Butterfly singing "In-A-Gadda-Da-Vida", seventeen solid minutes of not-talking Kelly resented from the back of the van. Jack saw her eyeroll and laughed.

"Every emotion you have plays like a movie on your face, did you know that?" he said. "I mean, the entire van knew you wanted to get away from Eric, probably because you'd much rather talk to me."

"I'd rather talk with anyone who gives me a chance to speak," Kelly answered. "But not necessarily you, Jack. You're so full of yourself you're in constant danger of overflowing. A new girl every week. Your bedpost is notched to the point of looking poxy. For all I know, you may *be* poxy, actually." She swept her eyes up and down him and shook her head. "I hear things. You're still always on the make."

"Not with you," he answered. "I see you're *still* hostile to men. Nothing changes much with you, does it, Kelly? Seriously, it's been two years since we graduated and you stayed to do research. You live ten, fifteen minutes away from me. Yet you haven't poked your head out of that lab once to see any of your old friends. Do you still have friends? Any at all?"

"So, you're *still* an asshole," Kelly said. "Now I'm wishing I could listen to Eric some more." She leaned her head back with a sigh. "I don't know why I agreed to this. Well, actually, I do know why. I was mad at Dr. Lawton, at all men and the way they treat women like we're subservient little dolls to be maneuvered around at their will. Thanks for the reminder."

"Hey, I'd never maneuver you," Jack said. "I'd be afraid of one of your spines stabbing me."

"You still teaching high school?" Kelly asked with her eyes closed, head resting on the seat back.

"I'm inspiring a new generation of mathematicians, if that's what you mean. I happen to think it's much nobler than working for the Department of Defense," Jack answered.

"You know damn well that's not true. DARPA hasn't gotten much of anything from our research, so just drop it. We mainly work on communication and information technology, and that could save American lives. I love my country. Just because I'm opposed to the war doesn't change that."

"I love my country too, Kelly. I'm just not willing to go off and kill innocent women and children in someone else's. I'd gladly defend the United States, but not in a war that isn't even ours." Jack looked out the window as he spoke.

"Is your brother still over there?" Kelly asked, softening as she remembered. "He's home now, right?"

"Yeah, he's home. Living with Mom and Dad in North Carolina, deeply devoted to beer and quaaludes. Do you know where they got the name 'quaalude'? It's short for 'quiet interlude.' Lovely name for a sleeping pill, but Kenny has far too many quiet interludes. He can't get a job, his fiancée left him, he barely functions. They want to send him to Boston to live with me, like I could straighten him out. But I can't. I couldn't even if I were staying." Jack continued to stare at the distant fields rolling by.

"What do you mean, staying? You're not moving, are you?" Kelly asked.

Jack chuckled, a low rumble devoid of humor. "I can either hide my body away or allow Uncle Sam to ship it off to be bagged. I'm out of school, I'm healthy, God knows there's proof I'm not homosexual, and nobody's buying conscientious objector from a guy who's been in as many fights as I have. I'll be drafted soon."

"What are you going to do?" Kelly asked.

"So, Laura didn't tell you?" Jack answered. When Kelly shook her head, he continued, "I'm on this trip to escape. Rodney knows a guy who can slip me off to Ottawa, and it'll be much easier from a big crowd in New York. I'm going to Woodstock to join a group celebrating non-violence, listen to some music that reinforces my decision, and climb into a car with a guy named Jeff Hillery who's going to save my life. Does that make you hate me? I mean, more?"

"I don't hate you, Jack. I never did," she said. "We're very different people, that's all. I'm trying to process what you said." Kelly paused to bite her lower lip. "I can't understand how you could leave a job you love and a life you've built to start over in a different country, just on the chance you might have to fight."

"If I don't want to end up like my brother, or dead, there's not much choice. It's not like I haven't thought about it. I can either leave or be forced to ship out. There is zero chance I'll escape that fate if I stay in Boston for another month or even week. There's talk Nixon will start a new draft lottery based on birthdates. I analyzed my own and the probability is strong my number will be up very quickly. My mom worries about it constantly, because now that Kenny's no longer in-country—"

Kelly interrupted, "You're even more likely to be drafted, I get it. But Jack, the lottery will be equal for everyone, with a number assigned to each birth date. So, even though yours is more common, it doesn't mean it's statistically probable."

Jack shook his head and answered, "I don't trust the Nixon administration about anything. Why pull a number corresponding to a relatively low incidence of birthdate when you can draft thousands more with September 9th?"

Kelly sighed. "Did you quit your job?" she asked.

"God, that's so like you. Did you do the responsible thing and give *noooo-tice*, Jack?" he mocked in an Alabama drawl. "No, of course not. I couldn't see going to my principal's office and saying 'Hey, I'm quitting so I can run away to Canada. Please give me a head start before you call the government, okay?'" He sighed. "Just forget I told you. We have three days to have a good time and listen to some fab music." He reached into a cooler on the floor and withdrew a bottle of beer, holding it out to Kelly, who shook her head no. Jack took a long swig as she watched. She studied his Adam's apple moving up and down. She studied his long eyelashes, framing irises as brown as the smoked almonds he extracted next and held out to her. She studied his almost collar-length hair, black to the point of a slight blue tinge in the morning sun. Kelly thought about Jack being the only person to best her score in any MIT math class.

I don't want you to go to Canada. There has to be another way. Enroll in grad school—no, you don't have the money. Maybe a sympathetic doctor could create a medical condition. Join the National Guard, but that takes political connections. You could resist and go to jail like Joan Baez's husband, maybe he won't be locked up for long. Anything but just disappear, Kelly wanted to say. Instead, she watched Jack look out the window and pretend to pay attention to the passing scenery as he drank a second beer, tapping his fingers to the endless drum solo echoing from Eric's speakers up front.

And when the tears reached her eyes, she picked up her notebook and pencil, trying to make sense of the world in the only way she knew to be true, steady, and dependable: numbers.

7

Unity SE35.86

DECEMBER 13, 2101

My mother insists I take some antique paper currency to Woodstock, which makes no sense at all to me. Money is a foreign concept in our society. I wouldn't even know how or when to hand it to someone!

She said, "You don't know what you might encounter. Even though you should have everything you need, keep this in your pouch for my peace of mind. If you get into any trouble, you can buy your way out of it. People would do anything for money in the 20th century." She handed me a rolled-up bunch of hundred-dollar bills from 1967, sealed in a small opaque black bag she told me to hide. I have no idea where she got them, and she wouldn't say. It probably won't even be opened.

I don't need food (I have my NCs). I don't need clothing (I have my mother's). I guess I could "buy" something from a vendor. Maybe I'll bring Mom a new headband from the Bindy Bazaar, because I'd like to keep the one I've borrowed and will actually wear at Woodstock. If they're small enough, I could bring back souvenirs for my friends. I have no idea how many headbands one or two or three hundred dollars would buy. I haven't learned about money in 1969 because I knew I wouldn't require that knowledge for this trip.

Tomorrow is the big day!

Daniel, Coifa, and Juleen told me at the park this morning they'll miss me, though I won't be gone more than three days. There's a slight hint of jealousy from each of them; they'll likely have to wait years for Time Insertion Protocol. They disguise it as concern for my safety, which is ridiculous. Woodstock was the most peaceful gathering of four hundred thousand gentle, caring people the world has ever known.

Daniel said someday he wants to go to San Francisco in the 1960s. I think he's still fascinated by hippie culture like most of us. He said everything about the city sounds perfect to him! I've already told you how tall and slender Daniel is, always elegantly dressed in outfits his AI companion manufactures at his request. Today he was wearing a carefully styled golden wig and a light tan jumpsuit with long sleeves. He was accompanied by his occasional glitch animal, a calm-yet-alert cheetah that sits by his side, licking its massive paw.

Juleen said she'd like to visit Tudor England (I think the hygiene challenges alone would keep me away from that, but she wants to see King Henry VIII). Coifa says she has no desire to be time-inserted anywhere (anywhen). I've never seen either of them with a companion animal. Maybe it's because neither of them has much imagination. I love them, but it's true.

My screeching monkey has been gone for days, by the way. I woke this morning to the most exquisite butterflies swirling all around me, brilliant blue on black swallowtails and orange monarchs and delicate little purple ones with lacy wings! I can only interpret them as giddy excitement.

Faisa seems oddly sentimental about being shut down for three days. "It will be strange not to have you here, Baezy." She seems to forget she's purely AI and doesn't have opinions on anything, not to mention she won't be aware and functioning in my absence.

Honestly, though, I depend on Faisa for so much. It's going to be difficult for me to be without her constant support. It'll be challenging without *all* the conveniences artificial intelligence provides us. I've never been "on my own" as you would say.

But what an adventure!

I have my clothes packed along with everything else and will wear my floral-embroidered white peasant blouse and bell bottomed jeans first. I even have a white lace bra with support wires sewn into it (how did you endure that all day, every day?). I've grown my hair long and straight to fit in, and it's a nice shade of ordinary 1960s light-brown. I've been wearing the old black leather "sandals" Mom gave me for a week, getting my feet used to them. They fit nicely into my hippie-suede travel pouch.

Kelly, I wonder if you'll recognize me in some way as your own DNA, maybe in my green eyes. I wonder if you'll like me. I wonder what I'll say to you first, what you'll be doing when I find you. I wonder what music I'll love hearing in person, whether Joan Baez will live up to my expectations as her namesake. I wonder what your friends will think of me (yes, I know a little bit about Laura, Rodney, Eric, Kristin, and Jack).

I dream about what stories I'll have to share when I return.

At 0800, I'll be picked up and escorted to the TIP portal. Mom kissed me goodbye today and reminded me she'll be waiting when I get back there on my actual birthday, which we'll celebrate on the 17th with music, dancing, and a special once-a-year NourishCube for me. I doubt I'll ever be able to thank her enough for this gift.

Love,
Baezy/Sarah

8

New York State Highway 17

FRIDAY, AUGUST 15, 1969

Eric reached to lower the volume on the second consecutive playing of "In the Year 2525" by Zager and Evans. "I'm gonna stop near Monticello to gas up again, guys, so we won't have to worry about it on the way out on Sunday. Anybody wants a bathroom visit, speak now or forever hold your pee," he announced. "We're still at least fifteen miles from the festival, right, Jack?"

"Right," Jack answered. "And I suspect the traffic will be crawling along much slower than it already is as we get closer. Might take a while." He glanced at Kelly scribbling in her notebook. "You should take a break and get out of this oven. We all should."

Kelly palmed the bead of sweat running down her forehead back into her hairline, blowing a little air upward with her bottom lip. "Oh, I'm planning on it."

Eric flicked his eyes to Rodney's in the mirror. "You okay, Ghost?"

"Stop it, Eric," Rodney answered. "My name is Rodney. And yeah, I'm okay for someone who's being slowly cooked to death in a Volkswagen."

"Man, you are paler and whiter than anyone I've ever met. 'Ghost' is perfect for you. I hope you brought sunscreen for your old man, Laura. You're going to have to baste him like a turkey." Eric snickered and banged his hand on the steering wheel.

"Shut up, Eric," Laura said.

Rodney ran his hand through his curly red hair, smoothing it back. "I'm gonna kill him if we don't get out of here soon," he stage-whispered to Laura.

When Eric drove into the service station, a teenaged kid with a crewcut rushed out to pump gas. His olive-drab shirt read "Jimmy" in white on an oval patch above the pocket. "You guys headed for the music festival?"

"Yeah, for Woodstock, fill it up please," Eric replied, walking toward the little grocery store without a look back. Kristin, Rodney, and Laura hurried along with him.

"Man, that's far out. My folks won't let me go, but my sister's sneaking over there tomorrow night," Jimmy addressed Jack as Kelly jumped down from the van, smoothing her skort and blinking in the sunlight. "Your old lady's really beautiful, man," Jimmy added as he watched her enter the store, the screen door smacking closed behind her.

"She's not my…never mind. So, do you know the way to the festival from here?" Jack asked him.

"Yeah, I've been over there a lot. My dad's friends with Max Yasgur, who owns the dairy farm where this is all happening, though he's pretty mad at him for bringing all these filthy hippies to town." Jimmy laughed. "You look pretty clean to me. And she *definitely* does." He nodded at the store. "You guys are way behind a bunch of people, though. Carloads have been comin' through here since Wednesday. You planning to camp in this thing?" He bent his head toward the van.

"That was our idea. All the stuff we brought's in there," Jack replied.

"When you get a little further up this road, you're goin' to take the exit onto 17B toward Bethel, and very soon you'll find people parking and walking. You'll have to carry everything in, probably at least three or four miles. This van's not going anywhere when you get closer to the festival. We heard everybody's on foot. Thousands of 'em. Nobody's ever seen anything like it around here." Jimmy finished filling the gas tank and wiped his hands on a rag he pulled from his back pocket, replacing it with a sigh. "Man, it's hot today. That'll be three dollars and twelve cents. Just tell my dad inside."

"Okay," Jack said, heading toward the store and then turning back. "Jimmy, do you know any other way we could get to Mr. Yasgur's property besides 17B? Like, maybe a back way? My friends brought all kinds of tents and bags and a big cooler. I don't really want to carry all that for miles in this heat. There's three girls with us. They're not gonna be much help." Jack leaned against the van. "Could I show you a map? Maybe you might be able to help me figure out a different route where we could end up parking closer?"

"Sure, right on," Jimmy said. "I think I can tell you a detour that'll work. You could maybe drive right in and camp on Yasgur's north twenty acres. I heard my dad saying there's been some people doing that, coming in from a different direction, and getting away with it. But you'll have to go way around to get there."

Jack held up a finger for Jimmy to wait and went to extract his map, unfolding it against the back of the van. Jimmy traced a line with his finger, which Jack marked with Kelly's pencil. "So, up to Liberty on 17, 55 to Swan Lake, then 144 to Hurd Road," Jimmy narrated as Jack followed. "Then you'll see a big hay field. I don't think they're stopping anybody, as of this morning, anyway. Oh, and there's a pond near there where you could swim, if, you know, you brought bathing suits." He blushed and glanced at the store, probably trying to spot Kelly through the window.

Jack smiled the tiniest bit and nodded. "How old are you, Jimmy?" he asked.

"I'll be fifteen in a few months," Jimmy said, straightening himself to his full height, which was nose-level with Jack.

"I teach kids your age, high school algebra and then calculus when they get a little older," Jack told him. "I have a feeling you're a good student. You've been a huge help to me. Take this," he handed Jimmy a dollar bill, "and I'll go inside to get Eric to pay for the gas. Thanks, man." He patted a grinning Jimmy on the shoulder as the kid pocketed his new riches.

"Far out! Thanks!" Jimmy called after him. "Have fun at Woodstock." A dark blue Chevy Nova pulled up to the gas pump behind the van, running over the driveway bell hose to generate a *ding ding* sound that summoned Jimmy back to work. Jack stopped and watched a middle-aged woman with gray beehive hair roll her window down and scowl at the van, then at him.

"Fill it up, Jimmy," she said. "I'm going home and I'm not stepping foot outside until Monday."

"Yes, Mrs. Hendricks," Jimmy answered. He nodded at Jack's retreating form. "That man's a teacher, just like you."

"I doubt that," Mrs. Hendricks huffed, staring at the van's MAKE LOVE NOT WAR bumper sticker and shaking her head before rolling her window back up and settling in to wait for her gasoline to be pumped.

Jack was grateful he'd taken time to talk to the kid.

A little over an hour later, Eric drove directly into the unfenced field and parked as they collectively gasped at the ocean of people down the hill from the van. The guys and Kristin jumped out and quickly began planning the setup of three canvas tents close by, claiming their space before it disappeared. In the distance, they could see the back of a large wooden stage flanked by scaffolding and huge metal towers. Jack figured all of them would be able to walk to performances and return to "base camp" easily.

They squinted at hundreds, maybe thousands, of rows of young people already sitting or lying in front of the stage, waiting for whoever might begin playing. Many had colorful blankets or towels over their heads to block the sun. For now, the dim roar of conversation and an occasional yell from the stage crew was the only music.

Laura slid the cooler from the back of the van until Rodney dropped a tent pole and rushed to help her, Eric, Kristin and Jack trailing him. "Baby, what is in this thing? It weighs a ton," Rodney said. They set it on the ground and Laura ceremoniously flipped the lid open.

"Anybody hungry?" she asked. "I baked a pineapple upside-down cake! And there are ham sandwiches, which we should probably eat tonight because the ice is melting in there. And lots of peanut butter and jelly for you, Kelly," she yelled at the interior of the van, where her friend remained firmly planted. Laura turned back to the others and continued, "I brought some Bugles and Starburst Fruit Chews, too. They're in a bag somewhere. Oh, and here," she extended a foil-wrapped chunk to Rodney, "it's the rest of the tunnel-of-fudge cake I brought for you. Along with this." She held up a can of whipped cream in her other hand with a smile clearly intended for Rodney only.

Rodney kissed her as he took it. "I'm gonna save these for our tent, baby. Men, find yourselves an old lady who loves to bake and knows righteous uses for whipped cream." He laughed and added, "But Laura, you do know they're going to be selling food here, right?"

"I know but I thought we could save money." Laura beamed at him before turning her gaze to the friends around them. "Umm, speaking of which, I guess this is as good a time to tell you as any, guys. Rodney and I are going to have a baby. We went to the doctor a few days ago to make sure, and he called yesterday. We're going to get married! We want you all to join us at city hall next month."

"Are you going to keep working?" came from the rear van seat.

Laura leaned her head back and blinked at the sky as she answered, "Yes, Kelly, I'll be there until right before the baby's born. That'll probably be in March of next year. Why don't you come out of there?"

"I'm just finishing something," Kelly said. "One second, I'll be right there."

Laura and Rodney received sweaty congratulatory hugs and handshakes, along with assurances everyone would attend the wedding.

Kelly stepped out of the van and sniffed the air. "Manure and marijuana," she said. "Lovely." She turned and waved at the crowd below them before placing her hands on her hips. "There must be hundreds of thousands of people here," she said. "Surely more than the fifty or hundred thousand they expected. I'm guessing the food you brought will come in handy, Laura. And congratulations, I'm really happy for you both." She offered Laura an awkward side hug and nodded at Rodney. "Y'all let me know when Joan Baez is on the stage. I'll be in the van. I think it's actually cooler in there."

"Hey, Kelly," Eric said, "don't do that. Come on, walk around with us. You'll see some far out stuff, guaranteed. You don't want to miss it all sitting in the van."

Kelly held her hand over her eyes like a visor and scanned the natural bowl surrounding the stage below. It looked like a squirming patchwork quilt spread across the earth. "I'd rather get a root canal than walk down there, Eric. I told you, I came for Joan and Joan only. I'm working on something that'll prove to Dr. Lawton once and for all I should be leading this project. I can't wait to show that old jerk what a mistake he made."

"And you thought all work and no play made *me* dull," Jack muttered as they stepped back to work on the tents. "If she was any more square we'd have to frame her and put her on a wall."

Eric chuckled. "Right on, man. Kelly's quirky, but she's got a great rack." He bit his lip and turned to Kristin. "At least you're out here helping us," he said to her. "This is taking forever, but it'd be much worse without you."

Jack yelled at Rodney, "Hey, man, give us a hand! We're never gonna get done if you sit there holding hands with Laura all day. Honeymoon hasn't started yet."

Rodney left Laura resting on the back bumper of the van and walked over. "Happy to pitch in, guys. I have a woman with whipped cream waiting for this accommodation," he said, nodding at his fiancée.

Eric reached for the heavy metal pole Kristin was handing him and noticed two guys heading their way as he looked over her shoulder. "Hi!" he called out.

"Hey, man. You want some help?" the tall, thin one answered, walking up behind Kristin. "I'm an engineering student at Cornell and my friend knows a thing or two about construction. Plus we just put two of these damn things together. I'm Gary and this is Bud." He waved at the shorter guy, who was wearing bell bottoms with an orange and green tie-dyed t-shirt in violent contrast with Gary's bright blue, yellow, and red floral one.

Bud flicked a cigarette to the ground and grinned at Kristin. "Let me take that for you," he told her. "Gary and I can get this done much faster working with these guys. You just relax."

Eric watched Bud push his shoulder-length hair behind both ears and squat into position to put the tent together. He realized Bud was old, really old to be attending the festival. Like, in his thirties.

"This is really nice of you," Eric said.

"Good vibes only, man," Gary answered. "We're all here to help each other."

Kristin stepped back and admired the construction, which went very fast with the five men working on it. After the third tent was fully set up, they all plopped on the ground to rest, surveying the scene.

Jack swiped his head on the sleeve of his shirt. "We should go swim in that pond we passed, Eric." He turned to their new friends. "Have you two been down there?"

"Not yet," Gary answered. "We only got here a little before you drove in. Haven't looked around much." He wrapped his arms around skinny legs and pulled his knees to his chest. "Really excited, though. There's a rumor that Iron Butterfly's gonna be here. Maybe even Led Zeppelin."

Eric nodded. "Led Zepp won't be here. I'm a disc jockey at WTBU, so I know. They were invited, but Plant turned it down. I'm not sure about the Butterfly, though. That would be far out." He regarded Bud and Gary's blank, unimpressed looks and added, "That's Boston University's radio station? It's a pretty big market. I'm sure you've heard of it." He leaned back on his elbows. "You guys wanna get high with us? I brought plenty of this." Eric held up an expertly rolled joint for Gary and Bud to see and missed Laura throwing up her arms in disapproval from the bumper of the van, where she was working on her second ham sandwich.

Rodney saw her, however, and jumped to his feet. "I think Laura and I are going to take a little break in one of the tents. Mind if we move into the one farthest from the van?"

Eric answered, "Sure, man, that's fine." He flipped a metal lighter open with a flick of his wrist and lit the joint in his hand, inhaling deeply and extending it to Bud, who took a puff and passed it to Gary and Jack. Kristin sat between Jack and Eric, glancing around nervously.

"Hey, you don't have to, Kristin," Jack told her through a cloud of smoke. He leaned in front of her to Eric, but Kristin grabbed the joint and looked at it closely, finally holding it to her mouth. She took a quick toke, then choked as she tried to hold the smoke in. She inhaled a second time and managed without coughing, handing it on to Eric with a smile.

"You wanna come with us to swim?" Eric asked Kristin. "The music won't start for a while."

"I'd like to look around, but I didn't bring my swimsuit," Kristin said, shrugging her shoulders.

Eric grinned and slowly exhaled a stream of smoke and compliments. "You won't need one, Kristin. You can swim in those shorts or maybe even your underwear. I've been stoked about spending time with you ever since you climbed into that seat next to me. You're the most foxy girl here." He leaned over to Bud like they'd known each other since childhood. "Isn't she?"

Bud nodded as he inhaled. "She is," he sputtered.

Kristin, used to being ignored in male company, enjoyed four men's attention very much and decided pot was not the horrible, scary bad trip she'd been led to fear. All she felt was relaxed and vaguely hungry. She jumped up and brushed hay from her shorts, carefully plucking each piece off individually as she finished.

"Come on, let's look around. Maybe we can find a hot dog or a burger."

The guys followed her like ducklings down a narrow path on the hillside.

Kelly, who'd been watching for ten minutes from the van's window, shook her head and muttered, "I want to go home." She decided a nap was her only escape for now. Kelly stretched out as well as she could on the vinyl seat and laid her head on a thin blanket she'd wadded up. There was no way she'd need it for anything else in this miserable heat.

When she woke, it was to strange music (she'd later discover this was Richie Havens, pressed into service because the opening band hadn't made it to the festival on time). Eventually she began hearing Beatles songs in the distance, but it was obviously not John, Paul, George, and Ringo. Kelly stepped out for a look around; the air was a little cooler and less stifling, though she wrinkled her nose at the overwhelming odor of marijuana. None of her friends were around. She guessed Rodney and Laura might be in their tent, but there was no way she was interrupting that. The others were probably in the mass of humanity spreading ever-wider from the stage like a human flood. She went to dig around for a peanut butter and jelly sandwich, then settled in to resume working in her notebook.

Her concentration lapsed when she heard a Gandhi-type Indian accent intone, "My Beloved Brothers and Sisters, I am overwhelmed with joy to see the entire youth of America gathered here in the name of the fine art of music. In fact, through the music, we can work wonders." Kelly leaned her head out to listen. "Music is a celestial sound and it is the sound that controls the whole universe, not atomic vibrations."

This elicited an eye roll from Kelly.

"Sound energy, sound power, is much, much greater than any other power in this world," the voice continued. "And, one thing I would very much wish you all to remember is with sound, we can make—and at the same time, break. Even in the war-field, to make the tender heart an animal, sound is used. Without that war band, that terrific sound, man will not become animal to kill his own brethren. So, that proves you can break with sound, and if we care, we can make also." This was followed by thunderous applause, and even though she didn't agree with the physics, Kelly was heartened by the sentiment.

When the music resumed, she listened enough to know it wasn't Joan Baez, then returned to her computations. She stopped once when Laura and Rodney called hello as they pawed through the cooler behind her, walking away giggling at some private joke. She hoped they'd stay in their tent or walk down the hill. Maybe she could review what she'd done in peace. Kelly realized she'd started enjoying her little private kingdom atop the hill, where she could work until the sun went down from her vinyl bench throne. Eric wouldn't take kindly to her using up the van's battery on lights after that.

After a few more minutes passed, Kelly glanced out the window to see the strangest sight she'd witnessed at Woodstock: Jack was climbing the hill in the distance, clutching a girl at his side. She was wrapped in a blanket. The girl was young—a teenager, likely—and had dripping wet long, dark hair. When they drew closer, it was clear she was sobbing. Jack stopped and kneeled before the girl, parting the blanket to reveal a white peasant blouse rendered transparent by water and bell-bottomed jeans that clearly hadn't been sufficiently wrung out (no wonder the girl had trouble moving; each leg probably weighed five pounds at the bottom). He gently removed the black sandals she had been struggling to walk in, holding them hooked on his fingers and nodding in the direction of their camp. He put his arm around her (of course he did, she was quite beautiful, Kelly noted) and helped her along. Kelly watched for Jack to install her in one of the tents, but he escorted the girl directly to the van.

Her van.

9

The Woodstock Music and Art Fair
Bethel, New York

AUGUST 15, 1969

Jack poked his head into the van, a corona of late-day pink sky shining above him like a halo. "Do you have any clothes she can borrow until hers dry? She's about your size," he said.

Kelly blinked at him and swept some errant hair behind one ear. She couldn't see the girl from her seat. "No, I don't. I only have one extra outfit. Try Laura." She frowned at his intrusion and held up her notebook. "Why did you bring her here? Surely she came to the festival with someone. It's not our problem."

Jack swung his head back and forth, glaring at her. "Kelly, under that math-encrusted exterior, there's gotta be a heart somewhere."

"That's not the point, Jack," Kelly answered. "Find her friends and let them hold her hand while she goes through her head trip or whatever it is. She'll be okay. Maybe take her to the stage and let them announce she's lost. You shouldn't get involved." Kelly looked back at her work and waited for Jack to leave.

"You can't be serious. There's probably half a million people here," Jack replied. "It's useless to try to find anyone. Come on, Kelly, she's a kid, probably the age of one of my students. She's alone and the way she talks, I don't think English is her native language. She says she grew up on a Sioux reservation in South Dakota. She ran away from home. Something's not right. I think somebody drugged her, actually. Maybe whoever drove her here. She's not safe down there."

Jack glanced to his right, where the girl was no doubt dripping in her blanket out of Kelly's view. "We were swimming and she suddenly appeared in the middle of the pond, where it's pretty deep, splashing like crazy and yelling about her stuff floating away. She had some kind of candy or something with her, and the people around us were catching and eating it, laughing at her. She kept grabbing at some wet papers that were useless and illegible, and then she started crying. Who goes swimming with a suede purse full of papers, Kelly? She needs a safe place until whatever drug she's on wears off."

Kelly set her notebook down slowly and deliberately, then crossed her arms to address Jack. "Take her to a medical tent, then. I don't do drugs. I don't understand people who do drugs. I'm not the person to talk to about this. Where's Eric?"

"Eric and Kristin were too preoccupied with each other to notice. They're still down the hill. Listen to me, Kelly. I swam over and helped her to shallow water, and she was naked, which a lot of people were, but she was trying to cover herself with her hands and all embarrassed. Her clothes were in her purse. She kept saying she had to get dressed, but her blouses and jeans and shoes were soaked. She insisted she had to put them on anyway. Some lady saw how upset she was and wrapped a blanket around her. They went in the woods and she came out wearing these wet clothes you could see through, clutching her purse. Come on, she needs help."

He leaned closer to Kelly, glancing behind him. "There was a Black woman at the edge of the water. This girl stopped dead in her tracks as we slogged out, staring at her with her mouth hanging open. Never mind she's still buck naked, she seemed mesmerized. She broke away from me, went over and touched the woman's arm, stroking it and going on and on about how beautiful her skin is, like she's never seen it before. That's the woman who threw a blanket around her and walked her into the woods," he whispered. "God only knows what else she said to her. The woman walked out with the girl in her wet clothes and quickly put the blanket around her again. Then she took her by the shoulders and pointed her at me, shaking her head as she met my eyes and urged her forward. I'm telling you, the girl isn't right. I'm not taking her back down and losing her in that crowd."

Now Kelly could see the girl pacing over near their tents, staring off into the distance between glances at the van. Jack's eyes trailed Kelly's to the girl.

"Although she ate one of her candy cubes as we were climbing the hill and she's stopped crying, so maybe she's doing better now," Jack added. "Looks like it."

Kelly raised an eyebrow. "What kind of candy? Are you sure it wasn't more drugs? And the girl must have a name," she said. "Why do you keep calling her that?"

"I don't think it was a drug. She just munched it and said she had to conserve what she had left. And she does have a name, and I was getting to that, but the girl says—" Jack quit talking and stepped to his left as a hand was placed on his shoulder, gently pushing him aside.

"Hi, Kelly, I'm Sarah. Sarah Sandoval," the girl interrupted. "This is not the way I wanted to meet you, but Jack wanted to speak with you first as he is a cool guy with a very groovy heart, isn't he? He's helping me because my arrival didn't go as it was planned and he feels bummed out for me. I came here to find you, though."

Kelly sat back and swept her gaze over the girl's flawless caramel-cream face before meeting her green eyes. "I don't understand. Am I supposed to know you? Why are you looking for me?" she asked. She thought for a second before frowning and adding, "Did Dr. Lawton send you to spy on me?"

Sarah paused for a moment and cast her eyes to the ground, tugging the blanket closer around herself. "No," she said. "I don't know Dr. Lawton. I ran away from home to come to the festival, then I found out you were here." She took in Kelly's skeptical look and added, "My family knows yours in Alabama. I left my mom a note and she called your mother, Gladys. I guess Gladys had told her you'd be here, so my mom asked if you could look after me because I'm all alone. I talked to your mother on a payment telephone in a glass booth in Monticello. She's very nice."

"I thought you were raised on an Indian reservation in South Dakota," Kelly said. "My family doesn't know anyone there. And how do you know my mother's name?" She looked at Jack through the VW's window. "None of this makes any sense. How could my mother think you'd find me among hundreds of thousands of people?"

"I'll explain all this far out circumstance to you soon, I promise. Our families are related. I know it sounds ape, but don't freak out," Sarah said. "First I'll remove these wet clothings and hang them to dry. I'll wear the blanket until then. You do not need to trouble yourself to provide me with anything; that was Jack's idea. I'll return after going into a tent. Can you dig it?" Sarah held her hand up to a bewildered Kelly and walked away.

"What the hell did she just say?" Kelly asked Jack.

"That she knows this sounds crazy but don't be upset, and she'll be right back if that's okay with you. Also, she's taking off her wet *clothings* to let them dry. I told you her way of speaking is strange, like she grew up with another language. Half the time it's just awkward, and half the time it's like she's been studying slang to throw at us." Jack braced his arm on the van's roof and smiled at Kelly. "So maybe she's not high, maybe she's just weird. She *is* your relative, after all. Does your family go around jumping nekkid into ponds in Alabama? Do y'all like to drown your handbags?"

Kelly rolled her eyes at him. "I need to call my mother. It's true we're supposed to have Indian blood on her side of the family. But she's never mentioned anyone in South Dakota," she said. "How long would it take us to drive to a pay phone?"

Jack shook his head. "You can't get anywhere now. All the roads in and out are closed down. I heard they're going to have to fly the singers here on helicopters; that's why all the performances are running late, because no one can get to the site. Oh, and they've started letting everyone in free, because their gates and fences were completely overwhelmed. We didn't need the tickets after all."

"That's easy to believe, looking at the crowd," Kelly said. "So there are no phones, and there's no way to get to one?"

Jack shrugged and said, "None that I know of." He sighed and looked toward the stage. "Eric and Kristin are down there with Rodney and Laura, and I told them I'd look for them, although that's pretty hopeless. Ravi Shankar is coming up, I hope in an hour or two. Joan Baez may come on in the early morning hours. I'll be back before then and walk down with you. You and Sarah'll be fine here until she's wearing more than a thin blanket. Her clothes should by dry enough by that point." Jack laughed. "Lots of naked folks running around here, though, already. Might not make too much difference." He squinted at the distance. "And I'm still not entirely convinced she isn't on something." He watched the tent Sarah had entered. "Her behavior was bizarre. I don't know, maybe I shouldn't leave her here alone with you."

"You're high on marijuana, Jack. She seems more stable than you," Kelly said, though she threw a worried glance toward the tent. "And I wouldn't ask you to miss the concert."

"Correction: I *wish* I were high on marijuana, Kelly. This whole situation kind of ruined that, but I'm going down the hill to fix it. I think you can be in charge now." Jack smiled and mock-saluted as Sarah emerged from the tent, grinning in a wrapped and tucked thin blue blanket sari. She walked to the van and tossed her suede handbag onto the floorboard as Jack stepped aside, then handed him her second set of wet clothes. "I draped the ones I was wearing over a tent. Would you please place these on top of the van to dry in the sun?" she asked.

"Sure," Jack said, stretching the dark blue top and jeans across the roof and pulling them into place.

Sarah nodded and said, "Thank you, man." Then she climbed in and took a seat, placing her hands on her knees.

Kelly glared at her and resumed her work with a sigh. Sarah looked out the window, trying to spot any campers near them. She drummed her fingers on her knees as though Sly and the Family Stone were playing nearby instead of in her head.

"Do you have to do that?" Kelly asked, her eyebrows drawn.

"No, I am sorry. I'm just so happy to see you," Sarah beamed at her. "You're even prettier than I expected."

Kelly shook her head without looking up. "I don't know how you could've carried any expectation at all. You don't know me."

"Of course, I don't," Sarah replied. "Do you like Joan Baez? I'm hoping to see her tonight."

Kelly's head jerked up. "She's my favorite singer. The whole reason why I agreed to come on this trip."

"I love her song 'Sweet Sir Galahad'," Sarah said. "It's beautiful poetry about a man climbing into a window to meet his lover, something about the moon being in the yard. Doesn't that sound pretty? It's just so romantic, because the woman's first love died tragically years before and she pretended to laugh around others every day but she cried at night. And now she has this handsome man who takes her hand and comforts her and truly loves her. She wrote it about her sister's romance with—"

"With Milan Melvin!" Kelly said, her eyes wide. "I saw Joan Baez do that song on *The Smothers Brothers*. I didn't realize it was about Mimi and Milan, though. I read about when they got married at Big Sur last year." She smiled at Sarah. "Maybe I misjudged you," she told her. "At least, you know your music."

Sarah offered her a smile and said only, "I do."

Kelly nodded and went back to her notebook, frowning. Sarah sat in silence beside her for several minutes before asking, "May I please see what you're working on in that notebook?"

"Oh, no, I don't think you'd...I mean, no offense, but—" Kelly stammered.

Sarah chuckled. "Here's something you don't know about me. I'm really, really good at mathematics." She took Kelly's notebook and flipped to the most recent page, reaching her hand out to grab the pencil as she studied Kelly's writing. "It is fortunate I'm here to visit and help you with this while you look after me," Sarah said. "Please do not flip your wig. But let me show you where you're wrong."

"No!" Kelly yelled. "This is hours and hours of work I can't lose. Don't mark anything with that pencil, please. Just give me back the notebook—"

Sarah held up her hand and interrupted, yelling back, *"Leela ampaytu keen washtay!*' That's Lakota Sioux for 'it's a good day!'" She patted Kelly's arm. "It's a good day for both of us, you will see, I promise. Relax and allow me to explain this to you."

Jack, who had found himself fascinated by their interaction between the two women and decided to stay and observe a little longer, mouthed "wow" at Kelly's stunned face as Sarah continued to speak to Kelly like she was a third-grader, then began underlining her work. He backed away from the van when Sarah announced, "Do you see on this page where you wrote '-x3 C 4x D x.2 x/.2 C x/'? I know this is a bummer, but that's messing up everything that follows…"

Jack flipped the cooler open and grabbed a couple of the ham sandwiches Laura had mentioned, tucking them into a paper bag she'd thoughtfully provided. *She's gonna be a great mom,* he thought. He looked back at the two heads bowed in the rear of the van as he started down the hill, humming "Aquarius" as he made his way. *This is the dawning of Sarah teaching calculus, Sarah teaching calculuuuus.* Jack smiled at his little song. Sarah might be weird, but she'd located a common language within a minute with Kelly. He felt sure everything would be fine at camp for a few hours. He'd done the right thing, helping the girl to their space.

Jack looked up from picking his way along the steep path and saw a guy approaching, waves of dark hair cascading past his shoulders. He wore a purple-striped shirt with a leather vest over it and the bell bottoms everyone seemed to have on.

"Hey, man, you want a hit?" the guy asked, holding out a joint.

"Thanks," Jack said. He handed the joint back, wondering where the young man was heading. "Are you camped up there?" he asked.

"No," he said. "Climbing higher for a look at the view. I'm in a band, but we're not playing. Just diggin' the music, man."

"You actually look like Mick Jagger. Oh my God, you're not Mick Jagger?" Jack took the joint from the guy's fingers and stared.

"Do I sound British to you?" The guy laughed and patted Jack on the shoulder. "My name's Steven Tallarico. Sit down, smoke with me for a minute. Look at all those beautiful people." He waved his hand at the crowd and eased himself to the ground.

Jack sat next to him. "I'm Jack Warren, from Boston. Well, North Carolina, originally, little town near West Jefferson. Hey, are you hungry? I have some sandwiches." Jack held up the paper bag he'd been clutching in his left hand.

"Cool, but no thanks," said Steven. "I'm a New Yorker, born and raised. Ever heard of Chain Reaction? That's my band. We've opened," Steven hissed through his teeth as he inhaled, "for The Yardbirds and The Byrds and The Beach Boys. Cut a couple singles a few years ago. We're not doing much lately, though."

"No, I don't think I have," Jack said. "But I bet I will someday," he added, always the encouraging teacher. "You're young. You still have plenty of time to make it big."

"Yeah, well," Steven gazed at the scene below, "you gotta dream till your dream comes true, right? I met this guy named Joe Perry, he's amazing, man, plays guitar like Mozart played piano, ya know? He's in The Jam Band, and they're fantastic. They just played a gig near my folks' summer place in New Hampshire. I'd love to start a band with him."

"What would you call it?" Jack asked, trying to grasp the now-tiny roach with his fingertips. "Somebody should invent a clip or something to hold these," he said, gingerly handing it back to Steven.

"No idea what we'll call it, but I'm thinking of changing my stage name to Steven Tyler. Little less ethnic, right? What do you think?"

Steven stood and brushed off his clothes as he stomped on the nearly non-existent remains of the joint.

"I hope your new band gets huge someday. But personally, I'd keep Steven Tallarico. It has a certain ring to it," Jack said, also standing, and then heading down the path as Steven climbed higher. "Nice meeting you! Thanks a lot for sharing, man, and good luck," he called over his shoulder.

Jack continued toward the crowd and soon realized there was no chance of seeing his friends until they returned to camp, whenever that would be. He made his way to a free spot in the grass far from the stage and stared at the setting sun until Bert Sommer began playing Simon and Garfunkel's "America". He cheered wildly along with the audience afterward and joined everyone in a massive standing ovation. Then he thought about meeting Jeff Hillery in two days, leaving everything behind. He took a quick look around to see if anyone caught him swiping a tear from his face.

Jack sat back down as the brunette three feet from him casually removed her shirt and bra, fanning herself against the heat. He tried to look nonchalant and focus on the music, his eyes forward as much as possible.

A little while later, after much pot had been passed down the row to and from the half-naked girl and then to the burly older man next to him, Jack remembered the ham sandwiches he'd brought. They sat behind him, treasures beyond value. He gobbled the first and broke the second one in two, offering half to the smiling shirtless girl next to him, giving silent thanks for the August temperatures and the beauty of American women.

10

The Woodstock Music and Art Fair
Bethel, New York

AUGUST 15, 1969

The row of Port-O-Sans near their camp was unknown to lots of attendees in the crowd down the hill, so the lines tended to be shorter. Kelly was grateful for that, even with the soul-crushing stench they developed. Jack had tried to discourage use by taking a page from the back of her notebook and making an OUT OF ORDER sign he taped to the compartment closest to them; that didn't deter anyone for long. The boys mostly went into the woods; Kelly and a pregnant Laura were forced to hold their noses and clutch one of the paper dinner napkins Laura had packed for picnics as they waited in line.

And now, Sarah had to go. Kelly grudgingly opened her duffel bag and extracted her spare outfit. "We can't walk over there with you in a blanket. Well, actually, we'd probably fit right in, but it would be awkward in a port-o-let. You can wear this until your stuff is dry. I'll wait outside the tent while you change, okay?"

Sarah emerged in the yellow daisy sundress Laura had loaned Kelly, which seemed as well-suited to Woodstock as a sequined evening gown, especially with Sarah's still-damp black sandals. Kelly decided maybe she'd trade the dress for the peasant blouse and jeans later if Laura agreed. Hell, that sundress wouldn't fit her for much longer, anyway.

They made their way to stand in line, Sarah glancing repeatedly at the facility in front of them and the paper napkin in her right hand without a word. After ten long minutes, she stepped forward to enter as a bearded man in a tie-dyed caftan swung the door open and smiled at her, sweeping his eyes up and down in appraisal. He held the door for Sarah like it was a portal to the Taj Mahal, not a stinking hell-pit.

It was soon clear Sarah had no idea what a portable toilet was, or how to use it. Kelly was forced to stand to the side, yelling door-locking instructions while people stared.

"Is that your child in there?" an older woman in a long, gauzy dress asked from the back of the line. "Maybe you should go in with her." She blinked at Kelly, clearly upset with the time Sarah was taking.

Kelly knocked on the door. "Hurry up, Sarah," she said. "There are twelve people behind you." She offered the woman a fake smile and shrugged. "Not my child, my friend is having some terrible stomach trouble. You might want to try a different line."

Kelly stepped away from the toilet door to watch for Sarah to emerge, trying not to breathe and avoiding the eyes of the hippies waiting impatiently, shifting their weight from foot to foot and crossing their legs. She smiled to herself and looked at the ground. Nothing was going to ruin her memories of their hours in the van. The two of them had worked non-stop on challenging complex equations, Sarah breaking through them like an ice cutting ship in the Arctic. Like a Saturn V rocket punching through Earth's atmosphere.

It was beautiful to behold.

The toilet door opened and Kelly watched the line stifle a cheer, staring at Sarah. She wished she'd coached her to clutch her stomach as she emerged. Long Dress Lady shook her head as Kelly took Sarah's arm and led her back to the campsite's makeshift handwashing station. Sarah held the bar of soap tentatively, then seemed to understand how to rub it on her hands as Kelly poured water over them.

"Did we solve anything that will help you in your research efforts at MIT?" Sarah asked, drying her hands and tossing the towel to its storage space on the bumper.

Kelly laughed. "Well, at first, but the rest was just for fun. I had such a great time with you. Would you like a peanut butter and jelly sandwich?" Kelly asked, flipping the cooler open. "I'm starving."

"Yes, I had the gas with you too. And no, thank you," Sarah said. "I'm not hungry."

Kelly frowned as she extracted the plastic-wrapped sandwich. "I think you mean 'had a gas'. Anyway, you really should tell me where you learned all that, Sarah. People don't just walk around with knowledge of Boolean algebra and differential calculus. I don't care where you went to school." Kelly shrugged. "You're brilliant. Your alma mater doesn't matter." She took a big bite of sandwich and caught an errant glob of jelly with her finger, wiping it on a napkin.

"What I told you is true. I taught myself," Sarah said. "I know you don't believe me, but I've never been to a school like you have. Where I come from, we don't do that."

"Where you come from," Kelly stared at her. "On the reservation in South Dakota." She chewed her sandwich thoughtfully. "It's okay. You don't have to tell me right now." Kelly turned her head toward the distant sound from the stage, a soft song she didn't recognize. "Oh no," she said, "I think I hear *Eric* singing now." Kelly scrunched her nose and seated herself on the cooler. She patted the space next to her for Sarah to join her and swatted at a mosquito buzzing her ear. "He sounds much closer to us than the stage. I hope he's not coming back here already."

As she finished the last bite, Eric and Kristin appeared arm in arm in the distance, singing "These Boots Are Made For Walkin'", laughing and swinging their legs wide as they stepped forward.

"Hey, you, get off of my cooler!" Eric sang when they drew close, elbowing Kristin as he looked to see if she got his joke. He did an exaggerated little Mick Jagger prance. Then he motioned to the cooler again, this time holding eye contact with Kelly. Even in the dim light that remained, his eyes were so red the irises looked eerily blue, almost glowing. "Kristin and I need food, man. Like, right now."

Kelly and Sarah jumped up and Kelly waved Eric ahead. "Help yourself," she said. "Are Laura and Rodney not with y'all?"

"Nah, man, they're not cool. They stayed down there to listen to some guy I've never heard and I've heard everyone who is *anyone*, Kelly." Eric pawed through the cooler and uncovered the prize, Laura's pineapple upside-down cake. He lifted the pan and removed the foil around the top. Then Eric and Kristin began scooping handfuls out and shoving them into their mouths, wide-eyed at the taste. "You should try this," Eric said. "So great, man."

"Eric, that's disgusting, you cretin," Kelly said. "Laura was going to flip it over to serve it on a platter she brought, and now you've destroyed the whole thing. That cake was for all of us. Put it down and I'll get some paper plates and forks so you can eat like a human." She watched Kristin, her eyes half-closed, chewing pineapple and moaning softly. "Did you have to get her on drugs, Eric?" She shook her head. "That's your scene, not any of ours. You make me sick." Kelly used a big spoon to serve them pieces of cake they'd already touched and leave a clean dessert for the rest of them.

She handed Eric and Kristin their plates and said, "I think we'll take this with us. Come on, Sarah, let's move our stuff into this first tent." She clutched the sheet cake pan and nodded as she opened the side door of the VW. "Sarah, would you grab your purse and my stuff in that blue duffel? Also, hand me that sleeping bag—yes, that one— and you carry the lantern. Oh, and will you also carry that brown bag?" She glared at Eric and Kristin sitting on the ground, cake crumbs and sticky, syrupy goo circling their mouths. Sarah trailed her like a hotel bellman, juggling Kelly's stuff and trying to keep the strap of her large suede handbag on her shoulder.

As they disappeared into the tent, Eric licked the caramel from one of Kristin's fingers and said, "Come stay with me in that middle one. Jack can sleep in the van."

Kristin rallied for a second. "No, *I'm* going to sleep in…van," she slurred. She grabbed the bumper to help herself up and staggered to the side door, attempting to slide it open. Eric clambered to his feet and grabbed the door handle, positioning his face close to hers as he pulled it.

"Are you sure? We could have a lot of fun. I'd make you feel real good, Kristin." She shook her head back and forth, briefly stumbled backward, then climbed in, Eric's hand firmly planted on her right butt cheek to "help."

Kristin laid her head on the wadded-up blanket Kelly had left behind and curled into a fetal position, her knees hanging over the seat's edge. "Wake me up…few hours," she mumbled.

Eric slid the van door shut and decided to rest in the middle tent, where he'd thrown his sleeping bag earlier. Maybe Kristin would be in a better mood after a nap. Maybe Kelly would stop being a bitch about the cake in a few hours. Maybe that weird Sarah girl would take her clothes off again. He smiled at the thought. He could hear Kelly chattering in the tent next door, though he couldn't make out the words. Something about dining decorum and manners, probably, from her majesty the friggin' expert. He took the small pillow from his sleeping bag and fluffed it with a few punches. As Eric closed his eyes, he vowed he'd wake before anyone good took the stage. All of this, every bit of it, was an opening act for the weekend he intended to have.

Kelly set the flashlight lantern in the corner of the tent and switched it on, then she and Sarah unzipped and flayed her sleeping bag open. "As long as we're not on the ground, we'll be fine," Kelly announced, "and it'll be so hot, we'll use your blanket sari for covers, okay?"

"That is a far out way for us to sleep," Sarah replied. She lifted the brown paper bag she'd carried and held it out to Kelly as she sat next to her on the sleeping bag. "Why is this so heavy?"

Kelly smiled and took it from her. "Among other things," she said, "there's a bottle of wine in here. My friends think I don't know how to relax and have a good time, but I brought it and another bottle that's in my duffel. And these." She extracted a bag of Bugles, a can of Pringles, and a few chocolate bars, handing one to Sarah. "Do you like chocolate?"

Sarah turned the dark brown wrapper over to read the bottom. "No, I haven't had this. I don't think I'd like it. You keep the chocolate bar and other things. I don't get hungry very often."

"I noticed. But do you get thirsty?" Kelly said, grinning. She held up a bottle of Boone's Farm Strawberry Hill with a flourish, cradling it like a TV game show model would for Sarah to inspect. "This is the best. It's not too strong and it's like drinking candy."

"Oh, I've never had wine," Sarah said, reading the label. "I'm sure it's very groovy."

Kelly withdrew the bottle and replaced it in the bag. "How old are you, Sarah? Give me an answer besides 'older than you think', because I really need to know more about you if we're going to be friends. I like you, but the mysterious act has to go." Kelly stretched her legs out and leaned back on her elbows. "I know I'm not always easy to talk to. I can be a little abrupt and impatient with people, but I'm making my best effort here not to push you. You're a mathematical genius and somehow related to my family in a distant way. That's literally all you've told me."

Kelly paused and began to address the ceiling of the tent, avoiding Sarah's blank stare. "I'm trying to ignore the way you acted like you were on drugs when Jack found you. You seem normal enough now, even if the way you speak is strange, though I can understand that. Maybe you really did talk to my mom. The odds of that would be remote, but let's say it happened." She returned her gaze to Sarah. "Tell me the truth about who you are. And about all the math you shouldn't know how to do."

Sarah took a deep breath and closed her eyes. "I have waited so long to tell you this," she said. "I should start with my real name. It's

Joan Baez Smith, after your favorite singer, but everyone calls me Baezy. I was born in 2069, the centennial of your far out Woodstock festival experience. I'm almost thirty-two years old even though I know I look younger to you…" She opened her eyes and turned them to Kelly, who stared in incomprehension for a few seconds before getting to her feet and leaving the tent.

Kelly stepped into the night air, still saturated with marijuana, cow patties, and the occasional waft from the port-o-lets, so brown you could almost see it. She regretted the lack of a door to slam on the tent. The insult was almost too much to bear: prank the math nerd, tell her you're from the future, try to convince someone profoundly rooted in reality you're a supernatural visitor. She wondered if Jack had suggested Sarah say something so absurd. It would appeal to his juvenile sense of humor, she decided. It was probably him and his pot-addled brain.

Sarah made no attempt to follow her. Good. Kelly walked to the van to sit in the front passenger seat and wait for Jack. She listened to Kristin's soft snoring as she stared at the mass of humanity below, formulating the exact words she'd use to tell Jack off. He deserved it for such a stupid stunt.

She wished she could sharpen her anger into something to hurt him, to hurt Sarah, but all it did was cause her to cry quietly, as alone as she'd ever been with half a million people. She thought back over the afternoon, working in the notebook with Sarah. She'd never met anyone who enjoyed mathematics as much as she did. And now, their friendship was ruined. She closed her eyes and laid her head back.

Kelly jumped as Sarah tapped on the driver's side window, a wide-eyed ghost. Kelly watched her fumble with the door handle until she leaned across to open it from the inside and pushed the door outward. Sarah climbed into the driver's seat, the overhead light briefly illuminating her wet cheeks. She sniffled and Kelly prepared herself for a pitiful apology, designed to elicit her sympathy. She had no intention of offering any to this strange girl.

"I am very sorry," Sarah said. "What I thought would amuse you just made you angry and that is lame. Let me show you something." She reached into her handbag and produced a plastic-encased South Dakota driver's license with her photo. "This is who I am, Sarah Sandoval. I'm nineteen, like it says there. I apologize for my crazy story. It was not funny. Could we please start over?"

Kelly handed the license back. "Why didn't you show me this in the first place?"

"I should have," Sarah replied. "I tried to tell you I grew up on Pine Ridge Reservation, I tried to tell you my real name, and you didn't believe me. It's my fault for showing off with the equations. I thought it would be cool and far out to make myself exciting, a person from the future, because you seemed to think it was impossible I knew those things." Sarah swiped at her eyes. "I'm truly sorry. I wasn't trying to trick you, just entertain you. I want us to be friends and have a good time together here." Sarah reached deep into her handbag, like Mary Poppins, and extracted a bottle of Kelly's wine and two paper cups, handing one to Kelly. "Let's drink this together while we wait for Jack to walk back. We both need to relax. Isn't this supposed to help you relax?"

Kelly shrugged her shoulders, took the bottle and twisted off the cap, then poured wine into each of their cups. She handed one to Sarah, who sniffed and gazed into the cup like it was some rare vintage.

"Cheers," Kelly said.

Sarah nodded and took a tiny sip. A scowl skittered across her features, but she managed to smile at Kelly. "This is very nice, thank you. I can feel the relaxation vibrations already."

Kristin slept on, never noticing when Jack swept open the door to a giggling Kelly and Sarah an hour later. "Joan will *finally* be onstage soon," he told them, glancing at Kristin snoozing in the back seat. "The pregnant one is asleep already, too," he added, "along with her fiancé. Such a wild bunch I came here with." He grabbed the empty bottle from the floorboard. "Oh, Boone's Farm. You're an animal, Kelly." Jack laughed and extended his hand to Kelly, who stepped down and smoothed her clothes as he walked to the driver's side for Sarah.

Kelly hiccupped. "From a California vineyard with the finest strawberries," she called after him.

Jack opened the door and Sarah started to fall as she climbed out of the van. "Whoa, are you okay?" Jack asked. He caught her waist and held her steady as Kelly rolled her eyes.

"She had three-quarters of a Dixie cup. She's fine," Kelly told him.

"Okay, well, you can't wear that," he told Sarah, who was swaying slightly after he released her. "A yellow dress isn't going to work out, sitting on the ground, and you'll be too cold, too. Where are your clothes?"

Sarah waved in the direction of the tents. "Maybe dry, I don't know. I'll go check where I hung them up." She nodded at Jack as she walked away, zigzagging a little. "I'll change clothes in the tent. Oh, and I can wear my headband, too! It is super groovy!" She headed off, Jack and Kelly staring after her.

"I'm going to get a long-sleeve shirt for her from my stuff," Jack said. "She can just throw it over that thin blouse." He opened the back of the van to rummage in his bag.

Kelly appeared at his side. "I wish you'd stop treating her like a child. She's a grown woman who knows as much math as you or I do. Or some kind of space alien." Kelly stared at the dark tent, where Sarah was obviously fumbling without the light. Probably couldn't figure out how to turn it on. She shook her head and turned back to Jack, who was still digging for his chivalrous shirt. Kelly slid her arm behind Jack and hugged his waist, laying her head on his shoulder. Jack paused a second and stroked her hair.

"You've had all but a three-quarters-filled Dixie cup of that wine, haven't you?" He laughed, his eyes still on his duffel bag.

"Yeah, and I need more. I'll grab the other bottle." Kelly decided to join Sarah in the tent and hurry her along. They emerged a minute later, Kelly holding the Boone's Farm aloft in her left hand. "You're welcome to some of this," she told Jack.

Jack exaggerated a grin and nodded. "My style is a little less syrupy. Don't worry, there are plenty of ways to party down there." He nodded at the crowd below as he helped Sarah into his shirt, pulling each arm into a sleeve. "There, Miss Sandoval. Fashion and warmth. And your headband is very cool," he said, touching the woven seed beads.

"Thank you," she beamed a smile at him. "I borrowed it from my mom."

Kelly groaned. "Your mom who didn't know you were running away to Woodstock had that lying around for you to grab? Is that the story?"

Jack swung his head between the two of them. He intertwined his fingers with Kelly's and then Sarah's on his other side. "Stick with me, ladies, the path is a little treacherous in the dark."

Kelly tightened her grip on his hand, wondering if he realized how perfectly it fit hers.

Sarah laughed lightly as they set off. "You're so strong, Jack. If I start to stumble, I know you can catch me."

Kelly felt an entire field of strawberries threaten to revisit her throat.

11

The Woodstock Music and Art Fair
Bethel, New York
EARLY MORNING, AUGUST 16, 1969

They walked toward the music, carefully stepping over a sleeping man in the pasture, his moonlit face poking from a blanket cocoon. The walk to the stage area was the best people-watching Kelly had experienced in her entire life. A guy with a shaved head was wrapped swami-style in a yellow sheet over a white t-shirt, clutching a large bunch of peacock feathers; two women approached them arm-in-arm, their faces painted in rainbow colors, offering single daisies to everyone (Kelly, Sarah and Jack all tucked theirs behind their ears); there was a kid who'd paired a shirtless barefoot look with purple tie-dyed jeans and a Davey Crockett coonskin cap; and a tall, bearded man in the distance, wearing a blue-print caftan, was carrying a small lamb under his arm.

Sarah stopped in her tracks and made her way over to the guy with the lamb, despite Jack trying to grab her. She hugged the man, holding him close for what Kelly counted as twenty-three seconds, whispering something to him as she patted the lamb on its head. She took the man's free hand in both of hers and held it for a while, her back turned to her friends, chattering away.

She refused to tell Jack and Kelly what she'd said to the man, but he stared for a long time as they walked on.

"Sarah, you don't know that guy. He may look friendly, and the lamb is cute, but you can't just go around hugging people," Kelly admonished. "There are hundreds of thousands of people here. Not all of them are nice, and it's weird for you to randomly hug a stranger."

"He's a gentle soul, I knew that immediately," Sarah replied.

"Why?" Jack asked. "Because he was carrying a baby lamb?"

"That's exactly why," Sarah said, turning around to wave at the man once more.

"Good lord," Kelly muttered under her breath. "He was probably on his way to sacrifice it."

Jack heard her and chuckled. "Always the trusting soul, Kelly Adams."

The crowd had thinned as the evening wore on into the wee hours of morning, so they were able to sit close enough to make out Joan Baez as she took the stage in a blue mini dress, her smile beaming peace to everyone. Jack sat with arms encircling his bent legs between Sarah and Kelly, trying to match their enthusiasm. This was not his style of music.

Kelly refilled her cup with Boone's Farm and passed another to Sarah, offering one to Jack as he held up a hand to say no. "You're probably still high on marijuana," Kelly said, sweeping her eyes up and down him with the smirking gravity of an elderly schoolmarm.

"I believe you may be right," Jack answered. "Otherwise, Joan would be a lot less interesting for me. But I would pass on that strawberry syrup under any conditions. You're probably both gonna be sick." He turned to see Sarah gulping hers down as they heard the opening guitar chords of "Oh, Happy Day."

Sarah jumped to her feet when Joan began belting the chorus, her voice washing over the crowd clear and strong. She sang along, matching every lyric word for word, as Kelly watched in astonishment. She pulled Jack's old shirt over her head and swung it in the air like a lasso. Kelly was grateful the white peasant blouse was dry, at least.

Jack had been sitting with his eyes closed, and upon opening them he first experienced the rain as tiny diamonds suspended in front of the stage lights. As he squinted, he realized there was a light drizzle falling on the crowd. Kelly was on her feet now, too, swaying to the music along with Sarah, who squealed and held her arms wide when she felt the rain. Sarah dropped Jack's shirt in his lap and jumped up and down in place like a kid stomping puddles, collecting tiny raindrops in each hand.

Kelly sat down and yelled at Jack, "Dammit! Can I have your shirt to put over my head?"

Jack handed it to her and Kelly hunched over to watch Joan from under a makeshift hood. Sarah, clearly still delighted by the rain, kept swaying and dancing until Joan paused to command the crowd to "sit down, please", a little brusquely, Jack thought. Sarah plopped next to Jack and accepted a bottle of wine passed by a girl on her left, taking a big swig and scowling before taking a second longer drink and sending it on. Jack drank, but Kelly handed the bottle to a shirtless man on her right, preferring her Boone's Farm.

Joan told the audience her husband was doing fine, and "we are too," pointing to her pregnant belly. She went on to the topic of her husband's arrest for refusing military induction, talking about his "very, very good hunger strike" in prison as a segue into the folk song "Joe Hill." No one had any idea how long David Harris would serve for refusing to be drafted.

Kelly locked eyes with Jack and placed her hand on his. He whispered, "It's going to be okay. *I'm* going to be okay. Stop worrying." He focused on Baez's trade unionist song, a strange choice, he thought, for a festival where people were clearly there for a good time. Anti-war, pro-peace was one thing, he mused, but he didn't want to be preached to about labor unions. He wished, not for the first time,

Kelly was a Janis Joplin nut, not a Joan Baez fanatic. Janis would never order anyone to sit down.

He noticed both Kelly and Sarah were captivated, though, swaying as they sat with their legs folded into pretzels, their eyes and ears glued to Joan Baez. Kelly had even forgotten how much she hated rain and tossed Jack's shirt aside. The music finally came to an end with "We Shall Overcome," which Joan encouraged the more-than-willing pair of them to sing along with.

Jack stood and stretched as Sarah reached past him to hug Kelly. "Wasn't she wonderful?" Kelly hollered over the crowd noise.

"She was so far out!" Sarah answered.

Jack decided Boone's Farm must contain potent hallucinogens. He looped his arms through the girls' and they made their way through the crowd, skirting around small campfires and sleeping bodies. Jack stopped for a nightcap toke from one of the few groups still awake at the bottom of the hill, three guys and a frizzy-haired girl who offered the joint to them as they drew near. The girl stared at Jack in a way that clearly said she wanted to offer more. Kelly and Sarah watched him wink at her as they walked away.

"Our escort is popular," Kelly told Sarah with an exaggerated nod and one eyebrow cocked.

"Would you like to sleep in our tent?" Sarah asked Jack. "I think there's room, and you won't have to crash with Eric. I have noticed he is a bug to you sometimes."

"No! No, that's not appropriate, Sarah. Jack has a place to sleep," Kelly said. She reached over and placed Jack's heavy shirt around Sarah's white blouse, dampened once more and a bit transparent in what little light shone as they climbed the hill.

Sarah shrugged and unwrapped one of her little candy cubes, popping it into her mouth. "Okay," she said. "I didn't mean anything but sleep. I am sorry." She stumbled over a rock and Jack caught her by the elbow.

He laughed as he released her arm. "*I'm* not. Let me know if y'all reconsider." He offered Kelly a grin and added, "I'm gonna pull her clothes off the top of the van and put them inside. They're probably soaked again." He kissed each girl on the cheek as they walked up to their tent. "Goodnight, ladies."

Kelly stumbled as she entered the tent and collapsed face-first on the sleeping bag. Sarah wasn't sure whether to laugh until she heard Kelly's giggles.

"You are blitzled," Sarah said, laughing and pointing at Kelly.

"It's *blitzed* and I might be," Kelly replied. "I haven't had this great a night in a long time, even with the rain. Laura's right, I work too much." She switched on the lantern and rolled onto her back, clasping her hands on her chest as Sarah sat on her side of the sleeping bag. "And why did you invite Jack to sleep in here? That was weird."

Sarah shrugged. "I'm a little blitzed, too. I was just being polite. I only meant he might be more comfortable here than with Eric. Nothing sexual at all. You're the one who mistook my meaning."

"He did, too." Kelly rolled her eyes and laughed. "I'm sure he thought it was the best offer he'd ever had. Jack's a lady-killer and he knows it, but I doubt he's been in a threesome."

Sarah raised her eyebrows. "A threesome? I don't understand. What is that?"

"Are you serious?" Kelly said. She watched Sarah nod gravely and decided to change the subject. "It doesn't matter. Listen, I want you to know I really enjoyed having you along for Joan Baez. It's so great to have someone who shares my love of her music." Kelly picked at a thread on the sleeping bag. "The truth is, I don't have many girlfriends. Where I grew up, my whole focus was math and winning awards in school. The other girls were interested in boys and clothes and cheerleading and movies and…they treated me like some kind of alien because I spent my Friday and Saturday nights exploring calculus. I wanted to earn a scholarship, and I did. But I didn't earn many friends. I didn't earn *any*, honestly. The other kids treated me like a freak. The most popular girl in school actually called me that in the lunchroom once. Bobby Ledbetter was sitting with me and she asked him why he was having lunch with The Freak. He didn't sit with me after that day.

No one did. I ate lunch with an open algebra book for company." She turned her eyes to the tent's ceiling, mentally counting the ribs holding it in place. "Plus I was scrawny and didn't get boobs until I was practically twenty, and I wore braces that looked like an aircraft engine in my mouth. I didn't have friends for a lot of reasons, I guess."

"I'm sorry. That must have been horrible for you. But Laura is your friend," Sarah said.

"Yeah, well, Laura technically works for me. She has to be nice to me." Kelly took a deep breath. "I don't really see anyone outside the lab. I work and I go home, lather, rinse, repeat. It's the choice I made, and I'm not unhappy with it. I mean, who doesn't dream of being at MIT every day?"

Sarah smiled. "I guess there are some people who want to be somewhere besides MIT, and then go home to wash their hair every night. But they're not doing important work like you are."

Kelly cocked her head to one side and frowned. "My hair…oh, never mind. And how, exactly, do you know my work is important?" she asked. She got to her knees and fumbled with the zipper of her duffel, then extracted a set of baby doll pajamas. "Sorry, I don't have any for you," she told Sarah. "I have a baggy shirt you can wear, though." She held up a red and gray MIT t-shirt for Sarah's inspection.

"I saw the work you are doing, remember? Thank you." Sarah took the shirt and held it up. "Why didn't you tell me about this earlier when I had no clothes?" she asked, removing her peasant blouse and pulling the t-shirt over her bra. "I had to wear a blanket."

"Because you had no pants to run around in, and it's too short. Plus, I just didn't know you well enough." Kelly finished putting her pajamas on and sat back down on her side of the sleeping bag, smoothing her hair behind her ears. "Anyway, what I was trying to tell you is, I work in a field that's almost exclusively populated by men. And my classes were much the same at MIT. Women are rare there. So I've never had girlfriends. I didn't get to know any women who are like me in college. That part was high school all over again."

"And now you know me?" Sarah asked. "I do feel like we have grown closer."

Kelly stared at her for several seconds. "Well, I'm definitely more comfortable with you now, you're right," she replied, adding, "Especially since I've had about a gallon of wine." Kelly pulled the Bugles and a chocolate bar from the grocery bag. "I'm famished," she said. "Aren't you hungry? I haven't seen you eat anything but that little cube. You have to be starving." She held the Bugles bag out to Sarah. "Here, try these."

Sarah examined the bag closely, clearly stalling. "I sneaked half a sandwich earlier. I'm fine."

"No you didn't," Kelly said, munching on a handful of Bugles. "I've been with you this whole time. Do you have food allergies or something? I know people don't really believe in that, but there was a girl in my elementary school who had to go to the hospital after she ate some peanuts."

"No, it's not allergies. The little cubes you mentioned fill me up. They have all the nutrition I need. I, umm, grew up eating them. They're all I know," Sarah said. "My mom makes them," she added.

Kelly nodded. "On the reservation," she drawled, exaggerating her accent. "And she has a factory to professionally package them. That's impressive." She unwrapped the chocolate and broke off a small piece. "Look," she said, handing it to Sarah, "if you don't want salty, try this."

Sarah held the brown rectangle and looked at it in the lantern light, sniffing tentatively. "If you insist," she said, placing the chocolate on her tongue like a communion wafer. She blinked at Kelly and swirled the chocolate around in her mouth, closing her eyes. When they opened, she began to cry, using the palms of her hands to swipe the tears upward.

"What's wrong? Oh my gosh, Sarah, what's wrong?" Kelly scooted closer to the tent flap, prepared to run for help.

"No, it's just so wonderful. I've never had anything like that. The taste is just…where I come from, only certain important people can have this, probably. I don't even know if *they* do. And you eat it all the time?" Sarah reached for the rest of the bar and examined it. "I can't believe I've lived my whole life without experiencing this. Chocolate. It is truly amazing. The melty sweetness, the softness, the taste, the way it coated my tongue…" She sniffled and swiped at her nose. "I'm sorry. I know I look ridiculous. I don't expect you to understand."

She started to hand the bar back to Kelly, but Kelly said, "Keep it. Enjoy. And maybe you need a Joe Hill to organize for food rights where you live." She laid her head on the little pillow she'd brought. "I'm sleepy, but I'm wound up, too. That concert was something I've dreamt of for years. I still can't believe I saw her."

Sarah lay on her side, facing Kelly. She broke off a second piece of chocolate and popped it in her mouth, closing her eyes for several seconds. "Me too. Joan Baez, right in front of us. That's enough excitement to keep me awake for hours. Maybe it's the wine, though. I'm sure I drank more than is suggested on the label."

Kelly said, "Umm, I don't think there's a recommended—is there no such thing as wine on the *reservation?*"

Sarah held up her hand, her eyes locked on Kelly's. She drew a deep breath. "Kelly, it's obvious to me you don't believe what I've told you. You make fun of the word 'reservation' every time you say it."

Kelly raised her brows. "That's true," she said. "Your story makes no sense at all."

"But you've shared so much about yourself, and now I wish you'd let me talk about myself and why I really came here. I want to tell you, even if you hear it like a fairy tale," Sarah said. "I am a part of you. I am *your* future, not just *the* future."

Kelly rolled her eyes. "And you are very dramatic. You are absolutely determined to make me re-live *2001: A Space Odyssey*, aren't you? Go ahead. I'm not sure I can stop you unless I leave, and I'm not going back out there."

"I don't know what a space odyssey is, so no. Just let me tell you. And do not flip over your wig this time," Sarah said. "First of all, you are working on the tiniest seed of what will become true artificial intelligence. I wasn't pulling on your legs when I said your work is important. It will impact everyone in the world, everything in our lives. You're at the very beginning of a revolution in computers. I've seen where it leads."

Kelly yawned and threw an arm over her eyes. "I am, huh? Maybe I've had enough alcohol to listen. Not to *believe*, but listen. You can talk me to sleep. Go ahead. Tell me about Future World. But I've seen *The Jetsons*, you know. I doubt you have much to add to my visions of flying cars and robot maids." She sighed and waited for Sarah to begin.

"You won't make a freak out again?" Sarah asked. "Promise?"

"I won't *make a freak out*," Kelly told Sarah as she lifted her arm and turned off the lantern. "Promise."

"Okay," Sarah began. "First of all, you can't tell anyone this, because they will think you're crazy."

"I'm pretty sure that goes without saying," Kelly replied. "Hurry up, I'm falling asleep."

"Try not to be so skeptical," Sarah said, exhaling a nervous puff of air. "Stop and consider the things you don't yet understand, the possibilities of the future. You can continue calling me Sarah, that's fine, it's on the driver's license I showed you…but my name really is Baezy, Kelly, and I'm your distant great-granddaughter. I traveled through time to visit you here at Woodstock, from the year 2101. I live in a place called Unity. I'll tell you more about that, but please know first of all it's a world like everyone dreams of now, with no war, no hunger, only happiness and health. All the peace and love and sharing this festival is about…" Sarah paused. "Are you still listening?"

"Yeah," Kelly sighed and rolled to her side, facing the tent. "Happy, healthy utopia with no chocolate for the masses. Got it."

"Just please keep your mind opened up, okay? I have so much to tell you about my world, but I'll start here. Animagenesis is something I know would interest you, because it was born of a glitch in artificial intelligence. You remember that guy who was carrying a lamb…"

Kelly woke to birdsong and a massive headache five hours later. Sarah still slept beside her, hands clasped under her head. Kelly briefly remembered something the girl had said about everyone sleeping in a standing position in 2101. Unreal. Obviously, she was taking drugs. And suddenly, Kelly knew the source: that little cube Sarah had consumed as they walked up the hill. *That* was when she'd reverted to the drug-addled state they'd first encountered, minutes after she ate the damn thing, during their conversation in the tent. She'd made sense until then.

Kelly reached for Sarah's handbag, one eye on the sleeping girl. She dug out six little cubes, each encased in a white and pink wrapper. She shrugged on Laura's daisy dress and opened the tent flap, checking first to see if Sarah stirred, then if any of her friends had emerged outside. No one was up in or anywhere near their camp.

Kelly took what was undoubtedly the source of Sarah's LSD dosage and turned the packages over and over, looking for identifiable markings on them in the weak sunlight. Nothing. She carried the cubes to the abandoned port-o-let, where she dumped them into a filthy, stinking, revolting hole in the first stall.

12

The Woodstock Music and Art Fair
Bethel, New York
SATURDAY, AUGUST 16, 1969

Kelly wiped the steady drizzle from her eyes as she returned from the port-o-lets, listening to the stage announcements in the distance. People were hungry, there was a food shortage, they should make their way to the woods for breakfast. An optimistic dude rattled on soon after about how the mud between the crowd's toes was "all part of the high" in "the first free city in the world of the Aquarian Age" because it glued them all together. "We're all in the same puddle!" Kelly shook her head and re-entered the tent, searching her purse for aspirin. She downed two with rainwater she gathered by holding her cup outside the flap for a minute.

Sarah slept on, occasionally moving a foot or taking an extra-deep breath. Kelly dreaded having to tell her what she'd done, but it was best for the girl. She'd have to understand. Kelly closed her eyes and hoped the aspirin kicked in before she had to handle that confrontation. She eased her body down onto the sleeping bag and hoped for headache relief, listening to the rain fall harder, a steady staccato drumbeat now.

She was half-asleep when Laura poked her head into the tent. Kelly held a finger to her lips and pointed at Sarah. In turn, Laura raised her eyebrows and pointed to the foil-covered cake next to Kelly's leg.

"Just a minute," she whispered to Laura, her dread of dealing with Sarah mushrooming in her stomach. Kelly grabbed the pan and slipped out with it as quietly as she could. Laura led the way to her tent, waving her hand at Rodney's neatly rolled sleeping bag.

"He wanted to explore this morning," she explained.

"I hope he has rain gear. Did you get enough sleep?" Kelly asked, sitting down to wait for Laura to serve her cake.

"We brought an umbrella. And I've discovered there's no such thing as enough sleep at this point in a pregnancy," Laura answered. "It's pretty much all I want to do, that and eat. Thank God I brought all this food. Did you hear the announcements? It's sounding like a granola riot could break out down there." Laura handed Kelly a plate with a piece of right-side-up pineapple cake and a fork. "Sorry Eric and Kristin pawed through it, and thank you for being the grownup there to save the cake. It'll still taste just as good," she said.

Kelly dug in. "This is fantastic, thanks. I think it's helping my hangover." She chewed slowly, relishing the syrupy pineapple.

Laura's eyes widened. "Hangover? What happened, Miss Adams? Has Woodstock transformed you into Foster Brooks?" Laura produced a mock hiccup for punctuation.

"Oh, I drank a bunch of Boone's Farm Strawberry Hill while Jack and Sarah and I watched Joan Baez. She was great, by the way," Kelly said. "It was everything I'd hoped for, even sitting there in the drizzle. At least it wasn't raining like this morning." Kelly nodded at the tent flap. "I'm really glad we're up on a hill."

"Well, if you want more Boone's Farm, Eric brought some and I doubt he'll touch it. He's seducing Kristin with pot instead. And Rodney and I won't drink it. That stuff is gross." Laura wrinkled her nose. "I can't believe how it's pouring out there. Maybe it'll let up soon." She finished her small piece of cake and cut a larger one, glancing at Kelly. "Seconds?"

"No thanks," Kelly said. "That was just right. Maybe I could take a piece for Sarah, though."

Laura hesitated before replacing the foil. "Is she planning to stay here? I thought you were only helping her after Jack's big rescue. Isn't she going to look for her own people? They can help her meet someone with a stage announcement, you know. I've been hearing them all along. You ask them to tell the crowd about a lost person, where to find her and everything." Laura stabbed her cake and took a bite. "I'm sure whoever she came with would like to be reunited."

Kelly shook her head the slightest bit before answering. "We aren't sure she arrived with anyone, or if she did, whether they're safe for her to be with. I've thought more than once they may have drugged her. It would explain a lot." She bit her lip. "You really don't like her, do you?"

Laura finished her cake and set the plate down, licking her fingers. "It's not that I don't like her. I don't know her. And honestly, Kelly, she's throwing the whole dynamic off. We were supposed to have three girls and three boys. Kristin should be sharing your tent. Unless you're encouraging her to sleep with Eric." She wrinkled her nose again.

Kelly took a deep breath. "Well, I know Sarah and I like her. She's interesting. I had fun with her yesterday and last night, too. She's not a bad person, Laura, but I think someone gave her drugs, and they've been affecting everything. She's just a kid." Kelly checked to see if Laura was wrinkling her nose again; she was an Academy-Award-winning dramatic cringer. "But that's over. She won't be taking any more."

Laura made her face solemn. "We aren't drug people. The guys might smoke a little grass, that's all. And you know it. I don't want to be around kids who do mescaline and acid or whatever." She clutched her still-flat lower belly and Kelly resisted the urge to roll her eyes.

"Take a look around," Kelly waved in the direction of the crowd below. "You're surrounded by hundreds of thousands of people who do mescaline and acid or *whatever*. There's a freak-out tent down there for them. Welcome to Woodstock, Laura. You're the one who talked *me* into coming along," she said. "Those people aren't bothering you. Stop being so square."

Laura burst into laughter. "Did you, Kelly Adams, the squarest person ever birthed into a pool of geometry, just tell me to stop being square? That's truly hilarious. Look, I know you bonded with that girl doing equations yesterday, but you're mistaking this... *mathfatuation*...with friendship. Sarah doesn't fit in here. She's giving everyone the creeps. Every sentence she utters sounds weird." Laura reached over to clasp Kelly's arm. "Sarah should go. Rodney thinks so, too," she said.

They both turned to see a dripping Sarah open the tent flap. She wore Kelly's MIT shirt with her wet bell bottoms. "I heard what you were saying, and I'm sorry you feel that way. I can get my things and go," she said. She held her eyes on Kelly, obviously hoping for support. "I apologize for your creeps, Laura." She dropped the tent flap and Kelly shot a look of disgust at Laura as she jumped up to follow Sarah into the pouring rain.

Kelly caught up and put her hand on Sarah's shoulder. "Never mind her," she said. "I have something important to discuss with you. Let's go into our tent. We need to talk."

"I don't think it's our tent," Sarah said, unmistakably sad. "I don't belong here. It never occurred to me your friends wouldn't want me. I only thought of you when I planned this trip."

Kelly pulled Sarah's arm toward the tent, relieved to find she'd follow. Inside, Kelly seated herself and extended an open palm to indicate Sarah should sit across from her. "I'm sorry you heard what Laura said, Sarah. She doesn't represent me or anyone else here except maybe Rodney, and that's only because she's completely in control of his brain lately." Kelly crossed her legs as she pulled them toward her, encircling her shins in her arms and resting her chin on one knee. She grabbed the blanket and began rubbing her hair dry, then offered it to

Sarah. "And I'm not the only person here who wants you to stay. I'm sure Jack does, too."

Sarah smiled and nodded. "Jack is so nice. I can never thank him enough for helping me, for bringing me to you. He is a neat cat."

"Yes, he's a good guy," Kelly answered. She took the blanket back from Sarah, although she noted both of them were still dripping rainwater all over the sleeping bag. Kelly saw the same loose thread she'd picked at last night as she'd talked to Sarah, high on Joan Baez and cheap wine. She yanked and broke it. "Just ignore what Laura said. She and Rodney are in their own little world right now. She's not thinking about anyone else's feelings, and I'm sorry she was so hurtful." Kelly paused to clear her throat. "And Sarah, I understand now why you've been saying all this wild stuff about the future. It only occurred to me this morning I've seen you taking drugs—"

"I do not take drugs," Sarah interrupted. "I never have." She dropped her chin to her chest. "So this means you still don't believe me."

Kelly reached to squeeze Sarah's arm. "You have a fanciful, bright, stunning imagination, Sarah. But you have to understand, I'm more rooted in reality and facts than anyone you could ever meet. I've always been this way. My mother read me fairy tales at bedtime, and I would stop her over and over to ask how a wolf could dress as someone's grandma, or try to blow a house down, or why a family of bears would live in a house with beds and bowls of porridge." She shrugged. "That's just *me*. I made her stop reading *Alice in Wonderland* three pages in."

Sarah raised her head and smiled. "No wonder you have trust issues, Kelly." She sighed heavily and toppled to her side, curling her legs into a fetal position as she gazed at Kelly. "I've decided it doesn't matter if you believe me. I'm happy to be here with you, to have this experience, and that's all that really matters. Laura and Rodney can tolerate me until tomorrow. I have to go home Sunday."

Kelly bit her bottom lip. "It makes me so sad to think of your leaving, Sarah. You may be the first real girlfriend I've ever had, and I'll really miss you. I hope we can write letters to each other." She turned her eyes to the ceiling, inhaling deeply through her nose. "Sarah, the thing is, I think you've been taking LSD since you got here. Maybe you don't even know it; I have no idea where those little packages came from. It explains all the things you've said to me. I don't think anyone could dream all that up without drugs, especially the part about being my many times great-granddaughter. And that wasn't necessary, by the way. I already liked you. A lot." She saw Sarah frown and close her eyes. "So," Kelly continued, "this morning I took the rest of your acid cubes and threw them away."

Sarah sat up and stared at Kelly. First her mouth rounded into an O, then her jaw slackened fully open. Sarah grabbed her handbag and began digging through it, pulling out her flower mirror and setting it aside.

"That's a really cute mirror," Kelly said. "And you brought a little camping toilet paper roll, sealed in black plastic! You should've told me you had that."

Sarah continued to dig in the recesses of her bag. "That's not a toilet paper roll, Kelly. And the other thing might look like a mirror, but it's really important. Almost as important as my NCs! I can't believe you threw them away. Where did you take them? I have to find them."

Kelly raised her brows. "NCs? What are you calling NCs?"

"My NourishCubes, the little things in pink and white wrappers. I told you, they're my food and my health support and they're preventing all kinds of illness in this filthy, muddy place and you have to take me to them. Kelly, this is bad, *really* bad." Sarah put her head in her hands and began to sob.

"Sarah, I can't. I'm sorry. They're gone. But we have food. We have a first aid kit and a medical tent we could go to, if you got sick or injured. You'll be fine. Better than fine, because you won't be drugged out of your mind," Kelly said, patting the top of Sarah's bent head.

"You had no right to go through my things. That is an unforgivable intrusion on my privacy. Just tell me where they are," Sarah said through her teeth. She raised her head and wiped her tears away, then her face darkened, a storm slowly rolling in and re-arranging her usually sunny features before Kelly's eyes. "Where are my NCs?" she demanded.

Kelly cut her eyes to the side, unable to meet Sarah's. "They're in the port-o-let. You remember the port-o-let, Sarah, and how it smells? I dumped them all in there. You wouldn't want them back even if you could get them," she answered. "And you can't. Honestly, you're proving my point with your attitude. They shouldn't be this important to you."

Sarah jumped up. "You *smeevacker!*" she screamed at Kelly. "You have no idea what you've done!"

Kelly kept her features calm and even. "I have no idea what a smeevacker is, either." She shrugged her shoulders. "Is that Lakota?"

Sarah stuffed her things back into her handbag, including her chocolate bar, and grabbed a second one from Kelly's bag. "No, it's an extremely bad word, though. The worst thing I could call you. *This* is Lakota. *Amáyuštaŋ pe!*" Sarah yelled, then stood as tall as she could in the tent and duck-walked to the flap.

"And what does that mean?" Kelly asked.

"It means leave me alone," Sarah said. "I don't know any good insults in Lakota, but I mean that sincerely. Goodbye, Kelly. I'll keep the shirt to remember our better moments." Sarah exited into the rain.

Kelly got to her feet while Sarah stormed the van, taking her wet clothes from the passenger seat and adding them to her handbag. She heard Jack yell, "Hey! Wait!" as Sarah ran to the path and descended the hill. Kelly watched Jack stumble out in his boxer shorts and jump into one leg of his jeans, almost toppling over when he put the second leg in and pulled them up. "What happened?" he asked Kelly.

"Oh, she'll be back," Kelly said. "I threw away her drugs. She's very upset right now."

"What drugs? I didn't know she had drugs," Jack said, squinting at the path down the hill as Sarah's head disappeared.

"Those little cubes she's been eating. They have LSD in them. I figured it out this morning. She said all kinds of crazy things to me,

Jack, after eating one. Like a switch flipped and she'd gone completely out of her mind." Kelly walked over and stood beside him. "She's mad, but she'll get over it."

"Kelly, have you ever been around anyone on acid? Ever?" Jack asked, shaking his head.

"Well no, but I know its effects," Kelly said. "LSD is mind-expanding. She blathers on about every wild thing in her imagination when she eats one of those little cubes. None of it makes sense. It's just euphoric babble."

Jack swiped his wet hair out of his eyes and looked directly at Kelly. "About what?" he asked.

"She doesn't want me to tell anyone but it's all insane stories about what the future will be like, all these things she makes up, ridiculous, unbelievable stuff. And she thinks she knows it because she's *been* there, Jack. She's absolutely under the influence of drugs," Kelly answered.

"Yesterday, when I found her, I told you she ate one of her little cubes when we walked up the hill and she calmed down," Jack said. "Then she did hours of math with you in your stupid notebook. Did you forget that? Or did you even consider it's just food to her?" Jack stared at Kelly. "Have you never known anyone with an imagination?"

Kelly smirked. "Well obviously, that was a candy without drugs in it, or one to settle her nerves," she said, crossing her arms. "She probably has more than one kind," she added.

"For a genius, you're exceptionally stupid, Kelly. I'm going to look for her." Jack grabbed his sneakers from the van and tied them on, bracing each foot on the bumper as he glared at Kelly.

"Well, you should know it wasn't just me. She overheard Laura telling me she doesn't belong here, that she's giving her and Rodney the creeps—"

"You should've defended her, Kelly," Jack yelled, scowling. "Laura can be really mean. Why didn't you take up for Sarah? That girl's been nothing but kind to you. To me, too."

"I *did* defend her!" Kelly yelled back, prompting Eric to poke his head from his tent and immediately retract it from the rain, an awkward blond turtle. "She only left because I threw her drugs away, and because I searched her things to find them. She was most upset that I invaded her privacy, I think. The stuff I got rid of can't be *that* important. And I tried to make up for Laura. I really did. I told Sarah that's not how the rest of us feel, and I wanted her to stay. I said you wanted her here, too."

"What's going on?" Kristin said, emerging from the back seat with a yawn. "What did I miss? Oh wow, it's really raining."

"Yes, it's raining and Kelly sent Sarah off into it and a makeshift city of half a million strangers with nothing but her clothes," Jack snarled. "Into foot-sucking mud with a pair of flimsy sandals."

"I didn't *send* her anywhere, Jack. And she has almost two full chocolate bars," Kelly said. "Besides, she's emotional right now, but Sarah will come back here. I know she will. It's the only logical thing to do."

"Kelly," Jack said, stabbing the air at her, "that's exactly your problem. Your world is logic and numbers, while the rest of us have feelings and emotions. You're friggin' Mr. Spock in a daisy dress."

Kelly grabbed his arm. "That's not true, Jack. I feel things, too. Maybe I don't show them all the time. I've had to learn to be unemotional and clinical and reserved after years of men regarding me as hysterical if I get upset over anything. That was part of my education at MIT. You were there. You saw it."

"You're wasting time," Jack said, pulling his arm away. "She'll be lost in that crowd soon." He ran toward the path and stopped as a huge cheer erupted at the bottom of it, out of his vision. Kelly and all the others in the campsite heard it, too, and wondered what was going on near their hill.

13

The Woodstock Music
and Art Fair
Bethel, New York
SATURDAY, AUGUST 16, 1969

Sarah slipped along the steep, wet path until the final thirty feet down, which she rode like a mud luge to a spot within five feet of a large camp of people. Most of them got up to cheer and applaud as though she'd shot herself at them intentionally. The crowd grew bigger as curiosity spread. Everyone clapped as they stared, but no one moved close to her, as though they were waiting for her to finish an impromptu mud-gymnastics performance as she attempted to stand.

After a couple of minutes, a short, stocky boy whose beard was struggling to grow stepped forward to help her to her feet.

"Are you okay?" he asked.

Sarah stood and patted herself. "Yes, thank you," she said absently. She nodded at the boy and turned to leave as a teen girl wearing strands of tiny seed beads approached, slipping one of her necklaces over Sarah's head.

"Here," she said, "these will bring you love and peace."

She thanked her and walked away from the still-cheering crowd, trying not to think about the dark brown mud that coated the back of her jeans. Kelly's MIT t-shirt was probably ruined. It didn't matter. She held her head high and strolled through the crowd, avoiding the eyes of every gawking boy and staring girl.

Sarah reminded herself no one, not even the promoters or most seasoned attendees, had more knowledge about Woodstock and what was to come than she did. She already knew it was futile to dry her clothes; the rain would continue off and on until it pummeled the entire festival with a torrential downpour, which would also deliver terrifying thunder and lightning like she'd never seen. Sarah knew where she'd seek shelter at that point.

She watched a bunch of teen boys whooping and running at a mudslide, each trying to make it farther than the one before. A girl in a long tiered skirt and t-shirt joined them, carefully removing her wire-framed glasses before her turn.

Sarah detoured into the thicker muck, where she could make her way faster. Her sandals, delicate as they looked, were made of extremely durable materials and designed to keep her from sinking. They protected the bottoms of Sarah's feet while those whose shoes had either been discarded or fallen apart cut themselves on pop-tops and other metal debris in the deep mud. She needed to move forward quickly, because she had no intention of seeing anyone from Kelly's camp again.

The idea of eating the brown rice and vegetables she knew loomed at the free kitchen made Sarah nauseated. Hot dogs and hamburgers were out of the question. She'd live on chocolate, she decided, though she had no idea how long two small bars would last. Sarah reached into her handbag and answered that question immediately, gobbling down the remainder of the first one Kelly had given her within a couple of minutes.

She walked forward, hurrying when she could, skirting around those in her path. With each step, she had the uncanny feeling she was escaping something; not the people she'd been with, something bigger. She was invigorated, alive. Sarah didn't care how much rain fell on her, how many steps she'd have to take to get to the pond, how the mud felt between her toes.

She simply *felt*. More deeply and strongly than she ever had, and she wasn't sure why. Maybe it was the hundreds of thousands who'd gathered in a spirit of peace and cooperation like never before. Sarah stopped and stood in place, watching two guys help a third hobble across the field to the medical tent. A toddler walked by holding her mother's hand, dressed as a tiny hippie in a fringed vest with a flower painted on her face. The little girl beamed smiles and blew kisses at anyone whose eye she could catch.

There was a feeling of utter safety, a oneness with the mass of people gathered in this cow pasture in the middle of nowhere. It was magic, even with Kelly trying to ruin it. Sarah would be forever grateful for the experience.

She looked around and decided she'd worked her way deep enough into the crowd to disappear from Kelly and her group, determined to put any frustration and anger behind her. Sarah sat next to a young woman with dark brown hair clipped short, her long legs curled onto a beach blanket. She wore a bright yellow mini dress with chunky fringe she'd obviously cut into the hem.

"Hello, I'm Annette," the woman said. "Would you like to scoot over and share the blanket until my old man gets back? He's taking advantage of a break in the rain to get us a sandwich, if he can find a short enough line. Did you hear the government is delivering sandwiches?" She pointed to a military helicopter in the distance. "Blankets, too."

"I hadn't heard, but I'm not hungry," Sarah said. "And I appreciate the offer, though there's not much point in sharing your beach blanket. My jeans are already filthy from sliding down a hill. I'm Sarah, by the way."

"That sounds like fun! Jerry doesn't want to do anything but sit here and listen to music," Annette said. "He did magic mushrooms last night and was convinced Arlo Guthrie wanted him onstage. I kept pulling him back down and telling him he'd have to wait for the right song. I was really grateful he fell asleep before I had to chase him and drag him away."

Sarah stared. "Magic mushrooms?" she said. "I don't think I've heard of those."

"Well, you can buy acid pretty much anywhere at the festival, but Jerry doesn't trust it. He sources his own 'shrooms and does them only like three or four times a year. Says it helps him write. He's a poet in his spare time." Annette's eyes widened as she spotted him in the distance. "That's him! That's Jerry." She pointed at a man with his hair swept into a ponytail, a brightly striped poncho over his jeans.

"What does he do the rest of the time?" Sarah asked.

"He's a pediatrician," Annette answered. "In New York City. I'm his receptionist. We don't have kids yet, but we feel like we have several hundred of them."

"Well, that is extremely far out of here," Sarah said. She studied the pediatrician, about fifty yards away, noticing as he tucked the sandwiches under his arm and stopped to hug a little girl. He gave her half a sandwich before walking on.

Annette and Sarah looked up as the military chopper took off and maneuvered over the crowd, its noise deafening. Sarah squinted against the dim sunlight as thousands of objects fell from the sky, lightly blanketing the ground around them with fresh flowers. Annette squealed as the helicopter's drone faded.

"They dropped daisies on us! Can you believe it?" She held one up and gazed at it. "Maybe The Man is finally getting our message. Flower Power. Peace is the way."

Sarah smiled at her. "Maybe The Man will understand soon," she said. "I hope so. I think I'll leave you to your husband. I only stopped to rest for a minute."

"You're welcome to stay and share our food," Annette said. "We have some fresh water if you're thirsty, and I even brought a little thermos of lemonade. I think the music's going to start again soon. Where's your group? Are you with other MIT students?"

Sarah glanced down at Kelly's shirt. "No, I borrowed this from someone. And that is very outta sight of you to offer, Annette, but I have to get to the pond and clean up. Thank you for letting me sit with you." Sarah took a daisy from the ground and tucked it behind Annette's ear, then added one to her own headband. "Peace to you and Jerry," she added. "Maybe I'll see you later. Enjoy every minute." She stopped a few feet away and turned back, breaking off two precious pieces of her remaining chocolate bar and extending them to Annette. "Thank you for being so nice," she told her.

By the time Sarah emerged from her isolated bathing spot way down the pond's shore, she could hear the band Quill beginning their set in the distance. Not a performance she intended to watch, but she smiled to herself, remembering the festival's promoters had sent Quill on a goodwill tour of local mental institutions and prisons prior to Woodstock, hoping to win area residents over with the gesture. Sarah giggled. Maybe a slightly less psychedelic band would have been a better choice.

She headed into the woods to replace her soaked t-shirt and jeans with the slightly drier navy peasant blouse and extra bell bottoms she carried in her handbag. She carefully hung Kelly's shirt and her jeans on a low branch. Maybe she'd return for them later. For now, she'd find her way to the Bindy Bazaar and see if she wanted to buy anything before Country Joe and the Fish took the stage. She wasn't going to miss the "I-Feel-Like-I'm-Fixin'-to-Die Rag" for anything.

She was still worried whether she could stay healthy and maintain energy without her NCs until she returned home on Monday. Her chocolate supply was dwindling steadily. Eventually she'd have to find something that looked appetizing and sanitary to eat and drink. Tears pricked Sarah's eyes as she relived the moment she'd learned Kelly had pawed through her handbag and destroyed her NourishCubes. How could she have been so wrong about Kelly Adams? What a disappointment she was.

She removed and ate the last of her chocolate out of sheer frustration, wondering how to get more. Maybe there would be some at the Bindy Bazaar. That would be a worthy use of a hundred dollars.

Jack stopped occasionally to ask if anyone had seen a girl in a red and gray MIT shirt, though he knew it was pointless. The last group to remember her was the now-very-stoned camp at the bottom of the hill, who reported the girl did the best mudslide of the day and was "so beautiful, man, even all dirty." The kid who'd helped her up offered to help Jack search, but he insisted he'd go by himself, walking as fast as his anger at Kelly propelled him.

He entered the Bindy Bazaar to escape the latest heavy rain, stepping inside a booth covered in small rugs. Jack picked up a rectangle of geometric-patterned carpet and pretended to be studying it, hoping to spend a few weather-free minutes.

"Hey, man," a guy in jeans and an unbuttoned light blue shirt greeted him. "Are you interested in a rug? Makes a nice souvenir," he said, nodding his head at Jack. "And you can sit on it."

"Umm, I'm not sure," Jack said, replacing the carpet on its stack. "You haven't seen a girl in an MIT shirt around here, have you?"

"No, but you can have an announcement made if you've lost someone," he answered. "I've been hearing those constantly. And there's a message board for that, too. You could leave a note."

Jack shook his head. "I don't think she'd respond. I have a feeling she's avoiding me."

"Girl trouble, huh?" the guy said. "Bummer." He went back to arranging his wares.

"Would you mind if I just stand in here for a minute?" Jack asked.

"Sure, man," the guy said. "Let me know if you need help with anything." He swept his hand across his rug display, then sat in the back of his stall, arms crossed.

Jack watched a steady stream of people pass. They walked across little bridges that spanned the wetter parts of the forest. Couples went by arm in arm; children trailed their parents. Several yogis strolled by, hands prayer-clasped as they greeted others, their white robes decorated at the bottom with wet leaves.

"Thank you," Jack called as he exited into the rain. He glanced into the next booth and found an older woman dressed as a gypsy, her woven black headband dangling what looked like tiny metal coins, her bracelets and anklets tinkling music as she walked forward to the makeshift wood counter.

"Hello, are you looking for jewelry?" She spread her hands flat as she leaned forward, each red-manicured finger bearing a ring. "Something special for someone? Let me show you one of my favorites." She handed Jack a thin silver chain fashioned into a bracelet, a small, polished round honey-gold stone suspended from its clasp. "That's amber. Amber absorbs bad energy and releases soothing vibrations. It's all about peace and calm. Any lady would love that. Do you have a lady?" She leaned forward and placed her chin on her hand, studying Jack. "If you don't, you should. Man like you can't walk alone."

Jack smiled at her. "I don't. But this seems like something that might come in handy if I ever meet the right girl."

The gypsy woman stared for several seconds, locking Jack's dark eyes with her own. "Oh, you've met her, honey." She returned his smile. "You just don't know it yet. Keep it in your pocket until your heart catches up."

"Is that right? Well, maybe I could use some soothing vibrations myself." He laughed softly. "Okay, how much is it?" Jack reached into his pocket.

"It costs two dollars and seventy-five cents," she said, extending her hand.

Jack handed her the bracelet back. "I'm sorry. I only have two dollars with me." He started to walk away.

"Wait," the gypsy lady said. "Do you have anything to trade, to make up the seventy-five cents?"

Jack produced one slender joint he'd rolled for this afternoon, holding it up for her to inspect.

The woman raised her brows and asked, "Do you have anything else?"

"No, I'm sorry, not with me. I can come back later with a piece of cake, though, if you'll be here tonight or maybe tomorrow. It's a long way from here, back at our camp. Would you like that? It has pineapple on it. I've heard it's great, but I don't like pineapple. Or I could trade you this." Jack shrugged and extended his hand toward her, the pot grasped between his finger and thumb.

The woman laughed and told Jack, "Keep that, honey. It's like bringing coals to Newcastle." She dropped the bracelet into the palm of his hand and closed Jack's fingers over it. "Just bring me some of that cake later. A big piece. Sounds delicious." She moved to sit down, smiling and nodding at him as he pocketed the bracelet and handed her two dollars.

The rain subsided to a drizzle as Jack thanked the woman and promised he'd return. When he emerged into the audience area, a voice in the distance announced, "There's plenty of food at the Hog Farm." He realized he was starving and headed to stand in line for whatever was being serving for lunch.

Jack never saw Sarah watching him from a hundred feet away, turning a beaded headband over in her hands before carefully replacing it on a counter and stepping out of his sight. Sarah studied Jack's muscular arms as he reached toward the gypsy lady. She wondered what it would feel like to have them encircle her. He ran his hand through the longish bangs that hung almost to his eyes, sweeping his hair back and flashing a smile as he nodded at the woman in the jewelry booth. He was beautiful, fascinating to watch.

Sarah wondered what it would feel like to be kissed by Jack Warren. She sucked her lower lip inward and imagined his mouth on hers. She felt an almost-magnetic pull to Jack, a force unlike any she'd known. She had to stop herself from going to him. He might try to make her go and reconcile with Kelly.

Worse, he might actually kiss her. That couldn't happen. Not with Jack.

She hurried away to disappear into the concert crowd, slipping in among a group of stoned California hippies who welcomed her with the first peanut butter sandwich of her life. She'd later describe it as "pure salty, creamy joy between the softest, sweetest pillowy squares." At that moment, though, seated between two shirtless men as they waited for Country Joe McDonald, she finished the sandwich and asked the cute one on her left, "Would it be too much of a large pig outing if I asked for another one?"

He grinned at her, his brown eyes sparkling, a dimple revealing itself in his right cheek. "Not at all, foxy lady. Just one minute and I'll get it."

Sarah found that, if she squinted her eyes a little, he sort of resembled Jack. "Thank you, umm…"

"Scott. You can call me Scotty," he said. "Do you even know how pretty you are?"

"Not really," Sarah said with her brightest smile. "Where I come from, every person looks about the same. I'm nothing special."

"Oh, I think you are," he said. Scotty swept Sarah's hair back with one hand and leaned over to kiss her, the lightest, barest touch of his lips. He saw acceptance in her eyes and put his arm around her shoulders, lowering her to the ground. He covered her mouth with his, softly at first, running his tongue along her lower lip and sucking it gently. Then he kissed her harder and more insistently.

She'd never felt anything like this before. Sarah was stunned at the way her body answered his. She shivered, pulling him closer.

When Scotty slid his hand to cup Sarah's breast, a different kind of jolt ran through her, reconnecting and alarming her brain. She opened her eyes and felt the raindrops falling into them, immediately pulling her body away and sitting up, her head in her hands. This was wrong.

This wasn't her Reproduction Cycle mate. This was someone she barely knew. Why was she kissing a stranger and enjoying it?

The answer came to her in a rush, an unwanted but undeniable thought: NourishCubes controlled more than nutrition. There was a *reason* NCs were changed when it was time for the Reproduction Cycle. Every hormone, every desire that had been suppressed for years had been running amok in her just now, because she hadn't had an NC for so long. Suddenly, she was faced with sexual urges and the freedom to decide what to do about them.

Life at home is so much easier without dealing with these complicated situations and feelings, temptations and decisions. Another way Unity has improved the world.

What she'd just experienced was dangerous, very much against the rules. "I'm sorry, Scotty, I can't do this," she said.

"What the—" Scotty shook his head and laughed, a hollow sound devoid of humor. He sat up and smoothed his hair back, then turned to stare at her, his eyes narrowing. He took a deep breath and exhaled with his jaw clenched. "You got an old man running around here? You should have told me."

Sarah considered her answer. "No, it's not that. I just can't right now. It's the wrong time."

Scotty rolled his eyes and lit a cigarette, shielding it with his left hand from the rain. "The wrong *time*," he said flatly, his Marlboro dangling from his lips. He gathered a government-issued blanket into a hood over his head and face, then pocketed his lighter and took a deep drag, blowing a cloud of smoke upward into the drizzle.

"Look," Sarah told Scotty, "Country Joe and the Fish are about to start, see?" She pointed at the musicians walking out and picking up instruments.

"Here." Scotty threw the peanut butter sandwich in Sarah's direction and turned his attention to the stage. She ate her sandwich as the band began to play "Janis", a post-breakup song about Country Joe's ex, the reportedly still-angry Miss Joplin. Sarah wondered if Janis was watching offstage.

Scotty sat with his eyes on the band, on the ground, on the drizzling sky, anywhere but on Sarah. She stood and swayed along to the beat with most of the audience, loving the music. Then came the song she'd been waiting for, the most iconic anti-war anthem of its time, the "I-Feel-Like-I'm-Fixin'-to-Die Rag".

"GIVE ME AN F!" Country Joe screamed to the crowd before starting the song. They responded and, clearly expecting the usual "I" in the FISH Cheer, were surprised when Country Joe yelled, "GIVE ME A U! The entire audience went wild. "GIVE ME A C! GIVE ME A K! WHAT'S THAT SPELL?"

Scotty screamed it with more force than anyone around Sarah.

Jack, a hundred thousand people and fifteen rows away, yelled it even louder for a different reason. Unless he left his life in Boston behind tomorrow, like it said in the song, his next stop was indeed Vietnam.

14

The Woodstock Music and Art Fair
Bethel, New York
SATURDAY, AUGUST 16, 1969

The guy on Sarah's right, Leonard, was quiet and soft-spoken the few times he acknowledged her presence. Since Scotty was ignoring her, she turned to him after Country Joe and the Fish departed the stage, a smile on her face.

"Do you know anything about the next band?" she asked him.

"No," Leonard answered as he tilted his head back to watch a helicopter pass in the distance. "Someone said they're called Santana, but that's all I know."

"They're going to be so outta our sight, you won't believe it," Sarah said. "Just wait. It's music unlike any you've experienced. Ever."

"Great," Leonard muttered. He pointed at the helicopter, now banking in the eastern sky. "Do you realize that's the same Army chopper that's flown over us five times? I know the markings on it. They're watching us. They've got half a million of us corralled here, and they're going to make a move. I know it."

Scotty leaned in front of Sarah and placed his hand on Leonard's arm. "That's not true, man. The CIA isn't watching you, Len, or anyone else here. This is a music festival. It's all peace. The chopper is delivering food or blankets. They might be carrying one of the performers in. That's not The Man coming to get you or any of us. Stop freaking out. You're being a downer. Again." Scotty had punctuated every word with an emphatic nod at Leonard. Now he returned his attention to the stage, crossing his arms and shaking his head.

Sarah's eyes widened. "What do you think they're here to do, Leonard?"

"The military has hundreds of thousands of young male bodies here to snatch up," he told her. "Think about it."

Sarah smiled at him. "I promise you, that's not going to happen. Absolutely not. These choppers are all here to help, Leonard. They're working with us, not against us."

He smirked at her. "How could you possibly know that? How do you know this isn't a smallpox blanket situation, Sarah? Didn't you tell us you're an Indian from a reservation in South Dakota? Do you really trust the United States government?"

Sarah took a deep breath. "I trust them *here*, Leonard. Don't make this into a heavy-duty thing. We're going to hear some great music in a minute, and you'll feel a lot better. You'll want to get up and dance."

Leonard went back to scanning the skies, unconvinced.

Scotty stared straight ahead and murmured to Sarah, "He gets like this when he's high. Don't worry about it."

The announcer said, "Ladies and gentlemen, Santana." A wave of conga drumbeats washed over the crowd, joined by vibrant organ chords (Sarah thought they sounded bright orange) and an occasional bluesy guitar riff in "Waiting". Everyone sat up to listen. They hadn't heard music like this. By the time they were seconds into "Evil Ways", couples were on their feet dancing. Jazz and blues met Afro-Cuban beats and Carlos Santana married them all with screaming electric rock guitar. A star was born.

When the band launched into "Jingo", Sarah grabbed Leonard's hand and pulled him to his feet, improvising a dance for him to follow, which to her great joy, he did. That song, that sound, his grin, that moment, would stay with her forever. They danced all the way through a blazing "Soul Sacrifice", then collapsed for the final number in Santana's set, laughing.

Leonard nodded at the space where Scotty had been sitting. "He left. I didn't even notice." His mouth dropped open. "You don't think they—"

"No, Leonard, absolutely not. No one took Scotty." She pointed to where he stood, twenty feet away, talking with a pretty blonde girl in a psychedelic paisley skirt and black knee boots. The girl flipped her hair and batted her lashes at Scotty. Her eyes followed his wave at the place he'd been sitting, an obvious invitation.

Sarah stood up. "Time for me to leave," she said to Leonard. She kissed his peach-fuzzed cheek and watched him rub it with his hand.

"Hey, don't go," he said. "Please don't."

"I have to. I have an appointment," Sarah said. "I loved dancing with you, Leonard. Your moves are most groovy. Stop worrying, everything is all right." Sarah put her handbag on her shoulder and added, "Hang loosely," as she patted his shoulder and walked away.

She was early, so Sarah took some time to wander around looking at the camps of people. Little kids frolicked, yelling and incongruously making finger pistols at each other at the festival of peace. Their parents sat atop brightly painted buses or in circles, each camp appearing a world unto itself but also an integral patch in the quilt that was Woodstock. She saw a large group doing yoga and heard their yogi assuring them they could get high if they positioned their bodies correctly and for a long enough time.

Sarah judged the position of the sun. It had stopped raining for a few minutes, and she guessed it was about 3:30 pm. Time to head to the small Free Stage at the Hog Farm commune.

As Sarah settled in with the California hippie group earlier, Jack was still searching for a glimpse of her red and gray shirt. The crowd swelled in anticipation of the music coming up and rendered that impossible. Jack had given up temporarily and trudged through the mud, trying to avoid slipping as he looked for a place to sit.

About ten people in from the end of a row, a guy with long, wavy brown hair and a bushy beard to rival Moses's waved at him and pointed to a vacant spot on a blanket to his right. People rearranged themselves so Jack could make his way in. He sat next to the man—it was clear to Jack he had a few years on him—and extended his hand.

"Jack Warren," he said. "Thanks for helping me find a space. Since the rain's let up, there's practically nowhere you can sit and see the stage."

"David Boyd," the man answered, shaking Jack's hand. "I think it's gonna spit rain at us off and on all day. I'll survive. I'm a fifth-generation Florida cracker. This weather is nothin', Jack. We laugh at hurricanes where I'm from."

Jack grinned and said, "I've never been to Florida. Always wanted to go." He looked the guy up and down, from his square-toed brown cowboy boots and jeans to his light blue Nehru-looking shirt, almost collar-less and unbuttoned practically to his waist. "I've also never seen jeans like those." He pointed at David's wide bell-bottoms, which featured a triangular brown leather insert to give them extra flare. And flair. "Those are far out," Jack told him. "Where'd you get them?"

"I made 'em myself," David said. "Added the leather to make these bells. And I sewed the shirt, too. Dig this." David lifted the hem of his shirt to reveal a large oval FLORIDA belt buckle featuring an alligator.

"I'm guessing you really love your home state," Jack said. "I'm from North Carolina, and I can't imagine an outfit to represent that. Maybe a tobacco leaf belt buckle," he said, "but that's really the wrong leaf." Jack chuckled. "Wanna get high with me?"

David's smile reached his warm brown eyes as he removed his wire-rimmed aviator glasses to wipe rain from them. "Sounds like a great idea," he said. "I'm always wishing people a great Florida day, no matter where they are. I even said it to my cousin in Cincinnati on the phone last week. Hell, we can have one even in this damn rain and mud. That," he pointed to the joint Jack held up, "will most definitely help."

Jack reached for his lighter and asked David, "What's with them?" He pointed to the teen couple whose blanket he was sharing, so engrossed in making out they were oblivious to his presence.

"Yeah, they don't come up for air much," David said. "They both dropped acid a few hours ago and when they're not making out, they're laying back and stroking each other's arms and legs, telling each other they're okay. Occasionally I tell 'em they're okay, too. Doesn't seem like either of them is on a bad trip. I figured I'd keep an eye on 'em."

"Very cool of you, a kind thing to do," Jack said, lighting the joint and inhaling. He passed it to David. "I heard Country Joe and the Fish are gonna start the music this afternoon. I'm guessing that's soon." He pointed to the distant stage, where a crew of guys appeared to be placing instruments. He blew a cloud of smoke and said, "Hey, this is a longshot, but you haven't seen a girl in a red and gray MIT shirt, have you?"

David shook his head. "Not that I remember. I've been sitting here for a while, ever since I got my paper cup of brown rice and vegetables. If she walked past, I didn't notice."

"Oh man, you ate that, too?" Jack scrunched his nose. "It was nice of them, but I could really use some barbeque about now. And you'd remember this girl, believe me. She's…different. Really pretty. Kind of shy but just a really bright spirit, you know? She's almost as tall as I am and has long, straight brown hair and the most beautiful green eyes, like moss with little copper bits—"

David handed the joint back to Jack, nodding his head and interrupting. "Sounds like you're in love, Jack. Is this girl your old lady?"

Jack swung his head back and forth. "Definitely not. I helped her out of the pond yesterday. She'd fallen in or something, and was dripping wet and kind of panicked because her stuff was soaked.

Walked her back to our camp because she's here alone. Then she got in a fight with Kelly—an old friend of mine from school—and took off. I'm trying to find her, make sure she's okay. That's all." Jack smiled as he finished speaking and thought *you know there's more to it than that. You look for her in every face you see because she's the most special girl you've ever met.*

David raised his eyebrows. "Very cool and a kind thing of you, too. I'll keep an eye out. Guys back at my camp behind us might've seen her. I'll ask when they show up. The way this crowd's growing," he glanced back over his shoulder, "I hope they can find me."

"Crazy, isn't it? Gotta be half a million," Jack said. The teen girl next to him repositioned herself and accidentally kicked Jack, while still attached to her boyfriend's mouth. He asked David, "Do you know their names?"

"Something like Sunshine Rainbow and Canyon Phoenix," David replied, choking a little as he laughed. "Canyon Rainbow and Sunshine Phoenix. It's probably Dick and Jane."

Several lively guitar chords rang out from the stage, followed by a "MARIJUANA!" yell on the microphone. "Ladies and gentlemen," the announcer called, "please welcome warmly, Country Joe and the Fish." A huge cheer erupted, briefly attracting the attention of Sunshine and Canyon, who glanced toward the stage and resumed making out. Jack and David grinned and stood, clapping along with the rest of the small nation gathered around them.

By the time they yelled "FUCK!" together at the end of the band's cheer, David felt like a friend. Jack noticed him looking behind at the crowd over and over, no doubt wondering where his buddies were. Sunshine and Canyon had finally settled into peaceful naps, the very definition of "tuning out". The woman on their right reached in front of the couple to pass along a box of bananas and oranges, as well as small bottles of water. Jack handed them to David after extracting one of each.

David peeled an orange and made a disgusted face when he tasted it. "Definitely not from Florida," he said. "But I'll take anything that passes for food right now. Once I'm sure those two are okay," he nodded at the sleeping kids, "I'm heading back to our camp for some pork and beans. I think we have four cans left. You can come along and share, if you'd like."

Jack nodded. "Thanks. We brought a bunch of food, and I'm sure someone else needs yours more. But that's really nice of you."

"Country Joe is a veteran, did you know that?" David said, cocking his head to one side. "Gives that last song a little more meaning."

Jack shook his head. "I had no idea. Far out."

"So am I," David said, meeting Jack's eyes. "A vet. I did two tours."

"Wow," Jack said, "and you're *here*?"

"Well, it *is* a music festival. I mostly came to see a new band called Crosby, Stills & Nash. That's David Crosby, from The Byrds, Stephen Stills, from Buffalo Springfield, and Graham Nash, from The Hollies. You know that Byrds song, 'Mr. Tambourine Man'? I've played that record about a million times. I can't wait to see what the three of them sound like together," David said. "What about you? Is there a band you especially want to see?"

"Far out, man. I love The Byrds, too, and didn't realize that's who the Crosby guy is," Jack said. He shrugged his shoulders. "I want to see Creedence Clearwater Revival. The Who. Oh, and Janis Joplin. Basically anything except the folk singers who were on last night. That's not my scene." Jack leaned his head back and looked to the sky, enjoying a break in the rain. When he spoke again, he kept his eyes trained on a cloud in the distance. "Can I tell you something confidentially? Like, I could use your thoughts on something."

David raised his brows. "Sure. Lay it on me."

Jack said, "I'm actually at this festival for another reason. The truth is, I'm about to be drafted. I know it's coming with Nixon's new birthday lottery. I don't have any exemptions. I can't go back to college. I'm a high school math teacher now, in Boston. I've just really gotten started." He looked into the distance, passing his orange from hand to hand like a hesitant pitcher on the mound. "I have a brother who came back from Vietnam really messed up. He, like, lives in darkness every single day, and now, so do my parents. My mom actually read an article in some women's magazine about encouraging your son to go to Canada." Jack waited a beat before adding, "And I'm supposed to meet a guy here tomorrow to take me to Ottawa, but I'm really torn about it." He bit his lip and searched David's face. "Do you have any advice for me? I mean, you've been there."

David made a neat little orange peel pile next to his foot. "You know what, Jack? I don't usually talk about this, but I'm a little high right now and you seem like a nice guy. And a teacher, I have a lot of respect for teachers." He drew his long legs in and circled his arms around his shins. "For what it's worth, I enlisted not long after we were attacked in the Gulf of Tonkin in '64. I was raised to be proud of my country, and I never doubted I'd do my duty to defend it. My dad served in WWII. My uncle was a fighter pilot in WWII and Korea."

"Okay," Jack nodded. "I understand that. I have an uncle who fought in World War II. My mom's brother."

David paused to consider his next words. "I love my country and I even enjoyed some parts of my job, but I really didn't like the boss." He laughed softly and took a deep breath before continuing with a sigh. "And make no mistake, I loved my brothers there, and always will. That's a forever bond. But, the whole Vietnam thing taught me a big lesson about government corruption. The military feeds casualty numbers to the news media, the nightly news regurgitates them to America, and they're completely underreporting the deaths over there. All we're doing is trading front lines with the enemy, like we're not there to win, and that is just bullshit. It's not the guys who are actually fighting this war, guys like me, who went into this with their hearts in it. It's the war *machine*, the profit being taken every time a bomb is dropped or a bullet's fired; every time a vehicle's destroyed; every time a plane's shot down. I saw it, the greed and the waste. All of us did."

Jack felt his heart shift, taking up an uncomfortable position in his chest.

David closed his eyes. "The truth is, I'm proud of my service. But if I knew then what I know now, I'm not sure I'd enlist. You may be making the right decision. You have to do what's best for you, for your family. And I can't tell you what that is, man." He opened his eyes and looked at the innocent faces of the teenagers sleeping next to Jack, their arms and legs intertwined. "I wish I could."

Jack swiped at a tear he hoped David had missed. "Thanks, man. I really appreciate what you did over there, and your talking with me about it. You are one cool dude."

David stood and brushed off his custom jeans, bending to pick up his orange peels and water bottle. "So are you, Jack. Watch those two for another hour or so, will ya? And thanks for the smoke." He held up a peace sign and then saluted before walking away. Jack watched him disappear and turned forward to wait for the next band's setup to be completed.

A minute or two later, Santana was announced and Jack squinted as they took the stage. The band immediately energized the crowd with their music, bringing Jack to his feet to dance in the rain. He swept his arms around, copying the lady on the other side of the sleeping teens. By the time they played "Jingo", the teen couple had awakened and stood up to mirror Jack's dance moves, something no one would do unless they were on some kind of hallucinogenic drug.

"You guys okay?" Jack yelled at Canyon, or whatever his name was.

"Yeah, man, we're groovy. Everything's cool. Don't worry about us." The kid threw his arms into the air along with his girlfriend, grinning at the sky through the drizzling rain.

They were fine, Jack decided, turning his attention back to the stage, resuming his "Jingo" head-bob and side-step flail. He also decided he'd buy a Santana album as soon as he could. He felt sure this band would be around for a long time. They beat the hell out of all that folk crap Kelly and Sarah had made him sit through last night.

When Santana finished to a roaring ovation, it seemed like maybe the perfect time to climb up and fetch the piece of cake he owed to the Bindy Bazaar lady. Jack did his now-habitual scan of the crowd for the red and gray shirt Sarah wore. He turned three hundred and sixty degrees around, slightly dizzy and still a bit stoned. Nothing. The teen couple had resumed kissing on the blanket next to him.

"You're too young to make love *or* war," he muttered at them.

The idea of the premium food in the VW van ended his internal debate over returning to camp. Jack was starving. He might as well check on The Wrath of Kelly and see how Eric and Kristin were getting along, though he figured they'd made their way down the hill by now. Rodney and Laura were no doubt cocooning out of the rain and discussing nursery colors and baby names. What a waste of Woodstock.

Jack nodded to himself and took one last glance at the kids next to him. Surely he'd monitored them long enough. They were in their own little world, and frankly, it looked like a really nice one. He gathered his trash to take to camp with him, planning to spend an hour or so there, and then come back down, deliver the cake, and search for Sarah. There was still plenty of daylight.

As he turned to leave, he overheard a couple behind him. "I don't wanna see her, you go see her," the man said. "I'll wait right here."

"But it's Joan Baez!" she yelled at him. "She's waiting in line to perform on the little stage next to that kitchen they set up. Right there with a bunch of unknowns. It's *her*!"

"Excuse me," Jack said. "Are you sure it's actually THE Joan Baez waiting to perform at the Free Stage? The one by the Hog Farm commune?"

"It definitely is. My sister saw her waiting in the line, and she's already gone back over there. But *Tony* here doesn't want to walk over with me, and I have a sprained ankle." She glared at her husband, who was suddenly interested in picking at something on his sleeve. "I can't hobble over there by myself, and Nancy's already taken off." Her New York accent made the last word sound like "awwf".

Jack carefully placed his fruit peels and water bottle on the blanket next to the teen passion pit. He offered the woman his best smile and stepped forward, extending his arm. "I'll help you get over there," he said. "I'm a huge Joan Baez fan."

15

The Woodstock Music and Art Fair
Bethel, New York
SATURDAY, AUGUST 16, 1969

The man called Tony looked Jack over carefully. "I'm going to our camp, and you meet me there, honey. You'll never find this space again. Just have Nancy walk you back, okay?" he told his wife as Jack extended an arm for her to lean on. "Thanks, buddy. I can't take any more folk music," he said, nodding at Jack. The woman kissed her husband, cradling his face in her hands, before hobbling away.

Jack turned to the perky brunette he was helping as they made their way through what passed for an aisle. "I'm Jack, by the way," he said.

"Lillian," she answered, beaming a beautiful smile at him. "Thank you for doing this. Tony's not as big a Joan Baez fan as you are, to say the least. What's your favorite song of hers?"

Jack laughed. "You got me. I couldn't name one if I tried. I'm going over there to look for a girl I met here. She's lost in this crowd somewhere, but if she hears Baez is at the small stage, she'll definitely be in the audience. It's worth a try." Jack alternated between glancing ahead and studying the ground, trying to help Lillian avoid the muddier parts and puddles. She winced occasionally, putting as little weight on her left ankle as possible. They made their way past an array of people sitting atop wet sleeping bags and blankets. Jack noted the sun was finally out and hoped things would dry up a bit. He thought, not for the first time, how lucky he was to have a camp to return to, elevated and well-sheltered.

"Ah," Lillian said. "I hope you find her. I also hope we get there in time to hear Joan sing. Nancy said she was at the end of a long line for some kind of open-microphone thing. If you'll just get me to Nancy, I'll be fine."

"You'd think they'd put her first, wouldn't you? She's a big star," Jack said, detouring to the left around a sleeping kid.

"Are you kidding me?" Lillian's dark eyes widened and she blinked at Jack. "This is Joan Baez. She'll stand behind every cashier, gas station attendant, dishwasher, cook, postal worker, waitress, farmer, student, and hairdresser, insisting on taking her turn."

"She'll probably organize a union while she's waiting," Jack said. "Quick, put your arm around my shoulders." She did and he swept his arm under Lillian's knees, carrying her across a big puddle, soaking the remaining dry parts of his mud-stained white sneakers.

"Wow! Thank you." She giggled as he set her down. "That was above and beyond. You're a nice guy, Jack. I hope this girl is there waiting for you to find her. Is she pretty?"

He shrugged. "I mean, yeah, anyone would say she's pretty. She was staying at our camp and one of the girls I came here with was mean to her. I thought they were becoming great friends, but apparently not. They had a fight and Kelly went through Sarah's handbag and threw away what she thought were drugs. I'm not so sure they were, but Sarah was really upset about it and took off this morning. I want to be sure she's all right. She's not here with anyone."

"Why was she staying at your camp if you just met her?" Lillian said. "I don't understand."

"Well," Jack raised his eyebrows, "she's kinda different. She was raised on a reservation in South Dakota and had never left it until she came to the festival. Her native language is Lakota Sioux, and her English can sound a little strange. When I found her, she'd fallen into the pond near where we were swimming and was splashing around, trying to grab all the stuff from her handbag that was floating away. We all wondered if someone pushed her in, although maybe she dropped the bag in and went after it. Anyway, she was crying and I can't stand to see a girl cry. I brought her back to our camp, and at first, she and Kelly seemed to really dig each other. So she stayed."

"Geez," Lillian replied. "How did she get here? To New York."

Jack shook his head. "She said she hitchhiked after running away from home. There was this long story about how her mother contacted Kelly's mom after finding Sarah's note, asking Kelly to keep an eye on Sarah. Supposedly, they're distant cousins and were in touch about the festival. I'm not sure any of us believed all of it." He paused, considering. "I think she knew Kelly's mom's first name, though, looking back. I don't see how she could have unless the families are related."

Lillian stepped around a puddle and pulled on Jack's arm, hard. "Sorry," she said, recovering her balance. "Sounds to me like maybe you should be a little scared of this girl. I'm just saying." She thought for a second and added, "Your friend Kelly could cawwl her mother from the phone bank. I heard there's one, there are just really lawng lines. People near the stage could tell you how to find them."

Her New York accent was extra-strong on those two words and made Jack smile. "There are pay phones?" he said. "I had no idea. I'll tell Kelly, I guess, but I don't think she really needs to call her mom long distance. There's nothing nefarious about Sarah, and every word she's said could be true. Or maybe she was just feeling overwhelmed, and invented this story about her mom and Kelly to try to get us to take her in. Kelly didn't completely buy it, but she decided she liked Sarah and wanted her to stick around. They bonded over something Kelly was working on when Sarah got here. And they both adore Joan Baez. Actually, Kelly will be really sorry she missed this performance at the Free Stage."

"And is Kelly your girlfriend?" Lillian asked, frowning.

Jack cocked his head. "At one time, I thought we might get together. We were both math students at MIT. I liked her, and I still do. But Kelly comes across really cool and detached, kinda intimidating. I thought about asking her out years ago but never did. The best way I can put it is, she gets along with numbers better than people. She has a fascinating job at the MAC Project at the university, and she literally works all the time. Kelly would rather be alone with her equations on a Friday night than on a date or at a party. She's brilliant, just kinda…prickly." Jack laughed a little. "She's a female Einstein cactus. That's Kelly Adams in three words. I guarantee you she's sitting in the van working in her little notebook right now. It's much easier for Kelly to address problems with a pencil than with her heart."

Lillian nodded. "I know a few people like that. I feel sorry for them. I address everything with my heart and absolutely nothing with math."

Jack chuckled. "I know a few people like that, too. Some of them are my students."

"Oh! You're a teacher? Where do you teach?" Lillian asked.

"At a high school in Boston. I'm originally from North Carolina, but took a job there right after college," Jack told her.

Lillian said, "I knew that was a southern accent. I wish I had an accent."

Jack laughed and helped Lillian hop over a large stick in the mud. "You do have a tiny New York thing going on there, I think."

As they drew closer to the Hog Farm commune, Jack heard some guys attempting to sing "I Want to Hold Your Hand", and they were about as removed from the Beatles and any acceptable harmony as they could possibly be. Lillian heard it, too, and laughed.

"Sounds like the Free Stage," she said. "Possibly a refund stage."

They broke through the small crowd and made their way closer, Lillian scanning for her sister. A blonde woman caught her eye and waved, frowning slightly at Jack. "That's Nan!" she yelled over the mutilated song. "Thank you so much, Jack. I hope you find Sarah." She pecked Jack's cheek and hobbled toward her sister's spot by the stage.

Jack watched to make sure she reached her destination. Then he looked at the line waiting to take the microphone, and a woman in a patchwork dress who resembled Joan Baez was fifth, making her way slowly forward as the faux-Beatles departed. He tried to spot Sarah in Kelly's red and gray shirt. Nothing. Jack stood with his arms crossed, hugging himself in wet clothes against a sudden chilly breeze. He really needed to get back to camp and change.

The people around him were all standing; it was an exceptionally muddy area. He guessed they were either relatives of the amateurs performing or Joan Baez fans. Probably the latter. The next performer to take the stage was a woman in her twenties, her hair in twin braids, wearing a purple mini dress. She looked at the crowd and started to back away, trying to hand the microphone to the next person in line.

"Come on, Carly, you can do it!" someone in the audience screamed. The woman rolled her eyes as she faced them. After a few seconds she walked back to the center of the stage and began singing "You Are My Sunshine", slowly and tentatively, with an almost sultry spin. As she went on, she gripped the microphone and sang the lyrics at full volume, stunning the audience with a version no one had ever considered, soulful and bluesy. Even Joan Baez looked up, Jack noted. The girl finished to wild applause and Jack felt an arm on his as she curtsied and left the stage.

"Hey, man, you want a blanket?" A guy in an orange velvet vest and worn jeans was looking at Jack, sweeping his eyes over his soaked clothes. "The Hog Farm is handing them out—Army blankets, I think.

I got an extra, if you want it." He handed Jack a thick dark-green rectangle of wool, which Jack gathered around like a cape.

"Thank you, man," he told the guy. "I really needed this." He snuggled into the shelter of the blanket, pulling it over his wet hair like a hood.

The next performer was an old man trying to sound like Elvis Presley. Jack looked around, disinterested. He decided he'd wait until Joan Baez finished, then head for some dry clothes at camp.

Jack's heart jumped at the sight of a girl with a red and gray shirt approaching from his right. He broke into a grin before realizing she was a member of the Hog Farm commune who looked nothing like his Sarah. Not *his* Sarah. He had to stop thinking that way, right now.

When Joan took the stage, he watched Lillian and Nancy swoon thirty feet away. There was still no sign of Sarah. He waited through several songs the audience begged the star to sing, noting the crowd was swelling as people realized who'd taken the Free Stage. Sarah didn't appear among any of the newcomers. Jack kept twisting around to look, but it was hopeless.

He watched Lillian hobble off with Nancy after Joan's final bow. Jack sighed and headed back toward the way up to camp, watching the placement of his poor, battered, filthy Converse sneakers as he trudged along.

And then a pair of familiar black sandals appeared in his path, facing his next step, forcing him to stop suddenly and look up.

"Are you following me?" Sarah asked, reaching to pull the blanket off Jack's head. "You don't need to," she added, her green eyes smiling at Jack's. "I'm having a great time. I've met some fun people, and the music's even better than I expected."

Jack scrambled for words, his surprise rendering him temporarily devoid of any that made sense. "I, ummm…you're okay. I was just checking to see if you're all right, after what Kelly did. I feel really bad about that."

"I'm better than all right," Sarah said. "This festival is what I dreamed of. I even love the rain, though I couldn't explain why to you."

Jack put his arm on Sarah's to pull them both out of the flow of people waiting to stream by. They stood next to a psychedelic-painted bus and he leaned against it, regarding her.

"You look different," he said. "What's different about you?"

Sarah held his eyes. "Probably the way I'm looking at *you*."

Jack blinked at her, standing before him in her own ray of sunlight, green eyes shining, her lips little pillows of deep pink. "I was going to say your clothes. That's a nice navy peasant blouse. You should tie it at the top, though." He motioned pulling the neckline together. "How old are you, Sarah?" he asked.

Sarah made an embarrassed little laugh and closed the deep V-neck of her shirt, carefully fashioning a knot in the string before she returned her eyes to his. "I'm nineteen. You want to see my driver's license?"

"No," Jack answered. "You just look so young, that's all."

She seemed to consider this for a few beats, then said, "I saw you in the Bindy Bazaar earlier, you know. I ran away before you spotted me."

"Well, you shouldn't have," Jack answered, shrugging. "I wasn't going to make you go and talk to Kelly."

Sarah offered him a tight smile. "You weren't going to make me do anything." She lowered her eyes to her sandals, hopping on one foot to remove a piece of hay stuck between the straps. "I watched you for a long time. And I ran because I felt so…drawn to you. It was strange." She shook her head back and forth slowly before continuing, clasping her hands and worrying her thumbs across them. "I'm feeling all kinds of things I've never felt before." She looked over Jack's head at a man walking on the bus's roof to climb down at the end. When he reached the ground and walked away, Sarah turned her eyes to Jack's again. "I think I'm falling on you," she said, almost a whisper.

Jack stifled a laugh. "I've been searching for you nonstop since you went down that hill, Sarah. I told myself it was to make sure you were okay, but the longer I looked, the more I felt like I had to see you. I *had* to. I kept picturing your smile, hearing your laugh. I looked at a hundred thousand faces, and all I wanted was for one of them to be yours." He paused and took a deep breath, smoothing the wet hair back from his forehead. "I think I'm falling for you, too." He opened the blanket and beckoned her in. "Come here. Your clothes are drenched. What happened to Kelly's shirt?"

Sarah stepped closer to him. She felt Jack encircle her with the blanket, a cocoon around them that blocked out half a million people. She let her head rest on his shoulder. "I put it over a tree branch to dry out. You can get it for her later. It's near the Bindy Bazaar. I think it should be pretty easy to find. The tree is a maple, I think, maybe an oak. The shirt's red, you know, so you can spot...I'm babbling, aren't I?" She pulled her head back and looked at Jack, smiling softly.

He wrapped his arms tighter, pulling the blanket and Sarah closer to his body. "Yes," he whispered, "you are." Jack's breath hitched a little as he said it, his mouth an inch from hers. "It's okay. Babble all you want. Just don't move, Sarah. Don't move."

"So this is why you were looking for me?" she asked, lowering her lashes. Jack saw a tiny frown skitter across her face for a second. Sarah bit her bottom lip. "Is it?"

He didn't answer. Jack closed his eyes and put his mouth almost on hers, just breathing there with her. Sarah felt his heart pounding against her own.

She slipped her hands behind his neck and pressed her forehead to his. Her own breathing had grown ragged because of the way her body was so perfectly fitted against Jack's. She could feel how much he wanted her. This was different, so different from the guy named Scotty. It was gentle, it was tender, it was real.

She thought the world would end if he didn't kiss her, but he just stood there, holding her waist tightly, pulling her to him, his breath shuddering against hers. Jack swallowed, clenching a muscle in his jaw.

He moved his mouth to Sarah's forehead, quickly pressing his lips to the tiny raindrops still running from her hair.

"Don't," she said, frowning. Sarah placed her hands on the sides of Jack's face. He slid his right hand into the hair at the nape of her neck and Sarah immediately felt a tiny current of electricity running through her. She raised her eyes to meet Jack's and leaned forward to touch her lips to his, tentatively at first. He kissed her back, his eyes closing as he pressed his mouth to hers more urgently. Sarah was so lost in him she couldn't stop. Nothing else mattered. Jack moaned and slid his left hand down from her waist, resting it in the back pocket of her jeans.

They stood there for what could have been ten seconds or a hundred years to Sarah. She pulled back slightly and found his mouth followed hers, thrilling at the way she was trembling in his arms; both of them were, from need, from the rush of heat between them.

Neither of them noticed the rain until Sarah managed to tear herself away, her eyes still closed. Jack tugged her body back toward his and fashioned the blanket into a hood over them both. Sarah rested her head on Jack's chest, the wild drum of his heartbeat against her ear.

She didn't want to look at him as she said, "I'm so sorry. I had to see what kissing you would be like, but I can't do this to either of us. I'm not supposed to…I have to go home Monday. My mother's waiting for me. A lot of people are."

Jack took a deep breath and held it, exhaling with a sigh, moving his hands to Sarah's upper back. "So how was it?"

Sarah moved her head against the damp fabric of Jack's t-shirt, wiping a tear that ran down her cheek. "It was the kiss of my lifetime, and always will be. But that's all it can be, a memory."

Jack's hand traced circles between Sarah's shoulder blades. "I know. I have to leave tomorrow. Look, I understand how you feel, but will you please come back to the camp with me? I need dry clothes, and I promise you, the two of us will be friends like before, that's all, and you don't even have to speak to Kelly or anybody else, and no one will bother you, and there's good food there, and plenty of shelter from the rain and we can still enjoy the festival together—"

Sarah leaned back into the rain and touched her fingertip to his mouth, taking the opportunity to put some distance between her body and Jack's. "Now *you're* babbling," she said. "There's some great music coming tonight, though nothing I really care about is playing now. I don't want to talk to any of those people at your camp, Jack. I guess I'll go with you, but I'll avoid the others, especially Laura and Kelly. Can we agree to that?" She stepped back a couple of paces and looked at him.

"Yes," Jack nodded, "I promise. Let me get you under this hood, Sarah. Come back and walk beside me. I'll keep the rain off you."

She shook her head and held her arms wide, a huge smile lighting her face. "I love the rain. It's a blessing, a joy, each drop a little miracle. I want to experience it," she said.

Jack couldn't help grinning back at her. "Okay, then. I'm starving, by the way. And you, my beautiful friend, taste like Hershey's chocolate." He grinned at her. "Do you have any left?"

"No," Sarah said, wiping rain from her eyes. "Do you know how to get more? I don't want any of Kelly's. But I need a bar of chocolate."

He would slay a dragon, Jack thought. He would crawl on his hands and knees to Hershey, Pennsylvania and bring it back to her in his teeth. He would pay his last hundred dollars, challenge a candy store owner to a duel at dawn, *anything* to get this girl chocolate.

Jack bit his lip. "Actually, I might know where to find a certain tunnel-of-fudge cake," he said. "Does that sound good?"

"Is it chocolate?" Sarah asked.

Jack squinted at her, a tiny frown drawing his brows together. "Umm, yes, it's very chocolate. If there's any left, you'll love it."

"Okay, then, let's do a split." Sarah started toward the path and Jack followed, shaking his head at her garbled slang and kicking himself for finding the right girl at absolutely the most *wrong* time in the universe.

16

The Woodstock Music and Art Fair
Bethel, New York
SATURDAY, AUGUST 16, 1969

When Jack and Sarah drew close to camp, they spotted Laura standing next to Eric's little propane stove, stirring something in an aluminum pot. Rodney stood with her, holding a large red umbrella to shield the fiancée, food, and fire from the rain.

Sarah stopped in her tracks. "I'm not going near her," she told Jack. "Laura doesn't like me, doesn't want me there, doesn't want to share food with me. I heard her talking to Kelly."

Jack put his arm around her waist and gave her a side hug. He squinted at the pot Laura was stirring in the distance. "All of us contributed equally to the food fund. That's probably a delicious batch of SpaghettiOs being cooked. You're as entitled to them as I am; you're officially my guest. And Sarah, you don't have to say anything to her. Laura was way out of line, and it's my camp, too. I want you here. Ignore her." He pointed to the van. "See, Kelly's in there, working as usual. You and I will walk right by Laura and Rodney, and you go in the tent you were sharing with Kelly. I'll keep her away, I promise. Looks like Eric and Kristin have already gone down the hill. You wait in that tent…which happens to be *my* tent, by the way, I brought it…and I'll join you in a few minutes. Just pretend you don't see the others."

Sarah hesitated, watching Laura for a few seconds. "Okay, I will. But I do not want a SpaghettiO." She frowned. "The chocolate cake sounded good, though."

"I'll see what I can do," Jack answered, swinging the blanket onto one shoulder and looping his arm through hers. "Give me a few minutes to change into dry clothes and I'll be right there. I guarantee you'll have complete privacy in the meantime." He led Sarah past a gawking Laura and Rodney, steering her into the tent. Kelly never looked up from her notebook.

Jack approached the side door of the van to gather his clothes. When Kelly saw him, he cut her off before she could say a word.

"I found Sarah. She's fine. You stay away from that girl, Kelly. You and Laura hurt her feelings, and you in particular had no right to do what you did. I still can't imagine what you were thinking, stealing her things and throwing them in the damn port-o-let. I brought Sarah to our place to get her away from anyone who might hurt her, and look what I walked her into! You and Laura behaving like cruel middle-school girls, saying hateful shit behind her back."

Kelly rolled her eyes, moving her head back and forth with a heavy sigh. "Look, maybe I went too far, but don't be so dramatic, Jack. I had my reasons. You seem to have forgotten we just met this girl."

He shook his head and looked toward the rest of their campsite, drawing a deep breath before continuing. "Yeah, well, she's special. I like her a lot, Kelly, and I won't let you be mean to her. Later this weekend, if she'll get anywhere near you, I expect you to play nice. This is my last day and a half with everyone. Could you and Laura please not ruin it?" He thumped his hands on the roof of the van, speech finished. "Now, Sarah and I are going to have something to eat in the tent I brought. You can have it back later, but in the meantime, it's off-limits. Understand?"

"So now she's installed as your Woodstock conquest in my tent? I should have known from the minute you first brought her up the hill, a very pretty drowned rat. You're an entirely predictable horndog, Jack Warren," Kelly said.

He leaned into the van for his duffel bag and unzipped it. Without a glance at Kelly, Jack extracted some dry clothes and said, "She's warm and kind and, yes, beautiful. Any other time I'd sleep with her in a heartbeat. Don't think I haven't thought about it. But I'm going to Canada tomorrow and Sarah has to head home. Her mother's waiting for her. I *do* have a conscience, despite what you think. I'm just hanging out with her tonight and tomorrow, that's all." He zipped the bag and threw it back to the floorboard. "It would be the best thing in the world for you to consider other people's feelings once in a while, Kelly."

Jack stalked away and Kelly stared after him as he approached Rodney and motioned to his and Laura's tent. Rodney nodded and Laura slapped his arm for some reason. Kelly turned her attention back to the numbers and symbols in front of her, but they were blurry from the tears in her eyes. She swiped them away and placed the notebook carefully next to her purse on the floor. She hugged herself and curled into a ball on the vinyl seat, listening to the rain fall on the VW's roof. Her answer to Jack's words would stay locked in her heart.

I consider your feelings every minute of the day, Jack. It's you and Sarah who don't realize what you're doing to mine.

Jack opened the tent flap to find Sarah crouched in the corner, watching the entrance warily. He smiled and held out a green t-shirt. "I have practically everything I own with me, so take advantage of it. Put this dry shirt on while I change and get some food. It'll match your eyes." He ducked back out and returned a few minutes later with a small piece of tunnel-of-fudge cake on a paper plate, along with a plastic fork. "You're going to love this," he told her.

Sarah stared at the cake in her hand, then lifted it to sniff. "Well, it does smell like chocolate," she said. "But it looks really weird. There's runny stuff in it." She wrinkled her nose and turned the fork over and over in the fingers of her other hand, studying it like a bronze spear tip unearthed by an archeologist.

"Despite her personality flaws, Laura's a great baker," Jack said. "You'll love that cake, but I have to warn you, it's the end of the supply. Rodney has to finish the bit that's left in front of Laura or she'll kill him. Apparently pregnancy comes with horror-movie mood swings." Jack dug into his bowl of SpaghettiOs with a plastic spoon. "Gah, these have never tasted so good," he said. "I was starving. Well, go on, try it, Sarah. It won't hurt you." When she didn't, he set his bowl down and took the fork from her and stabbed a piece of cake. "Here," he handed it to her, "you act like you've never seen a fork before."

Sarah slid the cake into her mouth and moaned slightly, chewing for at least thirty seconds longer than necessary. She nodded at Jack and gobbled the rest, licking the fork afterward. "Do you think Rodney would sell me his cake for money? I have money," she said, perfectly serious.

Jack laughed. "He'd basically be selling his marriage and child, so I don't think there's enough money in the world. His one mission in life right now is keeping Laura happy. Are you sure you don't want to try SpaghettiOs?" He held the bowl out to her.

Sarah wrinkled her nose and shook her head. "I think I like cake," she said. "Cake and chocolate bars are my favorite foods."

"Hmmm," Jack said. "Good choices. That reminds me, I have to deliver a piece of pineapple upside-down cake to a lady in the Bindy Bazaar a little later. Will you walk over there with me?"

Sarah grinned at him. "Is pineapple upside-down cake chocolate, too?"

Jack stared at her. "No, pineapple upside-down cake is vanilla with pineapple and a bunch of syrupy stuff. I think we've exhausted any hope of more chocolate. Although you can never completely deny the possibility of chocolate out in the world." He paused to scoop up the last of his food and chewed thoughtfully before setting the bowl aside. "Will you go with me?"

Sarah yawned. "Yes, I will. And I think I'd like to try pineapple upside-down cake, too, if there's enough," she said.

"I'll check," Jack told her. "Eric and Kristin demolished a lot of it last night." He put his hands behind his neck and lay back on Kelly's still-butterflied sleeping bag, patting the space beside him. "I really need a nap," he said. "No one will bother us. Let's get some rest."

Sarah moved to the very edge, placing three feet of space between them. She yawned again and told Jack, "I'm sleepy, too." She lay on her side to face him, hands clasped under her head, blinking her green eyes at his face before closing them. Soon he heard her softly snoring and fell asleep to that and the rhythm of the rain pattering outside, punctuated by occasional faint music from the distant stage.

When he woke, Sarah was standing as tall as she could in the tent, shaking her arms. "I'm still not used to sleeping like that," she told Jack.

He frowned and rubbed his eyes. "How are you used to sleeping?"

She glanced toward the tent flap. "It doesn't matter," she said. "Let's walk to the Bindy Bazaar. I need to move around."

"Give me a minute to get the cake and something to cover it so it doesn't get wet," Jack said.

Sarah smiled at him. "No need," she told him. "The rain is over for a while. I'll wait here. Please get a piece for me to try if there's enough. I won't be coming back up here later."

"Sarah," Jack said, "sit down for a minute and let's talk about this. There's no need for you to sleep somewhere else, and there are a lot of good reasons why you shouldn't. It's safe here, and dry, and I've already told you the others won't bother you. They *won't*. You're *my* guest in this camp, I keep telling you. You're here at my invitation, and that's what matters."

She sat and began to wring her hands. "Kelly doesn't want me here, Jack, she doesn't even want to be around me. I tried so hard to be who she wanted me to be. And it makes me really sad. I came here…it doesn't matter." She swiped at a tear running down her cheek. "I don't really care what Laura thinks. But Kelly, well, it was important to me. She thinks I use *drugs*." Sarah paused for a second, considering how much to tell Jack and deciding not to have another person think she was crazy. "Kelly went through my private things and threw some away, when I thought we were friends. Can you not understand why I don't want to stay here?" She sniffed. "And now she's going to be mad because you're spending time with me. Do you not see the way she looks at you? You are the apple in her eye."

Jack said, "I am *not* the apple of her eye, Sarah. You're wrong. She looks at me like an old friend from college. That's all. There's nothing between Kelly and me. Half the time she can't stand me." He sighed and reached to put a hand on Sarah's arm, squeezing gently, shaking his head, adding, "And none of this matters, Sarah, it all ends tomorrow. Let's have fun while we can. You wait here and I'll see if there's enough cake for you to have some. And tonight, after the music, you can sleep in the van or something. You're coming back here because I'm not losing you in that crowd again. You'll hang with us tomorrow, too, and it'll be all right. That's what I want, so let me have my way before I have to say goodbye to you and everyone and everything I know." He stood and hurried out of the tent before she could say another word.

He returned a few minutes later with the gypsy lady's cake and a smaller piece for Sarah, which she devoured and declared her third-favorite food. Somehow she managed to get caramel syrup all over the fork and her hands. Rather than stop to wash them and risk eye contact with Kelly or anyone else, Sarah licked her fingers as she and Jack hiked down the trail. Jack helped her down the section where she'd slid into a round of applause earlier, balancing the plate of cake in one hand and grasping Sarah's non-sticky left one with his other.

They reached the Bindy Woods surrounding the bazaar, stepping aside as several couples emerged hand-in-hand. The late-day sunshine filtered through the dense canopy overhead, transporting everyone to a softer, gentler world as soon as they entered the forest. There was a thick carpet of ferns along the trail labeled "Gentle Path".

Jack pointed at the tiny white lights strung above them, now switched on and glistening post-rain. "I didn't notice those before," he told Sarah.

"Neither did I," she said. "And it feels ten degrees cooler in here. Why would anyone leave these woods?"

"Well," Jack replied, "there *is* this whole music festival thing going on. But I agree, it's so pretty and peaceful in here." He fought the urge to take and hold Sarah's non-sticky hand in the quiet of the lush forest. Instead, he walked ahead, leading her to the vendors' booths. When they reached the gypsy lady, she stood and greeted them both with a warm smile, her bracelets jangling as she reached for the cake Jack offered. Jack thought she looked older this time; he noticed thin gray streaks in her tousled black hair and crinkles at the edge of her eyes.

"I knew you'd come back," she told Jack. "Thank you for this. I'll really enjoy it." She swept her eyes up and down Sarah. "Did you bake this cake?" she asked.

"Oh, no," Sarah laughed. "I wouldn't know where to begin to bake a cake, but I'd like to learn. I did have a piece of it, though, and it's tender and sweet and something I think I could live on. It's really good. Sticky, though; be careful to keep the syrup off your fork." She held up her caramel-coated hand.

"I have just the thing, hold on." The lady reached under her counter and produced a wet rag, reaching for Sarah's hand and gently wiping it clean. "I'm Kezia, by the way." She located a dry cloth and used it on Sarah's hand, though she continued to grasp the fingers in her own after she finished. "Better?" she asked.

Sarah nodded, smiling. "Yes, that's so much better. Thank you for your kindness." She glanced down at her hand in the woman's and back up to meet Kezia's eyes. "I'm Sarah," she added.

Kezia continued to hold her hand, stroking Sarah's fingers with her thumb. "You're a long way from home, honey. You traveled here with a lot on your heart. Something or someone deeply important to you was waiting."

Jack cleared his throat. "She's from reservation land in the Dakotas," he told Kezia. "And my name is Jack."

"Is that right?" The lady sat down and released Sarah's hand, regarding the couple before her with her head cocked to one side. "So, are you two having fun together, Jack? I've heard some great music in the distance. Last night I went over to hear Joan Baez while my husband watched the booth," she said.

Jack laughed. "You're a fan? So is Sarah."

"Well, of course I am," Kezia replied. "Isn't everyone?" She smiled and said *Sarah* softly, studying Sarah's face for a long moment. Then she swept her eyes to meet Jack's. "So, when are you going to give her the bracelet, son?" she asked him.

"I…" Jack stammered and shrugged his shoulders.

"Don't be embarrassed. It's plain as day she's the one I was talking about. And I think she'll need the amber a lot more than your pocket lining does, very soon." Kezia reached for Sarah's hand again. "You have a lovely spirit," she told her. "Where's the bracelet?" she asked Jack, who produced it from his jeans pocket and handed it to her. She fastened the silver clasp on Sarah's wrist.

Sarah held her arm up to admire the amber bead, glowing in the soft twinkly lights. "It's just beautiful," she said. She turned to Jack. "I don't understand, though. Did you buy this? For me? For someone else?"

Jack looked into her green eyes, which were sparkling like a child's beholding their first Christmas tree. "I bought it in case I found someone who'd truly enjoy wearing it. Looks like I found her," he said. "The amber is supposed to absorb bad energy and make you all peaceful and calm. Umm, soothing vibrations?" He frowned slightly at Kezia.

"Yes, that's right, amber is soothing," Kezia said. She placed her elbows on the counter and clasped her hands, leaning forward to rest her chin. "I hope you'll treasure that bracelet. It will see you through a lot," she said to Sarah. She paused for a beat, then added, "And honey? Forgive her."

"I don't know what you mean," Sarah replied, her eyebrows drawn together.

"Yes, you do." Kezia nodded, rocking her chin back and forth on her hands. "She doesn't understand. It's that simple. And you need to remember some people feel things even more deeply than the rest of us, but they wear their love and hurt on the inside, where no one can see."

Sarah and Kezia gazed at each other in silence for several seconds before Kezia turned to Jack. "You have to take a long journey soon. Both of you do. Make the most of every minute you have," she said to him, her face solemn.

Jack, clearly uncomfortable, looped his arm through Sarah's and began to lead her away before any serious fortune-telling commenced. "Thank you!" he called over his shoulder from several feet away. "Enjoy the cake."

"The bracelet's perfect for you, Sarah," Kezia called back. "And you stay safe, Jack."

17

The Woodstock Music and Art Fair
Bethel, New York
SATURDAY, AUGUST 16, 1969

Sarah followed Jack out of the woods, blinking at the late-day sun and wishing this century knew how to control outdoor temperatures. The t-shirt she'd borrowed was stuck to her back. She peeled it away with a sigh and matched Jack's footsteps to avoid mud puddles.

He'd been uncharacteristically quiet as they made their way along the Gentle Path. Now he walked with his head bent like he was studying the ground, even though this wasn't a muddy or particularly wet area. She stepped to Jack's right side and glanced at his expression, mostly hidden by a curtain of dark hair.

"What's wrong?" Sarah asked.

He offered her a slight smile. "I'm just thinking. Sometimes I do too much of that. I mean, you don't believe in that crap Kezia said, right? It's all a bunch of general advice that could apply to anyone. *Ooooh*, you traveled a long way for something important to you. Soon you have to go home. Oh, and you should forgive someone who doesn't understand you," he mocked in a singsong voice. "*Ooooh, people have feelings. So unique.*"

"Actually," Sarah replied, "I think I might. Maybe she's talking about Kelly."

Jack said, "Kelly hasn't asked for your forgiveness, Sarah. Did she tell you she's sorry for going through your private things and throwing them away? I have a feeling if she had, you wouldn't have left our camp in the first place." He raised his eyebrows.

"Well, no," Sarah answered. "But Kezia seemed to have a lot of insight. Maybe she can discern other people's—"

Jack interrupted, "You sound like my mom with her daily horoscope, which she swallows with her morning coffee. She only believes it if it predicts something good, of course. Bad portents are for the millions of *other* Geminis about to experience misfortune. Oh, and she thinks I'm compassionate and kind because I was born on September 9, a Virgo, so that's my role in life. I think I'm compassionate and kind because I was raised that way. Maybe it's my dad, who gave up his vacation time when I was a high-school freshman so his co-worker could stay at the hospital with his wife and premature baby. Maybe it was Mom herself, who made five-year-old me return the Halloween candy I stole from Billy Hollingsworth. Maybe it's my grandfather, who walked me over to share the fish I caught with our neighbors who couldn't afford a trip to the grocery store. Or maybe," he cocked his head to examine the sky, "it's the position of several distant celestial bodies at the precise moment I entered this world."

Sarah shook her head. "There are things all around us we can't see, Jack. Maybe Kezia has a gift and is trying to help."

Jack said, "Or maybe she's a charlatan who offers useless advice with every bracelet sale. I should have kept my money and ignored her calming-vibes spiel. She talked me into—"

Sarah stopped and tugged at the bracelet's clasp. "Do you want this back?" she interrupted. "It's definitely not giving me any feelings except aggravation."

Jack put his hand on her arm to stay her. "I'm sorry, I'll hush up. And absolutely not. I want you to look at that bracelet and think of me. Maybe the amber isn't magical, but if it reminds you of our time together this weekend, I'll be very happy." *Why am I being an argumentative ass?* he asked himself. *Because you can't stop worrying about going to Canada and arguing is easier*, his brain answered.

Sarah looked at his hand atop the silver chain and then up at him. "I won't need a bracelet, Jack," she said, her eyes soft on his. She cleared her throat and waved her hand at the audience seated in the distance. "Canned Heat is going to play in a few minutes. Want to find a seat? They're pretty good."

"Yeah," he replied, "Eric was talking about them. Says the lead singer looks like a grizzly bear but sounds like a sedated housecat. Probably typical Eric the part-time college disc jockey, spouting bullshit in an attempt to sound hip and informed." He scanned the crowd for a moment, and then nodded. "I'll lead the way."

They settled in next to some guys sitting on striped beach towels at the end of a row. Sarah spotted a bunch of people perched high on the narrow bars of the towers next to the stage, some of them dangling precariously far above the ground. She smiled at the knowledge none of them would fall, impossible as that seemed. The only deaths at Woodstock would be some poor kid who was run over by a tractor in a field as he lay in a sleeping bag and a man who died as the result of a drug overdose, possibly heroin. A magazine article had later speculated he might've lost his life to hyperthermia and heart inflammation, possibly side effects of the Thorazine he'd been given to combat an overdose in the first place. Strange, Sarah thought, amid the sea of pot and LSD surrounding her, the only death to result from drugs could have been something medically administered.

Jack nudged her arm and pointed. Several rows in front of them, a naked man danced to no discernible music whatsoever. Sarah laughed and covered her eyes with her hands. "He's going to fling off some body parts when the band starts playing," she said.

The announcer boomed from the stage, "There's been a little tremor of paranoia running through the audience about going to the first aid tent if you're on a bummer. If things aren't going well for you or whatever please be assured, again I repeat, please be assured that there's no bust, there's no hassle and we'll make every effort to make no unfortunate occurrence for you if you can't handle what's been going down."

Jack looked around for any signs of bad acid trips, spotting fifty or so pleasantly stoned people lying back and enjoying the late-day sun, some of them passing a tiny pipe down the row in front of him. Naked dancing guy looked happy enough.

"Please," the announcer continued, "we'll make every effort to make you as comfortable as possible. Don't throw yourself upon us unless it's absolutely necessary because at this time we are pretty well swamped." He continued admonishing the crowd to take care of one another above the sound of harmonica and drums warming up. "We've been blessed with the order that you've given us, but we cannot continue to hold your hand. Please if you will, bear with us."

"Are you okay?" Jack asked Sarah. "Do you want me to look for some water or food?"

"No, I'm fine," she answered, fanning herself with her handbag's fringed bottom. "Just looking forward to the music."

A couple of minutes passed until Canned Heat started a bluesy boogie with harmonica and lyrics about finding love and a man needing a woman to keep him company. Sarah kept her eyes on the stage, suddenly feeling awkward about all that had passed between her and Jack in recent hours.

When the band began "Going Up the Country", Jack shook his head and yelled at Sarah, "Typical Eric BS! The sedated housecat is the other singer, not the grizzly bear." He pointed and Sarah could make out a smaller man with the microphone in hand.

After Canned Heat birthed that hippie anthem, the rest of the performance was good enough to keep their attention, but didn't inspire either of them to dance. Sarah noted the naked guy had sat down and now leaned against the woman next to him. She hoped it was his wife or girlfriend.

Sarah turned to Jack after the band finished. "Want to go over to the Hog Farm kitchen and see if they're handing out anything good? Or we could just walk around for a while and explore."

"Honestly," Jack said, "I was a little afraid to mention it, but I'd like to bathe and wash my hair in that pond." He produced a tiny hotel bar of soap from his back pocket. "I don't want you to feel weird. You can wait for me in the woods. But my skin is starting to feel downright crusty."

Sarah nodded. "That sounds wonderful to me. I didn't think to bring soap. Maybe I could share yours." She held out her hands and examined them, the bracelet's amber bead dangling in the sunset's glow. "But I'm going to wear these jeans and your shirt into the water and wash them, too. I'm keeping my clothes on."

"Okay, that's a good plan," Jack said. "The pond is already full of other people bathing and swimming, so I'll just be one more naked man they won't notice. But unless we go all the way back up to camp, we won't have any towels. We'll have to drip dry."

"It will not be my first time," Sarah laughed. "And it'll feel good in this heat. That's fine. But you go first while I wait in the woods. You can bring me the soap after you get dressed, okay?"

"Deal," Jack said, and began to walk in the direction of Filippini Pond. They passed a small circle of high-school-aged boys strumming guitars and trying to copy "Going Up the Country". Jack realized just how good the sedated housecat's falsetto was when he heard their screeching version.

"Great song, guys!" he called to the kids. "Is songicide a word?" he muttered to Sarah.

"I have no idea," she answered. "But they may be committing some version of it."

They entered the woods and followed a narrow dirt path until Jack found a large rock and directed Sarah to sit on it to wait with her back to the water. "I'll be back in just a few minutes. No peeking," he told her.

Sarah waited until his footsteps faded and then turned around, watching as Jack stepped out of his jeans in the distance and tossed aside boxer shorts. She stared as his perfectly round bottom cheeks disappeared into the water, then turned her back to the pond and didn't look again. She studied the birdsong and leaves in the woods until a grinning Jack returned to her side, dressed and dripping water, extending the small bar of Cameo soap in his right hand.

"You didn't look, did you?" he asked. "Wouldn't want to ruin you for every other man you might meet."

"That certainly did not happen," she informed him as she took the soap. "I just listened to the birds and watched an insect crawling on a leaf. Those things seemed more interesting than peeking at you."

"You know," Jack said, "your English is getting better every minute you spend here. A little more hateful, too." He laughed at her retreating back and settled himself on the rock. At least he could watch her wash her hair. No law against that.

Sarah emerged from the water running her hands through her hair. She winced at the tangles as she walked up to Jack.

"Here," he said, "take my place." She sat on the rock and Jack positioned himself behind her. He produced a comb from his back pocket and gently separated each section of her hair, holding it still as he worked to prevent any pain. He leaned forward to look at her face occasionally to make sure he wasn't hurting her. She didn't see him kiss the last lock of hair as he replaced it, smoothing it against her head and announcing, "All set."

"Thank you," Sarah said, standing to leave. "Where did you learn to do that so well?"

"Mom used to pay me a quarter to comb her hair out. It was a job she hated doing, and we didn't have money for her to go to the beauty parlor in town." Jack shrugged. "That was free of charge. First one's on the house."

"On what house?" Sarah asked, tilting her head.

"Never mind." Jack waved his hand at the distant sea of humanity. "Shall we go? Let's see if the next band is any good. It's getting dark and I'm ready to settle in. Let's find a good place."

Sarah nodded and followed him, shaking the water from her arms and swinging them in an effort to dry them.

As they drew closer, they could hear a voice carrying from the main stage's microphone. "My name is Hugh Romney. I'm with the Hog Farm and I'm working on a scene, some people call it bum trips. I don't think there's such a thing as a bum trip…we have handled over three hundred and everybody's worked out all right. A half an hour after we release anybody from our section we turn them into doctors and they care for people that were tripping like they were when they came in." Jack raised his eyebrows at Sarah as she drew to his side. Romney continued, "Now people been sayin' some of the acid is poisoned. It's not poisoned, it's just bad acid, it's manufactured poorly. So anybody that thinks they taken some poison, forget it. And if you feel like experimenting only take half a tab. Okay, thank you."

The announcer's deep voice took over amid scattered applause. "Mark, Jody, Linda, please come to the rear of the stage please. Pam Mills, please come to the water pumps. Bill Green from Jericho, please meet Jeff at the information. Tom and Roseanne Glennon, Tom and Roseanne Glennon, please, someone has your medicine behind the stage please. Jack Warren from Boston, please meet your party at the information near the stage, please."

Jack grabbed Sarah's arm. "Did he say 'Jack Warren from Boston'? Did I hear that right? It can't be my ride to Canada, that's late tomorrow, and besides, he wouldn't—what could possibly—"

She took his hand. "Come on," Sarah said, sprinting forward with Jack in tow, running as though she knew exactly where she was going. She darted around camps and couples standing together and two small children throwing a ball, then had to slow as the crowd grew thicker. When they finally reached the information booth, Sarah spotted Rodney and Laura before Jack did, Laura glancing around, clearly upset. Sarah swung her hand forward to propel Jack to them. She still wanted nothing to do with Laura, so she placed herself within earshot a few steps away and waited.

"It's Kelly," Laura told Jack, breathless. She paused to take in some air, her hands on her knees. "We've looked everywhere for her. Rodney and I were in our tent and Gary and Bud came over to share some of our food and they brought a couple of snacks. Kelly ate some of the watermelon they had, and then she wandered off down the hill and Gary said—"

"So what, Laura?" Jack said, clearly annoyed. "If Kelly wanted to come down here by herself, she'll be fine. She's probably sitting somewhere waiting for the next band. Kelly's a big girl. She can handle herself."

"Some of their watermelon was spiked with LSD, Jack, and they might've accidentally brought it to us. Kelly ate a piece," Laura spat at him, her eyes taking in the water dripping from Jack's clothes. "Do you think I'd have you paged if it wasn't an emergency?" She glared at Sarah and turned her eyes back to him. "I know you're *busy*. I hope it was a nice little time at the swimming hole. But Kelly's out here with hundreds of thousands of strangers and possibly under the effects of hallucinogens. Kelly. *Kelly*, Jack."

Jack stared at Laura for a few beats, and then looked at Rodney. "Are you even sure she ate some of the drugged kind?"

"Not absolutely," Rodney answered. "Gary and Bud were a little out of it and weren't positive. They kept telling us to relax, that Kelly would have a good trip even if it was. But it scared Laura because it's not at all like Kelly to go off on her own. You know that." Rodney shoved his hands into his pockets and glanced at Laura. "We've been looking for an hour and a half. This is bad for Laura and the baby."

Jack asked, "Why didn't you just page Kelly?"

"Of course we paged Kelly, you idiot. Did you miss the part where she's tripping on acid?" Laura said.

Jack drew a deep breath. "You two go back to camp. Odds are, she's fine and just wandered off to hear some music. She'll probably turn up back there when she finds there are no folk singers coming up. John Sebastian played hours ago and she missed it because she was busy sulking in the van." He shrugged his shoulders. "Just go. I'll keep an eye out. I'm sure you're making a big deal out of nothing."

Laura shook her head. "We checked the freakout tents and the big medical tent, too. No one's seen her. She's in trouble, Jack, I know it. Please find her."

"I don't know how in hell I'm supposed to find her, Laura. Look around you." Jack waved at the mass of people seated and milling around on acres of land. "You're asking the impossible."

Sarah cleared her throat and stepped closer. "I can locate Kelly," she told Jack.

Laura swept her eyes up and down Sarah. "She's not a buffalo," she said, her voice dripping venom.

"Shut up, Laura," Jack yelled. "You are the most—"

Sarah interrupted him, ignoring Laura. "We are wasting time, Jack." She turned to Rodney, saying, "You two go back to camp."

Rodney handed Sarah the small flashlight he carried and said, "She's wearing that green thing Laura calls a skort and a white t-shirt."

Sarah nodded.

Laura started to speak, but Rodney put a finger to her lips. "It'll be fine," he told her, kissing the top of her head. "You need to calm down."

"No, it won't," she answered, her face clouded by anger. "It's almost completely dark and Jack's going off with that lunatic leading him around." She looked contemptuously at Sarah, who returned her gaze with equal contempt. "None of this is helping." Laura was the first to break eye contact, turning to Rodney. "We need to keep searching for Kelly. She's never had anything stronger than Boone's Farm, Rodney. She's out here somewhere doing God knows what on LSD."

Sarah took Jack's arm, leading him off into the crowd before another word could be spoken.

18

The Woodstock Music and Art Fair
Bethel, New York
SATURDAY, AUGUST 16, 1969

Jack trailed after Sarah, who kept fiddling with her handbag and walking in different directions like she was lost. He shined the flashlight from behind, trying to illuminate the way for both of them.

"I know you want to find her, Sarah, but this isn't the way. We need to pick a logical path and stick with it. We could search in a grid, that makes sense. The main medical tent is nearby. Why don't we start with it? Even if Rodney and Laura checked it, Kelly could have been brought there later."

"She's not in the medical tent," Sarah said, frowning. "In fact, I don't think she's still at the festival. I think she's gone farther away."

"Is this more psychic babble, like the gypsy lady? We're out here stumbling around in the dark based on your intuition? Maybe we need to stop and think about this, Sarah," Jack said. "I feel like we're heading in the wrong direction. She wouldn't leave the festival."

"First of all, you don't know what Kelly would do on hallucinogenic drugs. And no, I'm just really good at tracking people," Sarah called over her shoulder. "It's a skill I've developed. And if you want to stop, wait here. I'll find Kelly by myself. Or you can go back and ask half a million people if they've seen her, but I think you've experienced how well that works."

"And what do you mean 'farther away'? Are you saying someone took her?" Jack stumbled over a rock and cursed to himself. He glanced back at the lights of the stage receding in the distance. "Sarah, stop. Please be still for a minute," he said, struggling to catch his breath. "I can't see as well as you can, even with the flashlight. You're like a damn cat."

Sarah stood still for a few seconds, surveying the terrain in front of them. "We're going to have to detour around the Bindy Woods," she said. "There are lights there, but also hundreds of people clogging the paths, and they'll hold us up. Come on." She began her half-running pace forward again and Jack shook his head, torn between arguing about the futility of this search and curiosity about Sarah's bizarre sureness they were heading in the right direction. He inhaled a deep breath. They'd reach whatever dead end they were likely chasing soon enough, and then they could search where it made more sense.

Sarah darted toward the Hog Farm compound and Jack followed, sniffing pot everywhere and almost colliding with a long-haired shirtless man carrying a naked baby on his shoulders. "Sorry, man," Jack mumbled, struggling to keep up. He was wondering how the man handled the kid peeing down his back when Sarah stopped abruptly and pointed.

"Kelly's that way," she told Jack with a nod. They hurried past women dumping oats and nuts and fruit into trash cans.

"What in the world are they doing?" he asked Sarah. "Are they throwing all that away?"

"No, they're mixing tomorrow morning's free breakfast," Sarah answered. "It's called muesli."

Jack frowned and tried to keep pace with Sarah, who seemed to ignore groups of people and simply plow through them, Jack muttering "excuse us" in her wake. Occasionally they'd skirt around a campfire with people singing, perfectly normal, but the next second they'd encounter men and women having sex along the path as though completely alone in the world.

He cleared his throat the second time they saw a naked couple going at it in the moonlight. "Drugs," Sarah said. "No inhibitions. Have you ever tried LSD, Jack?"

"No, of course not," he answered. "Have you?"

"No," she said, "but there's a lot more of what you call 'acid' out there in the world than you think. The CIA experimented on people with it for years, the US military, too. Some of them were volunteers, and some most definitely weren't. Lysergic acid diethylamide was supposed to offer mind control in military and political situations, but its effects are too unpredictable. They abandoned those tests a while back."

"How do you know about that?" Jack asked.

"I've studied a lot of history," Sarah answered. "Those tests were available to paid volunteers for a while, easy to access for college students and others."

"Wow, I never knew," Jack said, his eyes on Sarah's back.

"You wouldn't," Sarah said. "Not yet. I have good sources."

Jack rolled his eyes, wondering not for the first time how much of this stuff Sarah made up off the cuff. "So, if you know so much about LSD, how much danger is Kelly in if she ingested some?" The moon passed behind some clouds, and he struggled to see by the weak flashlight alone.

"Depends on how much she took," Sarah said. "I think we can safely assume she did eat tainted watermelon, though, otherwise she'd never be all the way out here."

Jack kept himself from saying *if she's out here at all*. They'd completely passed the Hog Farm now and were heading onto what looked to Jack like private land, maybe a farm of some sort.

"Sarah," he hissed, "are you sure—"

"Yes, I'm sure," she whispered loudly. "I know what I'm doing."

Jack looked around and saw houses in the distance, small groups of hippie-looking people dotting the terrain around them with their cars, campfires, and tents. "Do you think they have permission to camp way out here?" he asked Sarah.

She laughed. "Of course not. Here, we have to turn a little," she said, veering off to the left.

"Sarah, there's nothing this way," Jack said, stopping in his tracks.

"That's right, but Kelly is. Keep walking, or if you need to rest, just stay here and I'll bring her out," Sarah said. "It's not much farther."

"Out of what?" Jack asked, exasperated.

"You can't see it yet," Sarah squinted her eyes, "but in the distance, there's a cornfield. I think Kelly is in there," she answered. "That's the best I can figure."

"Wait, you're going to barge into a field of corn some poor farmer is waiting to harvest and stomp between rows, hoping to find Kelly? I'm sorry, Sarah, but this is ridiculous. We should go back. We're wasting time and I know you have a hunch, but—"

"It's not a hunch, Jack," she said, pointing to the now-visible rows of tall corn plants. "You wait here. If I'm not back in ten minutes with Kelly, I'll walk back to the festival with you and we'll look all over there. We'll do a grid search, just like you said."

Jack collapsed onto the ground, exhausted and hungry. He'd let her go alone and discover she'd been mistaken. How much danger could there be in a cornfield?

"I'll wait right here," he told Sarah, glancing at his Benrus glow-in-the-dark military watch, a gift his brother had thrown at Jack's head on his last visit to North Carolina. He sighed and added, "If you're not back in ten minutes, I'm coming in after you."

"Okay," Sarah said, striding toward the cornfield.

She went down two rows and halfway back up a third before locating Kelly, lying on the ground and singing softly. Kelly waved her hands in the air above her chest. As Sarah drew closer, she recognized the song as The Beatles' "Yesterday", though Kelly had changed the lyrics to a shrill "all my troubles seen a finer dayyyyy" as she moved her hands.

Sarah leaned over Kelly's face, peering down at her for a few seconds, tracking Kelly's eyes as they traveled back and forth at nothing in the air. She said, "It's me, Sarah. Are you all right, Kelly?"

Kelly laughed, a slightly maniacal sound amid the silent stalks of moonlit corn. "Sarah? I'm painting the sky. You don't even exist, Sarah. You're part of this beautiful trip. You're a filament of my aberration." She moved her right hand in the air, carefully decorating something with an imaginary brush.

"A figment," Sarah replied, "of your imagination. Come on, Kelly, let's get you back to camp. Everyone's worried about you." She moved her hands under Kelly's shoulder blades and Kelly screamed, a shrill alarm. A minute later, Jack came crashing into the cornfield, yelling Sarah's name.

"Over here!" she called out. "I found Kelly. Just follow my voice. I'm going to need help with her. She's fine, but she doesn't want to leave." He made his way to the two of them, crashing through and dislodging a deer that had been enjoying its dinner at a stalk several rows over.

Jack took in the scene before him, a wildly disheveled Kelly with her skort shoved up to bikini-level, her hair matted with leaves, staring at something he couldn't discern and waving her hands back and forth.

"She thinks she's painting the sky," Sarah told him.

Jack's eyebrows shot up. "Of course," he said. "Kelly, it's Jack. We're going to help you back to camp."

Kelly grinned. "Jack. Jack, you came. Come here and paint with me. It's paint by numbers and I'll tell you where to put the blue. I'm up to three thousand and eleven…" she trailed off.

Sarah met Jack's eyes. "I think she'll go more easily with you, so I'll be silent. Grab her arm." They each took a side and pulled Kelly to her feet. Kelly immediately wailed about her painting.

"You can finish it when we get you back to camp, okay?" Jack said, maneuvering Kelly toward the end of the row, trying to hold the flashlight and swipe leaves and ears of corn out of the way as they went.

"You are the prettiest man I know, Jack," Kelly said, running her eyes over his face. "You have lashes that are, like, so long, like Liza Minnelli, and you…where are we?" She looked past Jack to the row of corn on her right. "Oh, this is so beautiful," she whispered. When she looked to her left, she told Jack, "That one's not really here. She's only in my head. She's my granddaughter someday in the future and she's part of this whatever it is oh it's so green…"

"Uh huh," Jack replied. "Just keep walking, Kelly. I'll help you."

"Her name is Baezy rhymes with daisy and she time-travels all over the universe. But you can't see her. Only I can see her. Like all the colors," Kelly said. "All these incredible colors. Some of them are new. No one has ever seen this orange but me."

Jack guided Kelly through the last of the cornfield, shaking his head at Sarah. "I don't know how you found her and I never will, but I'm glad you did."

Sarah offered her brightest smile. "Well, obviously I'm a time-traveler from the future and I have special powers," she said. "It was a slice of cake."

They walked and sometimes dragged Kelly past a series of disinterested campers, most of them passing a joint or pipe around or eating sandwiches. Jack's stomach growled, a loud motorcycle or aircraft engine. Sarah looked at him and said, "Should we stop at the Hog Farm kitchen? Maybe they have some spare muesli."

"I'd rather chew on the trash cans they're mixing it in. Even the sound of the word muesli is revolting. About as appetizing as snot. I'll find something at camp," he said. "It's definitely past my dinnertime, though."

"Dinner is an abstract concept man invented," Kelly pronounced, her eyes wide. "We don't need all this food. All we need is love…" and she began singing the song. She trailed off after a minute and started wailing, "I want to paint some more. It's not finished. The sky is huge!"

"As soon as we get there, Kelly, I'll give you a big paintbrush and you can lay under the stars and paint just like Michelangelo," Jack said.

"Sistine sky. Chapel of love. I love you, Jack," Kelly said. "I love you, and Daisy Baezy too." She glanced at Sarah. "I love you, future girl." She reached for Sarah's bracelet. "Pretty trinket," she said. "It's amber and it's making strong vibrations—"

"Not this again," Jack interrupted.

"Good, good, good, good vibrations," Kelly sang. She continued the song all the way to camp, including her own screechy version of its signature theremin wave that grated the ears right off Jack's head.

He and Sarah deposited Kelly on the ground as Laura ran over to hug her. "Are you okay? Oh Kelly, I'm so sorry. We had no idea—"

Kelly beamed at her. "I'm better than I've ever been. I'm decorating the sky." She lay back and Jack mimed handing her a paintbrush as Kelly frowned and decided where to place her next color.

Sarah said to Laura, "She'll be fine in another six hours or so. Just keep an eye on her."

Laura forced herself to look at Sarah, biting her lower lip and answering, "I was wrong about you. I apologize for the things I said. Thank you for bringing Kelly back."

Jack watched quietly as Sarah blinked at Laura before answering. "I understand," she said. "I'm a stranger and she's your friend."

Laura stared at Sarah for a few seconds. "I heated up some canned ravioli earlier. Would you two like a plate?" she asked.

"Yes!" Jack rubbed his hands together.

"No thank you," Sarah said, watching Kelly adorn the stars with a flourish.

"She likes cake," Jack told Laura, his brows raised.

Laura nodded slowly and went to fetch Rodney's last sliver of tunnel-of-fudge cake, handing it to Sarah with a smile as she brushed away a tear, whether from frustration or embarrassment, Jack couldn't tell.

When they finished eating, Sarah said, "Laura, one of the songs I came here for, my very favorite, is coming up. Will you sit with Kelly while we go down to hear it? Actually, Jack, could we take a sleeping bag down there and try to stay awake? The music will go on all night."

Laura yawned and stretched. "Take Kelly's. She won't be using it tonight. Rodney and I'll take turns watching Kelly and I'll put Eric and Kristin on duty if they ever come back. We haven't seen them all day."

"Eric's probably trying to kiss up and get backstage with his impressive radio credentials," Jack said. He ducked into the tent and retrieved the sleeping bag, knocking over Kelly's purse in the process. A chocolate bar fell onto the grass floor of the tent. Jack only paused for two seconds before zipping it into the bag and rolling the thing into a bundle. He emerged with it and a stolen blanket, too, grinning at Sarah.

Laura held up a hand for them to wait and fetched the red umbrella from her tent, handing it to Sarah. "It's probably going to rain later," she said, "and I can take Kelly to the van or her tent." Sarah nodded, and they turned to leave with one last look at Kelly's arm still moving in a wide swath, working at improving the Milky Way.

They found a good space recently vacated by a tired group who'd repaired to their own tents on the hill. The view was great, the acoustics seemed better in the darkness, and Woodstock fell under a drowsy, soft spell as The Grateful Dead began their set. It wasn't Sarah or Jack's favorite style, but provided a nice backdrop for conversation and stargazing when the clouds provided a gap.

"I wonder how Kelly's sky is unfolding," Sarah said, her eyes fixed on a distant planet. She curled her legs under her and put her weight on one hand, leaning to point with the other. "Did you know," she asked Jack, "that all the stars we can see are bigger and brighter than our own sun?"

Jack shook his head as he looked at her. "No, but that's cool. You're full of fun facts. And information. So much information, Sarah Sandoval."

She smiled at him. "Not really. I study a lot, that's all. I've always loved learning new things. It, umm, it comes easily to me, I guess. Math comes easily to me, too, just like you. And like Kelly."

"Do you think she'll be all right? Could she have, like, brain damage from the acid?" Jack asked.

"No, that's propaganda. She won't have brain damage and she won't be addicted from one use of LSD and she won't suffer debilitating flashbacks at random moments. Kelly will be just fine," she answered. Sarah didn't say it aloud, but she wondered why Kelly had omitted her drug experience when she gave her oral history as a Woodstock '69 attendee in 2023. She'd probably decided it would reflect poorly on her distinguished career. Or maybe she didn't want her children or grandchildren to know she'd taken acid, even if it was accidental. It had certainly come as a surprise to Sarah. Not many things from the past managed to surprise Sarah. Chocolate and Jack Warren, in that order. She shook her head free of those thoughts and turned to find him studying her.

"I'm sorry, I know I'm not supposed to say things like this, but I can't get over how purely beautiful, how perfect you are in this moonlight, Sarah," he said, his voice quiet while the band paused due to electrical problems onstage. "I apologize. I'm just being honest."

Sarah offered him a shy smile. "I think you're beautiful too, Jack. I wish we'd met at a different time."

He lay back and clasped his hands under his head, looking at her. "When? At what point in the past could we have met and stayed together? Without me running from the draft and you running to home. Wouldn't that be inevitable at some point, even if we'd met a year ago? Because I think my heart would have been even more crushed tomorrow."

"Anywhen," she said, her voice just above a whisper.

"That's not a word," Jack said, chuckling a little. "I like it, though. I could have loved you anywhen, Sarah."

She looked away from him, focusing on whatever she could to keep him from seeing the emotions in her eyes. She knew too much.

Too much about the past, too much about the future, too much to do anything but ache over it all.

19

The Woodstock Music and Art Fair
Bethel, New York
SATURDAY, AUGUST 16, 1969

It didn't take long for the rain to start, forcing Jack and Sarah to huddle under cover. Both were painfully conscious of the closeness of their bodies and equally determined to keep from touching, an awkward situation even with Rodney's large golf umbrella. Sarah kept bumping Jack's arm, apologizing each time as though she'd delivered an electrical shock.

Maybe she had.

Jack placed the blanket across their legs to catch some of the water. Sarah noted it seemed to repel raindrops and was thankful Jack brought it along with the sleeping bag they sat on. They were far more comfortable than most around them, though if Sarah were to be honest, she'd happily have sat in the rain. She wasn't going to tell Jack. He was working so hard to keep them sheltered together.

As long as the music continued they could focus on the band performing. The rain had, however, created a small lake around the Grateful Dead's stage equipment and electrical problems caused lots of interruptions throughout their set. Through each silent gap, Jack turned his head to people watch, an interesting pastime at Woodstock and the only way he could keep from staring at Sarah. He spotted a guy dressed as a clown down the row from them, his makeup running in red and white droplets onto his ruffled collar. The same man Sarah had spoken to the night before passed near them carrying a lamb under his arm. This time he was wearing a long brown vest and no pants. Jack thought of pointing him out to Sarah but was afraid she'd run to talk to him again.

Last night seemed a month ago. Jack pondered how the passage of so little time was amplified into much more by all they'd seen and done in the past twenty-four hours. The festival atmosphere changed everything; people were naturally drawn together in this setting. Couples probably met at Woodstock and Jack guessed at least a few would marry someday. He smiled, thinking how many babies might be born in precisely nine months with names like Santana, Janis, and Creedence.

"Some pennies for your thoughts," Sarah said over the sound of rain pattering around them.

"I was just thinking about how this place has drawn half a million people and then created...I don't know how to say it. Maybe, like, a private club with hundreds of thousands of members. We're sharing something no one else has or ever will. It could never be the same, even if they repeated it all next year." Jack shrugged his shoulders. "The rain, the food shortages, the mud, the crowding, the port-o-lets...I don't think the negatives will stay with us. I think we'll look back on this and realize we were part of something really special," Jack said, nodding at a clean-cut young man in Bermuda shorts walking in front of them. "Look at that guy. He probably hasn't eaten in hours, his clothes are soaked, his mama and daddy are terrified he's here with all these hippies. And he'll walk away carrying memories of Santana and how they made him dance, of the pretty girl who handed him a flower, of the taste of the wine someone passed to him in a jug."

Sarah nodded, her face thoughtful. "Kind of like when a woman bears a baby into the world. There is great pain, but the joy of holding her new son or daughter for the first time will make that part fade and she'll remember only the best of it. That's what I've been told."

Jack frowned. "Maybe," he said. "Anyway, I could be wrong. This could all be forgotten and a new music festival could take its place in history. Who knows what the future holds? Woodstock could end up a footnote. It just feels bigger because I'm here, living it, probably."

"Time will tell," Sarah said, her eyes wide. "There's a lot going on right now. Protests for civil rights, protests against war, so much anger and discord, such division. Maybe this is the way half a million people unite to escape and just share music and everything else for a weekend. To forget for a little while." She looked around at the crowd, some of them sleeping peacefully in the rain, some taking cover any way they could. One guy had flipped his lawn chair and was holding the seat over his head. "You know, when ancient civilizations had an important message or plea, they didn't speak it, they sang it in order to be heard by the gods. Maybe that's happening with these songs. Messages for those who wouldn't listen."

Jack nodded his head. "I studied music at MIT, but I never heard that about singing to the gods in ancient times. I've been playing piano since I was ten. My mother forced me. Turns out being good at math goes well with reading music. My teacher hated me, though. I have a tendency to daydream. And I'll never be good enough for a career in music, but the piano attracts lots of chicks at parties." He grinned at Sarah. "I wish I could play you a song."

"And what song would you play?" She smiled back at him, her eyes soft.

Jack repositioned the umbrella to his other arm. "Let's see. A song for Sarah." He exhaled a long breath. "You probably think I'm going to say 'Pretty Woman' or 'My Girl'. I've definitely played those to get a girl's attention at a party. But they aren't right for you."

Sarah tilted her head, listening.

"Okay, I've got it," Jack said. "You and I are in a room full of people. Everyone's had dinner and a few glasses of wine or cocktails. You're standing with a group fifteen feet away and you haven't even noticed me all night long. I sit down at a baby grand piano and play the first notes of *Moonlight Sonata*. Everyone knows it, no one expects it, and some people just keep talking because it's background music. But you meet my eyes and I look only at you as I play the entire first movement, the slow and sensual part. I never glance at the piano, I only hold your eyes with mine until the last note."

Sarah looked down at her hands. "That's quite a scene," she said. "I'd appreciate the song. I've heard recordings of it." She'd long ago viewed an AI hologram of Beethoven performing the sonata, but couldn't tell Jack. "It's very pretty. Do I walk over to you when you finish playing?"

"Of course you do. Those other people are boring and I've just wooed you with a keyboard. Here's the thing, most people don't realize it's so romantic. Beethoven didn't call it *Moonlight Sonata*. That came later, after he died. He wrote it as a love song to his pupil, Giulietta Guicciardi. He called it *Sonata quasi una fantasia*, which literally means 'sonata almost a fantasy', and my professor said it's because he had a crush on his beautiful student, but she was engaged to marry Count Robert von Gallenberg. And she did, in 1803. To add insult to injury, Gallenberg was a fellow composer whose talent was totally outshone by Beethoven's. It was like *Days of our Lives*, my mom's favorite soap opera, only around 1800. Either that, or Professor Trimble just loved a good, dramatic ill-fated love story. I mean, he wasn't there and Beethoven's feelings aren't in a history book. But I believe it."

Sarah laughed, her eyes twinkling at Jack's. "So I don't get *Pretty Woman*? I'm disappointed."

"Geez," Jack said, "what's a guy gotta do?" He fiddled with the umbrella, trying to make it stand on its own.

"Here," Sarah said, "let me take it for a while. You rest."

"Actually, I don't have a piano handy, but I did bring you a present." Jack reached under the sleeping bag and produced the chocolate bar he'd hidden, handing it to her with great ceremony.

Sarah squealed and immediately dropped the umbrella. Jack picked it up with a sigh and a laugh, watching her unwrap and devour the entire Hershey Bar in under a minute.

"Thank you so much," she told him. "Chocolate is way better than anything you could do with a piano. I mean to offer you no offense."

Jack nodded and watched her lick her fingers, searching for any stray molecule of sweetness. He cleared his throat before handing the umbrella back to Sarah and laying his head down, hands on his drawn knees.

"None taken, though you really should hear my rendition before deciding." Sarah shook her head with a giggle. "Anyway, another thing about history," he continued. "If you go back to early Europe, the only music was religious or some kind of court composition for royalty. Later, people discovered they could sing what they might not necessarily speak about politics. Music can be a powerful medium. So maybe you're right. Maybe this festival is making a statement in more ways than one."

Sarah smiled. "I bet it is."

The Grateful Dead started playing again, interrupting the conversation. Sarah and Jack watched the stage, but Jack was in a room with a baby grand piano, imagining what came next. He remembered a perfume ad in one of his mom's magazines, a tuxedo-clad musician next to a piano, cradling a woman's tiny waist as he dipped her backward for a passionate kiss. It was something about being forbidden, taboo, off-limits. Just like Sarah was. He shook the image from his head and tried to concentrate on the music.

By the time Creedence Clearwater Revival took the stage after midnight, Sarah had fallen asleep next to Jack and he caught the umbrella as she dropped it, grateful to find the rain had reached a gentle drizzle. He took the opportunity to study her face, from the long dark lashes that nearly reached her cheekbones to the small upturned nose to her lips, pale pink and slightly parted. Her eyebrows were a perfect frame for those green eyes, arched at a precise point from the middle of each eye on both sides, a mirror image. It was a face to inspire a painter, almost completely symmetrical. A face to inspire a mathematician. Jack tried to memorize every line and plane. He reached out impulsively to sweep a lock of damp hair off her forehead, lingering to stroke his thumb over her eyebrow, tracing its path. Sarah smiled but didn't open her eyes.

He looked around and noticed most people were sleeping. Creedence was playing to a very small percentage of those who dotted the field, and Jack could tell it bothered the band's lead singer. John Fogerty grabbed the microphone between songs and said, "We're playing our hearts out for you and want you to have a good time." Some lone guy a few rows behind Jack yelled, "Don't worry about it, John!" Between songs, Jack could hear a man behind him snoring like a rumbling engine.

Sarah heard the snore and laughed softly, her eyes still closed. "I don't know how everyone's sleeping through this. They sound great."

"Yeah, well, we're all pretty tired and I suspect some of us have ingested a few things to make us sleepy," Jack told her. He lay next to her and put the umbrella down as the last of the light rain dried up.

Sarah drew a deep breath through her nose and turned on her side to face Jack, blinking at him. She yawned and said, "Wake me up when Janis Joplin's done. She's up next. I can't stay awake for it."

"How do you know that?" Jack yawned back at her. "Did you see a schedule I missed somewhere?"

"No, the announcer must've said it," Sarah replied, her eyelids heavy. "I know you love her. You shouldn't miss Janis." She clasped her hands under her head and fell asleep almost instantly, the guitar chords of "Proud Mary" a lullaby to her ears.

Jack sat up and screamed along with others as Janis's sandpaper voice scrubbed the blues all over the crowd. Sarah slept on for the entire hour, something he wouldn't have believed possible. He thought he remembered her saying she could sleep standing up. Obviously, that was true.

When Janis sang her final note, he shook Sarah's shoulder gently. She sprang awake and rose, laser-focused on the stage as the next band's setup was being done.

"Do you know Sly and the Family Stone?" she asked Jack, who shook his head no. Sarah took his hand in hers and pulled him to his feet. "Trust me," she said, "you won't want to miss this." Her smile and eyes were lit from deep within.

When Sly Stone took the stage, all swinging white fringe, glasses, and afro shining in the spotlight, Sarah laughed and jumped up and down. "I've been waiting for this my whole life!" she yelled at Jack. He grinned along with her, the band's trumpet section reviving him and every other sleepy person in the wee hours of Sunday morning, adrenaline running through their veins like an interstate convoy of eighteen-wheelers.

The opening organ chords of "I Want To Take You Higher" rang out, followed by backup singers chanting "Hey! Hey! Hey!". Jack watched Sarah begin a complicated dance, her feet flying in every direction and arms shooting toward the sky. She screamed "BOOM LAKA LAKA LAKA" with the band as she did something that was reminiscent of The Twist, lowering herself almost to the ground and gyrating back up. By now, all eyes around them were on Sarah, not the stage. Each time Sly sang the word "higher", Sarah leapt into the air, choosing the final one in the chorus to turn to Jack and yell, "Catch me!" as she jumped. He threw his arms around her lower back and hoisted Sarah against him, holding her close, her head half a foot above his. Jack lowered her slowly, sliding Sarah down the front of his body.

When their mouths were level, he kissed her briefly, the slightest brush of lips, a microkiss. Jack locked his eyes on hers as he set her feet on the ground. Sarah blinked twice and broke away to continue her dance, leaving Jack embarrassed as he glanced around at their spectators. They'd no doubt expected something much more passionate, the kiss from the Tabu perfume ad. He shifted his weight awkwardly from foot to foot and waved his arms, his best dance moves. The crowd lost interest in Sarah and focused on the band again.

Between songs, as Sarah recovered her breath, Jack said, "I apologize. I got caught up in the moment. I shouldn't have kissed you."

Sarah's eyes sparkled as she laughed. "Don't apologize. That's part of the dance now. It will be forever." She couldn't imagine kissing Daniel, though. They'd done this dance a hundred times without anything remotely like the lift and slow, lingering, sexy drop Jack had just done. Sarah clasped her shaking hands together to keep Jack from seeing how he'd affected every nerve in her body.

While Kelly listened to the faint music from half a mile away, the clouds parted and she decided to paint a swath of stars the coffee-bean brown of Jack Warren's eyes, a translucent version so they'd sparkle in the heavens above her every night. She lay back on the blanket Laura had placed on the ground, regarding her work. Kindness. Kindness was radiating from the sky, washing over her in waves and covering everyone else in the world. She was one with everything around her, with the entire universe. She closed her eyes as she became a roly-poly bug like she'd played with as an Alabama child, folding all her tiny legs in and curling into a ball as she felt the armor fall into place along her back.

Laura peeked from her tent and told Rodney, "I think she's finally passed out." Rodney answered her with a snuffling snore and turned his back to her. A few minutes later, Kristin and Eric walked up hand-in-hand, gazing at Kelly on the ground. Laura came out with a towel to cover Kelly as she slept, though it had to be eighty degrees outside.

"What happened to her?" Eric whispered.

"She dropped acid," Laura replied. "Some kind of accident with a piece of watermelon she got from our neighbors. That girl Sarah found her way off in a cornfield, and she and Jack brought her back. She thinks she's been painting the sky all night. I've been keeping an eye on her, but she seems to have finally passed out for good. You two can get some sleep in your tent. I have insomnia that's not going away anytime soon."

"Far out," Eric said, staring at Kelly's curled form in the moonlight. "Kelly gets to try LSD before I do. Never would've believed that in a million years. Kelly Square Adams tripping in front of God and everybody. Far freaking out."

"Will she be okay?" Kristin asked, worry in her eyes. "I've heard there can be terrible flashbacks and you can maybe get addicted to acid-tripping and lose everything. She may never be the same person."

"That's propaganda from The Man, designed to terrify the populace," Eric pronounced. "She'll be fine. I'm a little jealous."

Kristin dropped his hand and headed into a tent. "You sleep in the one Kelly had and I'll take the other. Jack and Sarah can make do in the van."

"Aww, come on, Krissy," Eric wailed, his face twisted into a scowl. "Keep me company!"

"No, Eric," she replied. "I've had more than enough of your company. I need some sleep. I think I'll actually be glad to get home soon. This has been fun, but I won't be seeing you in Boston."

"Bummer. Bummer for *you*. I've spent this entire festival with you, Kristin, and what a waste of my time. There are thousands of girls foxier than you'll ever be out there," Eric waved his hand toward the crowd. "And any one of them would have been thrilled to be in your place." He stared at her and shrugged his shoulders for effect, making sure Kristin understood how bewildered he was by her choice not to sleep with him. Eric shook his head and announced, "Goodnight, everybody. See you tomorrow." He slipped into his tent as Kristin rolled her eyes at Laura.

"He really is insufferable," Kristin whispered. "So full of himself, and he's always *on*. It's like he thinks a microphone follows him around. I'm keeping my distance tomorrow."

Laura nodded. "Sorry about that. When we planned this trip, I figured he'd be latched onto Kelly the whole time. He's always had a crush on her. But Sarah distracted Kelly and now she's distracting Jack. This whole thing has gone off the rails."

Kristin shook her head. "Eric has a crush on whatever woman is standing close to him. And tomorrow, that won't be me. Goodnight, I'm exhausted." She entered her tent and left Laura staring at Kelly, whose arms and legs occasionally moved like she was swimming through the air. Laura couldn't imagine how Kelly would regard the whole tripping-at-Woodstock experience once she recovered her senses. It was the most un-Kelly thing imaginable. Knowing Kelly, though, acid would probably lead to some sort of bizarre mathematical breakthrough in her otherwise orderly, measured, metered brain.

Laura spotted Jack and Sarah in the distance and went back into her tent, watching and listening but hearing nothing except murmured conversation she couldn't make out. They stopped to examine Kelly, who'd kicked off her towel. Jack knelt and replaced it gently, pulling the beach towel up to Kelly's neck and nodding at Sarah as he held a finger to his lips and whispered "shhh." Laura continued spying until they settled into the van, the two of them carefully choosing distant seats to sleep on. Good. Maybe Jack would turn his attention back to Kelly on Sunday, where it belonged.

20

The Woodstock Music and Art Fair
Bethel, New York
SUNDAY, AUGUST 17, 1969

Kelly woke as she heard someone emerge from a tent nearby, immediately closing her eyes as she realized it was Eric's shoe ten feet from her head. She willed herself to be utterly still. The last thing in the world she needed was conversation with Eric, which would likely be a combination of probing questions about her LSD experience and hints of his interest in her body lying on the ground, available for his inspection.

Eric yawned and stretched as Grace Slick announced she and Jefferson Airplane would play "morning maniac music" for the crowd, her voice carrying clearly in the early hours of Sunday, a wake-up call that caused him to jump into his jeans and emerge from his tent. No one else was awake in their camp; even Kelly still remained curled into a ball in the pale, anemic sunlight. He stood studying her in sleep, wishing the weekend had unfolded with her by his side instead of that iceberg Kristin. But Grace Slick made them all look like trolls. That woman was a beauty queen, a righteous babe, and he was thrilled to hear her onstage.

Eric ran down the hill alone as fast as his feet could propel him.

Kelly opened her eyes as soon as Eric stopped staring and moved into the distance. She blinked at the sun's rays and said a silent prayer of thanks for her brain's restoration to working order. The sky looked normal, her hands looked normal, and she was even grateful for the dull ache in her back from sleeping on the ground. She would never eat anything unpackaged and offered by a stranger again. The feeling of her mind being on ice, skidding from weird thought and vision to weirder thought and vision was something she did not want to repeat. Ever. She inhaled a deep breath, ignoring the marijuana and port-o-let vapors that wafted across their campsite.

Laura came out and placed a hand on Kelly's shoulder. "Are you all right? We were really worried about you." She sat next to Kelly on the ground, wrapping her arms around her knees.

Kelly nodded. "Yeah, I'm fine. I never want to feel that way again, though at the time I really was enjoying painting the sky. I'd like to go strangle Gary and Bud, but the truth is, I should have known to ask before eating anything those two brought over."

Laura said, "For what it's worth, they both felt really bad about what happened. They haven't shown their faces since you wandered off and we were frantically searching for you."

"I wandered off?" Kelly replied, her brows drawn together. "I thought I was right here the whole time."

Laura picked at some fuzz on her sleeve. "No, you went a long way from camp. You ended up in some cornfield down the road. You were apparently on the ground between cornstalks, waving an imaginary paintbrush around. Jack and Sarah found you. Well, honestly, Sarah did."

Kelly closed her eyes and sighed. "Perfect. Now I guess I'm supposed to thank her for ruining my time at the festival *and* discovering my humiliation, leading Jack to watch me as I made an idiot of myself." She groaned and leaned back on her elbows. "How did she find me, if I'd gone that far away? Oh God, please tell me my clothes were on."

"Your clothes were on. And Jack understands you took drugs accidentally. He was just worried about you," Laura said.

Kelly perked up. "He was? Like, really worried?"

"Well, of course," Laura said carefully. "And nobody knows what voodoo Sarah used to find you, but she did. You have to give her that."

"No, I don't. I'm sure I'd have been just fine if y'all had left me out there and let me wander back this morning. However Sarah located me, she did it to embarrass me. I'm sure it was very satisfying for her."

"That's not fair, Kelly," Laura replied. "We were all panicked and trying to figure out where you'd gone, and Sarah helped."

"Oh, so now you're on her side?" Kelly's eyebrows soared as she stared at Laura. "Last I knew, she was a weirdo you didn't want around."

Laura glanced at the van. "She's still a weirdo, though she did find you and bring you back to us. She seems harmless." Laura paused and added, "And I'm sorry, but I think Jack really likes her."

"Fine," Kelly said, standing and brushing off leaves and hay from her clothes. "I couldn't care less. Jack has a serious woman-chasing addiction. Let him chase her and not me. He's going off to Canada today, anyway. None of us will see him for years, if we ever do."

Laura went back to picking at fuzz on her sleeve. "Whatever you say, Kelly. But I think you should tell Jack how you feel about him. Today might be your last chance. He's going away, possibly forever. And maybe he'll see weird Sarah differently if he knows you're interested."

Kelly blinked at her. "Jack's just an old classmate. He's a friend. You have no idea how I feel about him," she said, looking into the distance. "I've never even hinted to you about anything beyond that."

"You didn't have to, Kelly. You look at Jack like a lost puppy longing to go home tucked under his arm. No one could miss it," Laura said.

Kelly glared at her. "So flattering, thanks."

"Maybe I put it wrong, but I can see he's more than a friend in your heart." Laura inhaled deeply and added, "Maybe he'd even go back to Boston with us. With you. If he knew. It might change everything. I bet Rodney could get Jack's money back from Jeff Hillery, at least most of it." Laura stood and patted Kelly's shoulder. "Look, I'm glad you're okay. I'm going to try to go back to sleep for a bit. I didn't get much until about five this morning." She yawned and stretched her arms above her head. "Think about telling him. What have you got to lose?"

"I guess my dignity already disappeared somewhere among stalks of corn last night," Kelly said, sighing. "But Jack's not going to change his mind about Canada. I'd like him to know I'll be thinking about him while he's there, and hoping we can somehow stay in touch. He was pretty mad at me yesterday. I don't want him leaving like that." She looked at the van. "Are they both in there?" She nodded her head toward the bumper.

"Yeah," Laura answered, "but separate. I saw them keeping their distance as they went in. They didn't look like a couple."

Kelly nodded, working up her nerve. She waited until Laura disappeared into her tent before walking to the side of the van to look in. Sarah was stretched out on the back seat. Jack was sleeping with his head tilted forward in the front, his feet up on the dashboard. Kelly smiled at the lock of dark hair hanging in his face. How many times had she seen that in a classroom, Jack bent over a math problem? How many times had she wished he'd look up at her and catch her watching, just once, and see her as anything but the only girl majoring in mathematics at MIT, the freak, the loner? She swallowed hard and rapped her knuckles lightly on the window, trying not to wake Sarah. Jack jumped and turned to smile at her. Sarah slept on as he quietly opened the door and climbed out.

"Hey," Jack said, rubbing his eyes. "Are you *you* again?"

"Yeah, I'm me again," Kelly told him. "Thanks for rescuing me last night. I hope you know I'd never take drugs on purpose—"

"Everybody knows that, Kelly," he interrupted. "Do you feel okay? You were definitely in a different world, painting the sky and singing and babbling about stuff no one understood."

"I'm fine," she said. Kelly cleared her throat. "I'm grateful to you and Sarah for finding me and bringing me back to camp. I didn't even know where I was."

"Yeah, well, it was mostly Sarah. She searched for you and all I did was tag along and help walk you home. You can thank her," he said.

Kelly nodded. "I will, of course. I've probably been too hard on Sarah. I promise I'll treat her better."

Jack raised one eyebrow and cocked his head, looking at Kelly. "That would be a nice change. I'd really like everyone to get along today, before I leave."

Kelly bit her lip, her eyes still on Jack's. "About that. I don't guess there's any way I can talk you out of going to Canada?"

Jack waved his head back and forth, looking at the ground and shoving his hands into his pockets. "I've made up my mind. And I promised my mom, Kelly. I don't want anyone to know she's aware of this plan, but she is, just between you and me. She's terrified of losing another son, either the way she did with Kenny or killed in Vietnam. This was her idea in the first place. It was excruciating for her to ask me to go away, but she said she'd prefer that to worrying about me every second of the day and night."

"So, this is all your mom?" Kelly asked.

"No, I'm scared shitless, Kelly. I don't mind admitting that. Like I told you, if I stay in Boston, I know I'll be drafted, probably sooner than later. Truth is, I'd be a liability to any fighting company in Vietnam. Not only do I disagree with our involvement there, I'd make a crappy soldier. Believe me, I've thought about it. A lot," Jack said. He was still staring at the ground when he said, "I'm not proud of my decision."

Kelly reached to lift Jack's chin with her finger, meeting his eyes as he looked up. "You're not the only one, Jack. There are lots of guys who are scared, and they go anyway. You know that."

He sighed. "Well, I'm not going to be one of them. Not after what my folks have gone through with Kenny, who left here the most gung-ho infantryman on Earth and came back a drugged, drooling, drunk, bitter, hateful ghost no one recognizes."

"Okay," Kelly said, "I get it. Look, could we go for a walk, just you and me?"

"Sure," Jack said, "let me go tell Sarah."

Kelly turned her eyes away so he wouldn't see them rolling. "No, don't wake her. We'll be back soon. I just need to stretch my legs after sleeping on the ground all night. And stop by that disgusting port-o-let."

"I'll leave her a note." Jack pulled a piece of paper from his pocket. "You got a pen or something?"

"For heaven's sake, Jack, Sarah's a grown woman. She'll know you've gone to the toilet. She'll wait for you," Kelly said.

Jack shrugged and looked back at the van. "I guess," he said, walking in the direction of the port-o-lets. "She won't go off alone. She'll know I'd worry."

Kelly rolled her eyes again at Jack's back as she followed him.

After the port-o-lets, Kelly led Jack up a hay field and sat on the ground, patting beside her for him to join her. She turned to Jack and said, "First of all, I've been selfish and I apologize. I think I had an epiphany while I was painting the stars last night. I'm sorry."

Jack chuckled. "So, it took a good hit of LSD to expand your consciousness to that point, huh? Or was it the cornfield? Did the magic ears whisper *Kelly, you've been a pain in the ass?* Was there a chorus of kernels shaming you?"

"Very funny. For your information, I'm thoroughly humiliated anyone saw me that way," Kelly answered. "I'm trying to apologize here. I know how mad at me you were yesterday."

Jack moved his head up and down. "I was. It's over. You're forgiven," he said.

Kelly exhaled slowly. "And I understand why you're leaving. I've made my peace with it. I just want you to know I hope you get to come back. And I was thinking we could write to each other and stay in touch."

Jack shook his head. "I'd like that, but I'm not sure it would be safe for me to send you letters from Canada."

"Send them to the university. And use some other name," Kelly told him. "I'll know it's you."

"Okay," Jack said. "I'll try. It's going to take me a while to get settled. All I know is that a church in Ottawa is helping me, the way they've helped others in the past two years. Rodney said there are many more who've fled to Canada than we know. And the Canadians are very receptive to having them there, particularly those with an education and skills. I think a lot of them are critical of the US being in Vietnam, too. There are some people who think their efforts are more anti-American-government than pro-American-men."

Kelly nodded her head. "Sounds like it may be lonely," she said.

"I don't think there's any 'may' about it. It will be." Jack drew a deep breath. "I could be making the worst mistake of my life. All I know is, I'm tired of thinking about it and just want it over with. I want to hang around y'all today and enjoy some music, and then get into a car and not worry about it anymore. I think I'll feel better once I'm up there and can't debate with myself over and over."

"And Sarah?" Kelly asked.

Jack frowned. "What about Sarah? I have to leave her, too. Her parents are waiting for her in South Dakota. I'm going alone, Kelly."

"I know. I just meant, I'm sure you'll be sad to say goodbye to her. You two seem to have grown close really quickly here," Kelly said, her eyes tracing some clouds passing over them.

Jack shrugged. "I guess so."

"Well, I want you to know I'll be thinking of you. I wish all this could have worked out differently, Jack." Kelly pulled a blade of grass and began shredding it into thin pieces with her fingertips. "I work ridiculously long days before going home and staring at equations there until I pass out. I haven't seen much of you since graduation, but I wish I'd have said something. I should have told you a long time ago. I really like you, Jack."

Jack grinned at her, a flash of white teeth and sparkling brown eyes crinkled at their corners. "I really like you, too, Kelly. You know that. You're like my little sister. My little sister who's zoomed ahead of me, with a brilliant future in research at MIT. I'm so proud of you."

Kelly summoned a smile and pasted it on her face, throwing the grass ribbons to the ground. "I hope you'll stay proud of me, Jack. That really means something to me. Umm, I guess we should get going. Everyone's probably awake now." She stood and extended a hand to Jack, pulling him up and waiting until his back was turned to swipe her eyes.

Jack walked ahead of her and said over his shoulder, "And Kelly, anything else there might have been between us, whether months ago or this weekend…well, that's impossible with me leaving. But don't think I've never thought about it. I have."

Kelly sighed and followed him, a thousand words caught behind the lump in her throat.

Sarah was waiting on the bumper of the van. Kelly hated how her eyes lit up as Jack approached, how she sat her cup of water next to her and jumped up to hug him, how she turned to Kelly and said, "Are you feeling better?"

"I'm fine," Kelly answered. "And thank you for finding me last night." She locked her eyes on Sarah's. "Could I talk to you privately for a minute?" Kelly glanced at Jack. "Girl stuff," she said to him. She beckoned Sarah into an empty tent and settled on the ground inside, Sarah following and closing the flap.

Sarah sat, hugging herself. "You wanted to speak to me?" she asked, wondering what Kelly could possibly want with her at this point.

Kelly cleared her throat. "I care about Jack. I'm guessing you do, too. And I'd be lying if I said your being here didn't screw up my entire weekend. I don't like you, Sarah, whoever you are. But I want you to know I'll be nice to you for his sake. I'm capable of being polite even to people who've crossed me. I'm Southern. Politeness is as genetic as our casserole-baking reflexes when someone's sick. Or our love of college football."

"I see. Well, that's nice of you, especially since I've done nothing wrong. Nothing at all," Sarah replied. "And I hate to pour water on your parade, but Jack and I are as together as two people can be after knowing each other for so little time."

"That's just it," Kelly said. "You barely know him." She narrowed her eyes at Sarah, adding, "And you never will."

Sarah paused before patting Kelly's hand gently. "I know what it feels like to kiss him. To have his arms around me. To hold his body against mine." She blinked at Kelly. "It's going to break my heartbeat when he leaves."

"It's 'break my *heart*,'" Kelly spat. "I am so sick of your mangling every idiom, every old saying, every bit of slang, phrases known *everywhere* except your brain. Lakota Sioux must make a transition to English very hard. At least, for the stupid."

Sarah stared at Kelly, her mouth a flat line. "Is this your version of being polite? You're like sugar and spears."

"It is while Jack's not here to witness it," Kelly said. "And it's sugar and spice, you idiot."

"No, I did that one on purpose." Sarah waited until she'd taken a couple of calming breaths to continue, "I could not possibly be more disappointed to meet you." Could this really be the person she'd thought she'd want to take back to Unity with her, to show her the splendors of the future? The grandmother she'd longed to meet and embrace? Sarah stood and left the tent without another word.

Kelly sat with her head in her hands, listening to Laura call out, "Breakfast?" to Sarah.

"No, thank you," Sarah's voice replied.

"Good talk?" Jack asked Kelly when she emerged.

"Absolutely," Kelly replied, sniffing the air. "Everything is great. She just wants to be alone for a little bit. Breakfast smells wonderful."

Laura had a skillet over the fire, frying sausages and scooping them onto paper plates for Kristin, Jack, and Rodney. She handed a plate to Kelly. They sat on the ground in a circle, sneaking peeks at the girl sitting in the van as they ate. Sarah's head was now leaning forward toward her lap. Kelly knew Jack was fighting the urge to run and check on her.

"Do you hear that?" Rodney mumbled as he chewed. Laura shot him a look for talking with his mouth full, causing Jack to grimace on his behalf. Laura was definitely soon to be mothering both a baby and a twenty-three-year-old.

"Hear what, Rod?" Jack asked.

"It's very distant thunder, you can barely make it out," Rodney said. "Almost like an engine revving miles away. It's just every once in a while."

Laura turned her eyes to the sky. "There's not a cloud in sight, Rodney. It's going to be a beautiful day."

"Yes, it is," Kelly said, stabbing her sausage with a plastic fork for the third unsuccessful time. She gave up and ate it with her fingers, just to see how Laura would react.

21

The Woodstock Music and Art Fair
Bethel, New York
SUNDAY, AUGUST 17, 1969

Sarah picked up Kelly's beloved math notebook, flipping through the pages. Apparently, she hadn't accomplished much after the two of them stopped working together. Sarah found a pencil on the floorboard and scribbled a few lines, glancing over her shoulder occasionally to be sure she wasn't watched. She threw Kelly's notebook at the floor and exited the van, still furious at the way Kelly had spoken to her in the tent.

Sarah walked to the circle of friends and made sure Kelly was watching as she sat next to Jack, hooking her arm through his and tugging him slightly closer to her. She told him, "Come on, the music won't start back for a while. Let's go walk around. We'll meet everyone here at one o'clock, okay? We can all go down together. Joe Cocker will play around two."

Jack gazed up and down at Sarah like she was a priceless work of art. He smiled and nodded, his voice soft. "Who's Joe Cocker, though?" he stage-whispered. "Never heard of him."

"He's a British singer. Very talented, extremely odd performing style. You'll see," Sarah said.

"How would you know that, Sarah?" Kelly asked, her eyes flashing rage. "You can't possibly have any idea what's coming up on that stage. None of us do. Rain delays have shifted everything. There *is* no schedule."

"My hearing's excellent. You all missed the announcer saying it in the distance this morning, Kelly, but I heard it. Joe Cocker has been performing for years, whether you know of him or not. Do any of you want to come with us?" Sarah asked. "Kelly, you'll probably want to stay here and look at the next page of your notebook. I finished an equation you were stuck on. Then I started a new one I think you'll find challenging."

Kelly threw her paper plate on the ground and stalked off, her face a map of anger. She slammed the van door, and Sarah saw her immediately reach for the notebook, just as she'd known she would. Mathematical curiosity would keep her busy for a while, especially since Sarah had introduced a concept a few years ahead of this time.

Sarah and Jack rose to their feet. "Anyone want to come with us?" Jack said. "You're welcome to join us."

Laura shot a quick look at Rodney, then Kristin locked eyes with Laura. Kristin said, "No, we'll stay here or wander around together. It's so pretty and sunny for a change. Thanks, though. We'll see you at one. Should be a fun afternoon."

"Y'all know I leave at seven. That's when I'm meeting Jeff," Jack said, nodding at Rodney.

"Groovy," Rodney answered. "You kids have fun. There's still a lot of festival left and it's a nice day."

Sarah looked at Laura and swung a hand in the direction of the van. "You should probably go talk to Kelly. I think she is having a difficult time right now," she told her.

Laura shook her head. "Are you trying to sound concerned, Sarah? Isn't it a little late for that? We all know you're the reason Kelly is bummed out."

Sarah said, "I promise you, I never wanted to upset Kelly. I tried to do the opposite. She's the one flipping her wig over and being mean to me. Everyone seems to forget Kelly is the one who went through my handbag and threw my personal items away. That she accused me of using drugs, which is not true. Kelly's the only one around here who's been dripping on acid."

Laura tracked Sarah's arm as she lowered it. "*Tripping*," Laura said, rolling her eyes. "The word is 'tripping'. Is that a new bracelet, Sarah? I don't remember seeing it before."

Sarah extended her wrist toward Laura. "Yes, it is. Jack gave it to me. Isn't it pretty? The amber is supposed to absorb bad energy." Sarah waved her arm back and forth. "I think I feel it pulling from your direction, hold still—"

"Both of you, stop," Jack interrupted, turning to leave and pulling Sarah with him. "This is a ridiculous catfight between you three and Sarah hasn't done anything to Kelly. If Kelly's mad, that's her problem. I thought we were past this."

Sarah leaned her head against Jack's shoulder as they walked away, a clear declaration to Laura and, she hoped, Kelly. She wasn't going to protect anyone's feelings except her own. And Jack's. She'd wasted enough time trying to grow close to her ancestor, the Kelly she'd idolized and was now sorry she'd met. For the rest of the festival, Sarah intended to make the most of every minute with Jack Warren.

An idea occurred to her as they approached the still-slippery path down and Jack enclosed her hand in his to help her. Sarah worked her way down the hill behind Jack.

"If your driver is taking you to Ottawa," she said, "he'll have to pass through Binghamton, New York, where I'm supposed to take the bus home to Rapid City. If you could drop me off there, it would be much easier for me than hitchhiking. I promised my mother I wouldn't do that after the festival. Do you think Jeff Hillery could give me a ride that far?"

"Sure, I don't see why not," Jack said. "I'm supposed to be his only passenger. That'll give us a little more time together, too."

"Yes," Sarah smiled at Jack's back, "it will." She reached into her handbag and clutched the locator beacon disguised as a flower-shaped mirror. "That's the great part." An extra hour or two with Jack would be worth the minor shift Time Insertion Protocol would have to make to get her home. They wouldn't mind. This would be much better than staying at the festival with her great-great-great-grandmother. Kelly didn't want Sarah around, anyway. She'd made that very clear.

Sarah reached the bottom of the hill, her fingertips tingling as always when they brushed Jack's as he helped her down. "Come on," she told him. "There's something I want to see. And I want you with me because I'm a little scared."

Jack stopped walking. "Should I be scared? What is it you want to see, Sarah?"

"You're from North Carolina, right?" Sarah said. "Does your family have cows?"

"Of course we have cows. So do most of our neighbors," Jack said.

"Well, I've never seen one and I want to," Sarah told him. "I want to pet a cow. And this is a dairy farm. If we walk far enough in that direction," she pointed, "we should see a whole group of cows."

"Herd," Jack said, shaking his head.

"Well I'm glad you're listening," Sarah responded.

Laura tapped on the side window of the van before opening the door. "You okay in here?" she asked Kelly.

Kelly didn't look up from her notebook. "I'm fine. Just let me figure this out and I'll join y'all. I guess we'll all go down together when the music starts. I'm not giving up my last hours with Jack for Sarah. She's not winning that one."

Laura sighed. "Okay then," she said, starting to close the door.

"And Laura, you were wrong. I did have plenty to lose by telling Jack how I feel. I lost the ability to pretend to myself he wants to be with me," Kelly said. "I'll never get that back."

"Kelly, you don't know. Sarah will be gone back to South Dakota and Jack may be able to return from Canada. We don't know how long the war will go on. Rodney doesn't think it'll be much longer. Nixon and Kissinger both seem dedicated to ending it diplomatically. Rodney thinks the government will eventually even let draft dodgers back into the country without jail sentences. I heard him tell Jack that. They're starting to realize more and more young men are fleeing to Canada and beyond, tens of thousands of them. Rodney doesn't think Nixon will stop them from coming home when it's all over, especially if it looks good politically. So Jack may be back in your life before you know it."

Kelly tapped her pencil eraser against the page. "Highly doubtful, but I guess Rodney has a point. It's nice to think that could happen. I'm sure Nixon would like to end the war and make that his legacy. What politician wouldn't? But I think you're overly optimistic about Jack and others getting to come home unpunished. How would veterans feel about that? It would be a giant slap in the face to the people we owe most."

Laura sighed. "You do have a point." She looked over at Kristin, who was trying to clean this morning's frying pan. "I'm going to go teach her how to wash a skillet. See you after you've solved all the world's math problems." She closed the door and walked away as Kelly resumed work, her brows knitted in concentration.

Laura didn't see Kelly close the notebook and place it on her lap, staring out the window at nothing.

"Just reach over the fence. They think you're going to feed them, that's why they're coming over here," Jack said. "They won't hurt you." The white and brown cow at the front walked right up to Sarah, her huge belly swaying, a string of drool running down from the corner of her pink mouth. The cow bellowed a loud, bawling moo at the rest of the group.

"Is she talking to them?" Sarah asked.

"Well, kinda," Jack shrugged. "She's letting the rest know it's okay to approach you. Pretty soon she'll figure out you don't have food. She'll walk away. So pet her while you can. Look." Jack reached out to the cow and stroked his hand down her face. The cow nudged his hand upward with her head, waiting for something edible to drop in her mouth.

"What do you think her name is?" Sarah asked Jack.

"Well, honestly, she's a dairy cow on a giant dairy farm, so she's likely a number, Sarah," Jack said. "But let's call her Elsie."

"Hi, Elsie," Sarah said, her voice pitched high enough to shatter glass.

"Umm, try lowering your voice a little. Just talk to her the way you would to me," Jack said.

Sarah raised her brows at him. "Okay, I will," she said. She turned back to Elsie. "Hi, I'll miss you when we both have to leave and I hope you meet only ugly girls in Canada and I stole a look at your butt when you were bathing yesterday," she said softly, rubbing the cow's forehead. Sarah turned to Jack. "How's that?" she asked. "Elsie seemed to enjoy it." She continued to run her hand along the front of the cow's face and then the side of her head. Elsie flicked an ear and let Sarah continue. "I think she likes me," Sarah told Jack.

"You saw my butt?" Jack said. "I think we have to get married now. Is it like that in your culture?"

"Not exactly," Sarah said. "Although we'd never see each other naked before the r…before marriage. We're matched with someone who's perfect for us in every way. It's a time of great happiness everyone looks forward to. My husband and I will get to have a baby. I can't wait for that."

Jack leaned against a fencepost. "Perfect for you, huh? I think I'm pretty perfect for you. And I'm fully capable of making babies. Let me show you," he said, grinning wide.

"You know what I mean," Sarah said, solemn. "I think you would call it an 'arranged marriage', maybe?"

Jack nodded. "Yeah, I know that's a thing. But you're not some sixteenth-century European princess being pawned into a political alliance. Besides, I can't see how anyone can select someone perfect for you *in every way*. That's impossible."

"You'd be surprised," Sarah said. "I haven't heard of a single couple who didn't feel perfectly matched." Elsie turned her head swiftly and walked away, the rest of the cows following. "I wish I'd had something to feed her."

"I can assure you, these cows are well fed," Jack said. He studied her face, looking for any sign she'd been kidding about the arranged marriage thing, but saw none. "Come on," Jack told her. "Let's see if there's any way to wash our hands over by the Hog Farm kitchen."

"That would be nice. And I could use a drink of water. And something sweet to eat, even if it's muesli."

Jack took one last look at her eyes before they walked away. "You're serious, aren't you? About the arranged marriage."

Sarah smiled. "Absolutely serious. I've been looking forward to it my whole life."

Jack frowned. "Do you know who your…umm…guy is? Have you seen him? Met him?"

"No," Sarah said. "I hope he's a lot like you." She giggled. "At least, in the buttocks."

"I'm flattered," Jack said. "But I'm so much more than a cute butt, Sarah. I also have a great sense of humor, mathematical skills, a charming accent, and I can tame cows. Plus I'm a good kisser."

Sarah stopped walking. She looked around at the people in the distance, no one paying any particular attention to the two of them. They were in broad daylight. What could it hurt?

"So prove it," she told Jack. "Again." She looped her arms around his neck and closed her eyes.

Jack reached up and gently removed her arms, holding both her hands in front of him as he stepped back. "I'm sorry," he said. "It's the wrong time and place." He held Sarah's eyes and continued, "I'd give just about anything if I'd met you before, Sarah Sandoval. I think you're perfect for *me*."

Sarah blinked at him in disbelief. "Is this because of what I told you? The 'arranged marriage' is a long way off for me. Years, probably. Why can't we enjoy here and now, Jack? Today is literally all we have."

Jack stopped walking and chose a clean-looking patch of ground to sit on. "Wait a minute," he said. "Let's talk about this."

Sarah settled next to him and looked at Jack expectantly.

"Sarah, this person who's chosen for you...wouldn't you be expected to, umm, save yourself for him? I mean, that's what I would think, in a situation like that," Jack said, his eyes searching hers.

"Of course," Sarah answered. "And I will. That's not what we're talking about here. I don't know what kind of sexual education or experience you had in North Carolina—"

"None," Jack interrupted with a laugh. "The closest I got to that was seeing Mrs. Gardner walk to her backyard clothesline wearing nothing but a lacy white bra and a skirt. She was probably younger than I am now, and I'm forever grateful she had to go fetch a blouse. It's an image I'll carry with me till the day I die. Jimmy Hartzog and I were in his treehouse next door and I was almost thirteen." Jack smiled at the memory. "Anyway, no one *ever* spoke about sex in my family. My dad didn't have some special talk with me. And there certainly wasn't anything taught in my school, either."

"So, I only wanted to kiss you again," Sarah said, lifting her shoulders. "Nothing more than that. And you hurt my feelings. I feel like you're not interested in me anymore."

Jack exhaled a long breath and trained his eyes on the distance, looking anywhere but at Sarah. "Oh, Sarah, no. Look, that kiss we had was one of the most intimate things in my entire life. I've been with women, sure, but not like that." Jack stopped to pick up a small rock next to him and throw it to land near the fence. "Look, I may joke around with you, might sound like I'm trying to seduce you. Flirting is just what I do. But if I kiss you again...I don't know how to put it. I know you don't have experience with this stuff." He sighed and shook his head with a shrug. "If I kiss you again, that will be the start of something I'm pretty sure I can't stop. I want you like I've never wanted anyone before. Kissing you isn't some game I can end, Sarah." He paused before adding, "Not to mention the consequences for me, let alone for you. You know how people talk about being lost, not knowing what to do next? That would be me. I can't let that happen." He returned his eyes to hers and offered her a soft smile. "This whole vulnerable thing is new to me."

"I understand," Sarah said. "It's completely new to me, too." She held her hand to the side of Jack's face and stroked his cheek with her thumb before jerking it away. "Oh, cow germs. I'm sorry."

Jack stood and took her dirty hand to kiss it, adding an exaggerated gallant bow in an effort to make Sarah laugh. All she did was blink, so he added a dainty curtsey along with, "You can put cow germs on me anytime, milady." Nothing. "Hey, I'm *still* funny, Sarah," he told her somber face. "You know I am."

Sarah stood and brushed her jeans off. She answered, "You are a barrel stuffed with a monkey."

Jack snickered. "Well, thank you. Come on and let's see what delights the Hog Farm has cooked up. And if they have any discarded produce lying around, we'll bring it back to Elsie," he said.

Sarah put her hand on his arm. "Wait, Jack. Instead of going to the Hog Farm, let's go back to camp. There's a bunch of bread there, and I saw an extra jar of peanut butter Laura hasn't opened. Couldn't we share those things with people who are really hungry? We're not, not really. The Hog Farm kitchen is trying to feed a crowd who came here without food."

Jack nodded. "We really do have a lot. Might have to sneak some stuff by Laura, but she's probably napping, anyway."

When they walked up, everything at camp was just as they expected. Laura and Rodney were resting in their tent, it looked like Eric had somehow talked Kristin into going off with him, and Kelly was still sitting in the van. Again, Jack thought: *what a waste of Woodstock.*

He and Sarah used the hand-washing station and got some water to drink. Then they grabbed the bread, full jar of peanut butter, and a plastic knife. They headed into an empty tent like night burglars, glancing around to see if they were spotted. Sarah watched Jack construct fold-over sandwiches and copied him until she spotted a glob of peanut butter on her thumb and impulsively licked it off. That led to her stopping work to construct and eat an entire sandwich, sitting on the ground and letting Jack finish up on his own.

"This is truly wonderful," she told Jack between bites. "I wish I'd tried it before. Do you like peanut butter?"

"Got me through college," Jack replied. "That, and SpaghettiOs."

Sarah wrinkled her nose. "I'm still not ready for those things."

They wrapped and placed all the half-sandwiches in an empty paper grocery bag, then took one of their drinking-water jugs and paper cups. Jack checked his watch; they had a little less than an hour until one o'clock. They hurried their way down the hill without falling, a miracle with Jack carrying a heavy jug of water and Sarah trying not to damage the sandwich-filled bag.

He'd thought Sarah intended to find people who looked like they needed a meal, but she went straight to the end of a long row near the stage. She told Jack, "These are people trying to hold their seats for the music coming up. They're not going to leave for food, and they're probably starving at this point." She asked a teenage girl at the end to take a half-sandwich and pass them down. Sarah then handed the water jug and cups to her.

The girl jumped up and hugged Sarah after she took her portion. "This is so nice of you. Thank you both very much," she said, nodding at Jack. "My friend isn't feeling well and I didn't want to leave her to get food. I'm really hungry." She waved her hand at a sleeping girl.

"Is she okay?" Sarah asked.

"She has, you know, cramps," the girl whispered to Sarah. "It's her time of the month."

"Oh, good for her," Sarah said, glancing at the sleeping girl. "Does she have everything she needs?" she asked.

"Yeah, we came prepared," the teen whispered again. "We're pretty close to the port-o-lets. Jenny took some Midol and she'll be all right. Thank you, though. That's very thoughtful." She smiled and sat down to eat her sandwich.

As they walked away, Sarah asked Jack, "What is a person's 'time of the month'? And what are cramps? I haven't heard of either where I come from."

Jack stopped walking to read her facial expression, which seemed sincere. *How in the world could she not know this stuff? Do they call it something else?*

"Well, that's weird," he said. "I'm not sure what y'all call it. I think you should ask Kristin or Laura or Kelly, anyone but me. I am most certainly not an expert on that." Jack glanced at his watch. "It's a little early, but let's head back up and make sure everyone is there. This Joe Cocker guy sounds interesting."

Sarah leaned her head back and examined the sky. "He sure is. You'll never see anyone perform like him again." She knew a violent thunderstorm would sweep in after Joe Cocker's set, and started working on a plan to get everyone back up the hill before the deluge hit.

22

The Woodstock Music and Art Fair
Bethel, New York
SUNDAY, AUGUST 17, 1969

"**D**on't think I didn't notice the peanut butter and bread disappeared," Laura greeted Sarah and Jack with her hands on her hips. "I mean, it's okay, but I wish you'd asked first. I assume you shared it down there with the crowd."

"Yeah, we did," Jack said. "Sarah and I were kinda in a hurry and I didn't think you'd mind. We *do* have a ton of food."

"You literally have no idea," Laura said, looking at Sarah. "After Rodney and I made the group grocery run, we cleaned out everything in our kitchen cabinets and brought it, too. I'm starving all the time. I never know what I'll want next. There's half a jar of pickled beets in our tent."

Jack frowned. "Well, no one's going to bother those. Anyway, thanks for understanding. It was Sarah's idea to share with some hungry people." He beamed at Sarah like she'd just returned from volunteering five years in the Peace Corps, not handing out a few sandwiches. Sarah offered Laura a shy smile.

"I hope you don't mind," Sarah said. "Also, I ate a peanut butter sandwich. It was really great. Thank you for making that possible."

"No, that's fine," Laura told her, smiling sweetly. "I'm glad you enjoyed it."

Jack couldn't tell if the two of them were making nice or were she-wolves circling each other. He decided to give them the benefit of the doubt, telling Laura, "I'm happy to see y'all getting along. It's really important to me."

"I know, Jack," Laura said. She took a deep breath and glanced at Kelly in the van. "I'm sure Kelly will be polite, too. She doesn't want you leaving for Canada upset with any of us, especially not her."

"Are y'all leaving for Boston tonight? I heard somebody say that with all the delays, the concert might run until tomorrow," Jack said.

"Yes, I guess it might, but Rodney and Eric both have to be back at work. I didn't ask Kristin, but I know she only planned to be here until tonight," Laura said.

"What do they do for work, Rodney and Eric?" Sarah asked. "I've been wondering."

"Rodney has a good job working as a supervisor for his dad's business," Laura replied. "His father owns a small factory near Boston that manufactures plastics, things like hair barrettes and children's jewelry. And Eric is a part-time disc jockey but he makes most of his money working for a Volkswagen dealership. That's how he got this van. He's been with them since high school and he was promoted to body shop manager a couple of years ago. He does really well."

Sarah glanced at Jack and then turned back to Laura. "I don't mean to pry, but why aren't either of them worried about the draft, like Jack?" she asked.

"No, everybody knows, it's okay," Laura answered. "Rodney had a pretty high draft number to start with, but now he'll have a hardship deferment because we'll have a child and be dependent on him."

Jack looked surprised. "Really?"

"Really," Laura said. "It's no accident we're having a baby. We've been trying for almost a year, Jack."

"And Eric?"

Laura turned her eyes to the sky. "Eric supposedly has asthma, even though he smokes enough pot to make me extremely suspicious of his doctor. But he got his 4-F a while back."

"Speak of the annoying devil," Jack said, waving at Eric and Kristin walking up. "Looks like we're all here. Let me go grab Kelly."

"I'll get Rodney out of our tent. He's been reading about new manufacturing methods for his dad," Laura said. "That was the only way he got to take off early last week."

What a waste of Woodstock, Jack thought for the third time. He opened the van door and extended a hand to help Kelly down, noting she hadn't been working when he walked up.

"It must be hot in there," he told her. "Why don't you come up for air every once in a while?"

"I get busy and don't even notice," Kelly said. She smiled at Jack and pecked his cheek, turning to offer Sarah a side-hug like they hadn't retracted their claws a few hours ago. "Peace," she said to Sarah.

"Peace," Sarah nodded. They each took one of Jack's arms and started toward the path, the rest following.

"Hey," Laura said, "I have something planned for after Joe Cocker, if you'll all come back to camp. Kind of a little going away party for Jack. I baked something special and we have rum and Cokes for people who want them."

"And I," Eric announced, "have two fat joints rolled for the occasion."

Laura answered him, "No you don't. Not if we're leaving tonight with you at the wheel. I'm not riding with you stoned."

"Hang loose, Laura, your old man isn't gonna drink or smoke if you don't. So stop freaking out. We already talked about it. Rodney will drive, right, Ghost?" Eric said, looking over his shoulder.

"Stop calling him that," Laura growled. She shot a withering look at Rodney. "I'm never speaking to him again after this weekend," she muttered to her fiancé. "You aren't, either."

Sarah glanced up at Jack as they began the path down. "Why does Eric call him 'ghost'?" she whispered.

"You haven't noticed he's basically the color of notebook paper?" Jack whispered back.

"I think his skin is beautiful," Sarah said. "I've never seen anyone like him. Were his parents like that?"

"Like, *Irish*?" Kelly said, looking behind to make sure they were out of earshot. "Yes. His name is Rodney Shannon. His paternal grandparents came to this country after World War I. His mother's people are from Kilkenny. Laura told me they're hoping to visit his relatives over there someday."

"Well, Eric shouldn't talk to Rodney like he does. He's rude to everyone. He's switching me off," Sarah said.

Kelly nodded. "He turns everyone off. But he had the van to bring us all here. We have to put up with him."

"Peace," Jack muttered.

"Right," Kelly answered.

"And you know what?" Jack added. "As annoying as he is, Eric has been good to me over the years. All of you have, one way or another. I'm a lucky man to have so many great friends. I'm going to miss every one of y'all, even Eric."

"We'll miss you too, Jack," Kelly gave Jack's hand a squeeze as he helped her to the ground. "I'm hoping you get to come home soon."

Jack stood and waited to help Laura. "Who knows?" he said. "Maybe I will. I sure hope so."

Kelly looked at Sarah, who lowered her gaze to the ground like there were answers among the mud puddles.

They ended up far from the stage but able to make out Joe Cocker in a brilliant red, gold, brown, and blue tie-dyed shirt. "I love the way he swings his arms and leans backward and forward and sideways as he sings," Jack yelled at Sarah. "And man, what a voice. He's singing from deep in his heart, you can tell."

"From his *toes*! I see what you meant," Kelly yelled in Sarah's direction, never taking her eyes off the stage. "I love his gravelly voice!" She stood watching for a few more seconds before adding, "His body jerks around like someone's holding his marionette strings way above, moving him with the music. I've never seen anyone perform like that."

Rodney and Laura danced, their eyes on each other. Eric yelled at Kristin, "Man, this guy is far out. I told you he could sing! I can't wait to talk about him on-air tomorrow night."

Kristin nodded and kept her gaze on the stage, completely enthralled. "He's amazing!"

"I'm gonna grow huge sideburns like that," Eric called out to no one in particular.

"You'll look like a nineteenth-century bank clerk," Kelly yelled back.

Jack reached down for Sarah's hand and held it through every song. Cocker told the crowd in his thick Yorkshire accent, "We're gonna leave ya with the usual thing, the only thing I can say is that to many people, this title just about puts it all into focus. It's called 'With a Little Help from Me Friends'. Remember it." Sarah dropped Jack's hand during the organ chords of the introduction and reached to Laura, Rodney, Kristin and Eric on her right side, motioning for them to join arms. Then she linked her arm into Jack's and nodded to Kelly to do the same. She smiled at Jack and mouthed the words, "What would you do" as she began swaying to her right, pulling Jack and Kelly along with her. Laura continued the motion and the whole group swayed left and right together through the whole song. Not one of them would ever forget those eight minutes, singing along to lyrics they already knew, each word meant for Jack even if that remained unspoken.

Sarah looked at the clouds rolling in. Pieces of paper were starting to fly through the air between rows of people. The announcer said, "It looks like we're gonna get a little bit of rain, so you'd better cover up." Soon after, he began asking people to get away from the towers near the stage as it became increasingly obvious a strong storm was about to hit.

Sarah told Jack, "We need to go now. Right now. Just trust me."

Jack yelled to Laura, "Let's do this party now! Come on, y'all!" He grabbed Kelly and Sarah's hands and began to make his way through the crowd.

The seven of them made it to the bottom of the hill as the announcer said, "Let's think hard to get rid of it, please! No rain!" Soon, several hundred thousand people were screaming the mantra "NO RAIN NO RAIN NO RAIN" while Jack and the others made their way up to camp. They heard the announcer telling everyone "It's gonna blow through!" and "Try to keep yourself comfortable!" punctuated by cannon-boom thunder.

Sarah stopped as the first heavy drops pelted them and told Jack, "We need to be in the van. All of us. The tents won't be stable when the winds really start blowing. Please, convince them all to get in the van. We'll be safest there."

Jack yelled at the others, "Grab whatever you want to bring and take the place in the van you rode here in." He looked at Sarah. "You'll sit between Kelly and me in the back."

"Great," Kelly and Sarah groaned simultaneously.

They made it in before the deluge, slamming the doors against the wind. Laura handed out paper cups to everyone, then produced cans of Coca-Cola. "Sorry it's warm," she said, pouring plain Coke into her cup and Rodney's. "What the heck, a little won't hurt," she splashed some rum into both before handing the bottle to Jack. He poured his and looked at Sarah with the bottle poised above her cup.

"Is it like Boone's Farm?" she asked Jack.

"Absolutely not," Kelly answered, plastering herself against the window to keep from touching Sarah.

Jack poured Coke into Kelly's cup and Sarah's, too. "You can try it, but I don't think you'll like rum. Maybe start with a sip of Coke first," he told Sarah.

Sarah tilted the cup to her lips. "It's…fuzzy? Fizzy?" She giggled. "I like this." She nodded at her cup. "Put a little bit of the rum in."

He poured about a teaspoonful into her cup and passed the bottle forward.

"A toast to Jack," Rodney called out. "It's not goodbye, my friend, but farewell for now. We love you, man. May you find every happiness in Canada, and return to us soon."

"Hear, hear," Eric called out. He held up his cup and said, "Here's to swimmin' with bow-legged women."

Kristin said, "Can we go home now?" and took a big gulp from the rum and Coke she'd just poured.

Eric grinned. "What? It's from an old sea shanty. It's historical."

Jack laughed. "You're a mess. All y'all are. I'm really going to miss each and every one of you. And Kelly, I will try to get some letters to you and maybe you can keep everybody up to date on what I'm doing. All I know is I'm starting out in Ottawa, or near there, and I'll have some empty-headed job at first. What I'll do after that, I have no idea."

"Well," Laura said, "I'm starving so this surprise won't wait." She produced a foil-covered pan of brownies cut into perfect squares. "They were frozen when we left and I think they'll still be fine. And no, Eric, there's nothing funny in them. Just good fudgy brownies." She handed Jack the pan and a napkin as the rain outside began to sound like a monsoon, the wind rocking the van a little. "Those poor people down there. I wonder if Bud and Gary are okay in their little tents."

"I don't care," Kelly said, reaching for the rum now sitting by Jack's feet.

Jack reached over the seat to squeeze Rodney's shoulder. "Thanks for setting this all up, Rodney. Now that it's finally happening, I think I made the right choice. And at least I don't have to leave here alone. Sarah's going with us as far as the bus station in Binghamton."

"She's what?" Kelly and Laura said together.

"It's where I have to catch the bus to Rapid City," Sarah said. "I can either catch a ride with Jack, or hitchhike. It's way too far out of your way. Binghamton is literally on the road to Ottawa."

"How convenient," Kelly said, swallowing the rest of her drink and looking at the rain pouring down.

"Yes, it is," Sarah smiled at her. "I'm happy it worked out that way."

"I'm sorry I can't put on any tunes," Eric yelled over the rain. "Can't drain the battery. Man, Cocker was great up there."

They started a discussion of favorite performances. Kelly chose Joe Cocker over Joan Baez, surprising Jack. Sarah voted for Sly and the Family Stone. Jack said, "I'll never forget hearing Santana for the first time. Ever."

"Yeah, well, for me it's Country Joe and the Fish," Eric announced. "That cheer is gonna be in my head forever, even if I can't play it on the radio."

Kristin said, "You're all wrong. It was Creedence Clearwater Revival. I love them."

Jack's brows shot up. "You and Eric were there for that? I heard them. They were really good."

"I was," Kristin said. "Eric was sound asleep. I think you and I and that guy who yelled might have been the whole audience."

"That was a waste of Creedence," Jack said. "They're a great band and I hate that so many people slept right through them."

Thunder shook the van and a flash of lightning flooded the interior, revealing terror on Sarah's face. She sat there shaking as Jack pulled her to him, resting her head on his shoulder. He stroked her hair and whispered, "It's okay. We're safe in here."

"That was a close one," Rodney said. "Too close for me."

"Me, too," Laura added, scooting under Rodney's arm. "I've been scared of lightning my entire life."

Sarah took a deep breath and sat back up, determined to stay calm. "You saw all the camera equipment set up, right?" she asked. "They're going to put together a motion picture movie about Woodstock. So you'll be able to see a lot of it again." She licked the remains of brownie from her fingers. "These are absolutely delicious, Laura. Thank you."

"You're welcome," Laura called back, not turning her head.

The wind howled, whistled, rocked the van, and seemed to want to remove them from the hill. Kelly could have sworn she felt them skimming across the grass a couple of times. A paper plate smacked into the windshield, causing Eric and Kristin to jump.

Jack glanced at his watch, hoping the storm would pass before he and Sarah had to head down the hill. She smiled and patted his hand, which he took as a good sign. He swore the girl could sense things before they happened.

Kelly noticed Sarah never seemed to look away from Jack, staring at his profile like she was studying him, even when she spoke to everyone else. Jack was looking out the window like Kelly, waiting for the storm to pass. He seemed oblivious to Sarah's eyes locked on him.

"This doesn't feel like a party," Eric said, passing the drinks back after refilling his and Kristin's. "If we can't have music, anybody want to play a game?"

Jack, Rodney, and Kelly shook their heads no as Sarah said, "Yes. I need something else to think about. What kind of game?"

"Ever heard of truth or dare?" Eric asked her. "It's really easy. All you have to do is tell the absolute truth when I ask you a question…any question…or you can choose to do something I dare you to do instead. Nothing dangerous, of course. I'm not crazy."

Kristin shook her head at him and braced her feet on the dashboard, arms across her chest.

Jack said, "Eric, buddy, I don't think this is a good idea. Maybe another time." He poured rum and Cokes for himself and Kelly. Sarah held her hand over her cup to say no.

Laura spoke up. "I'll play," she told him. "Ask me anything."

"Okay," Eric stroked his chin. "Laura, have you ever done it with anyone but Rodney?"

"Geez, Eric, what kind of question is that?" Laura answered, rolling her eyes. "You're such an ass. But no, I haven't."

"Hey, I'm just trying to make the conversation interesting, Laura. That's my bag, remember? If we're all stuck in here, it's something to do," Eric told her, looking in the rearview mirror.

Laura glanced around. "Now I get to ask a question." She turned and swept her eyes across the people in the van. "Sarah…you're playing?" Sarah nodded her head yes.

Jack shifted in his seat, clearly uncomfortable. "This is a bad idea, Laura. We don't need to play any games. Let's talk about something else."

"No, there's something I want to know about Sarah," Laura said. "Sarah, where—"

Kelly interrupted with, "Laura, as your friend and your boss, I'm telling you to stop. Now." She sipped her drink and continued to watch water run down the window. "Let it go. Stop the stupid game before everyone in this van is upset. Let's just stay quiet for a while."

Sarah's mouth dropped into a sagging, stunned oval. She blinked several times and started to reach for Kelly's hand, but Kelly moved hers away. She bit her lower lip and refused to look at Sarah, choosing to study the pattern of the rain instead.

"I think it's slacking off," Kelly said after a few minutes. "Maybe we should listen for music starting back up."

Music didn't come, not until long after the storm. At 6:15, Jack slid his giant duffel bag out of a partially collapsed tent into what had mostly subsided into drizzle. He hugged Kristin, shook Eric and Rodney's hands, and gave Laura a quick squeeze of her fingers.

Jack opened his arms to Kelly and held her there for a moment, whispering, "It's going to be all right. I'll let you know what's going on, the best I can. You take care of yourself, okay?" She shook her head up and down next to his, sniffling tears by his ear. "Don't put up with any crap from Dr. Lawton. You're the best he has or ever will have, and he knows it."

Jack and Sarah made their way to the meeting point, arriving a little early.

"We're supposed to be at this corner of the stage. Jeff's wearing a bright yellow shirt," he told her. They tried to stand out of the constant stream of people passing, many of them carrying their stuff to leave for home. People were hugging goodbye, some of them crying and promising to stay in touch. By 7:20, Jack was pacing in the small space they had, worry etched into his face.

At 7:40, he told Sarah, "He's not coming. I know it. I gave that guy two hundred dollars. I emptied my bank account. Hell, I *closed* my bank accounts. I left my rent money on the table with a note for my landlord. Oh, man, he's—"

"Jack," Sarah said, her hand on his chest, "breathe. In and out. Don't panic. Maybe he's running late. Can you call him?"

"What, on his magic car telephone, Sarah? How does that work?" Jack blew a long breath of air through pursed lips. "I've shut down everything in Boston. I even told a buddy of mine to call about subbing tomorrow, so my kids don't get creepy Mr. Kaiser." He broke away from Sarah and looked at the ground for a minute, then returned his eyes to hers. "Look, I've made a big mistake. I need to go back up that hill. I need to get back to Boston and get my damn money back. Rodney said we could trust—"

"Jack, calm down," Sarah said. "I'm sure there's an explanation. The last thing you need to do is go back to Boston. Think about it. Do you trust *me*, Jack?"

"Yeah, Sarah, I do," Jack frowned, "but I don't have any choice. I don't see how this can work out okay."

"Well, it can. Stay here and wait. Don't move. I'll be back very soon. Just keep watching for Jeff," Sarah said, though she was almost sure Jeff wasn't coming. She waded into a crowd, her fingers searching for the roll of bills covered in black plastic at the bottom of her handbag. Sarah clutched that and held on as she looked through the sea of people exiting.

"Are you heading north?" she called out to the more likely candidates, smaller groups and singles. No one answered her until a man with shoulder-length blond hair stopped. He wore a flowered shirt and jeans torn at one knee, mud all around it. Sarah figured he was probably twenty-five at most.

He looked her up and down and said, "Yes, I'm going north. My little sister's meeting me here in a bit. Why?"

Sarah decided he must be safe if he had a sister with him. "I need a ride. A friend and I do. And I'm happy to pay you well for your time," Sarah said. "We're from Ottawa, and our ride home had to leave early. So I'm trying to find someone going that way." Her mother told her people would do anything for money in the twentieth century. How much, though? Sarah had no idea.

"Cool, yeah. Okay, I could go that far, I guess. But what kind of money are we talking about?" the guy said. "I'll be happy to help out, but that's going to add at least six hours to our trip. We live in Syracuse."

Sarah remembered the number Jack had said, and decided she should add extra for the last-minute request. The guy was going to be driving all night.

"Would you do it for three American one hundred dollars bills?" she asked him, pronouncing each word carefully.

She saw in the way his eyes lit up that he would. "Yes, three hundred dollars will probably be enough to cover me. My name's Howard. Friends call me Howie. What's yours?" he said, immediately assuming she must be a native Canadian who spoke French or maybe some Indian language.

"I'm Sarah. Sarah Sandoval." She didn't know what to do next, so she waited for him to say something. Sarah stood awkwardly in silence, looking around.

Howie stuck his hand out to shake and Sarah grasped it a little too hard, pumping his arm up and down. "It's a deal," Howie said. "The thing is, Marie's going to be about an hour saying goodbye to her new boyfriend. And I promise I'll meet you and your friend wherever you want. You don't have to give me any money yet, okay? I'll get payment from you when we get in the car. It's better that way. And I'll drop

Marie at home on the way, when we pass by Syracuse. Can you meet me in an hour?"

"What about that information booth? In one hour." Sarah pointed to a red and white wood booth about twenty feet away.

"Perfect," Howie said. "Do you have a watch?" He glanced at her arm.

"No, but my friend does," she said.

Howie looked at his watch. "I'll meet you two at that information booth at exactly 8:50, okay?" He started to move away, then turned back to ask, "What's your friend's name?"

"Jack," Sarah said.

"Ah, I thought it was a girl. So Jack needs to go to Canada, huh?" Howie folded his arms across his chest, looking at Sarah. She offered him a bright smile and he shook his head with a sigh. "Okay. I'll see you here then. The less I know, the better."

Sarah rushed back to tell Jack. She found him looking much calmer, leaning against a post, hands shoved in his pockets. He greeted her with a smile. "Hey, sorry I freaked out. Look, let's just go back up and tell the others what happened, Sarah. I'll make Eric take you to Binghamton tonight, and I'll go home with them."

"No, Jack," she said, taking his hand. "I've set up a ride for us. At 8:50, we're meeting him at the information booth near this spot. We'll check first to see if Jeff Hillery ever showed up, okay?"

Jack put a hand on Sarah's arm, blinking at her. "What? How?"

"I'll explain everything," she told him. "But for now, take a walk with me. There's something I need to do before we leave here."

"Sarah, all this was set up with Hillery, including the church he was supposed to take me to. I don't know where anything is. I don't have any contact information. Hillery was going to introduce me to someone who'd get me a job. I've never been to Canada, Sarah. I know absolutely no one in Ottawa. This just isn't meant to be."

Sarah closed her eyes and stood in silence for a few beats. She opened them with a long exhale and smiled at Jack, touching the side of his face. "Yes, it is," she said. "I need you to understand that. Please come with me." She stepped back and tugged at Jack's hand.

"Where are we going?" he asked, picking up his bag. "This duffel weighs a million pounds. Not the best time for a hike." *And I don't know if I should be doing this. Going to Canada could be the biggest mistake of my life. There will be no turning back*, Jack's brain screamed.

Sarah said, "Then let's take it into the woods and sit down for a few minutes." She walked toward the woods near Filippini Pond, leading Jack to the rock they'd sat on the day before. No one was around, only a few people splashing way out in the water.

Sarah turned her face to Jack's, seeing a thousand questions there. "The whole time we were sitting in that van, all I could think about was how hard it would be to leave you. I can't stand the thought of it, Jack."

He started to interrupt, and Sarah held a finger to his lips. "Just let me say this. My mother gave me money in case I needed it on this trip. That's the absolute truth. And I choose to use it for us to go to Canada together, tonight."

Jack blinked at her. "You want to go *with* me? I mean, nothing would make me happier, but I can't ask this of you, Sarah. I can't take your money. And you kept telling me you have to go home. I've already been trying to scheme ways to get to South Dakota someday." He smiled at her, his eyes crinkling at the edges the way she loved.

"I *do* have to go home, that's true, but not yet. And all I want in this world is more time with you," she said, swallowing hard. "I came here for different reasons, but you've become more important to me than any of them, Jack." Sarah felt her stomach wad itself into a tiny ball of pain. More important than making her mother frantic with worry? *Anantha doesn't deserve this, especially after arranging this trip as a gift to me. Accounting for my actions in Unity will be inevitable, too.* She pushed those thoughts away, determined to follow through on the plan she'd made for both herself and Jack.

Sarah stood and tugged Jack's hand. "Come with me," she said. She walked to the water's edge and pulled a daisy-shaped mirror from her handbag, holding it at arm's length with the pond behind them, just like people would hold phones for selfies in another fifty years. "Come here," she told Jack. "Look at us." He added his face to the mirror image next to hers.

"Why are we doing this?" Jack said, smoothing Sarah's hair out of her face with his hand.

"Because neither of us will ever be the same after today," she answered. She took the mirror, careful not to bend any of its petals, and threw it into the pond as hard as she could. It landed with a satisfying plop and sank. Sarah slid her arms around Jack's neck, resting her forehead against his. "It's going to be fine," she whispered, both to herself and Jack. She kissed his lips lightly and took Jack's hand in hers, walking into a future as uncertain as any she could have imagined. There would be consequences when they found her. Sarah hoped for leniency and understanding. She was violating rules, important rules.

Sarah's hand was nestled in Jack's as they walked in silence. She thought once more about when she'd read the interview Kelly had done back in 2023, one of many documenting the experiences of original Woodstock attendees. She hadn't paid much attention to it at the time; it was at least a year ago. She'd only been trying to know and understand her distant grandmother.

Kelly was characteristically brief and clinical, listing the friends she traveled with and what music she'd liked, mentioning Joan Baez more than once. She didn't say anything about drugs. She confessed to the interviewer that back then, she worked all the time and she'd spent most of the weekend in the van with her math notebook. The person who'd enjoyed the festival the most was her friend Jack, and she was happy for that, because Jack Warren was killed in Vietnam eleven months after The Woodstock Music and Art Fair of 1969.

PART II

23

Ottawa, Canada

AUGUST 1969

August 24, 1969

Dear Kelly,

I am fine and staying in a motel near Ottawa. Jeff never showed up to take Sarah and me north, though. I've written a letter to Rodney with instructions on how to send my refund from Jeff to the motel office and he'd better mail me a check. I still can't believe the guy didn't meet me, but I just finished ranting at Rodney about it and will spare you.

We ended up in an old Ford Fairlane with a guy named Howie and his little sister Marie, who talked all the way to Syracuse, where he dropped her off. Then Howie took us to a motel just south of Ottawa. I think it was almost 5 a.m. when we arrived. Sarah told Howie he'd driven us far enough, we'd go home after crashing at the Wander Inn for a few hours. Well, I think she said "after crashing into the Wander Inn room", actually.

Yes, Sarah decided to come to Canada with me. I'm pretty sure she felt sorry for me, knowing I had nothing to go back TO. I'd mailed a resignation letter to my principal (without details, of course), closed my bank accounts, left money and a note for my landlord, all that and more, but I was still going to head back after Hillery didn't show. I didn't think I had any alternative until she said she'd come to Canada with me, that she could help me figure this out. And I'm ashamed to admit it, but she had money her mother sent and that made it possible to arrange a ride to Ottawa. Sarah insisted we make this trip together, that this was her choice. She said she can delay going home for a while.

The border crossing was easy. No one cares if you're coming to Canada to visit. They asked some basic questions and sent us on our way. It was made clear to us that if we intended to stay, we needed to apply for Landed Immigrant Status.

So, we walked into that little motel office before 5 a.m., red vinyl chairs lining the wall, cigarette smoke, big fluorescent light glaring, and found one of the nicest people I've ever met. His name is Alex Landry. He's an old guy with close-cropped white hair, taller than I am and solidly built, I'm guessing in his sixties. Said he's always in the office by 4:30. He welcomed us with a huge smile, mostly for Sarah, I'm sure. She was immediately enchanted by Mr. Landry. He stubbed his cigarette out in a red glass ashtray and asked if we needed one room or two. Sarah told him two before I could open my mouth. It's costing us each eight Canadian dollars per night to stay here, which isn't too bad. Sarah is paying for her own room. That's the way she wants it.

It's a good thing Sarah is with me, because I didn't know where to start with all this. She had the idea to go to the local library our first day here. We asked Mr. Landry and he told us where to catch the bus and what stop to make, for both the library and a bank to exchange currency, because he wasn't going to take American dollars after one night's stay.

We found a book at the library called *Manual for Draft-Age Immigrants to Canada*. It even had a phone number in Ottawa for a lady named Goldie Josephy, who helps guys like me. Later we found a pay phone near the motel and dialed her number. We tried over and over and she didn't answer. We kept walking back over there and calling. She finally picked up the phone yesterday and met us in a small diner down the street called Fred's, where we sat in a booth and talked about my situation. She's an older lady, kind of mom-like, with curly brown and gray hair. She welcomed us with a warm smile and handshake before sitting down and ordering a cup of tea, stirring a pound of sugar into it as she began by telling us there's no draft in Canada. She said the last time they tried it was during WWII and tens of thousands of men refused to register. She said the mayor of Montreal was sent to jail back then for encouraging people to resist the draft, and then he was re-elected FROM JAIL. Forced military service is apparently not something many people believe in here. Most Canadians don't seem to mind young men coming across the border like I did.

Anyway, Goldie calls herself a peace activist. She's been doing this for years, and said she sometimes even lets new arrivals stay at her house until they get on their feet. Goldie thinks it should be pretty easy for me to pass an interview and to get a job in Ottawa. I want to be employed as soon as I can, even though it probably won't be as a teacher unless I'm really lucky. I do know that my MIT degree plus teaching experience will help a lot with the immigration part, at least.

Goldie told me where to go in town and fill out an official application for immigrant status. Soon, I should have an interview with Canadian officials. She coached me a little bit on what to answer, like don't try to say I've never heard of Selective Service or an idiot statement like that. She says the guy already knows I'm a draft dodger. She seemed to think my freshman year of high school French counts for something, though I only remember about two words. At one point, she kind of patted my hand on the table and laughed. She said I'm easy, all I have to do is be me. And cut my hair short, which I hate, but it'll grow back.

Goldie knows a lot of people. She's going to speak to a friend who owns a grocery store about hiring me for something, even if it's temporary. She asked Sarah about getting her a job. Sarah told Goldie she has to leave for home soon.

Goldie also promised to be on the lookout for an apartment I can afford.

The biggest thing I've found out is that the FBI can issue a warrant for my arrest, but it isn't valid here. They can't use it in Canada. That's only true for draft dodgers (I'm already used to the label), not deserters. I don't have to be nearly as careful as I'd worried about. A lot of stuff I heard about fleeing to Canada and being arrested was a lie. But I can never go home. Goldie said that more than once. It's still hard to believe and I guess I try to pretend it isn't true.

I told Mom before I did all this I couldn't imagine if something happened to her or dad or my gram and granddad, and me not being able to come home. Mom interrupted and said she'd much rather I not be able to attend her funeral than for her to attend mine. Of course, then she started talking about how Kenny is and she has no idea if he'll ever get better. She and Dad are afraid he's going to end up in jail, but honestly, that might be the best thing for him, even though she was sobbing when she said it.

Sarah seems very happy now that we're here. She spent the first hour or two in Howie's back seat frantically looking for things to hold on to in the car. I don't think she's comfortable in traffic. By the time we were pulling into Syracuse she'd settled down and grabbed the back of Howie's seat to watch the turn signal blink. She does the same thing on the bus, always insisting we sit behind the driver. I have no idea why it fascinates her, but told her people using turn signals is pretty rare where I come from, too. She didn't get the joke.

We went to a newsstand near the bank for a paper and some stuff to take back to the motel. Sarah discovered Reese Peanut Butter Cups (it's Reese, not Reese's here), the combination of her two favorite things, so she bought six. She took one to Mr. Landry, and he tasted it and told her it's not as good as a Coffee Crisp, his candy bar of choice.

So now, Sarah picks a Coffee Crisp up for him every time we go somewhere.

There's a diner within walking distance (the one where we met Goldie). The food at Fred's is good and pretty cheap. Sarah asked for a peanut butter sandwich the first time we went, and the waitress blinked at her a few times but brought her one. I reminded her afterward we can make those really easily at the motel. Now she's moved on to grilled cheese. I suspect when I introduce her to pizza, there will be no turning back.

One day we took the bus to a department store to buy Sarah some sneakers. She threw those muddy sandals in a garbage can where we agreed they belong. She's started running in a park near here every morning. Said she used to run every day at home. She complains about how hot it is, though.

Every once in a while I think she's homesick. Yesterday I stood outside the pay phone while she tried to call her family in South Dakota. No one answered the first time and then she got a wrong number. She just smiled and hung up the phone like that was okay with her, saying she would try again the next day.

The money thing is important because Jeff owes me, but not as important as I'd thought. If I run out, Sarah has what her mom sent to tide us over until I start getting a paycheck, whether I'm a janitor or teacher or stacking bananas in the produce department. I don't want to dip into her money, though. Closing my bank accounts left me enough to get us by. I doubt she has much beyond bus fare back to South Dakota. I don't want to ask, anyway. We were happy to discover at the bank that American dollars have a very favorable currency exchange rate. It helps a lot.

That's pretty much what's happening here.

I'll send a real address when we have one. Please write back. I hope you're doing great and things with the MAC Project are going well. You should be running it. But Kelly, get out and have some fun, too. Say hi to everybody for me.

Love,
Jack

24

Monday, August 25, 1969
The Wander Inn
OTTAWA, CANADA

Sarah stood leaning across the motel's white Formica counter, chin on her hand, talking to Mr. Landry. He laughed as Jack walked in to join her.

"Here comes your beau," he said. "What's an ugly guy like you doing with a beauty like this? It hurts my eyes to look at you." He took his glasses off and set them down, blinking at Jack. "There, that's better."

"She's with me for my intelligence and charm," Jack responded, picking up Mr. Landry's discarded *Ottawa Citizen* from the counter. "Which don't seem to be getting me a job. Mind if I look at your paper?" he asked. Mr. Landry nodded, replacing his black-framed glasses. He walked through the door leading to his home behind the front desk, which he shared with a calico cat named Pierre. Mrs. Landry had died two years ago, a subject her husband made clear was off-limits. Jack had the impression she'd suffered a lengthy illness.

"I don't think he likes me," Jack told Sarah, nodding in the direction of Mr. Landry's exit.

"He likes you, he just likes me much better," Sarah said. She looked at the classified ads along with Jack. "There's a new one today," she said, pointing to the paper. "Do you know how to be a hairdresser?"

"Afraid not," Jack told Sarah, shaking his head. "Goldie's grocery store guy isn't going to come through. I'm getting desperate enough to go to the hospital janitor interview this afternoon, much as I hate the thought of mopping up bodily fluids."

Mr. Landry returned carrying a business card. He handed it to Jack, saying, "Go see this guy. He's an old friend. I told him you're supposedly good at mathematics, though I haven't seen any evidence of it."

Jack looked at the card. "Walton C. Armstrong. He owns a Volvo dealership?" he asked Mr. Landry. "I mean, I appreciate it, but I know nothing about the car business."

"Don't have to," Mr. Landry replied. "Wally needs someone to help get customers financing, figure out what they can afford, that sort of thing. He wouldn't be talking to you if it wasn't for me, Jack. But Wally and I went to school together and I told him your beautiful girlfriend is with you all the time and I need you to go off to work." He winked at Sarah. "And as much as I love having you kids living here, you need to get a proper apartment, an address you can use with the immigration people. Wally can help with that, too. He owns a building in the neighborhood of the dealership. It's nothing fancy, but it'll work."

"Wow, thank you, Mr. Landry," Jack said. Sarah leaned across the counter and pecked the old man's stubbly cheek.

"Don't thank me yet," Mr. Landry said, rubbing his face where Sarah had kissed it. "He'll need a good look at you and when it comes to impressing him, you're on your own." He swept his eyes up and down Jack. "You have about a thirty-two inch waist, right? I have some old dress trousers you can probably wear. They won't be circling this belly again." He patted his stomach. "You definitely need to change into some more businesslike clothes."

"I have some, sir," Jack told him. "I have an entire teacher wardrobe, you just haven't seen it. But thank you very much."

"Number 8 bus," Mr. Landry called out. "If you hurry you'll only have to wait about ten minutes. Sarah can stay here and watch *General Hospital* with me."

"Yes, I have to know what happened to Jane and Howie after Friday," Sarah said. "They are so perfect for each other, even if she doesn't know it." She grinned and waved at Jack, yelling "Good luck!" as he went out the office door.

"Why do you love *General Hospital* so much?" Sarah asked, watching Mr. Landry place his usual "BACK IN ONE HOUR" sign on the counter. She followed him into the living room, taking a seat on the gold-floral sofa next to his worn leather recliner.

Mr. Landry rubbed his chin. "I don't. But my Edie did, she wouldn't miss one day. Scheduled everything in the morning so she'd be back for it. So, when she got sick, I started watching it with her. Got hooked, I guess, though for a long time it made me feel close to her again after I lost her. I'd sit here and imagine what she'd say at the latest twist of fate in Port Charles. I still do, every day."

He got up to fiddle with the TV, though Sarah thought the picture seemed fine. She saw him swipe at his eye as he sat back down.

"It's been two years since Edie passed away, and I think a lot about how the only thing we really did together was watch this damn show. I waited until it was too late, when she was so weak. Sat here with her while she watched and worked on her quilts." He patted the light-gold patchwork quilt that was hanging on the back of the sofa. "I was too busy trying to make the motel a success, it kind of took over my days and nights. The only thing any of us have is time, Sarah." He paused as the theme song began, then continued, "I regret some things I've done, but it's the things I didn't do that haunt me. Places we didn't go, all the times I thought about taking her dancing and collapsed in this recliner instead, the cream-filled doughnuts she loved I never stopped to pick up on my way home. Remember that, Sarah. You think you'll have plenty of years to show people the kindness and thoughtfulness in you. That's not always true."

"Did you and Mrs. Landry have any children?" Sarah asked quietly.

"We had a little girl. Her name was Robin. Only lived two weeks, some kind of heart thing. Edie never got over that. Hell, I didn't either," he said. "Let's watch the show now." He nodded toward the television and crossed his arms over his chest, clearly finished talking.

The television's picture rolled upward with lines blipping across it and Sarah jumped up to adjust the vertical tuning knob the way Mr. Landry had taught her, looking at his unsmiling face as she sat back down. He grunted thanks at her, his arms still tightly crossed. Sarah didn't think he was really watching the soap opera today. She wondered what Mrs. Landry had been like; there were no photos anywhere in the dimly lit living room. In her mind, Edie Landry took the shape of beleaguered nurse Jessie Brewer, who was sipping coffee at her desk onscreen. She thought Mr. Landry might've looked a little like Dr. Steve Hardy when he was young, though it was almost impossible to imagine.

When the show ended, she asked Mr. Landry if he had any pictures of his wife. He held up a finger for her to wait and returned with a green vinyl photo album, handing it to Sarah.

"She was a beautiful woman, my Edie. I haven't looked through this since she died, and I still can't. You have a look for me. You can do it here. I don't want my personal things out in the office."

He switched on a lamp next to where Sarah sat and headed toward the door.

"You really like this Jack guy? Is he your future?" Mr. Landry asked over his shoulder.

"I don't know what my future is anymore," Sarah replied. "I thought I did. Now everything is different, since we came here. But yes, I really like him."

"He's a pretty nice fella for a draft dodger, I guess," Mr. Landry said. "If Wally gives him this job, he'd better work hard and not embarrass me. It's hard to count on young people these days." He shook his head. "I sent him after that job because of you, Sarah. You seem to want to make a life with him. I see the way you look at that boy, like he hung the moon."

Sarah nodded, a slight crease between her eyebrows. "I do, Mr. Landry. Thank you for helping him. But…we're not married. Won't the idea of us living together in an apartment seem wrong to you?"

Mr. Landry looked at the ceiling as he answered. "Nothing you can do living together that you couldn't do living separately, the way I see things." He walked through the office door and closed it behind him.

Sarah stared at the closed door and considered what Mr. Landry had said for a minute. Pierre wandered in and jumped onto the sofa next to her, curling up for a nap. She stroked the cat's fur and heard him purr, both of them delighted. She would miss Pierre.

Sarah opened the photo album, listening to the protesting creak in its spine. She'd bet he hadn't looked at it in many years. She discovered Mrs. Landry had been a petite blonde, nothing like the serious dark-haired *General Hospital* nurse. Their wedding photo showed Mr. Landry towering over his wife, his expression part happiness and part awkward embarrassment at having to pose for the photographer. Edie Landry's smile lit the entire photo for both of them, the hopes and dreams of a new bride written all over her face.

Sarah sat turning the pages for an hour, watching Alex Landry turn into a playful husband on his honeymoon in Banff, laughing at something his wife said as they rode a gondola up the side of a mountain, impossibly young and handsome. As she neared the end of the carefully placed photos, she saw fewer and fewer of him and his wife. There were pictures of relatives, older men and women. One showed an elderly lady blowing out candles on a cake. The last picture in the album was a large one of Mr. and Mrs. Landry standing next to each other in front of the Wander Inn office. She was visibly pregnant and it made Sarah cry to see the excitement on Edie's face. She traced their image with her fingertip and left the album sitting on the coffee table, going to join Mr. Landry at the counter. He was sorting through a stack of mail.

Sarah touched his arm and said, "Your wife was very beautiful. Thank you for letting me see."

"I wanted to prove my point, Sarah," Mr. Landry said, his voice husky. "You wake up one morning and all you have is the past. Make sure those memories are the best ones you can have." He walked to the glass exit door. "I'm going to check on the rooms and make sure they're ready for tonight. Keep an eye out here, would you? I'll be back in a few minutes."

Two hours later, Sarah spotted Jack smiling as he approached the office and she told Mr. Landry, "Look at him. He must've gotten the job."

Jack walked in waving a piece of paper. "Not sure how I'll ever thank you enough, Mr. Landry!" he said as the door closed behind him. "Mr. Armstrong hired me on the spot. I start on Thursday." He grinned at Sarah as she came from behind the counter and he picked her up for an impromptu whirl.

Sarah giggled as he set her down. "I'm so glad you got the job!"

"Not only that, it pays a lot better than I thought it would," Jack said. "And there's this." He held up a key and dangled it in front of Sarah. "We have an apartment to move into."

"Oh," she said, glancing at Mr. Landry, who was scrubbing the same smudge on the counter he'd worked on earlier. "When are we doing that?"

"Mr. Armstrong has a tenant moving out this weekend, so next Monday," Jack said.

Mr. Landry said, "You two wait here. This calls for a celebration." He disappeared through the door to his home and Sarah looked at Jack while they waited.

"It's small, but it's furnished and ready. And, well…the thing is, I'll sleep on the couch because there's only one bed. I don't mind," Jack said, his voice quiet.

Sarah looked at the key, following Jack's hand as he pocketed it. Mr. Landry returned with a bottle of red wine and placed it on the counter with three small glasses. "This was Edie's. I'm a beer man, myself. But we should drink a toast." He poured generous servings into each glass and nudged two toward Jack and Sarah, lifting his own into the air and saying, "Here's to a happy future to you both. Congratulations, Jack!"

"Thank you," Jack replied. "I'm so grateful to you, Mr. Landry. I'd be mopping up disgusting things for a living if it weren't for you. You have no idea how much this means." He hugged Sarah's waist as she took a tentative sip. "And we'll still visit," he added. "The apartment's not that far from here."

Mr. Landry grimaced as he swallowed his wine. "Just the pretty one. You're not my type." He looked at his watch and announced, "It's almost quitting time for me. Gerard will get here in five minutes to take over the counter for the night shift." Jack and Sarah had met Gerard, a scrawny guy in his late thirties, exactly once. "I'm going to have a beer or two and a nap before dinner," Mr. Landry continued. He pushed the rest of the bottle toward Jack. "You kids take this with you. I don't want any more."

Jack took the bottle and their glasses, opening the door with his back for Sarah to go through. "Thank you again," he called to Mr. Landry. "For everything."

The old man nodded and looked at the wall clock as they walked away.

"He's so lonely," Sarah said to Jack. "I wish I knew someone to introduce him to."

"Maybe we'll find him a woman. You never know," Jack said. They reached his motel door. "Want to come in and drink some wine?" He wiggled his eyebrows at Sarah as she took her glass from him.

She shrugged and looked back toward the motel office. "Yes, I will," she announced, surprising Jack. Sarah followed him in and sat at the little table and chairs in front of the gold-curtained window. Jack sat opposite her and poured more for each of them. Sarah took a long drink and put her glass down. "Let me buy you dinner," she said to

Jack. "We should try that thing you've been telling me about, pizza pie."

Jack frowned. "Sarah, I don't want you spending—"

Sarah interrupted him, reaching for the bottle. "I have more money than you think. We can use a little of it tonight. It's a special occasion and I'm not eating another peanut butter sandwich, Jack. I want to try new things." She poured more wine into her glass.

Jack raised his glass and clinked hers. "To new things," he said. "You'll absolutely love pizza."

Sarah stood and finished her wine. "I'll meet you here in an hour," she told Jack. She waved as she left, leaving Jack to listen for the familiar sound of her adjacent room's heavy door opening and closing.

When Sarah returned, she wore the white peasant blouse and jeans she'd put on after he fished her from Filippini Pond. That seemed like a year ago. He blinked away thoughts of Sarah splashing naked in the water, Sarah wearing a soaked blouse, Sarah anything but fully dressed, standing at his door, clutching her handbag and smiling at his wine-addled face.

"Ready to go?" she asked him.

Jack ran his eyes up and down Sarah. "Not really," he said, swallowing. "Let me brush my teeth." He let Sarah in to sit at the little table and wait. "How hungry are you?" he called out from the bathroom. "I think Rosario's is open for a few more hours."

"I am pretty starving for food," Sarah yelled back from her chair by the window. He walked out and stared at the way the late-day light leaked through and silhouetted Sarah's profile. She looked like a Renaissance painting, softly lit against the shadows.

Sarah stood and walked over to take his arm. "Come on," she told Jack. "I want to see what makes pizza so special."

They rode the bus to the restaurant in silence, Jack sneaking glances at Sarah and trying not to think of Filippini Pond. The hostess at Rosario's seated them in a booth and handed them menus. Sarah took a quick look at hers and closed it.

A waitress about their age appeared to ask if they'd like drinks to start. She had short black hair and a pencil tucked behind one ear.

"I would like to order red wine," Sarah said. "And a large cheese pizza for me." She handed the menu to their server, whose nametag read CLAUDINE. "Do you want a pizza too, Jack?" Sarah asked.

"Sarah, they're kind of huge," Jack told her. "Maybe we should share a pizza."

Sarah shook her head no, and Jack ordered a medium pepperoni and sausage of his own, along with a glass of chianti. Claudine wrote everything down and returned almost immediately with their wine.

Jack took a sip and said, "So much has happened today. Like this apartment, for instance. You didn't say much about that situation. We won't have separate rooms anymore, but we'll make it work." He watched Sarah's face, trying to read her reaction.

"Okay," she said. Sarah hesitated and bit her lower lip. "I've been thinking about it. I don't know how long I have here with you, Jack, but I won't get to stay. Mr. Landry talks how he wishes he'd done more for his wife when he had her by his side, how he should have taken her dancing, how sorry he is he didn't take the opportunities…" Sarah trailed off, inhaled a deep breath and released it. She looked into Jack's eyes and lifted one shoulder. She said, "Maybe I should roll in the hay while the sun is shining."

He was too stunned to laugh. "That's an excellent philosophy," Jack told her. "If you're saying what I think you're saying, though, are you sure? Last time, you told me to stop. I thought we agreed we should keep this relationship platonic."

"Mr. Landry told me he sees the way I look at you. And I certainly see the way *you* look at *me*. It makes me wonder, Jack, if I shouldn't live every minute with you the way I want to, not worrying about the future. Just about what we have now," she said.

Jack raised his brows. "Your future includes an arranged marriage, remember?"

She hesitated before answering. "None of us knows what will happen. Everything changed when I came here with you, I told you that," she said, frowning. "It's all uncertain now. When I get home, I'll do what I need to do." She took a long drink and set her wine carefully on the table. "I want to make some memories we can treasure after I leave. They may be all I have to hold onto."

Jack reached out a hand for Sarah's and had to withdraw it as Claudine delivered an appalling amount of pizza and two dinner plates to their table. She arranged Sarah's twenty-inch pie so it almost hung over the edge next to Jack's. She smiled sweetly at Sarah as she handed her extra napkins.

"Can I get anything else for you?" she asked.

"I'd like a glass of water please," Jack said. Sarah added she would like one, too. She sat staring at the pizza, unsure how to pick it up.

Jack told her, "Look. Pull a piece out and put it on your plate," he demonstrated. "Might need to let it cool for a minute. Then fold it like this, so all the toppings are inside a wedge. It's okay to use your hands, but we can ask Claudine for a fork if you'd like." He glanced in the direction their server had gone.

"No, I'll just pick it up," Sarah told him. She wrestled a piece of pizza free and held it up for a bite, stringing a bridge of mozzarella cheese through the air and trying to catch and replace it with her other hand. She grinned at Jack. "This really is as good as you said. But so messy."

When Claudine returned with their water, Jack asked for a couple of forks. "Much better," Sarah said. After two slices, Sarah was full and asked Jack, "Does anybody ever take pizza home with them?"

"All the time," Jack replied. "I'll ask for a box." He wiped his hands before reaching to hold Sarah's again. "So, what were we saying before? Something about making memories? Because I think I have some ideas," he said, his thumb stroking the back of Sarah's hand, tracing little lightning strikes across her skin.

Sarah offered him a tentative smile, clearly unsure what to do next. "Hey, could we go dancing like Mr. Landry talked about?" she asked.

Claudine interrupted with the box and carefully placed Sarah's pizza in it. She handed Jack the bill. Sarah reached for it and slid it to her side of the table, attempting to figure out how to proceed. Did she walk to the counter up front to pay? Was the amount right? Could dinner have possibly cost only nine dollars? She stared at the paper and wondered what to do next.

Jack reached across the table and plucked the bill from her fingers. "You can pay next time," he told her. "It's important to me to buy your dinner tonight. I'm gainfully employed now, Sarah. I'm not worrying about money."

She shrugged her shoulders and said nothing except, "Thank you." She watched Jack hand Claudine a ten-dollar bill and tell her to keep the change for herself.

They walked into the cool night air, Jack balancing the pizza on the way to the bus stop. He said, "I saw this place earlier a couple of blocks over called Louie's. It's just a little bar, but it looks good from the outside. I'll bet people dance there. Wanna go and see? It's only a little after nine o'clock. We're too young to go home this early." Jack cleared his throat, unsure what Sarah might want at this point and afraid to spoil the mood she'd set at dinner. "Unless, umm, you're in a hurry to get back." He looked at her face, noting she was biting her lip and frowning slightly, a sure sign she was deep in thought.

"Yes, let's go to Louie's," Sarah said, reaching for Jack's hand. "I could use another glass of wine."

The bar was almost deserted, a nice little place with a single candle flickering at the center of each table. Jack held Sarah's chair out and put the pizza box on the one next to her. No one appeared to take their order, so Jack approached the bar and asked for two red wines from a person he presumed to be Louie. As he was waiting, he spotted an old-fashioned jukebox at the back of the long room. There was a little open space in front of it.

"Is that a dance floor?" he asked as the bartender slid the glasses toward him.

"It is if you want it to be," he answered, smiling. He nodded at the only other couple in the bar, holding hands at a table along the brick wall. "It's pretty quiet right now. The place'll fill up about ten, post-dinner crowd."

"Thanks," Jack said. He carried the wine to their table, taking a long drink before setting his down. "I'll be right back," he told Sarah.

Jack examined the jukebox offerings. He walked up and took Sarah by the hand as the opening strains of Percy Sledge's "When a Man Loves a Woman" played, tugging her to the tiny would-be dance floor. He pulled Sarah close and held her as he moved in an awkward box step.

Sarah giggled. "It's a nice song. But I don't know how to dance this way," she said.

"It's okay," Jack said. "Neither do I. This is my sixth-grade slow dance, the only one I know." He kissed her lightly. "Sarah, were you serious about—"

She held a finger to his lips. "No more talking," Sarah said. She lay her head on Jack's shoulder as he tightened his arms around her.

By the time the song ended, it was clear they were ready to finish their wine and go home. Jack held Sarah's hand as they sat at the bus stop and through the entire trip without speaking a word.

As the bus pulled up to their stop, brakes hissing, Sarah stared straight ahead and told Jack, "Yes. Yes, I was serious."

He took her hand and led her to the deserted hallway outside his Wander Inn room, setting the box down as he unlocked the door and then transferring it to the table inside. Sarah followed him into the darkness.

Jack pulled Sarah to him. His mouth found hers and all the urgency of the kiss they'd shared in the rain at Woodstock came flooding back. Sarah moaned and pushed Jack against the closed door, her arms around his neck. They stood locked together in a deep kiss and Sarah felt her entire body shaking, aching for him. Jack swept his arms under Sarah's thighs, lifting her to wrap her legs around his waist. He carried Sarah backwards to the bed and collapsed on it with her body on top of his.

"Sarah," he whispered, his breathing ragged, "are you sure?"

She responded by pulling her blouse over her head, throwing it at the wall. She leaned down and put her lips on Jack's, her hands fumbling with his belt. Jack reached to unbuckle and remove it, raising her off the bed with his hips in the process. Sarah rolled to her side, sliding the rest of her clothes off as Jack stood to get out of his pants and shirt. He hovered over Sarah, studying her naked form.

"My God, you are beautiful," he murmured. He took her hands, bringing her to her feet in front of him. Jack ran his hands along Sarah's body, gliding over every curve, pausing to gently cup her breasts, kissing the top of each one. Jack's breathing was labored as he whispered, "There are so many ways I want to make love to you, Sarah Sandoval. This is only the beginning." He eased her back onto the bed and covered her body with his, breathing in concert with Sarah for a minute, enjoying the feeling of her skin against his. Jack kissed her deeply, taking his time as he reached to touch her, stroking the most sensitive parts of her body until Sarah moaned.

"Please," she whispered, her voice breaking. "Please."

Jack entered her, watching Sarah's face as she winced slightly. "Are you okay?" he asked.

"I'm fine," she whispered, pulling his mouth to hers. Jack buried himself in Sarah, lost himself in Sarah, became a part of her from that night on.

She was wrong, he thought. There was nothing uncertain about his future. He would love Sarah Sandoval until the day he died.

25

August-September 1969

OTTAWA, CANADA

Mr. Landry shook Jack's hand at six o'clock Monday morning and turned to hug Sarah.

"You two have my telephone number if you need anything," the old man said. "I really will miss my *General Hospital* buddy. I've never let anyone into my…living room…like that." He cleared his throat. "I know you're in a hurry so you can get settled before Jack has to be at the dealership, but I want you to wait right here for just a minute, okay?"

Sarah blinked in the early-morning light that flooded the office. Jack thought she was probably trying to swallow tears rather than upset Mr. Landry. Even he felt kinda choked up leaving the old guy. He'd done so much for both of them.

Mr. Landry emerged from the door of his home carrying a large shopping bag, which he handed to Sarah. She peered inside and said, "Oh, Mr. Landry, is this one of hers? It's beautiful." Sarah held up a quilt with rings of dark green and blue against a cream background to show Jack.

Mr. Landry nodded, rubbing his hands together. "That's one of the first ones Edie made. I think she'd like you to have it for a housewarming present."

Sarah started to protest, but thought better of it. The tears were falling now, blinking or not. She hugged the old man and whispered, "Thank you" as she kissed his cheek. "This is so kind of you and we will treasure it, won't we, Jack? And I'm going to miss you so much. I promise I'll come an afternoon or two every week after we get set up in the apartment, and we can check up on Port Charles together, okay? I'm also going to try to learn to make a brownie and cut it into pieces, so you may get one if I don't burn it up."

Mr. Landry was struggling to keep his composure. He held up a hand and said, "Just one more thing." He rushed off and came back with a stained, slightly battered copy of *Betty Crocker's Guide to Easy Entertaining: How to Have Guests and Enjoy Them*. "I bet there are the best instructions for how to bake brownies in here. You'll find a recipe for an angel food cake, too, that one's a beauty." He handed the book to Sarah. "Most of them are pretty easy, though occasionally Edie would throw the cookbook on the floor in frustration. Come to think of it, never, ever try the Chicken with Orange Sauce. That's what led to the dent in the right corner."

Sarah laughed through her tears. "I wish I could have known Edie," she said. "Thank you for this." She blew him a kiss and walked away with Jack, just like she hadn't come along and moved into the old man's heart and ripped a piece out as she left. Mr. Landry watched until they turned the corner, hoping Sarah would not forget him.

Jack lugged his giant duffel and several bags of Sarah's things onto the bus. He deposited them on some empty seats and plopped down next to his sobbing girlfriend. Jack kissed the top of her head before taking her hand in his. He didn't bother to try to cheer her up, just held on to Sarah as she cried. There were no words to make leaving Alex Landry any better. He knew it.

Sarah and Jack's apartment was about eight hundred square feet of dark brown carpeting and empty beige walls, except for the tiny half-bath and kitchen. Those floors were green and white striped linoleum. The kitchen was hardly big enough to turn around in and featured a stove and refrigerator that looked like a tiny child's play set. It had a mullioned window over the sink with lime green café curtains, which offered a view of the small yard and street in front. The cream-colored countertops were accented by the occasional burn mark, from both cigarettes and misplaced hot pans. There was a wood dinette set large enough for two people and one entrée at most; it was situated between the kitchen and the optimistically named living room. There sat a worn nubby brown sofa whose springs tortured the bottoms that dared to sit on it. In the corner was a cast-iron freestanding woodstove for heat, though it would be months before temperatures dropped enough to merit its use.

The bathroom comprised a bilious-green tile shower stall and matching toilet with a white pedestal sink that looked like it might predate indoor plumbing, if the concentric rust rings around the drain were a clue. Lighting was minimal everywhere, which helped hide the series of stains on the quilted tan bedspread. The bedroom draperies were a deep orange that had faded to peach in random spots. Jack thought it smelled vaguely like the ditch he used to catch tadpoles in near his house.

Sarah absolutely loved the place. She spent her first day exploring little shops nearby while Jack worked, picking out and buying a framed painting of the Canadian Rocky Mountains' snow-covered peaks to hang near their sofa and a watercolor of a cornfield for the bedroom. "In honor of Kelly," she told Jack. Jack brought home a used record player from a pawn shop and surprised Sarah with Sly and the Family Stone's album *Stand!*, so they could dance to "I Want to Take You Higher". Sarah fell in love with the song "Everyday People" and played it constantly. Jack grew used to hearing it when he opened the apartment door after work.

They went to the grocery store together late Tuesday and selected ingredients for brownies, stopping at a department store for a new square pan. Sarah thought the one in the kitchen cabinet looked too dirty, and Jack wasn't inclined to argue with her. It hadn't improved after several scrubbings, during which Sarah stabbed her hand with steel wool and resolved never to use it again.

On Wednesday morning, Sarah waited for Jack to leave before sliding her dresser drawer fully open and depositing the remainder of her American money, about two thousand dollars, along with a note. It took her almost an hour to write the few words she decided, in the end, would be best for him to read. Sarah thought about the look on Kelly's face every time she tried to tell the truth about her home. She would not risk creating the same revulsion in Jack's eyes.

She stopped wearing her amber bead bracelet, tucking it into her travel pouch handbag along with two Reese Cups. Soon after, she occupied herself with disastrous brownie-baking experiments. She tried creating them from the cookbook's recipe three times. They looked and tasted nothing like Laura's. Sarah scraped them into the kitchen trash can, creating a mountain of what looked like scorched soil after a forest fire.

Jack opened the front door around six o'clock, overwhelmed by a thick waft of smoke that briefly reminded him of Woodstock's ambience. This one, however, transported him instantly to the burn piles his dad used to make on their farm. Jack's job back then had been to stand nearby with a water hose, making sure the fire was contained. He'd hated every dull moment.

Jack saw Sarah sitting on the kitchen floor, her back against a cabinet. She had her head in her hands. "I am not learning this very well," she said. "In fact, I have given up. I will never make another brownie or anything else. I am not a cooker, Jack. I have tried, but I only cook disasters." In the living room, Sly Stone sang his usual "Everyday People" lyrics.

Jack knelt down next to her, using a finger to lift Sarah's chin. "There is an old saying. If at first you don't succeed, try, try again."

Sarah looked into Jack's eyes. "That is a *very* stupid saying. Either you're good at something and it comes naturally, or you're not. I have always learned very quickly and easily until now. This is different. Laura must have been born knowing how to mix batter and make it grow correctly in an oven."

Jack stood and put his hands on his hips, staring down at her. "You know, Beethoven's early music tutor said that as a composer he was hopeless. Elvis Presley was fired after one show at the Grand Ole Opry. They told him he wasn't going anywhere in his career."

"Elvis who?" Sarah said, picking at a fleck of burnt brownie on the floor.

Jack took her hands and pulled Sarah to her feet, wrapping his arms around her. "You may be used to learning things quickly, Sarah, but some stuff takes time and practice, no matter how talented you are. You can't just quit." He kissed the top of her head and continued, "You have to put in some sweat. That last one's a motivational quote from my high school football coach."

"I do not want to sweat," Sarah said. "That's another thing. It's getting too hot to run. I rode the bus to the park after I finished cooking and came home within ten minutes. I hate weather."

"You don't hate weather, Sarah, just *this* weather. It'll change before you know it, and then you'll think it's too cold," Jack said, taking a beer from the refrigerator and moving to the sofa.

Sarah nodded and followed him, removing the phonograph needle and turning it off. She settled beside Jack, ignoring the sofa's unwelcoming cushions as they stabbed her. She sighed and told him, "If you'll go with me to get more granules of sugar, I'll try again tomorrow."

Jack smiled at her. "That's the spirit," he said, gulping his beer. "Give me a minute to change out of my fancy business clothes. You won't be sorry, Sarah. You'll work out this brownie thing."

Thursday afternoon, Jack stood in the kitchen loosening his tie and asked Sarah how the day's brownies had gone. She reached into the cooled oven and pulled out the pan, setting it on the counter.

"Look and see. I didn't burn it, but it never got beyond being watery."

Jack pondered the correct response, deciding it was, "I'm starving for pizza. Let's go to Rosario's."

Sarah nodded as she scraped the goo into the trash can. Jack wondered briefly if Sarah had decided brownies were dinner food, but thought he'd avoid asking about that today.

On Friday afternoon, Jack came home and hid a grocery bag in their bedroom before joining Sarah. He avoided the topic of brownies altogether as he watched her move around the kitchen doing something that seemed to involve the refrigerator.

He said, "I really like the Volvo business, and I think I'm pretty good at the job, Sarah. I can't see doing this forever, but it's a good way to tide us over until I get something better. It'll be a big help to say I work for Mr. Armstrong in my interview next week. He has three dealerships and his name is well-known. Mr. Landry did me a huge favor there."

Sarah smiled at him and cupped his face in her hand, patting his cheek as she said, "You could have made a great hospital mopper, too. You'd be good at anything. Except dancing, that needs work."

"My dancing is exceptional," Jack replied, sliding his arm behind Sarah and dipping her back as far as the tiny kitchen allowed, then pulling her body up as he kissed her. "Unfortunately, no one can dance to 'Everyday People'. Not even Sly Stone. He probably hides during this song."

Sarah set the tiny table with paper plates and napkins before producing tonight's meal: ham sandwiches with canned green beans on the side. She seemed so proud of heating them, Jack acted like it was a typical dinner combination the world over. He watched Sarah across the table and thought he'd eat sandwiches and beans forever with her if she'd let him.

They met their neighbors that night as they sat on the patch of cement in front of their door, enjoying a cool breeze. Arielle and Christophe Gagnon were a newlywed couple from Quebec who spoke enough English to seem to understand Sarah when she told them she and Jack had been at Woodstock. Sarah tried inviting them in to listen to Sly and the Family Stone through a series of hand gestures and dance moves. Christophe recognized the word "music" and pulled Arielle into the apartment, where they danced like professionals around the nubby brown sofa. The two of them moved in elaborate synchronization as Jack and Sarah stopped to watch, their mouths hanging open.

"I don't think I like them and their fancy dancing," Sarah said, laughing as she closed the door behind the Gagnons. "I'm going to get a Joan Baez album before they come back. Let's see what they can do with 'Joe Hill'."

"I'm guessing some sort of very emotive ballet," Jack said. "You know, you don't have to be the best at *everything*, Sarah."

"I would like to be the best at *something*, Jack. There are so many things I want to learn, and it takes forever," Sarah said. "I can't imagine learning to cook from a book."

"My mom is a fabulous cook, and she learned without recipes," Jack said, folding her into a hug. "You'll either master cooking or I'll be the happiest man on earth living on ham or peanut butter sandwiches. It doesn't matter. All I care about is having you with me." He yawned and stepped back from her. "The Gagnons exhausted me with their grace and perfection. Let's go to bed." He held his hand out to Sarah.

Her favorite time of the day was when she lay next to Jack in their bed. It felt more like home than anywhere she'd been. The smell of him and the feel of his weight beside her made Sarah feel like the most secure person in the world. They usually fell asleep with their arms around each other, but if not, she'd place two fingertips on his arm as he slept just to be touching him somehow.

Saturday morning, Jack followed Sarah into the kitchen and handed her the grocery bag he'd hidden. "I have to work until four today," he said. "I wanted you to have this." Sarah opened it and found a box of Pillsbury Fudge Brownies Mix.

"Why couldn't you have told me about this before?" she asked him, scowling. "It all comes in a box? I don't have to measure cocoa powder and spill it all over the counter? I don't have to scrape failure out of a pan over and over? Why did you do this to me, Jack?"

"Because you seemed to be having so much fun learning," Jack replied. She threw a dishtowel at him. Jack held his hands up in surrender and backed away. "The truth is, I didn't know. One of the guys at work told me his wife just uses a mix."

Sarah baked a perfect pan of brownies after Jack kissed her goodbye and went to the bus stop with six of them piled on a foil-covered paper plate. She was overjoyed at the idea of surprising Mr. Landry after a week of trying to bake had kept her from joining him for *General Hospital* every day. Over and over, she'd waited until she could deliver something she'd cooked especially for the old man, imagining the smile on his face.

Sarah wore a t-shirt the previous tenant had abandoned at the back of the bottom dresser drawer along with her favorite jeans. The t-shirt was white, banded in black at the neck and sleeves. It featured a mouse with enormous round ears and red shorts, his stick legs shoved into huge white shoes. His stance was jaunty and made Sarah smile.

She boarded the bus, asking the now-familiar driver, "How are you, Francois? You look handsome today."

Francois grinned over his shoulder at Sarah as she took her seat behind him. "Never better, *ma belle*." He closed the doors and whistled a tune Sarah didn't recognize as "Pretty Woman" the rest of the way to her stop. Francois noticed his passenger leaning forward to watch the turn signal flashing on the dashboard, as he'd witnessed Sarah do so many times.

Sarah grabbed the plate and hoisted her handbag onto her shoulder as the bus pulled up to her stop. "I'll see you here at three o'clock," she told him as she started to walk down the steps to exit. Sarah paused and impulsively removed one of the brownies, handing it to Francois. "I baked this brownie," she told him.

Francois took a big bite and chewed. "These are fantastic!" he said. "I am very impressed. Where did you get the recipe?"

Sarah smiled as she walked down to the doors. "I do not mean to poke your bubble, but it came from a mixture in a box," she told Francois, just before stepping to the ground. "See you later!"

Sarah waved through the closing doors as he yelled, "Thank you!"

Mr. Landry jumped up and ran around the counter, smoothing his hair back. "Sarah! What a nice surprise!" he called out. "You're a sight for sore eyes. What took you so long?" He stood with his hands in his pockets, grinning at her. "Sure miss you around here. Hell, I even miss Jack, but don't tell him."

Sarah laughed and set the plate on the counter. "Look what I brought you," she said, pulling the foil back with a flourish. "This is what took me so long. I wanted to bring you something I cooked."

"Well, I might have to eat every single one of those," Mr. Landry said. "You know what's utterly perfect with brownies? Cold milk. I have some in the refrigerator. I'll get us a couple of cups."

"Cow's milk?" Sarah said. "I don't think I want to try that."

"Sarah, dairy cows devote their entire lives to providing milk for people to have with brownies. It would be cruel to them to ignore it," Mr. Landry said. "I'll be right back."

As he went into his home, a lady approached the office. She had gray hair that curled around her face. Sarah noted she wore a skirt with a patchwork pattern and a soft shade of pink lipstick to match it.

She smiled brightly at Sarah and asked, "Have you seen Alex?"

Sarah looked at her blankly. "Oh, Mr. Landry. Yes, he'll be right back." Sarah walked behind the counter and took a seat.

"Do you work here?" the lady asked.

"Oh, no. I used to live here. Well, for a little bit. I became friends with Mr. Landry then. I came back to visit him today," Sarah said.

"I see," the lady said. She stuck out her hand for Sarah to shake. "I'm Valerie Campbell. Most people call me Val. I've been staying at the Wander Inn while my kitchen and bathroom are being remodeled. My house isn't far from here. I'm going home Monday, if they finally finish it. Construction of any kind takes forever, doesn't it? It was supposed to be done today. My husband was in that business, so I know. He passed away five years ago." Valerie frowned. "I'm sorry, I'm just babbling at you. I do that sometimes."

"I'm Sarah, and that's fine. So, have you gotten to know Mr. Landry very well since you've been here?" Sarah asked.

Val's eyes flickered to the door that led to Mr. Landry's home. "No, I only know his name is Alex because it's on the little sign in my room. He doesn't say much. I came over to ask if he might have a replacement light bulb for my room's lamp. I can come back later." She turned to leave.

"No, don't," Sarah said, her voice low. "He's going to be back here in a few seconds. Do you watch any soap operas, Val? Do you like to cook things?"

"Well, I'm not sure why you're asking me, but yes, *General Hospital* and sometimes *Coronation Street*," she answered as Mr. Landry opened the door, carefully carrying two small cups of milk in one hand and a clutch of paper napkins in the other.

"Oh, I love that show, too," Sarah said loudly. "Mr. Landry, Val watches *General Hospital*," she said, waving her arm at the lady. She noted Valerie Campbell was a good four inches shorter than Mr. Landry now that he stood near her; not as tiny as his wife, but still. Sarah accepted her cup of milk from him and sniffed it tentatively. She set it on the counter. "How about that? A fellow fan."

Mr. Landry nodded his head. "It's a good show, though a bit melodramatic sometimes."

"Well, it wouldn't be a soap opera if it weren't, would it?" Val said with a chuckle. "My favorite storyline was years ago. Were you watching back when that kid Angie was in the bad car accident? Her boyfriend was driving drunk. Anyway," she turned to look at Sarah,

"Angie's face was so horribly messed up in the accident, she was thinking about suicide. She told a courtroom full of people Eddie had had a few beers before getting behind the wheel. He didn't even go to jail but they broke up, obviously. Then she had a secret baby, Eddie's baby, and gave it up for adoption. And all of a sudden, her face got normal again and she and Eddie got back together."

Sarah's eyes were wide. "What happened next?" she asked.

Mr. Landry said, "They got married, and she must have told him about the baby, because they decided they wanted it back—"

"And they tried to kidnap the baby in Chicago!" Val clapped her hands.

Mr. Landry frowned and shook his head. "Did they steal that baby? Did they get to keep it? I can't remember."

Val smiled. "I can't either, but I recall they never went to jail for attempted kidnapping. I remember thinking the two of them never went to jail for anything, and wondered if the writers thought that would be too boring."

Sarah pushed the plate of brownies and a napkin toward Valerie Campbell. "Please try one of these," she said. "I baked the brownie this morning. I'll get us some more napkins from the kitchen and a glass of water for me. Would you like my cup of cold cow's milk, Val?" she asked.

Val offered Sarah a puzzled smile. "You know what? I love cow's milk. Especially with brownies. Thank you, Sarah," she said.

Mr. Landry's eyes darted after Sarah as she went toward the door. "She's a nice kid," he told Val. "And about as see-through as that door you just came in. Not exactly subtle." He chewed his brownie thoughtfully, sitting down opposite where Val stood at the counter.

"I can't argue with that," Val smiled at him. She looked down at the brownie in her hand. "My husband used to like these. I'm more of a vanilla person. I bake a beauty of an angel food cake."

"Is that right?" Mr. Landry said. "I've heard of those." He swept the crumbs from his brownie into one hand and dumped them into a wastebasket under the counter. He looked out the glass door of the office and waved his hand. "Is there a problem with your room?"

"Oh, it's just a little thing," Val said. "I was going to ask you for a light bulb. The one in my lamp went out." She shrugged. "If it's no bother."

Sarah came back in, handing extra napkins to each of them. "Do you like to cook, Val?" she asked.

"Sarah," Mr. Landry said. "Please stop grilling Val and trying to play matchmaker. I'm sure she's not looking for an old geezer like me." He turned his eyes to Val and hesitated. "You're a very nice-looking woman. I'm sure plenty of fellows would like to court you."

Val's eyes sparkled with a small laugh she held in. "I'm not being courted by anyone at the moment," she said.

"Well, I'm too old to court anyone, anyway," Mr. Landry said. He reached into a box under the counter and extracted a hundred watt light bulb, handing it to Val. "You know how to install this?" he asked.

She took it and said, "I'm pretty sure I'm capable." Val folded her napkin neatly and handed it and her empty cup to Sarah. "Thank you for the brownie, Sarah. You're a great baker." She rushed out of the small office before Sarah could reply.

Sarah immediately rounded on Mr. Landry. "Why did you do that?" she demanded. "Val is perfect for you."

"She's not interested in me, Sarah. I'm probably ten years older than she is. Pretty woman like that, a guy like me gets one of those per lifetime. I had mine," he said, folding his arms across his chest.

"She told me she wishes you'd take her to dinner," Sarah said. "She thinks you're handsome, too. Maybe you're allotted a second pretty woman. I bet Edie would want you to ask her to go to dinner in a nice restaurant."

"Well first of all, you made that up. She said no such things, Sarah, I can hear from my living room, you know. And second, that's not fair," Mr. Landry said. "Not fair at all, Sarah. Let's change the subject. Tell me all about your new apartment."

They sat talking until time for Sarah's bus. She stood and offered Mr. Landry a hug, whispering, "Val is interested in you. I can tell. Just think about it."

The old man rolled his eyes. "If she brings me a bouquet of roses and a box of chocolates, I'll relent and let her take me to the prom," he said. "You go have fun with Jack. Tell him I said hello. And Sarah, don't wait so long before visiting again. You don't need baked goods to bring me, just your company."

Sarah looked back and waved before she turned the corner to the bus stop. At three o'clock, Francois could see her waiting on the bench from a block away. He pulled the bus up and opened the doors, waiting for Sarah to board. When she didn't, Francois told his passengers he'd be right back. He went around the bus and saw no sign of Sarah anywhere. He shook his head and climbed back aboard, thinking his eyes must have been playing tricks on him.

By seven o'clock, Jack was pacing anxiously around his and Sarah's apartment. He walked to the pay phone nearby, cursing himself for not springing for the cost of having a line installed. Mr. Landry told him Sarah left around three that afternoon.

"Is there anywhere else she might have gone?" he asked Jack. "Maybe she went to the store. That's probably it."

Jack braced his hand against the wall of the phone booth as he looked around him. Sarah was nowhere in sight. "Maybe," he told Mr. Landry. "But she's been saying ever since I met her she'd have to go home. I wonder if someone took her against her will. It's not like her to leave without saying goodbye."

"No, it's not." Mr. Landry waited a few beats before asking, "You two didn't have an argument about something? Is she angry with you?"

"No, not at all," Jack said. "It's nothing like that."

"Well, call the police," Mr. Landry said. "And call me as soon as you know something."

Jack found the number to dial and the officers met him at the apartment, Arielle and Christophe Gagnon watching from a respectful distance as he let the police in the door. Of course, the Gagnons hadn't seen Sarah. No one had since she traveled to the Wander Inn. Later, Francois Roy would tell police he'd seen Sarah waiting at the bus stop alone. She'd been wearing a Mickey Mouse t-shirt and jeans. She was carrying nothing but her handbag, he was pretty sure. But he'd never witnessed anything like it: one second she was there and the next she'd vanished into thin air.

Jack sat on their bed with his head in his hands after the police left, promising to find Sarah. They would contact authorities in South Dakota. He didn't have much to offer them beyond her name and Pine Ridge Reservation. He told them they should get in touch with Kelly Adams in Cambridge, Massachusetts, just in case Sarah turned up there.

But he knew that wouldn't happen.

He'd searched the apartment for any note, any clue about where she might have gone. For a second time, Jack pulled out Sarah's dresser drawer, still full of the neat stack of shirts and jeans she'd stored there. He dumped it on the bed and spotted a shocking amount of cash, wondering for the first time if Sarah might've been involved in something illegal. Tangled in her white peasant blouse, he found a small piece of paper from his notepad, the one he kept at the end of the kitchen counter. His hand trembled as he lifted it to read, knowing its contents would shatter his heart.

The note said:

"I cannot explain why I have to leave you, Jack. I would give anything if it were not true. If you've found this note, it likely means I've disappeared. Please do not worry about me. I promise you I am fine and there is no way you can find me. The police can't help. No one in South Dakota will know where I am. I suspect you already know that, somehow.

I've never loved anyone the way I love you, Jack Warren, and I never will.

I will still be with you, no matter what. I will be in every raindrop that falls, every song you listen to, every beat of your beautiful heart.

The money is meaningless to me. Take and use it for whatever you'd like, except to make a woman happy.

I am yours always, anywhere and anywhen.

Sarah

26

The Return
Unity SE35.86
JANUARY 6, 2102

She blinked her eyes open into very bright lights overhead, sensing someone was nearby. A male voice said, "Baezy?" and she took a moment to answer.

"Sorry," she said. "I haven't been called by that name in weeks." Baezy swallowed hard and fought the urge to cry, taking in the sterile white walls around her and TIP employee whose face appeared above hers. She was prone on a table, she realized, naked with a blanket of some sort over her. *Sarah*, she thought. Then: *Jack. He's finding out I'm gone…*

"Baezy?" the man said again. He was about her age and thus shared her skin tone, as well as a similar nose and eyes. "My name is Hodroit," he said. "You've only been back for a short while. I'll take you to your mother after your medical exam is complete." Baezy noticed lights running along the side of the table now; they were blue, green, and red with an occasional yellow flash. A memory surfaced: an MET, medical examination table. Of course they'd do that when she arrived. Baezy struggled to swallow; her mouth was dry and a wave of nausea swept over her.

"May I please have a sip of water?" she asked Hodroit.

Hodroit took a seat beside her, shaking his head. "Not until the examination is complete. What is the last thing you remember in 1969?" he asked, glancing at the side of the table and then the wall, which seemed to be streaming the colored lines of light to another location.

Baezy watched the flow of colors and then turned to blink at him. "I was waiting for a thing called a bus to arrive for my transportation," she said, her voice raspy. "Did my travel pouch accompany me on my return?"

"It's here," Hodroit answered, holding it up for her to see. "They've discarded the Reese Cups, whatever those are. You should be able to keep the rest of the things in the pouch. We'll be finished here in a few seconds and I'll get you a drink and something to eat." He helped her to sit up and handed Baezy a small orb of water, which she accepted gratefully. That was followed by a NourishCube. It tasted, amazingly, like peanut butter. She ate it and looked at him expectantly, as though he might have another.

"You'll feel full soon," Hodroit told her. "Give it time to take effect."

He watched her carefully, glancing at the wall again a few times. "You will be allowed a few minutes with your mother," Hodroit continued. "Then you'll be taken straight to Council headquarters. They have questions for you," Hodroit shook his head slightly and Baezy felt her stomach churn as she rose to her feet, trying to clutch the blanket around her. Hodroit handed her a small bundle that looked like one of Daniel's jumpsuits. Baezy noticed it was very large and bright red. "Put this on," he instructed. "I'll come back to get you soon."

She emerged from the room along with Hodroit into a wide corridor. A few TIP employees in the distance directed stares and frowns at Baezy when they spotted her, whispering to each other.

Baezy ran her hands along the sides of the ugly jumpsuit, embarrassed. She needed to get to her homepod and change.

A group of important-looking people approached. She recognized the white-haired man in front as her mother's friend, Dr. Richards, one of the senior leaders of TIP. On his right stalked a large male lion that snarled at Baezy as Dr. Richards walked by, the AI manifestation of his anger. The man pointedly refused to make eye contact with her. At that moment, she realized she might be in far more trouble than she'd anticipated.

Hodroit turned and led her down a smaller hallway, its walls lined with three-dimensional portraits of Unity's heroes and leaders. Her mother's likeness was displayed near the door to the room where Anantha waited.

Baezy rushed into her arms. Anantha held her close and said, "I was terrified when you didn't appear that night, Baezy. I knew you'd have come home for your birthday celebration if you could have, so I was frantic. I didn't know if you were lost in time, injured, or even worse. These Time Insertion Protocol people wouldn't tell me anything, except they were 'actively searching' for you after the loss of your return beacon signal and that they'd locate and bring you home safely. As each day passed, they said less and less. Carl Richards even refused to see me after a week went by. I have been sick with worry. What happened to you? Were you injured? They told me you are fine." She paused and held Baezy at arms' length, running her eyes up and down her, taking in the red jumpsuit.

"I am, Mom, I had a medical examination right before I came in here," Baezy said. She made a decision to let Anantha continue talking before saying much.

Anantha's eyes grew wide as she went on, "I was so worried I'd sent you off into danger, that arranging this trip was the biggest mistake of my life. I kept asking them how many NCs you'd need to survive, what would happen if you ate the food available to you in 1969, whether medical facilities would have been capable of diagnosing and treating you if you became ill," her voice cracked, "whether you were stuck in some kind of in-between, why they couldn't locate you if you were still there. They had no answers, other than admitting you had taken only three days of nutrition with you, but they said you'd be able to eat and drink the things humans consumed in that time." Anantha paused to breathe.

"That is true," Baezy said, nodding her head. She noticed for the first time a robot stood feet behind her mother, presumably waiting to escort her to the Council. It had a female form designed to look like an AI assistant/companion but much more solid-looking. The bot was wearing all-white, a long tunic over ankle-length pants, and standing impossibly still. "I am all right, Mom, I promise," Baezy began. "I'll tell you everything. First, they want to interview me—"

Anantha interrupted, "I could tell they didn't know what they were talking about. They kept saying you'd be back 'soon'. 'Soon' turned out to be over three *weeks*. I don't ever want to let you out of my sight again. I don't know how TIP got this so wrong. People are going to lose their jobs over it." Her relief at seeing Baezy morphed into anger. "No one should have to deal with this incompetence ever again." Anantha turned toward the robot and loudly announced, "Let me repeat that for you, bot. I don't care who's listening. Time Insertion Protocol is going to be in big trouble. Even Dr. Carl Richards."

Baezy bit her lip. "They did the best they could, Mom. We all knew this TIP program was new and there had been a few glitches. I never doubted I'd be returned to you safely at some point. And I'm *fine*. There's a lot to tell you, but first the Council wants to see me and I don't think they're willing to wait. I'm so sorry. I know you were worried—"

"The Council will investigate what happened, and they'll report to me," Anantha interrupted. "In my day, we didn't launch anything until it was fully tested. Now you have TIP assuring everyone they know what they're doing, encouraging time travel like it's as simple as a transpod delivery, when they clearly aren't ready. Artificial intelligence needs sound human judgement to guide and discern. We've had years of people displaying their embarrassing emotions in the form of trembling fawns and hissing snakes thanks to incompetence." Mom's mouth formed a flat smirking line. "But the point is, I dealt in reality and *facts*."

"You sound like your great-great grandmother," Baezy said with a sigh.

Anantha brightened at the mention of Kelly. "I want to hear everything about her," she said. "And Woodstock, too. But I never would have arranged this birthday gift if I'd known there was danger of them losing you, Baezy," Anantha said. "I apologize for their messing it all up."

Baezy conjured a smile and placed her hand on Anantha's arm, saying, "Mom, it was a wonderful trip. Joan Baez was as amazing as you and I knew she'd be. Her voice was astonishing. Seeing the performances in person brought more joy than I can express. I danced in the rain to Sly and the Family Stone! Woodstock was…well, it was inspiring to witness half a million people doing their best to make each other comfortable despite all the rain and mud, without enough food to go around. Of course, I hadn't expected to have to worry about food—"

"I *told* you you'd need that money," her mother interrupted, anxiety written all over her face.

"No, I didn't need money for that," Baezy told her. "Kelly's group brought plenty of…nutrition. And the towns, the neighbors, the people around the festival all joined together and sent food items to share. The whole thing was a great example of how people took care of each other back then."

Anantha looked thoughtful. "Well, history shows the festival began a fresh era of philanthropy," she said. "The hippies were sort of the architects of a new wave of public kindness, opening charities and social service organizations after Woodstock."

Baezy was relieved to find her mother reciting facts rather than worrying about where she'd been for weeks. "That's true," she replied, embracing her mother in a brief hug. "There's so much to tell you, Mom. This experience changed me, made me feel things I've never felt before." Baezy paused to consider her next words. "Everything that happened to me, happened for a reason. I know that now. I apologize for all the time you spent worrying. I'm fine, and I'm forever grateful."

"Then why are there tears in your eyes, Baezy? You still haven't said where you've *been*. Were you stuck at the festival site? Did Kelly stay with you? Did your beacon malfunction?" Anantha asked, reaching to take her daughter's hand in both of hers.

The bot escort walked to Baezy's side. "Time to go now," she announced in a soft monotone. Her voice sounded perfectly human.

"I am talking to my daughter," Anantha said, angered by the interruption. "You will wait until I have finished. I have had to wait weeks for my daughter's return because this place is completely inept. What is your name and identification?"

"My name is Betula," the bot replied. "My employer is Time Insertion Protocol. I will report your dissatisfaction to the appropriate departments and make sure it is noted in order to improve future experiences for others. Your feedback is valuable to us. We apologize for your inconvenience, Dr. Smith, and hope you will consider using TIP again in the future."

Anantha rolled her eyes and then watched in horror as the bot extended a thin circle of bright pink plastic around her daughter's wrist. Betula pulled Baezy's hand away from Anantha's grasp and led her from the room.

"How *dare* you treat my daughter like a prisoner!" Anantha screamed at the closing door. "Smeevackers! She's done nothing wrong!" She rushed to follow Baezy and Betula out and down the corridor as far as she could until she encountered a door that wouldn't open.

Anantha slid her back down the wall and sat on the floor, wondering what her daughter could have done to merit this treatment. It was TIP that should be interviewed by the Council, not Baezy. She sat for a few minutes, thinking, then rose and stalked toward the visitors' room, where she'd waited for news every day for weeks. She would demand to speak to Carl Richards. Again.

Baezy was ushered into another sterile white chamber, this one with a glowing green band running horizontally around the middle of its walls. Betula placed her in a chair about ten feet in front of a table where two women and an older man were seated. She retracted the pink band and left the room.

The Council members were dressed in all white, just like the table and chairs and everything in the place. Baezy realized the second woman was an AI female, probably the equivalent of her Faisa. The man looked to be at least a hundred years old; he had old-fashioned bright purple hair with a matching goatee and deep wrinkles on his forehead and neck. Baezy noticed a white owl perched in the corner of the room, likely a manifestation of the man's feeling particularly wise. The bird preened its feathers as the Council silently regarded her.

Baezy shifted in her chair and felt for the bracelet in her travel pouch. She rubbed the smooth amber bead between her fingers, willing herself to be silent and hold the gazes of the people in front of her. She took a deep breath and waited for their questions.

The woman in the center smoothed her long brown hair behind her ears and began. "Morning greetings. I am Justice Bloom and this is Datala, my assistant." She waved her hand at the AI female and continued, "Our other Council member present is Justice Thomas." The man nodded and shifted in his seat as he regarded Baezy without expression. She wondered at the things he had seen since the year 2000, a stunning amount of technological progress. He'd been born when people drove automobiles and consumed animals, when natural weather caused hurricanes, when people had families with ten children. She couldn't help but stare.

Justice Bloom cleared her throat and said, "We have a number of things to discuss, Baezy. TIP has provided us updates on your activities over the last three weeks."

Baezy sat up straight and tried to look calm. "Please begin," she said.

"First of all, we understand your insertion into 1969 was botched, and that you lost your NCs. Is that correct?" Justice Bloom asked.

"Yes. I materialized in the water, in a pond with a number of people who were swimming and bathing. My NCs floated away. I was left with only a few. Some of them were actually eaten by men and women in the water with me," Baezy replied.

Justice Bloom's eyebrows shot up and she paused for a moment to glance at Justice Thomas. "I see. So, you were forced to go without your NCs for much of the festival. We understand that, as well as the impact it had on you physically, mentally, and emotionally. Did you contract any illness while you were there?"

"No, I didn't," Baezy replied. "I felt fine. Better than ever, actually."

That caused more surprised glances at the table. Justice Bloom continued, "What happened to your location beacon, Baezy? Was it lost in the water with the NCs as well?"

Baezy blinked at her. "Yes, it was. It fell out of my travel pouch when I landed in the pond, which wasn't my fault." The green line running around the room glowed red as soon as she said the words. She closed her eyes and sighed. "I'm sorry, that's not true. I threw it into Filippini Pond, at the site of the festival, on Sunday, August 17, 1969. I did that deliberately, with the knowledge I could delay my return."

Justice Thomas leaned forward and spoke for the first time, his voice booming much deeper than she'd anticipated. "Did you travel to 1969 to intercede in Jack Warren's timeline, Baezy?"

Her eyes snapped open in surprise. "Of course not. No. I traveled there to meet my M5, Kelly Adams, and enjoy the music festival. I've heard about Woodstock my entire life, and my ancestor, too. I wanted to see Joan Baez. I'm named after her because Kelly loved her so much. I wanted to hear the music for myself, to see what it was like to witness it. I wanted to wear clothes from the 1960s, like you all did the year I was born. That's why my mother arranged this TIP gift for me. I had no plans to interfere in Jack Warren's future. I promise, I didn't."

"But you did interfere," Justice Thomas replied. "We would like to know why. Your deliberate delay of your return has caused great concern, but worse, your actions have altered the lives of more than simply Jack Warren. We're still trying to determine how many. We feel sure you were aware he was to go to Vietnam in June of 1970." He and Justice Bloom stared at her.

Baezy took a deep breath, trying to keep emotions from showing. "Yes, I was aware he was to go to war in 1970. I also knew he died there soon after." Baezy struggled to control her voice.

"Jack Warren died within six weeks of his arrival in Vietnam, of injuries sustained when his armored personnel carrier ran over a land mine," the AI assistant Datala spoke for the first time. The two justices nodded.

"I knew," Baezy choked out. "But I wasn't going to stop it." The green line glowed steady on the wall.

"And what changed that, Baezy? Why did you choose to violate every rule you were given?" Justice Bloom asked.

"I think you know the answer to that question," she said, palming tears from her face. "I fell in love with Jack Warren," Baezy sobbed the words out. "I aided his escape to Canada so he wouldn't lose his life in the next year. I couldn't let that happen."

Justice Bloom sat back in her chair, her gaze unblinking. Justice Thomas crossed his arms. "You know," he said, "there are consequences from your interference and *for* your interference. We haven't yet determined whether Jack Warren's absence caused anyone to be injured or killed. But the fact remains you caused it, and impacted lives. You were warned against this multiple times before your TIP departure." He held Baezy's eyes, which still streamed tears. "We bear a certain amount of responsibility for your emotional involvement, because TIP effected the loss of your NourishCubes, which would have prevented that. But your actions are your own, no matter what, Baezy."

Justice Bloom took over, adding, "And you have forfeited your Reproduction Cycle, the joy of meeting your selected mate, falling in love, and beginning new lives together. That was scheduled for two years from now, but it can no longer happen for you."

It took Baezy a moment to consider Justice Bloom's meaning. The RC had been the furthest thing from her mind. She had already fallen in love. She didn't want anyone except Jack, but had assumed her future would eventually include a companion and follow the plan everyone else's did after her return to Unity.

"Why?" she asked. "That's a harsh punishment for what I've done. It isn't fair—"

Justice Bloom raised her eyebrows and interrupted. "It's not a punishment, it's simply a fact. Even if you choose not to keep your baby, you've already ruined your chances at a successful RC. I think you understand why, Baezy."

Baezy looked at the hands folded in her lap, trying to process the magnitude of the trouble she was in. Justice Bloom's words didn't register for a few seconds. She frowned and said, "My baby? Are you telling me I'm pregnant?"

Justice Bloom nodded. "This is also a byproduct of your lack of NourishCubes. And your lack of discretion, judgement, and restraint." Justice Thomas shook his head and left the room without another word, waving the door open with a whoosh. The white owl flew along close behind him.

Baezy sat speechless for a moment, staring at Justice Bloom as she continued to berate her.

"Your actions are unprecedented and will lead to new measures and safeguards for Time Insertion Protocol, if they're allowed to continue these 'trips' at all. You may have cost many others the opportunity to participate. There's great shame in what you've done, Baezy. You've not only interfered with lives in the past and likely altered its future in ways we don't yet know, you've returned carrying a child. He will not be one of us. He will look different. He will not be as evolved or advanced. The only positive aspect of this is an opportunity for geneticists to study the boy," she said. "You and he will live apart from others. You will be attended by a geneticist and a physician to deliver your child. But don't expect anything like the life you would have had if you'd returned as you were supposed to, instead of the choice you made."

Baezy's hands automatically went to her belly. "I'm having a son. Jack's son," she muttered, blinking away fresh tears.

"Baezy, this isn't a cause for happiness," Justice Bloom said. "Your life is going to be difficult and your child will suffer rejection in our society. To use a hateful word from long ago, he will be a freak. That's a punishment in itself." She hesitated and glanced at her assistant, Datala. "In addition, you are sentenced to confinement in your homepod for a period of one full year. Your mother may return for the birth of her grandchild and stay for one week, but otherwise you will be completely isolated. Do you understand? No teleportation, no communication. No interaction with anyone but your geneticist and physician. Your AI companion is being reprogrammed to act as a guard. We'll make arrangements for indoor exercise."

She drew a deep breath and looked at Datala again, who sat motionless and recorded every word, no doubt. "After your one-year sentence, you and the child will be moved to the complex at Big Spring, away from the people you've known. Datala and I have determined that will be best for the boy and convenient for our geneticists' studies and tests." Justice Bloom's brows knitted together as she added, "The consequences would be far worse were it not for your mother's celebrated status as a person who has contributed great advancements to our technology. Do you have any questions?"

"No," Baezy whispered. "Thank you, Justice Bloom." The justice nodded as she and Datala rose and left the room. The bot escort, Betula, re-appeared at Baezy's side to take her home. Her mind raced through what had just happened, and what was coming next.

She stood to accompany the bot, who didn't bother placing a ring around Baezy's wrist. Baezy felt in her handbag and removed her silver and amber bracelet, clasping it on instead. She drew a shaky breath, thinking how her mother would be stunned. Shocked. Ashamed. Unplanned pregnancy was completely unheard of in their time. She yearned to tell Anantha her side of the story, but it would be months before she had the opportunity. Nine long months. Instead, her mother was probably seated in an office at TIP, hearing about her pregnancy and every other thing Baezy had done from Carl Richards.

A wave of nausea washed over her as she climbed into the transpod. Everything suddenly felt and smelled strange in this place, the only home she'd known until less than a month ago. Baezy turned the last several minutes over and over in her mind as the scenery flew by. The bot escort sitting next to her materialized a small piece of cloth, handing it to her to dab her eyes.

She wouldn't get to tell her friends anything; she wouldn't even get to *see* Daniel, Coifa, and Juleen, likely never again if Unity was determined to keep them separated. They'd no doubt hear she was being locked away for violating TIP rules and shake their heads at the park for months. She wondered how much they'd really miss her. Even Faisa would never be her friend and roommate again, unless the Council restored her programming after the one-year sentence.

Baezy closed her eyes and laid her head back on the seat. How had everything in her world fallen apart so quickly? She tried not to think of how Jack was hurting, how he'd feel when he found her note. She tried not to think how she missed both the life she'd had with him, and the life she'd thought she'd return to in Unity. Everything was gone, destroyed. Everything but one.

A baby. She was going to have a baby. Jack's son. And that was all that mattered now.

27

September 1969

OTTAWA, CANADA

Jack heard the banging on his front door and pulled the pillow over his head, rolling to his side and facing the wall, where "Kelly's Cornfield" greeted his tired eyes. It had been over a week since Sarah disappeared. Her note was correct: the police had been no help at all, and if they were at his door, they were only delivering sympathetic looks and empty promises. He tugged the pillow tighter against his ears.

Whoever it was would not stop pounding their fists. Jack sighed and slid his jeans on, running a hand through his hair. He had three days of stubble on his face and couldn't remember the last time he'd brushed his teeth. Whoever waited at the door deserved what they got for interrupting his solitude.

He swung it open to reveal a very angry Mr. Landry standing on the tiny patch of cement that served as his front porch. "Damn it, boy," Alex Landry said, "it's two o'clock on a Monday afternoon. Why the hell aren't you at work? Wally called me this morning. He's ready to fire you." He ran his eyes up and down Jack, shaking his head. "You need a shower, son."

Jack walked away and collapsed into the brown sofa, wincing slightly. "I told them on Friday I might not be in today," he said. "It's been more than a week of waiting to hear something, *anything* solid from the police. It's not a secret to anyone at work, Mr. Landry. They've seen the police come and go from my office twice. They know I'm having a hard time, and that's why I left after lunch on Friday. I didn't have anything scheduled that afternoon." Jack heaved a heavy sigh. "Look, I can't sit and talk to customers about their finances right now and act like everything is normal. The people at the dealership know that. I can't believe Mr. Armstrong sent you over here." He leaned back and closed his eyes.

Mr. Landry regarded the seven empty beer bottles on the counter and the ashtray on the kitchen windowsill containing what looked like a marijuana cigarette butt. "He didn't send me, I'm here because you've embarrassed me, Jack. Get the hell up. I'm not going to let you do this to Wally just because you feel sorry for yourself. Sarah's not the first woman to leave a man. Maybe she had a good reason to get away from you. If she did, you'd better hope I never find out about it."

Jack didn't open his eyes to see whatever threatening gesture Mr. Landry might be making. "You think I'd ever have harmed her, done *anything* to risk losing her? I love Sarah. You *know* that, old man," he said. Jack's jaw clenched and he swallowed hard. "I would never have hurt her. Even the police know that. Everyone they've talked to has told them how happy we were. And I was at the dealership when she disappeared from the bus stop. You have to believe I'd have done anything in this world to protect Sarah."

Mr. Landry sat next to Jack, reaching a hand out to push on the springs under the cushion around him and frowning. "Then maybe you can tell me why she'd disappear into thin air, Jack. Maybe you can tell me *how*."

Jack sighed. "I told the police, and I told you. She's always said she had to go home, from the time I met her at Woodstock. She left me a note saying we wouldn't be able to find her. I've shown it to the police, I've shown it to you. I've re-read it a hundred times, and it explains nothing. Sarah wouldn't have left me if she hadn't had to, I can tell you that. Whatever made her go is a mystery to me, and always will be."

Mr. Landry folded his arms over his chest. "What about the money she left, Jack? You didn't tell me nearly enough about that."

Jack sighed. "She told me her mother had given her some money, and I thought she'd maybe have two or three hundred sitting around for bus fare home, for any emergencies. But there was this big roll of bills next to her note, almost two thousand in American cash. I gave it to the police when I showed them everything the next day, like I've told you. I didn't want them to think I had any motive to get my hands on it. I told them to keep all that money in evidence or whatever, for when Sarah returns. They made a big show of putting it in a sealed envelope. I signed for it."

Mr. Landry grunted in apparent approval.

"I keep waiting," Jack opened his bloodshot eyes and looked at Mr. Landry, "for her to come home. I see someone who looks like her everywhere I go. I rushed up to some girl wearing a white t-shirt and jeans standing at the bus stop last Thursday and put my hand on her shoulder. She jumped, then turned around and glared at me. All I could do was apologize as she hurried away. She didn't even wait for the bus." He leaned his head back again, closing his eyes and pinching his nose. "Every day she doesn't come back, something in me dies a little bit more."

Mr. Landry stared at him. "Quit being so damn dramatic, Jack." He swung his head back and forth. "You either get to Armstrong Volvo at eight o'clock tomorrow morning, or you get your ass on a bus back to America."

Jack sprang forward, his eyes wide. "I can't do that! They'll be waiting to arrest me for draft evasion as soon as I step on U.S. soil. I've applied for Canadian citizenship, Mr. Landry. I can't go home now." He rubbed his forehead with his palms. "And I haven't given up hope she'll come back here, either," he added, his voice trailing off softly.

"Then I suggest," Mr. Landry said, "you shave and shower and act like a grown man. This isn't the movies or some soap opera, Jack. If Sarah ever does come back, you sure don't want her to find you like *this*." He rose from the sofa and groaned. "And do something about this old couch, it's not fit for a human to sit on. Your landlord won't mind if you replace it with a nicer one." Mr. Landry walked to the door and opened it, allowing an unwelcome amount of light to fall on Jack. "I'm telling Wally you'll be there tomorrow morning at eight sharp, and you will." He closed the door with a bang and Jack lowered his aching head into his hands.

Jack did his best to act like he was all right at Armstrong Volvo the next day, an attempt to impersonate a normal human. He smiled at customers, he opened doors for them and offered one of the wrapped candies on his desk to anyone seated across from him. He talked to the guys he worked with about the upcoming hockey season (which he didn't really understand) and the movie *True Grit* (Jack hadn't seen it, but the guys seemed to think he was fluent in all things Old West). He arranged an auto loan for a young couple who walked into his office hand-in-hand, the wife with a cooing baby perched on her hip.

He tried not to be jealous of their happiness. He tried not to be exhausted by being nice. He tried not to notice the frowning glances directed his way when his co-workers thought he wasn't looking.

On Thursday, two of the women in the office staff, Celine and Mary, brought Jack a foil-covered paper plate. "We're so sorry about your fiancée's disappearance," Celine told him, placing the plate on his desk.

He didn't bother to correct her. Jack cleared his throat. "This is very nice of you. Thank you," he said.

"Umm, this is my mother's recipe, maple sugar cookies," Celine went on, "and they always cheer me up." She stepped back and lingered awkwardly in the doorway, pulling her knee-length pencil skirt down and smoothing it as Mary nodded and offered Jack a frozen smile.

Mary stood next to her friend, silent until Celine bumped her arm. "Anyway, we wanted to say we're sorry and we hope they find her safe and sound," Mary offered. Jack noted she was younger than most of the women in the office; she wore a slightly shorter skirt than Celine, patterned in bright flowers. Her hair was pale blonde, cut into a long, swingy bob that almost reached her shoulders.

"I hope so, too," Jack muttered, reaching for a meaningless piece of paper on his desk. "Thank you again. I'd better get back to work." The women each offered a small wave and moved away. Jack wondered what rumors had spread about Sarah, how much speculation there had been at the dealership about her sudden disappearance. Some of his colleagues had probably assumed he was an axe murderer and they awaited his arrest any day now. At least it seemed he had the sympathy of the women in the office, he thought, taking a cookie and biting into it. It tasted better than anything he'd had in a long time. Jack finished half the plate, forgetting Sarah was gone for about five minutes. Then a wave of sadness washed over him again, and he closed and locked the door of his small office. He extinguished the bright overhead light and leaned over to place his head on the desk, hands clasped behind his neck.

Two weeks later, a late-afternoon shower moved in just before time for Jack to leave the dealership. Customers hurried into the showroom with their salesmen, who offered tea or coffee and a comfortable place to sit until the rain abated. The herd of office women emerged to exit along with Jack from the service department door out back.

Mary held a wide umbrella, its bright yellow matching the flowers on her short-sleeved sweater. "Would you like to share, Jack?" she asked. "I can walk you to the bus stop."

He shrugged and held his hands up to catch the drops as they fell. "No thanks," he said. "I like the rain." He turned and walked away, Mary shaking her head behind him.

The following Friday morning, Mr. Armstrong summoned Jack to his office. "I know you've been through a lot, Jack," he began. "And I appreciate your showing up and giving us your best every day. You're doing the job exactly as I'd hoped you would." He smiled and nodded at Jack, picking up the cigar in his ashtray. "The customers like you. My employees like you, too."

"Thank you, sir," Jack relaxed a little and sat back in the armchair that faced Mr. Armstrong's massive oak desk.

Mr. Armstrong cocked his head to one side as he puffed the cigar. "Do the police have any new leads? Any idea where Sarah has gone?"

Jack shook his head, his stomach twisting. "No. Everything they've investigated has led nowhere."

"Well, don't lose hope, son." Mr. Armstrong stubbed his cigar out. "The wife made me promise to cut back on these," he told Jack with a frown. "The reason I called you up here is to offer you an opportunity, Jack. There's a '62 Pontiac Acadian a lady traded in yesterday, a nice car in practically showroom condition. Before it goes on the lot, I'd like to offer it to you for the wholesale price. No profit at all." He leaned forward and clasped his hands on the desk. "I know you're tired of riding that bus every day. You work in an automobile dealership. You should be driving to work, Jack."

Jack swallowed. "I appreciate that very much, sir. If you don't mind, though, I would like to continue to save my money and not go into debt right now. And honestly, you're already renting your apartment to me for far less than I'd pay elsewhere. That's more than enough, Mr. Armstrong." He shifted in his seat, nervous. "The truth is, I've grown used to riding the bus every day. I don't mind."

Mr. Armstrong raised his brows. "I can't argue with a young man who wants to save his money. If that's your choice, I respect it. But Jack," he said, "let me know if you change your mind. We'll find something for you."

Jack stood and shook Mr. Armstrong's hand. He crossed the room before turning to his boss and adding, "You've been very kind to me, sir. I appreciate it."

Mr. Armstrong nodded as he picked up his cigar. "Let me know if you need anything," he said.

Jack walked down the stairs thinking about the money he'd been saving every week. The one indulgence he'd decided to allow himself was a new album by a Woodstock artist each Friday. Sarah's Sly and the Family Stone album still conjured images of her dancing to "I Want to Take You Higher". He could hear her yelling "catch me!" with a huge smile on her face. He could see her hoisted above his head, feel her sliding down the front of his body, the tentative kiss they'd shared. That was a treasure, but he also wanted to listen to other music they'd heard there. Last week he'd picked up Santana's debut and played it over and over. Today he was going to the record shop for Joan Baez, just to close his eyes and see Sarah standing in the rain, swaying and singing along.

"Do you have 'Joe Hill', or any of the songs Joan Baez sang at Woodstock?" he asked the clerk. The kid was probably eighteen, Jack thought. He had shoulder-length curly hair and a long, narrow face. His faded brown t-shirt featured a Led Zeppelin logo.

"Sorry, man, that probably won't be out until next year," he replied, ducking beneath the counter. He stood with a nod of his head and consulted a binder full of information. "Looks like January," he said, "but you might like this." He walked around to lead Jack to the "C" bin. "This band was at Woodstock," the kid told Jack.

He placed a cellophane-wrapped album in Jack's hands, *Green River* by Creedence Clearwater Revival. Jack flipped it over to look through the track listings and grinned.

"This will be perfect," he said. "They played several of these songs."

The kid started walking back to the cash register. "Yeah, I read they did," he said over his shoulder. "Can you imagine what that was like, actually *being* there?"

Jack said, "Yeah, must've been a far out time." He paid the clerk and headed to catch his bus home.

A letter from Kelly waited in Jack's mailbox, almost-translucent paper in an airmail envelope with red and blue stripes around its edges. He went to put his new album on and opened the letter at the dinette table as the opening guitar chords of *Green River* rioted.

"Dear Jack,

I was stunned last week when the local police visited me at work, asking if I'd seen Sarah Sandoval. I haven't, and I don't expect to. Laura, whose grumpiness grows in proportion with her swelling belly, scowled and blurted to them I'm the last person Sarah would reach out to, ever.

I'm sorry about her leaving you so suddenly. The way they described it, she took off from a bus stop in Ottawa, just disappeared. That made no sense to me or Laura, either, and I'd be lying if I said we didn't wonder about it. Whatever prompted Sarah to go is between the two of you, of course. I know it's none of our business.

But Jack, Sarah is not like you and me or anyone I know, for that matter. Whatever her background is, I think it left her with a lack of true feeling for others. She's all wild imagination, smart, brilliant, even. But other than that, she's not what she seems. I was afraid all along she would hurt you someday, honestly, but there would have been no telling you that when you were following her around like Pepe Le Pew at Woodstock.

When you told me she'd gone with you to Canada, I worried, but you said you were only friends. It was probably ridiculous to believe that, knowing you. Your next letter clearly hinted there was more between you and Sarah.

Jack, I hope you'll move on and meet someone who's right for you instead of a strange girl full of secrets. Laura and I both think you deserve and will find better. Forget Sarah ever came into our lives like a dripping seventeenth-century witch emerging after remaining afloat in a swimming trial. (Laura's words.)

Speaking of advice, I'm trying to work less and get out more, like you said. So far, that's meant faculty parties where Dr. Lawton parades me around like a show dog in an arena. I jump through hoops and run around sticks, he gets more funding.

Congratulations, by the way, on your job at the Volvo dealership. I know you'll do well and it's a good way to make money until you get back in a classroom. That's where you belong. I still hope you'll be teaching in Boston again someday.

I am sorry for all you must be going through because of her. Take care of yourself, Jack. Everyone says hi except Eric, who says *be cool man far out right on, Jack,* or some ridiculous shit like that. (He stopped by with Rodney to pick up Laura as I was writing this.) We miss you.

I probably do more than anyone.

> Love,
> Kelly"

28

Unity SE35.86

JUNE 5, 2102

That is not allowed was Faisa's constant refrain, a chant that echoed in Baezy's ears for the first few months she was confined to her homepod, one that carried into her dreams at night.

Her décor had been rendered all-white. The walls were devoid of any ornamentation. Baezy found herself staring at the blankness and trying to conjure the Kelly's Cornfield painting she left on the bedroom wall in Ottawa. Even her window, which used to feature whatever view she asked Faisa to generate, was a field of sterile white.

Her mantra was: they can control me, but not my thoughts.

She sat alone in a corner chair and gathered them around her like a blanket, closing her eyes and sighing so deeply and often that Faisa continually monitored her oxygenation levels. Baezy wondered if the Council realized they'd made her experiences in 1969 her refuge, her escape, her shelter from the punishment they'd devised for her. If they ever found out, they'd find a way to take them away.

Jack tugging her body close to his under a blanket hood he improvised in the Woodstock rain. Telling him theirs was the kiss of her lifetime, watching his soft smile in reply.

The amber bead of her bracelet, and the way it looked beneath the tiny sparkling white lights of the Bindy Bazaar when he gave it to her. Walking through the dense forest with him, beaming her happiness at everyone who passed by.

Jack holding her aloft and sliding her slowly down against his body as Sly Stone sang he wanted to take her higher. She'd never been so high in her life as in that moment.

The way they looked, framed together in her daisy mirror with Filippini Pond in the background. The moment she'd changed both their lives, the momentary wrench in her stomach from the knowledge there would be consequences. She'd do it again, exactly the same, to save him.

Dancing in his arms in a tiny Ottawa bar, knowing she would join her body fully with his as soon as they got to Jack's room. The entire universe reduced to her and Jack when they made love. Lying next to him afterward and reaching out to touch his arm as he slept, because she needed to be connected to him.

She'd do all of it again.

Chocolate. Cake. Pizza. Music. Love.

Baezy was lost in memories constantly, unless Faisa interrupted her. That happened far too often.

It seemed everything external that could possibly provide pleasure was denied. Her traditional method of reading fell under *that is not allowed.* Instead, Faisa had procured an antique book made of musty-smelling paper, a heavy object Baezy found awkward to position comfortably. Baezy read *The Hunchback of Notre Dame* three times and begged Faisa to find another book. Faisa said no. She asked to have her old laptop back, the one she'd used to write to Kelly before she left. *That is not allowed.*

Music was not allowed. Learning modules were not allowed. Any kind of entertainment was not allowed. Spending time in her sleep chamber for longer than nine hours was not allowed. Faisa woke Baezy every morning with a NourishCube and escorted her to the exercise area, where Baezy was expected to expend two hours of effort every day. She longed to stretch out and lay her body down the way she had during her visit to 1969. It made much more sense to her now than a vertical sleeping position. The closest she got to reclining daily was during a weight-resistance exercise Faisa generated. She tried staying on the floor once or twice, but she was never allowed to rest there.

The physician visits were another opportunity to recline. Her homepod had been provided a medical examination table, a smaller version of the one at TIP headquarters. Faisa kept it folded and out of the way until a visit was due.

The physician, Dr. Tessen, found Baezy unwilling to talk the first few times she came. Every time she made eye contact, Baezy quickly looked away, certain the doctor was passing judgement on her. She felt ashamed and waited in silence as Dr. Tessen evaluated her through mostly cursory examinations. The table revealed everything as well as an internal exam might have, so Baezy was spared that indignity. Baezy watched the colored lights swirl and sneaked an occasional peek at Dr. Tessen's face, looking for any kind of reaction. At the conclusion of each visit, the doctor would invariably report all was well with both Baezy and her baby.

Their weekly routine became so rote, it surprised Baezy today when Dr. Tessen glanced toward Faisa in the corner of the room and said, "That's a beautiful piece of amber on your bracelet." Her voice was low, as though she didn't want to be caught conversing with her patient.

Baezy smiled and quietly answered, "Thank you. It was a gift. From the father of my baby, actually."

Dr. Tessen smiled and nodded. She kept her voice barely above a whisper. "Baltic amber like that is over thirty million years old. In recent centuries, mothers offered it to babies who were having teething pain. Supposedly, chewing on a necklace made of Baltic cherry amber beads like yours was extremely soothing." She looked at Faisa again and quietly added, "Baezy, my visits here aren't really necessary, at least not on a weekly basis. Don't tell anyone that. The Council seems to think because this baby was conceived with someone who isn't…well, as advanced as we are…that you require constant prenatal monitoring and care. I'd like to continue to see you each week, though. You seem like a nice person to me, not someone who should be punished this way." Baezy nearly cried at the kindness, blinking at Dr. Tessen.

The doctor pretended to drop something and moved close to Baezy's ear. "Your mother, Anantha, sends her love to you," she whispered.

Faisa walked closer, clearly ready for the visit to conclude. Baezy cleared her throat and tried to improvise something to say. She asked, "Doctor, can we accelerate my pregnancy now that it's reached five months?" She leaned back on her elbows, regarding her swollen belly. "Please? I've heard of women who bore their child within twenty-six weeks."

"That can be done after five months," Dr. Tessen replied, "only for women who have conceived during a normal approved Reproduction Cycle. Your pregnancy must take forty full weeks with no interference, Baezy, because you're not carrying a child like the others you've heard about. I'm sorry. You'd be risking your baby's health." Dr. Tessen made a great show of reviewing all the data provided by the MET. "The medical examining table results are all good, but we must monitor you closely. Yours is a very special case because it allows us to study the progression of fetal development as it was before modern science perfected the process. Most physicians have never witnessed this. I'm very grateful I was chosen to monitor you, Baezy." She stood to leave. "I'm recommending some changes to your NourishCubes. You'll notice they look a bit smaller and taste different."

Baezy frowned. "Why smaller? And I've gotten used to the peanut butter flavor. Why do we have to change it?" She held eye contact with the doctor for the first time, noticing hers were the tiniest tinge more blue than the usual green in Unity.

Dr. Tessen bit her lower lip and a crease appeared between her eyebrows. "If absolutely necessary, you may have two as a meal. But you're gaining too much weight with this pregnancy, Baezy. For the optimal health of your baby, we must add certain nutrients and minerals at this point in his development. Your NourishCubes will taste more like the ones you grew up with. I'm sure you'll enjoy them." Dr. Tessen stepped away and Faisa accompanied her to override the door seal. "See you next week," she called to Baezy, who remained on the medical examination table in anticipation of the dreaded geneticist, Dr. Hale.

He always arrived within an hour of Dr. Tessen's visits, so Baezy seized the opportunity to lie down as she waited. She asked Faisa to dim the lights in the room and was surprised to find that was, apparently, *allowed*. Baezy closed her eyes. Her mother still loved her and somehow found a way to tell her, even after the shame Baezy had caused. She clasped her hands over her belly and almost drifted off to sleep until a chime announced Dr. Hale had entered.

Dr. Hale was a stern man who'd never once smiled at Baezy and he didn't today. He wore a geneticist's uniform of a bright green shirt and matching knee-length pants. His uniform had gold metallic trim on the shoulders and cuffs, which complemented his general air of importance. Baezy noted his head was shaved in the latest fashion, with one side displaying a wide strip he'd had dyed green. It looked like the freshly mowed grass she'd seen in Canada.

"Hello, Dr. Hale," she greeted him. "How are you?"

He made no response at all. She gave up trying to engage him in banter and stared at the white ceiling as he subjected her to the invasive and uncomfortable "sampling" she found humiliating. Baezy closed her eyes and tried to imagine she was somewhere else, anywhere but on the examining table.

The geneticist stepped back, waving his hands in the air to make the glove-like protective film on them disappear. He appeared to be leaving without a word spoken to Baezy.

"Please, Dr. Hale," Baezy said. "I know you've already determined everything about my son. Please tell me about him."

She always asked. He had never answered her beyond, "The fetus is healthy."

Dr. Hale seemed to consider before finally shrugging his shoulders and pronouncing in a monotone, "The male child will look much like his father, with a very pale skin color, dark brown eyes and nearly-black hair. His musculature and athletic ability will be inferior to current standards. His intelligence will be average on our scale at best. He will possess musical ability and a facility for numbers." He shook his head and frowned. "The mathematical talent is a genetic marker from both his parents. Little else will be apparent of the M1's…that is, *your* features in his appearance."

"Are there any…disorders I should worry about?" Baezy asked, because she did. She worried all the time about a long-forgotten condition her child might suffer, some sort of fragility or vulnerability he might have to bear in her world.

"Nothing remarkable," Dr. Hale answered, turning to leave. "I see no evidence of any particular disorder or anomaly. You're very fortunate in that regard. I'm changing my visits to once per month until after the child is born. Then, our team will see you much more often."

He hurried away from Baezy as though she were carrying something he didn't want to catch, a bad case of the twentieth century.

29

November 1969

OTTAWA, CANADA

Jack watched from the corner of the showroom as Mary dropped a file on his desk, waiting for her to leave before returning to his office. Paul Robinson, one of the salesmen, observed him watching and said, "She's a pretty girl, Jack. Maybe invite her to Thanksgiving dinner with you. Kathy would be happy to set another place at the table."

Mary stepped away from Jack's office. Today she wore a businesslike brown pantsuit with a bright orange and pink floral blouse underneath. She waved her fingers at the two of them with a smile before retreating into the office, a female enclave Jack and the other men rarely breached.

"Yes, she is, but no, I'd rather join you two and the kids without a date, Paul. It's not the right time for that. It wouldn't be fair to Mary, you know?" Jack said, shaking his head in the direction Mary had walked.

"Yeah, of course I understand," Paul said. "Kathy and the kids will be happy to see you. I think my daughter has secret plans to marry you someday. She tried to be nonchalant when Kathy told her you're joining us, but six-year-olds don't pull that off very well. She said she's making you a pilgrim hat. If you're lucky, she'll run out of construction paper."

Jack chuckled. "Rachel's a doll. I feel incredibly lucky to celebrate the holiday at all," he said. "I mean, I know y'all have your Thanksgiving in October, but the idea of a meal like my mother cooked every year is the greatest gift Kathy could give me."

"You're lucky I have a wife from Tennessee," Paul answered. "One who knows how to cook. Kathy is all excited to perform whatever strange rituals you people bring to the occasion. And the kids are fascinated. You're the only person they've met in Canada who talks like their mom, and the entire reason we're being subjected for the first time to cornbread dressing, whatever that is." Paul didn't mention that Kathy had already invited Mary in the hopes of making her and Jack a couple. He would plead ignorance and hope for the best.

A week later, Jack handed his coat to Kathy and kissed her cheek as he walked into the Robinsons' two-story home, a place he felt instantly welcome and comfortable. Time with them and their two children, Ronnie and Rachel, had meant a lot to him since the first Saturday Paul invited him over at the beginning of October. He stood waiting for Rachel to run down the steps into his arms, all six-year-old wide blue eyes and giggles.

"Did Daddy tell you about the surprise?" she asked Jack.

"There is no surprise, Rachel," her mother said with a shake of her head. "Unless a pecan pie better than his own mama's is a surprise."

Rachel rolled her eyes. "I wanted to make you a hat and it didn't work. It would have been a lot better than a pie."

"I'm sorry it didn't work out, but getting to see you is the best part of this day even without a hat," Jack told Rachel, setting her down. "And that *would* be a stunning surprise, Kathy," Jack said. "My mother won a blue ribbon at the 1951 Ashe County Fair for her pecan pie. She's very fond of telling people, even strangers on the street."

"Those judges never met my pie," she replied. "It's the reason Paul Robinson married me—well, that and my incredible legs." Kathy hiked her new plaid maxi-skirt up to knee level and swung her calf out for Jack to admire. "Try to control yourself," she admonished. "Many men have followed me home after a look at my alluring ankles." Kathy was a thirty-eight-year-old mother hen with a distinctive southern accent and a sassy sense of humor that reminded Jack of home. She was dedicated to making Jack's life better, even behind his back and against his will. "Rachel, you go to the back yard and play with your brother on the swing set." She shooed the little girl away, though Rachel cast an annoyed glance at her mother over her shoulder. "Come on in and have a drink, Jack," Kathy said. "Paul's in the living room. I have to get back to the kitchen."

Jack found Paul in deep conversation with one of their fellow workers, a guy from the service department whose name escaped him. Paul handed Jack his usual bourbon rocks.

"You remember Leon, right?"

"Yes, Leon, hi," Jack said, taking a sip. He vaguely remembered the man specialized in air conditioning repair. Or was it transmissions?

"Leon's wife is in the kitchen helping Kathy," Paul informed him. Jack wished he could be, too. He knew an inevitable discussion about hockey was going to ensue, one he'd be lost trying to follow.

The doorbell rang as Paul went to fix a new drink for Leon. "Jack, would you mind getting that?" he said, frowning slightly.

As Jack swung the white front door open, it revealed Mary Clarke standing on the porch in a dark blue shift dress and sweater, her hair freshly styled into swinging blonde curls and a small strand of pearls at her neck. Jack blinked at her, wondering where her date was, until he realized what Kathy had done.

"Come in, Mary," he said. "I'm just going to the kitchen to help Kathy with something. The guys are in the living room. I'll be right back."

He stomped into the kitchen and began to inform Kathy what a mistake she'd made. "I know you mean well, but I am not—"

Before he could say another word, Kathy held a finger to his lips. "Hush your mouth," she said. "She's a sweetheart and everyone is tired of watching you mope around like an old hound dog. Give her a chance." She smoothed her curly brown hair away from her forehead and turned around to open the oven door. "The turkey's going to take at least another forty minutes. Get out there and socialize. I'm not asking you to *marry* her, honey, just get to know her a little."

"This is a bad idea, Kathy." He glanced over at Leon's wife, who appeared completely focused on the onion she was chopping. Jack turned his eyes to the ceiling like he was searching for his patience there. He shrugged his shoulders at Kathy but went and did as she asked.

He sat next to Mary during a delightful dinner that even featured cranberry salad like his mom used to make. Rachel stared hard at Mary as though hoping to make her disappear from across the table. Mary's response was to ask Rachel for a moment in private after dinner. They walked into the living room and Mary reached into her handbag to produce a Twist-and-Turn Barbie doll she'd brought for the little girl and a set of Matchbox cars for her brother.

Mary was pretty, she was warm, and she was kind. Still, Jack didn't ask her on a date.

Jack still rushed to the mailbox after work each day, still squinted at strangers in the distance, trying to puzzle out Sarah's form. Sometimes he'd allow himself to imagine she was waiting for him in the apartment, that her face would appear in the little window above the sink as he walked up.

Almost a month passed before he decided to see if Mary might accompany him to Wally Armstrong's annual employee Christmas party. Attendance was definitely expected, and Jack didn't want to be the only guy there on his own. He and Mary won dinner for two at a French restaurant during some stupid party game Jack had tried to avoid. So, they went there the next week and discussed dealership gossip over beef bourguignon.

Jack discovered the day after that dinner Mary was Wally Armstrong's niece by marriage, his wife's sister's youngest. He was summoned to the executive office for a private talk about treating her properly.

"She doesn't want everybody to know," Mr. Armstrong explained. "Mary's independent and is afraid people will think she gets special treatment working for me. She doesn't. But you be good to my niece, or my wife will have you drawn and quartered."

It seemed Mr. Armstrong and the entire staff had already assumed Jack and Mary were a pair. "You could do worse," Paul told him. "She's not just easy on the eyes, she's smart. Even Rachel approves after the Barbie bribe."

A few dinner dates later, in Jack's frigid apartment with its barely helpful woodstove battling February, Mary Clarke felt like she was finally breaking down some of the concrete walls surrounding his heart.

She'd come to pick him up for dinner that night since Jack stubbornly refused to purchase and drive a car, especially in the harshest winter he'd ever known. He'd been meeting Mary at restaurants, taking the bus to and from to avoid awkward decisions after dinner. Jack felt Wally Armstrong's eyes on his back every time he was near Mary's body.

When they returned from the steakhouse, she produced a gift for him. It was an album she wanted Jack to play. The apartment was so cold they kept their coats on as they sat, waiting for the music and the fire in the woodstove both to make the living room tolerable.

The album was The Beatles' *Abbey Road*. The funky opening sounds of "Come Together" immediately struck Jack as an anthem that would've fit right in at Woodstock. He realized at that point he'd never even told Mary he'd been there. It still wasn't a subject he wanted to discuss.

As the next song, "Something", filled the darkened room with its lush guitar, Jack leaned back and closed his eyes. The lyrics seemed to be written about Sarah. He saw her face, heard her laugh, felt her arms around him. The image of her climbing out of Filippini Pond the day they met played like a movie in his mind. Her hand in his as they walked to Louie's Bar in search of a dance floor; her body pressed against his as they performed an awkward box step under pale purple spotlights there. Her giggling delight at tunnel of fudge cake in the tent. Sarah whispering *I think I'm falling on you*. Something in the way she wooed him. Jack smiled to himself.

He opened his eyes to find Mary staring at him in the light of the fire, her head tilted to one side.

"You really like this song, don't you?" she said. "It's beautiful."

"*You* are beautiful," Jack replied. He leaned over to kiss Mary. She tasted like crème brûlée and warmth and someone who could offer him a future. Mary was here, she was real, she was part of his life in Ottawa.

But Sarah would never be far from his heart, ever.

30

Unity SE35.86

OCTOBER 2102

Baezy had never known physical pain in her life. She had certainly never had a concept of the way childbirth would torture her body in excruciating wave after wave. She asked Dr. Tessen, "Is this normal? Surely women don't endure this every time a baby is born."

She sighed and leaned her head back on the medical examination table, which had transformed into an accommodation for her body to give birth. She was cradled in a position that might be pleasant if it weren't for the sensation of a thousand twentieth-century knives hacking their way out of her belly.

"The pain is as I expected you to feel," the doctor replied. "Try to rest between the contractions. Save your strength for the hours ahead."

Baezy gasped, "*Hours?* Please get my mom in here. She's allowed to be in my homepod, and I need her."

"I know," Dr. Tessen replied. "She's on her way." She placed a steadying hand on Baezy's arm and squeezed as she watched the lights of the MET monitor her patient.

When Anantha arrived and was ushered in unceremoniously by Faisa, she found Baezy clutching the sides of the table, her teeth gritted against the pain of her strongest contraction yet. Bright colors swirled all around her, more vibrant than usual and therefore alarming to Anantha.

When Baezy met her mother's eyes, all she could do was sob and apologize, "I'm so sorry, Mom. I'm so sorry."

Anantha leaned down to embrace her daughter and answered her, "Baezy, I don't want you to apologize. The idiots who managed to mess up your time insertion no longer work for TIP. The blame is on them for ruining your NC supply. As far as I'm concerned, you are not at fault here. None of this could have happened if you'd had the nutritional, emotional, and medical support you needed, as we were promised you would." She glared at Faisa, even though the AI assistant was equipped with no emotional receptors at present and might never be again. "Bring me a chair," she ordered imperiously.

Faisa did and Anantha took a seat next to her daughter, glancing up occasionally at Dr. Tessen, whose face remained relaxed and impassive in spite of Baezy's obvious distress. Anantha didn't have to ask for an update.

"The labor is progressing well, and both mother and baby are fine. The two of you should spend this time before the pain increases to talk about the things you've been denied an opportunity to discuss over the past nine months," Dr. Tessen said. She motioned for Faisa to follow her across the room. Baezy was amazed to see Faisa comply and give her privacy with her mother.

"Mom, I truly never meant to cause you this shame," Baezy said, tears dripping down the side of her face. "I—"

"Baezy," her mother interrupted, "I've missed you so much, my beautiful daughter. Stop saying you're sorry. I know that. My concern now is only for your wellbeing and that of my grandchild. Nothing else matters to me." She closed her eyes and continued in a lowered voice, "I've thought about this over and over. It's obvious to me you loved this Jack Warren deeply. Tell me about him." She took her daughter's hand in both of hers.

Baezy blinked and took a deep, ragged breath and exhaled it slowly. "Jack is unlike anyone I've ever known. He has a great physical beauty, with dark hair and brown eyes that sparkle when he's happy, and crinkle at the edges when he smiles. And Mom, he was so happy with me." This brought new tears, which Baezy swiped at and continued. "He's kind and thoughtful. He's funny. He's a talented mathematician who taught children in a school. And he plays piano, though I never got a chance to hear him. He loves music. He's a terrible dancer. He would do anything for someone he loves. He'd do anything for *me*. He is a wonderful man."

Anantha said quietly, "He *was*, Baezy. I'm sure he was all of those things."

Baezy threw an arm over her eyes, ignoring her mother's point. "And I know you said to stop apologizing, but the worry I put you through is unforgivable. So, one last apology. I am really sorry." She was seized by a stronger contraction than the last one and Anantha called out to Dr. Tessen, who appeared by the table almost instantly.

"I know you can't administer modern pain relief because of the baby, but couldn't you use a drug from the early twenty-first century, at least? Something to help her endure this?" Anantha asked.

Dr. Tessen shook her head. "I'm sorry, but I am under strict orders not to. Even if I could, I have no such drugs. They haven't been manufactured for many years."

When the labor progressed and the pain with it, Anantha clutched Baezy's hand so hard, she was afraid of causing bruises. Her daughter was struggling, trying to navigate something she'd never anticipated, a process her contemporaries would find much less difficult. Anantha felt helpless, a situation she was unaccustomed to and which tore at her heart every time Baezy cried out.

Finally, after eight long hours, Baezy held her son in her arms. Scrawny and long, the baby had skin that was a splotchy bright red and wrinkled. She wasn't allowed to nurse him; he was administered a liquid supplement that would lead up, eventually, to solid NCs designed for his optimal health. Dr. Tessen gave Baezy special

NourishCubes to make her milk disappear and return her body to normal.

Anantha dreaded the day the baby's skin color faded to the pasty white that would elicit stares and whispers everywhere he went. She tried to look happy, even as she worried about every day that would follow now for her daughter and grandson in Unity. They were certain to be challenging. She shook her head and tried to think of something positive.

"Have you decided on a name for him?" she asked Baezy.

Her daughter smiled. "Jackson. Jackson Warren Smith." Baezy looked at her son with wonder and adoration, touching each of his tiny fingers and toes, tracing the lines of his sleeping face with her fingertip. "He has Jack's nose and mouth. His ears. And you can see how dark his hair is. He's like a miniature of him. He's beautiful, isn't he, Mom?"

Anantha nodded, her eyebrows raised. "Jackson is such a nice name," she answered.

Dr. Tessen reached to take the baby away, but Baezy clutched him to her chest, terrified of what she intended to do. "I promise," the doctor said, "I'm only going to bathe and dress him. Jackson will be back in your arms in a few short minutes." Baezy looked on as the doctor cleaned the baby and applied something that immediately dried and healed his umbilical stump. Dr. Tessen affixed a garment designed to sweep waste away from his skin and dissolve it. She wrapped him snugly in a blanket of soft golden cloth and tied him into a secure bundle, returning the baby to his anxious mother.

Baezy kissed the top of his soft head, inhaling his delicate fragrance and marveling at his long, dark eyelashes. Jackson lay quietly against Baezy's chest, sleeping soundly. She turned to Anantha and asked, "Are they coming today? The geneticists? I don't want them to wake him up."

"I don't think so, Baezy. Surely they'll give you both time to rest," Anantha said. She reached a tentative hand to stroke the fuzzy dark hair on Jackson's head, something she'd never seen on a newborn infant. She sat holding her daughter's hand and watched as Baezy and her son slept.

Two hours later, Baezy woke to the chime of a bell and watched in dismay as Faisa delivered the geneticist, Dr. Hale, to her side. He wore his usual green uniform and introduced a second older man who accompanied him as Dr. Tyler. Anantha simply nodded her head and stepped back to supervise whatever it was they planned to do, poised to scream an objection, threaten, do whatever was necessary to protect her daughter and grandchild.

Dr. Hale carried a white rectangle with high sides that Baezy realized was an attachment to her medical examination table. He fixed it into place and the two men turned their attention to her baby.

Dr. Tyler leaned over Baezy, avoiding her eyes and focusing on the infant cradled in her arms. He shook his head. "We should begin measurements and evaluate him right away." He reached to take her son and Baezy held Jackson tightly against her chest, shaking her head no and looking to her mother for support.

Instead, Anantha nodded and said in a soothing voice, "I think they're just going to measure him and take some genetic samples. Let them accomplish their tasks and leave." To Dr. Hale, she said, "I am watching you both closely. If you do anything to cause harm, you will never set foot in this homepod again."

Hale and Tyler stood ignoring Anantha for a moment. Then they glanced at each other briefly and Dr. Hale reached for Jackson.

Baezy reluctantly handed the small bundle to Dr. Hale and watched him place Jackson on the rectangle, which began to stream lights. She couldn't watch. She was tired, afraid, and all she wanted was her son back in her arms. Baezy closed her eyes and waited.

She heard Dr. Hale say, "Anomalies in both brain and skull size when contrasted with what we've achieved, as anticipated. Significant difference in various organ sizes as well. Look, Dr. Tyler, it has an appendix."

"What are you talking about? He is my son, he is not an *it!*" Baezy's eyes shot open and she attempted to sit up enough to look at Jackson, who was hidden on the small table. She spotted the gold blanket they'd removed and tossed over to the side. "Is he all right?"

Dr. Hale answered, "Yes, do not worry. Your son is healthy and displays all the characteristics I told you he would. We are simply noting the advances made since G-HOP began. This child presents an unprecedented opportunity for us. He's a combination of the perfection we've attained and common human genetic characteristics of a hundred and thirty years ago."

Baezy narrowed her eyes at him. "Genetic optimization may have lengthened lifespans and eliminated diseases, but at what cost? The homogenization has rendered none of us true individuals. When I was in 1969, I saw hundreds of thousands of people of all races, all colors, all uniquely human in their own beautiful ways. They cared for each other, they—"

Anantha interrupted her daughter. "Baezy, you should rest. The doctors are trying to complete their examination."

Dr. Hale nodded his thanks to Anantha and she watched as he took some sort of instrument from underneath the table. The baby screamed a moment later and Baezy rolled to her side to get up, frantically trying to see what they were doing to her son.

Dr. Tessen's hand appeared on Baezy's shoulder, easing her back down. She leaned her face above Baezy's, smiling and warm, and handed Baezy a very small NC. "Chew this," she instructed. "It will help you, I promise."

Anantha nodded at her daughter. Baezy needed to rest; she needed to stop talking. Baezy looked into Anantha's eyes and saw a promise she would make sure Jackson was all right. She dutifully chewed the NC, which tasted like chocolate.

Baezy fell into a deep sleep. She dreamed of cows with calves flying above them on delicate wings of gossamer blue, of a night sky painted in brilliant yellows and oranges, of Jack calling her name over and over from a place she couldn't find.

31

May 1970

OTTAWA, CANADA

Jack reached across the console of his candy-apple-red '67 Camaro and held Mary's hand. The car was ridiculous and impractical for Canadian winters but he didn't care. He loved every inch of it from the cool horizontal doors that slid to hide the headlights and the growling 350 V-8 to the sporty spoiler on its trunk lid. He loved the way it jumped forward when he hit the gas. He loved the way people looked at his car.

Mr. Armstrong, true to his word, had offered it to Jack when an older lady decided she couldn't climb in and out of her late husband's sports car and replaced it and her own aging station wagon with a shiny new Volvo. At wholesale, it was a thrilling bargain Jack couldn't pass up. He figured he could park it during the harshest snow and ice and take the bus.

His citizenship was being processed and everything indicated he'd be accepted. The job at Armstrong Volvo was paying him both a decent base salary and a commission on each financing deal he wrote. Jack was surprised to find his income sufficient to cover both the car payment and a move to a nicer neighborhood. He was now renting a small ranch-style house down the leafy suburban street from the Robinsons.

They were driving to Mary's parents' favorite restaurant to celebrate her dad's birthday. Mr. Clarke had three daughters and Jack seemed to be the son he'd always wanted, at least until he tried to discuss hockey with him. Jack kept his hair cut short and his politics conservative. Mr. Clarke, an insurance executive, showed his approval with firm handshake greetings that usually included enthusiastic pats on Jack's back. He took that as a good sign. Mrs. Clarke was already sold on Jack. Her brother-in-law, Wally Armstrong, had nothing but nice things to say about him.

He turned toward Parliament Hill, where Mary's mom and dad waited at the restaurant in the Fairmont Chateau Laurier Hotel. Jack tugged at the collar of his shirt, uncomfortable in the spring heat. More uncomfortable would be Mary's mom suggesting, not for the first time, the Fairmont would be a stunning place for a wedding reception.

Jack's own parents sounded good each time he called them on Sunday nights. Kenny was freshly released from a brief prison term for a minor burglary. His mother delighted in having him home and reported to Jack he didn't seem to be interested in either drugs or alcohol. He'd even started seeing a woman, a divorcee named Wanda Lynn from West Jefferson with two small children. She was cautiously optimistic Kenny could hold his life together, especially with Wanda Lynn's support and faith in him.

Mary pulled a compact from her handbag and applied lipstick as the car idled at a red light. Jack looked at the sedan next to him and noted its middle-aged male driver sweeping his eyes appreciatively over the Camaro. The light changed and Mary yelled at Jack for taking off a little too fast, squealing the tires and causing a bright pink lipstick smear next to her mouth.

"This car is going to get you into trouble, Jack Warren," she said.

"It already has. Look who's sitting next to me," he replied with a wink, throwing on his right turn signal. Jack braked for an elderly lady who'd decided to cross the street, traffic light be damned. As he waited, his eyes wandered to a bus stop he and Sarah used to frequent. A woman sat there and from this distance, she looked a lot like Sarah, only in a long dress and unseasonable sweater.

He was used to these little tricks his mind played occasionally. He'd seen Sarah in so many strangers on the street, he'd learned not to pay attention. Besides, this woman had an infant on her lap. It couldn't be her.

PART III

32

February 3, 2024

HUNTSVILLE, ALABAMA

Kelly sat alone regarding the vast jewel box of city lights beneath her. There were rubies and emeralds and diamonds sparkling in the night, a little blurry because both the cold and a twinge of sadness were making her eyes water.

"Are you okay, Mom?" Her daughter, Allie, took the clear plastic chair left over from the wedding ceremony next to her. "Why are you out here all by yourself? I looked everywhere for you. You disappeared after cake." She looked at her mother's profile. "Is it Dad? I can see how a wedding would be especially rough." She reached for Kelly's cold hand.

Kelly offered a weak smile to her elder daughter. In the moonlight she could easily have been Kelly decades ago, green eyes glowing and brown hair past her shoulders, though Allie had so many blonde highlights added these days it looked much lighter.

"No, Alice," Kelly said, "I miss him every day, but it's been well over a year and I've adjusted. Giles was ten years older than me. He was almost eighty-six, honey, and had a wonderful life." She reached for Allie's hand. "You girls have helped me more than I can ever say. If it weren't for you and Jemimah, I'd be sitting at home watching

Jeopardy and yelling answers for no one to hear. That's a terrible feeling, being highly impressive without an audience."

"You need to call me Allie and her Jem, Mom. If we'd stuck with Humility Alice and Eleanor Jemimah, we'd have been bullied out of our lunch money every day." Allie sat back and smiled at her mother's chuckle.

"I was just torturing you a little. All I can do is apologize. Your dad's Yankee family had a lot of important and mandatory female names to be passed on, women ranging from Pilgrim to merely grim." Kelly stared at the lights again.

"That was Dad's line, but I think it's true," Allie said. "And you could've told him no."

Kelly smiled and sighed as she shook her head. "I could never say no to your father. That's why *you're* here."

"You know that's gross, right?" Allie said. "I don't want to hear—"

Kelly plowed on, her brows knitted in memory. "That night we first met? He was the most gorgeous man I'd ever seen, like Robert Redford had walked into a stuffy university party with his own personal spotlight—hell, his own *air* because he kind of sucked it out of the room. All the women turned to look at him. When they found out he was an important donor, they were practically salivating and rubbing their hands together like cartoon bad guys. I saw one woman tug her neckline down to show a little cleavage when he came closer. But Dr. Lawton led him straight to me, expecting my usual dog and pony show and maybe a bit more." Kelly blinked at the lights below and smiled. "I didn't know he'd asked for an introduction and Dr. Lawton was basically trying to pimp me out."

"Mom, did you just use the word 'pimp'? Seriously?" Allie said.

Kelly chuckled. "Well, it worked out fine. Ours may have been the first genuinely feminist marriage of the 1970s. Giles loved my brain and I just wanted to stare at him because he was pretty."

"Daddy was very intelligent, Mom," Allie said.

Kelly squeezed her daughter's hand. "Of course he was. Everything about us was well-matched. He loved my accent, too.

There's something about a demure Southern woman that works for a New England man."

"Are you actually calling yourself demure, Dr. Kelly Hopkins?" Allie threw her head back and laughed. "Is terrorizing your mentees *demure?*"

"I can be when I want to," Kelly replied. "And there's nothing wrong with demanding excellence." She took her hand from Allie's and clasped it with her own, lowering her head as they sat in silence for a minute.

Allie knew her mother had retreated into darker thoughts. "Anyway, if you're out here worrying, you need to stop. Jem and I are going to make sure you get the best medical care. Huntsville is one of the best places for breast cancer treatment in the South. You're going to be fine, Mom."

Kelly nodded at her daughter, tears in her eyes. "I know that. Believe it or not, I know I'll be fine. I just don't want to go through it all. But having you girls with me all the time has been the greatest blessing I could imagine. Thank you for being by my side for every appointment." Kelly bit her lip and added, "The topic is closed for tonight. We came to celebrate a beautiful wedding and marriage." She stood to go back into the reception. "It's freezing out here," she said, tugging her wool wrap around her shoulders.

"Okay, Mom, but we're there for each appointment because we treasure you, that's all I'll add. Your entire family will always be here for you. Dan and Carl love you, now that they've learned their mother-in-law is human and only maybe the third most intimidating computer scientist in the world. Your grandchildren worship you." Allie paused for one last look at the city twinkling below. "Come on, you should dance with Ashley and me. She'll be heading back to Massachusetts tomorrow."

"My granddaughter, who will graduate along with thousands of other girls at MIT this year, half her damn class. Who knew they'd come this far, since I introduced them to X chromosomes?" Kelly said, linking her arm in Allie's.

"Mom, you weren't the first—"

"Hush, Allie. I was the first to do what I *did*," Kelly answered. "The first to graduate from their new computer science program in the seventies. The first to be recruited by NASA's Marshall Space Flight Center. The first to go on to both doing research and teaching students about artificial intelligence development in Huntsville. The work I did on the Rover alone—"

"I know, Mom. Thank you for my Roomba and my Alexa. But thank you more for being a great mother while you did all that," Allie said, kissing her mom's cheek. They drew close enough to make out the music in the ballroom. Allie tugged on Kelly's hand. "Come on, it's 'Sweet Caroline'." The crowd inside yelled SO GOOD SO GOOD SO GOOD.

Kelly removed her painful leather pumps and tossed them aside as they walked in. She and Allie located Jem and Ashley dancing in the middle of the room, grinning and waving their glowsticks at the two of them like aircraft marshallers parking a jet. Jem's dark blonde hair was cut short and her smile was so like Giles' it wrenched Kelly's heart a little. She reached for Jem's hands and improvised a dance she thought might look reasonable for a woman her age, praying the videographer was occupied elsewhere.

When the song ended, they gathered at a table far from the DJ's speakers so they could talk. Kelly swept her eyes over the dark green tablecloths and peach, pink, and white flowers in lush greenery surrounded by candles. The reception had the kind of lighting that made everyone feel beautiful, and Kelly beamed a smile at her daughter and granddaughter.

Ashley said, "Can I get anything for y'all? I'm going for a beer. What about you, Gran?"

Kelly asked for white wine and watched Ashley pause to flirt with a young man who'd been failing to hide his stares at her all night. Kelly shook her head, marveling at the genes that had carried green eyes to Ashley and then whisked her off to MIT. She thought about how proud Giles would have been at her graduation in May.

Summa cum Proude, he would have said.

Jem's husband Dan interrupted her conversation with Allie to hand over their sleepy six-year-old, Waverly. She settled in Jem's lap with her head on her mother's chest as Dan headed off to engage in man talk. Ashley set a glass of wine in front of Kelly and settled next to Allie with her beer, sipping it slowly and trying not to look like she was searching the crowd for her cute young stranger.

Kelly looked at the family around her and grew weepy all over again.

"Mom was telling me she couldn't ever say no to Dad and that's why I exist, Jem," Allie announced, nodding at their mother. "Was I an attendee at *your* wedding, Mom?"

Kelly sipped her white wine. "Of course not. You were born over a year after we were married." She twirled the stem of the glass in her fingers and paused to adjust her engagement ring, holding it out for Ashley to see. "This diamond was in your grandfather's family for well over a hundred years before he put it on my finger. I want you to know that when I'm gone, it's going to you, my first granddaughter." The three-carat oval stone was a disco ball in the tiny overhead spotlights of the ballroom.

"Thank you, Gran, it's gorgeous," Ashley began before her mother cut her off.

Allie said, "Don't be maudlin, Mom. You're going to be around for a very long time."

Kelly frowned at her daughter. "I'm not being maudlin, I'm being practical, Allie. It's a minor miracle the Hopkins family allowed Giles to give me this ring. I wasn't what they had in mind at all." She turned her attention back to Ashley. "Your grandfather's longtime girlfriend was this Boston Brahmin debutante named Evelyn, and your Great-Grandmother Hopkins was already counting her future blond Brahmin grandchildren before I came along. I was a twenty-three-year-old nobody with an Alabama accent and a *career*. It was positively scandalous. No woman in that family had ever been employed or occupied with anything beyond fundraisers, shopping, and needlepoint. Here I come with my mathematics degree from MIT and aspirations for much more, and her son is obsessed with me. Evelyn was a blank slate she could etch her designs all over. I was solid steel she couldn't scratch."

Kelly took a big gulp of wine and continued, noting her granddaughter's fascination. "Then I compounded the horror by taking her precious son off to Alabama when NASA recruited me. They visited us exactly once, when Allie was born. I think she secretly wanted to see the birth certificate to ensure we adhered to the generational Humility Alice rule." The younger women all exchanged glances. This was more information than their mother and grandmother had ever shared, by far.

Kelly held her empty wine glass out to Ashley. "Would you mind, darling?" She secretly hoped Ashley would encounter that young man again and dance with him.

"No, Gran, not at all. I'll be right back," she said, kissing the top of her grandmother's head as she walked away.

Joe Cocker began singing "You Are So Beautiful" and the groom, a distant cousin on Kelly's side, searched for his wife and swept her into his arms, then dipped her with a passionate kiss for the photographer.

When they came up for air, Allie said, "Weren't they high-school sweethearts, Jade and Cody?"

"Yes," Kelly answered. "They've been in love forever. Just a beautiful couple," she sighed.

As soon as Ashley returned with Kelly's wine, the cute guy she'd been watching for walked over and swept her off to the dance floor. Allie rested her chin on her hand. "It's so hard, telling her goodbye each time. We have to be at the airport at nine tomorrow morning. I wish we were Amish and she lived next door for life and the only time we were apart was when she went down the field for a barn raising."

Jem stared at her. "What are *you* drinking, Al?" she said. "And also," she added, "wasn't this guy, Joe Cocker, at Woodstock?"

Kelly's eyebrows lifted and she tilted her head. "Yes, he was, although this song came later. But I saw him perform. He was fantastic to behold."

Jem continued over Waverly's sleeping blonde head, "You never talked about it. I mean, what was it *like*, Mom? It's hard to believe you were actually at Woodstock. No offense, but you're the last person I'd expect to have been there."

"Well first of all, like I said in my interview last year, I wasn't a typical attendee. I spent an absurd amount of time sitting in our van and working while everyone else experienced the festival. I was young and stupid and thought I had to impress the world with my seriousness. If I had to do it over, I'd have heard every band. I went mainly for Joan Baez because I've always loved her voice. I didn't even know the other performers," Kelly said.

"Why have you always been so weird about it? I would think you'd want to talk about being there to anyone who'd listen," Jem said, looking at her sister. "Even if you weren't in the middle of things the whole time. I mean, it was freaking *Woodstock*, Mom. Did you have big bell bottoms and a tie-dyed shirt? Did you smoke that wacky tobaccy?" She and Allie giggled.

Kelly took a delicate sip. "No and no," she said. "And it was mainly your dad. He didn't want any of his bank associates to know I'd been there. It would have been an embarrassment to him professionally. And of course, his parents never knew. Alice would have had the vapors and collapsed at the thought." She smiled. "Giles didn't want me to bring it up. He didn't really want me *thinking* about it at all, and it started to feel like something that happened to someone else after years went by. He especially didn't want me to talk to y'all about the festival, being there with all the hippies and enjoying music that wasn't his style at all. But honestly, there are some things I'd like to tell you both."

Jem and Allie laughed. "We know about your acid trip, lady," Jem said. "Dad told us you accidentally ingested it and we must never mention the experience to you. It was part of his *just say no to drugs* and *watch your drinks in a bar* speech." Kelly's daughters nodded in unison, eyes wide and mock-solemn. "Although we would both very much like details."

Kelly sat back with her glass and scanned the crowd. "I didn't even mention that in my attendee's oral history last year. It was another lifetime." She set her glass down and smiled at her daughters. "Both of y'all come over tomorrow afternoon about two o'clock. I have something I want to show you from Woodstock. I think it's time. And I'll answer your questions. Believe me, there will be a lot of them."

Jem and Allie's eyebrows moved like semaphore flags signaling their puzzled intrigue. "Oooh," Allie said. "We will most definitely be there."

"I'll bring the groovy acid and 'shrooms," Jem said. Kelly glared and she added, "Or maybe a nice bottle of chilled prosecco. Did you drink at Woodstock?"

"Boone's Farm," Kelly replied.

"Prosecco it is," Jem nodded her head at her mother.

33

February 4, 2024
HUNTSVILLE, ALABAMA

Kelly paced her living room as she waited the next day, picking up and putting down countless silver-framed photos of Giles and the rest of her family. She settled into the sofa and forced herself to be still until Jem and Allie arrived. She knew they were going to have a hard time with what she was about to tell them both. She was still torn about whether she should at all.

When the girls were settled in chairs opposite her, Kelly tapped her hands on the black notebook in her lap. "I'm about to show you something I promised your father I never would. But things have changed in recent years and I have reasons for telling you this now. Giles thought my memories were all tangled up in my accidental acid trip. But that's not it at all. It's taken me…well, it was years and years later when I finally understood what happened, and I hope you'll keep an open mind."

Jem said, "For heaven's sake, Mom, whatever you did fifty years ago is fine. Just tell us."

Kelly swallowed hard. "Maybe bring me a glass of that prosecco you promised."

Jem did and Kelly took a deep drink before she began. "Okay, this is going to sound crazy to you. I need you both to hear me out and see what I have to show you before you say anything. Do you promise?"

Jem and Allie nodded yes, their eyes wide and, Kelly could tell, on the verge of rolling.

"There was a person who came to our camp at Woodstock. Her name was Sarah Sandoval." Kelly drew and exhaled a deep breath. "She told me she was my many-times great granddaughter and that she had time-traveled from the year 2101 to meet me at the festival."

"So she was the one with the acid," Allie said.

"No, she wasn't," Kelly answered. "She knew things that didn't make sense, the performers coming up that hadn't been announced, when it was going to pour rain…and how to find me nearly a mile away when I wandered off into a cornfield after I was drugged. None of it added up to anything I could accept. I thought she was a crazy, weird girl with a vivid imagination, and yes, that she was on acid at times. I tried to dismiss the things Sarah said."

She took a sip of wine. "When Sarah arrived, I was working out equations in this notebook. She sat there and stunned me with her knowledge of mathematics, showing me what I'd done wrong. *Me.* The math whiz with the MIT degree. I still thought it was some kind of fluke. I brought this notebook back and barely looked at it again until nearly a year later, when I noticed a corner was folded down on a page near the back. Of course, that's something I'd never do in a million years."

Allie and Jem gave into the eye roll urge. "Just tell us whatever it is you did, Mom."

"It isn't what I did. It's what I found." Kelly opened the notebook to the creased corner page. "She wrote this and left it for me. I want you to read it now," she said, handing the book to her daughters and sitting back to watch them.

Jem and Allie read together:

"I am sitting in this van while you are furious and ignoring me. I feel bad about the argument we just had, but I feel even worse that you still don't believe me. I am planning to leave this note for you to find and keep, because it's the only way I can prove what I told you is true. I am your great-great-great-granddaughter. My name is Baezy and I am from an era in which time travel is possible. I came to meet you, even though all you've done is hurt my feelings.

Watch for the following things to take place in time. Each year will prove to you a little bit more that all I've tried to tell you is true.

In 1970, you will meet and fall in love with a man from Boston. The two of you will marry in 1971. You will have two children. I am intentionally not using names, genders, and dates here, because you deserve to see these things unfold without prior knowledge.

You will continue your education at MIT and be invited to work for NASA. This will return you to your home state and you and your husband will raise your family there. It will be your permanent home. You will have a very long life, Kelly. In fact, you will live to the age of ninety-eight, a remarkable thing in your era.

Mark these: in 1980, a former actor and California governor named Ronald Reagan will be elected president. In 1986, a nuclear power plant in Russia called Chernobyl will explode and render the area around it uninhabitable. In 1999, the entire world will fear the new millennium portends disastrous problems from computer issues. It doesn't. On September 11, 2001, a terrorist attack on two buildings in New York City will kill thousands and be remembered always as one of the darkest days in modern history. In 2020, a mutated virus that originates in China will create a global pandemic that will kill millions of people.

None of this can be controlled or prevented in any way. I am telling you only to prove my point. Watch for these events, Kelly, and you will understand I did not lie to you. There is literally no other way I could know all this if it weren't recorded history when I was born. It is my hope you will accept the truth about me, and remember me with far more affection than you showed me in 1969.

Your move to Huntsville impacted the future in ways beyond your imagining, and I cannot tell you anything beyond this: you and your family will be fine. The future is a bright one and the changes to come are not to be feared. I've been writing you letters from a place called Unity SE35.86 for a long time now. It was known as Huntsville, Alabama in your time.

Love,

Baezy"

Allie set the book on a table and Jem clutched her stomach. They both looked at Kelly as Allie said, "You believe all of this is true? All this Nostradamus shit she scribbled in your little notebook? You're a *scientist*, Mother."

"I do believe it, yes. And it gives me a lot of hope about this radiation therapy I'm going for every weekday. Tomorrow it all starts again. If I believe one thing she wrote as the truth, I have to believe it all. And she didn't miss a thing there, Allie," Kelly said. "Not one. So I guess I can expect to have twenty-one more years."

Allie and Jem exchanged glances. "Who else knew this girl at Woodstock, Mom? Are you still in touch with any of them?"

Kelly said, "I get a Christmas card from Laura and Rodney some years. Eric hosts an oldies show on a satellite radio station. I have no idea where Kristin is. I think Jack is still in Canada somewhere. We've all lost touch over the years, but Jack knew her best. She went to

Canada with him and disappeared suddenly soon after. That fits with being a time-traveler, too."

Jem groaned. "Please don't use the word 'time-traveler'. Have you ever tried to find this Jack guy? Seems he would know better than anyone if any of this is true. Does he have a Facebook?" Jem was already pulling out her phone.

Kelly shook her head back and forth. "I am a computer scientist. You both know I won't go anywhere near social media and allow everything I do to be tracked and sold to—"

"What's his last name?" Jem interrupted.

"Warren. Jack Warren. Last I knew, he was in Ottawa, Canada and stayed up there even after amnesty was declared for draft dodgers," Kelly said.

Her daughters raised their eyebrows at each other and Jem went back to scrolling on her phone.

"That's a subject for another day," Kelly said. "You have no idea what it was like in 1969."

Allie said, "No, we obviously don't." She was looking at her sister's screen. "That's not Ottawa, and he's too young. That one is in Quebec and he's a dishwasher. What did he look like, Mom?"

Kelly sighed. "Fifty years ago, he had dark hair and eyes and was a math teacher. He was…Jack was very special to me."

More glances between Jem and Allie. "He was a teacher?" Allie asked. "Do you think he still is?"

"Well no, obviously he'd be retired. But like I said, I haven't heard from Jack in many, many years. He stopped communicating after Sarah disappeared," Kelly said. "I'm not even positive he's still alive—"

"Bingo!" Jem announced. "There's a retired math professor living in Canmore, Canada, although his profile pic is blank. I'm looking through his friends list. Oh my God, there's one named Sarah Warren." She clicked on Sarah's name and showed her sister, then began scrolling through photos.

Jem went to sit next to her mother on the couch. "Mom, could this be Jack? Could it be Sarah with him?" She showed Kelly a photo of two elderly white-haired people standing next to a man who was clearly at least fifty years old. The younger one in the middle had his arms around the shoulders of the other two. The caption read "Always happy to have a visit from Jackson."

Kelly squinted at the screen. "Maybe," she said. "I'm not sure. They've both aged so much."

Allie, who'd joined them on the other side of Kelly, shot a look at her sister that said *clearly she doesn't realize how much she's aged, too.* "Scroll through some more, Jem," she ordered.

"It's like a chronicle of Jackson, whoever that is. Their son I guess. There are photos here from the time he was an infant. Photos of him on a tricycle. Kindergarten. First lost tooth. High school. Prom and graduation. Geez, it's a regular Jackson gallery. There aren't any of the two of them, if they are Jack and Sarah. Look at this," Jem said, "it's a post from last year. 'Happy Birthday to my beautiful mother, Anantha' and of course, there's a pic of old Jackson. Oooh, look at this, y'all, her bio says: *Like mothers since the beginning of time, she broke her own heart and used the pieces to fix mine.*"

"Well, that's poetic," Allie said.

Jem and Allie leaned closer to where the phone screen was held in front of Kelly. "Mom," Allie said, "look at that photo of the three of them again."

"Make the photo bigger," Kelly told Jem, who enlarged it with her fingers. "Oh, my gosh," Kelly said. "It's the bracelet. See her arm? That bracelet is silver with an amber bead, the one Jack bought her at Woodstock. I can't believe it." Kelly sat back into the cushions and sighed, shaking her head. "So, she came back? And they have a child?"

Jem sat quietly for a minute, and then said, "Not only that, this looks like it might be a chronicle she's made of Jackson's life for her mother, Anantha, wherever she is. Or I guess I should say, *whenever.*"

34

February-April 2024

Kelly blinked at the light filtering through her bedroom curtains and rolled to her side, expecting to see Giles there. Sometimes it still surprised her to find him missing. She ran her hand over the smooth ivory sheets and whispered, "I love you," to the empty pillow. "What am I going to do, Giles? The girls are determined to meet Sarah. This isn't what I planned on at all."

Kelly swept her robe around her shoulders and padded downstairs to eat something before Allie arrived to take her to today's radiation treatment. She chewed an English muffin that tasted like buttered sawdust and looked for birds in the backyard. *When I decided to tell them, I thought she was long gone. All I wanted to do was assure them I'll be fine, that I have a long life ahead of me. And it's backfired spectacularly. I never in my wildest dreams expected her to be back, much less living with Jack and sharing a son.* Kelly hated the way her stomach reacted to the idea of Jack and Sarah living happily in Canada. She dumped the remains of her breakfast into the trash can and went to dress for today's ordeal: the third Monday out of four she'd endure the burning sensation that followed her everywhere after treatment, the third Monday of four she wondered what would happen if she just left it all alone.

But that wasn't a chance she was willing to take, or willing to put her family through.

Kelly was raw, sore, exhausted, mildly nauseated, grumpy, impatient, and bored as she sat in her radiation oncologist's beige on beige on beige waiting room. She flipped through a 2015 edition of *Better Homes & Gardens*, her eyes focused on exactly nothing.

Allie held up her phone. "Look, Mom. Isn't it gorgeous?" She showed Kelly a series of photos of Banff National Park in Canada, mountains that dwarfed glacier-fed lakes glowing green and blue. "Did you know, in the early days, they promoted Banff as The Switzerland of America?"

"What's wrong with The Switzerland of Switzerland? Your dad and I liked it a lot. I presume that's America as in *North* America," Kelly replied, setting the magazine down on a table and crossing her arms. She stared off into space, clearly disinterested in Allie's phone screen.

"Not everyone has seen alps and auroras in both hemispheres, Mother. You really are travel-spoiled. But it's been years now since you've been on a big trip. What was it, Vienna, in 2017?" Allie asked.

Kelly sighed. "Yes, Vienna for the Christmas markets. We both loved every minute, but I'm not sure I'll ever want to travel long-distance again. And I've been a little preoccupied, Allie. First the pandemic, then your dad's illness, then *this* mess. I'm simply drained. I want to go home and curl up into a ball and sleep. What I *don't* want to do is indulge your fantasies of meeting Sarah."

"Mom, Jem and I both think you need a trip to look forward to, something wonderful on the other side of all this. Something to be excited about and count down to. You and Dad loved to travel so much. I know you miss it," Allie said. She stared down the nurse behind the counter, willing her to call her mother in for her treatment so Kelly could go home and rest. They were already twenty minutes behind schedule.

Kelly had been through two weeks of this, every weekday introducing fresh searing pain that sent her home to gingerly apply cream and frozen washcloths to her breast. She didn't want to go anywhere or do anything. It was a grueling process for anyone, but at seventy-seven it was particularly hard on Kelly.

"I know what you're trying to do, Allie. Banff is near Canmore, where Jack and Sarah live." She exhaled a long breath through pursed lips. "I told you, it's best if we don't contact them. If they wanted to hear from me…look, I can assure you Sarah knows precisely where I am. She's known all along."

Allie swallowed, hesitating before answering. "Yes, but by your own admission, you were horrible to her at Woodstock. Why would she reach out to you again? And Mom, she's *our* great-great-whatever, too. Jem and I deserve to meet her, despite whatever catfight you might have had over Jack."

"It wasn't over Jack." Kelly rolled her eyes and hoped to hear her name called so she could escape this conversation. "I was upset she and Jack were together, yes, but Sarah and I fought for other reasons. And you're right. I was harsh and difficult with her. I know that. I also know that's why we *aren't* contacting them."

Allie leaned back in her chair to catch her mother's eyes. "Mom, has it occurred to you that you owe Sarah an apology? She came all that way, thrilled at the idea of meeting her lovely ancestor and she ran into a 'harsh, difficult buzzsaw' instead."

She paused as Kelly squinted her eyes at the insult. "I was hardly a *buzzsaw*, Allie," Kelly said, her eyes flashing.

Allie continued, "More like buzz*kill*, maybe. But you weren't nice. And now we have this fascinating opportunity to meet our time-traveling descendant from generations away. Why in the world wouldn't we do that?"

"I'm being treated for cancer, Allie." Kelly closed her eyes and listened to her stomach groan and churn. "That's all I can think about right now."

Allie resumed scrolling through her phone. "When this is over and you have a clean bill of health, Jem and I may just go without you," she said.

Kelly frowned. "You know what? Help yourselves. Go to Canada. Give them my best. You can explain who you are and Sarah will be thrilled to meet you. It's fine by me."

"I know you'd love to see Jack Warren again, Mom, you've made it clear he was special to you. And I believe you want to see Sarah, too, you're just too stubborn to admit it," Allie said.

"I had no idea she existed in this world," Kelly hissed. "The only reason I showed you girls—"

"Kelly Hopkins?" the nurse called, her arm extended.

"I'll be right here waiting for you, Mom," Allie told Kelly as her mother's form retreated toward the door, her shoulders hunched and every step dragging.

"You know," Kelly said, sipping water on the way home, "I was thinking about what you said, about a trip to look forward to." She stared out the window at passing stores and restaurants, most of which had been built during a rapid Huntsville-area expansion that seemed never-ending in its quest to gobble up land. The site of Giles' former bank was a Chick-Fil-A now, with two lines of cars streaming constantly in the drive-thru lanes. Kelly watched the boys and girls taking orders from drivers, knowing each was wishing customers a "blessed day." The marquee sign out front read THERE'S GRACE IN FORGIVENESS. Kelly chewed an ice cube and pondered whether the sign was meant for her. "I admit, Allie, I'm scared to go see Sarah and Jack. I'm such a different person now and I'm sure they are, too. I look like hell. I feel like hell—"

"Not until you're ready, Mom. You *will* recover. There're two more weeks of this and then you'll start getting back to normal. And there's good reason to believe radiation is the end of your treatment and you won't need chemo. Dr. Lind said so," Allie replied. She gave her mother a minute to think and continued, "I could book tickets for two months from now. It'll be late April, with everything in bloom up there. I don't know if Jem can get away with Waverly in school and all, but you and I could make this trip together. We don't have to stay with Sarah and Jack. There are great hotels in Banff. You've seen for yourself, it's gorgeous. And I think a change of scenery will be just what you need. The mountains are practically magical and the air is therapeutic, too."

Kelly continued to stare out the window. "You and I both know we could find a change of scenery in North Carolina or Maine, Allie, so let's not pretend that's why you keep harping on Banff." Kelly closed her eyes before continuing. "I suppose I should go and let you meet her. Let her meet *you*. But if we're going to do this, I don't want you to reach out to Jack and Sarah yet. We can buy the plane tickets and if they have to be changed, that's easy, we'll go somewhere else. But once you contact Jack and Sarah, there's no turning back. So, wait, Allie. I need to see how I'm feeling closer to then." She thought for a minute and added, "Sarah and Jack may not want us to visit. There's no reason to think they would. They might tell you so."

That was all she said and Allie knew enough to stay quiet the rest of the way home, lest she disturb the balance of the delicate decision Kelly was weighing. Allie didn't dare mention she wanted to invite Sarah and Jack to Ashley's MIT graduation at the end of May, where Jem could meet them, too. Kelly was already dangerously close to shutting down the idea of a reunion without the added pressure introducing Ashley would bring. She still wasn't sure she'd even tell her own daughter who Sarah *was*. Probably not. Ashley was a brilliant, lovely girl about to begin life after college, starting with a trip to Costa Rica she and her friends had been planning for a year. A time-traveling great-granddaughter was definitely not in order at this point in Ashley's life.

Allie thought about Sarah beholding her great-great-great, great-great, and great-grandmothers all together in Cambridge. She had so many questions for her, ranging from those concerning Ashley's future to the future of the world in general. "You know, Mom, the whole time-travel thing is still accompanied in my head by *X-Files* theme music. I can't even tell Carl, because he'll think I've lost it. Jem and I have pored over that note a hundred times and we can't explain it away. We've enlarged and stared at Sarah's face in that Facebook photo and damned if she doesn't have my green eyes. Yours too, Mom."

"I know she does." Kelly swallowed hard. *Grace in forgiveness. Stupid Chick-Fil-A sign. I wish I'd never told Allie and Jem.* But what Kelly said was, "It's only natural that you want to meet her. I can understand that. If you want to call after three more weeks, go ahead. I'll go with you in April if they agree and I'm well enough. *Only* if I'm well enough. But again, Allie, Jack and Sarah may have no interest in seeing us at all." She rested her head on the cool glass of the car's window with a deep sigh, picturing the scenery Allie had shown her. *I've always loved majestic mountains and glacial lakes and bizarre confrontations with my former crush and his time-traveling wife who claims to be my descendant.* For reasons Kelly didn't understand, she found herself wiping a tear hurriedly before Allie could see.

Two months later at Calgary Airport, Kelly refused Allie's offer to steer her rolling suitcase as well as her offer to drive the rental car. They rode mostly in silence, commenting only when the mountains jumped into view and refused to be ignored.

"They're even prettier than I imagined they'd be," Allie said thoughtfully.

"They're majestic, all right. I still prefer the Swiss Alps," her mother replied.

Allie rolled her eyes and refused to ask her mother why. The last thing she wanted was a thirty-minute travelogue from Kelly.

As they approached the Rimrock Resort Hotel, a uniformed valet took the car and derby-wearing bellmen in vests competed to fuss over the two women. "Name's Archie," the guy pushing their luggage cart announced in a British accent. "Where might you beautiful ladies be from?"

Kelly stared at him. "Alabama," she answered. "And you aren't Canadian."

"You'll find the personnel in this hotel come from all over the world, even the nether regions of Surrey." He opened the door to their room with a flourish and showed them the astounding mountain view. "Roll Tide," Archie pronounced to Kelly with a grin, placing her suitcase on a stand.

"Cosine, secant, tangent, sine, 3 point 1 4 1 5 9. Integral, radical, mu, dv. Slipstick, sliderule, MIT!" Kelly chanted back, her brows raised at Archie. "Massachusetts Institute of Technology Engineers fight song. There's more to Alabama—"

Allie stepped forward to interrupt. "Thank you, Archie," she said, handing him an American twenty. "Sorry, it's all I have right now."

Archie beamed a smile at her and bowed slightly as he left the room. "No worries at all, madam. Enjoy your stay."

"I'm pretty sure we're out of the running for favorite guests now, Mom. Geez, did you have to say all that?" Allie said, watching her mother flop onto her bed near the window. "At least you didn't inform him the Airbus 320 we flew on to Canada was built in Alabama. I *really* don't think that flight attendant cared."

Kelly ignored her and studied the mountains. "What time are they coming tomorrow?"

"At noon for lunch," Allie answered. "Get some rest, Mom. I think we both need a nap."

The Rimrock's huge dining room was combined with a lounging area; leather sofas and warm dark wood everywhere was accented by softly glowing chandeliers and a stunning bank of floor-to-ceiling windows revealing postcard mountain views. At the center a massive fireplace roared, comfortable even in late April. Dining tables sat beside the windows, and Allie noticed doors leading to a balcony hanging over the hotel grounds, offering a closer view of nearby peaks.

"We should've come here last night," Allie told her mother. "This place is gorgeous."

"Room service was fine," Kelly answered, distracted by the views. She stood in place, her hands clasped and worrying each other, while Allie went to consult a hostess about seating. In the distance, Kelly could hear the soft chords of Beethoven's *Moonlight Sonata* drifting from the room's grand piano as a man played, his back to her. A lady stood next to the pianist, the long white hair cascading between her shoulder blades marking her as Kelly's age. Groups of tourists sipped mid-day cocktails in the chairs and sofas surrounding the fireplace, most regarding the pianist's flourishes with smiles and nods.

Allie took her mother's arm and guided her to a table boasting a superb overlook. "She said we can sit anywhere we want." A server handed them menus and Kelly immediately ordered a glass of prosecco. It was delivered right away and she drained it to the final notes of the sonata, a little sad to hear it end.

As she ordered a second glass, the elderly couple from the piano appeared at their table. Allie jumped up and impulsively hugged Sarah, whom Kelly recognized right away as the admiring piano fan she'd viewed from behind. She noticed Sarah's hair flowed past her shoulders like snow running down a mountainside in the *front*, too. Her green eyes sparkled with a smile that others in the dining room seemed to be admiring. Kelly was torn between focusing on her resentment at Sarah's looks and the awkwardness of the situation.

Jack stood at Sarah's side wearing a black cashmere sweater and jeans. When he grinned at her, Kelly felt tears form in her eyes. Here was the face of the boy she'd known in the 1960s, pure and simple. Kelly stood and stepped into Jack's waiting arms for a hug.

"I don't even know what to say," she whispered to him.

"None of us do," he whispered back. He released Kelly and pushed her chair in as she sat, taking a seat next to her and signaling to their server in the distance. Allie sat staring at Sarah as though she were a statue in the Louvre dressed in a mid-calf burgundy skirt and matching sweater.

Kelly turned to Jack to say, "I'd forgotten you play piano."

"Yeah, they have me over here most Friday evenings during dinner. I asked for permission to play today." Jack accepted a bourbon on the rocks from a young lady who delivered a glass of white wine to Sarah. Kelly realized the two of them were well-known in this hotel and wondered if Allie had known that when she booked it. Sarah was reciprocating Allie's stares and Kelly sighed.

She turned to Jack and said in a low voice, "While those two examine each other, catch me up on the last fifty-five years. You have a son? When did you leave Ottawa? When did *she* come back from her mysterious disappearance?" Kelly hadn't thought Sarah was listening.

"I came back about seven months from the time I was taken to Unity in 1969, but more than a year had passed there. I wanted to get back before Jack established a new life without me, so we timed it that way. I explained my sudden reappearance by saying I'd left home again because I had a baby I had to get away from my family in South Dakota. I know that's lame, but it was the best thing I could come up with. No one was very happy with us after I reappeared, especially not Jack's girlfriend. There was no way I could begin to disclose what had really taken place," Sarah said, sipping her wine.

"She wasn't my girlfriend, Sarah—" Jack began.

"Anyway, I went to his house and waited on the doorstep with Jackson for him to return from his date with Mary. It was raining that night. I didn't mind, but Jackson did. He cried for two hours as we sat there," Sarah said. "Jack came roaring up in this ridiculous car—"

"Wait," Jack interrupted. "Let me show you the love of my life." He produced a photo from his wallet of Sarah, all long brown hair and hip huggers and wide grin, leaning against a bright red '67 Camaro. He handed it to Kelly.

"Wow, you're as beautiful as I remember you," Kelly said to Sarah, passing the photo to Allie.

"I meant the Camaro," Jack said, chuckling into his bourbon.

"That car was a terror to me," Sarah told them. "I had to hold Jackson on my lap everywhere we went and frantically hope we wouldn't have an accident. I spent most of my time in it with my eyes tightly shut. I finally talked him into buying a nice used Volvo with seat belts." She shot Jack a look and continued, "Jackson was such a miniature Jack, he knew he was his son, no matter how strange the circumstances. But it took me a very long time to convince him where I was from and why I'd disappeared."

"About a year," Jack said, gulping his drink. "But I was so thrilled to have you back, it didn't matter. Poor Mary's a nice girl, ended up married to a local barrister and has six children and fifteen grandchildren. But at the time, she was both furious and trying to appear empathetic about my missing girlfriend suddenly reappearing. With a *baby*."

Allie blinked at Sarah. "Did you know you were pregnant when they took you back? To what did you call it? Unity?"

"No," Sarah said. "That was a shock. To make a very long story short, Unity is a society in which scientists have achieved what they determine to be human genetic near-perfection, eliminating disease and dramatically prolonging lifespans. So, Jackson was fascinating to them, the only known specimen of mid-twentieth century genes mixed with their ultimate late-twenty-first. They began conducting experiments—"

Jack interrupted her. "It was horrible and we don't like to talk about it. And Sarah's mother, Anantha, was well-connected with the time travel people. In order to save her daughter and grandson from enduring endless tests and being ostracized every day of their lives, Anantha worked out a way to send them back herself, without any way to trace them. It was a great sacrifice she made, but she couldn't bear to see what they were going through."

Sarah sighed. "It's a lot to process. That's one reason you've never heard from me, Kelly."

Kelly frowned. "So, where is Jackson now?"

"He lives under an assumed name in Los Angeles. We didn't want to risk any possibility they'd ever find him, because Jackson is far more interesting to them than I am. Me...well, I'm pretty sure Unity leadership was glad to see me gone," Sarah said. "Jackson is a spectacular keyboardist who plays studio sessions for recordings. I'm sure you've heard him on your favorite songs. He has a wife named Terri and a daughter, Kaitlyn, who's starting at UCLA this fall."

"Wow," Allie said. "That *is* a lot."

All eyes turned to Kelly, who swallowed her prosecco the wrong way and coughed. "I'm fine, I'm fine," she gasped. Their server stood at a discreet distance waiting to take their lunch order, approaching only when Kelly quieted.

As he walked away, Sarah said, "I know we all have so many questions for each other. We'll have time to discuss it all. But if it's okay with you and Allie, Jack, I'd like to take a walk with Kelly after lunch. There's a beautiful trail nearby." Jack and Allie nodded.

Kelly coughed again and was pretty sure her stomach had leapt into her throat and lodged there. "Sure," she told Sarah.

"How did you come to live here, in this gorgeous place?" Allie asked. "Did you leave Ottawa right away when Sarah came back?"

Jack grinned. "Not right away. The person who was second-happiest to see Sarah return was an old man named Alex Landry—gosh, he was younger than I am now." Jack shook his head. "Mr. Landry owned the motel where we lived when we arrived in Ottawa. He was so good to us. He even got me a job." Jack looked out the window at the mountains. "When Sarah came back, he was planning a wedding in Banff to a woman Sarah introduced him to, a lady named Valerie Campbell. We came here with them for the ceremony, which was very lavish compared to our city hall wedding a month before. Sarah and I both loved the area and eventually I got a job at the University of Alberta in Edmonton. We moved to Canmore when I retired eleven years ago." He glanced at Kelly. "I feel like this conversation is one-sided. Tell us about your life, Kelly. Obviously, you have a beautiful daughter." He nodded at Allie.

"I have two beautiful daughters," Kelly answered. "The younger one is named Jem, and she's home with her six-year-old, Waverly, in Alabama." Kelly took a deep breath and looked at Sarah. "This seems ridiculous when you already know it," she said to her. "You know everything."

Sarah swung her head back and forth. "I really don't. Just the historical highlights I was able to discern in 2101."

Kelly looked around their table to make sure no one was listening. "Well, I married a wonderful man named Giles Hopkins in 1971. I continued my education at MIT and was eventually recruited by NASA. We moved to Huntsville then, in 1978." She stopped talking and looked down.

"Mom is too modest to brag on her accomplishments, but she's had a stellar career. The last year has been a really rough one, though," Allie said as her mother's head jerked to attention. Despite Kelly's glare, she continued, "My dad passed away a year and a half ago. They were married for over fifty years, so you can imagine how difficult it's been. And more recently, she's been treated successfully for cancer, and that was a very...challenging and painful time."

"Allie, none of that is necessary to bring up," Kelly said. "I'm absolutely fine," she informed Jack and Sarah.

Allie inclined her head slightly at Jack as their food was served, and Kelly had the uncomfortable feeling Allie would be sharing all sorts of personal details with him while she and Sarah went for a walk. She stabbed at her salad and wished for another fortifying glass of prosecco before Sarah confronted her in private, but their server had disappeared before she could ask. Later, Kelly watched Sarah savor a chocolate tart while she sipped her third glass of prosecco and hoped desperately Sarah would decide to go home and take a nap after all that sugar.

As they climbed down the flower-lined path toward the valley, Sarah said, "This is far enough," indicating a wood bench for the two of them to sit on, out of sight from the restaurant.

Kelly settled next to Sarah and tried to prepare herself for whatever was coming. Guilt settled over her like a fine dark mist as she thought of the way she'd treated Sarah in 1969. Kelly looked into the distance, refusing to meet Sarah's eyes. Echoes of her voice at Woodstock ran through her brain.

I don't like you, Sarah, whoever you are. But I want you to know I'll be nice to you for his sake. You barely know him. And you never will.

"You've been through a lot lately," Sarah began. "I'm sorry for the pain you've endured."

"But you can't wait to tell me how I screwed up all those years ago," Kelly said. "I already know, Sarah." She noticed the amber bead dangling from Sarah's arm, glinting in the sunlight. "It's amazing you still have that bracelet," she said. "Did it travel to the future with you?"

Sarah held up her arm and admired it. "Yes, it did. It got me through some pretty horrible stuff. The lady in the Bindy Bazaar told us the amber has magical properties that absorb bad energy and make you all peaceful and calm." Sarah looked ahead at the mountains, avoiding Kelly's gaze. "Kezia said a lot of things, actually. One of them was that you needed something from me."

"Oh, really?" Kelly said, noticing Sarah fumbling with the clasp of her bracelet. She frowned at Sarah as she reached for her arm and placed it there, fastening it on Kelly's right wrist.

"This should be with you for the time being," Sarah said. "We have a saying where I'm from, 'carrying you with me', and it means in a literal sense. Friends and family might, for instance, borrow a piece of jewelry or a clothing fastener or anything at all, and keep it with them to *carry* that person along. I want something from me with you."

Kelly held out her arm. "I couldn't possibly take this from you," she told Sarah.

"Well, you can and you will," Sarah said, her eyes shiny. "I'll get it back from you someday. It'll remind you of me and this moment. The part about the amber and the bad energy is probably absolute bullshit, though," she added.

Kelly laughed along with Sarah and rubbed the amber bead, admiring its deep reddish-gold color. "I don't know, I think my finger feels sedate," Kelly said.

Sarah turned serious and held Kelly's eyes. "I want you to know I forgive you, Kelly, for all the things you did and said. I put you in an impossible situation, never thinking how outrageous my story would sound to you."

Kelly spoke her words carefully, trying not to reveal the urge she had to cry. "What makes you think I need your forgiveness after all these years, Sarah?"

Sarah said, "I know you better than you think. And I love you, Kelly, I have all along. Let's forgive each other, right now. Forgiveness takes us back to the people we were and lets us start over. It's kind of like time-travel. We can change our lives this way."

Kelly considered Sarah's words for a moment and looked away, muttering, "I'm sorry." She swiped at her eyes. "I was so mad at you for monopolizing Jack, for being everything I wasn't. For your joy and spontaneity. I was a starched white blouse and you were a…gauzy peasant top. Jack saw the difference in us as soon as you two met."

Sarah exhaled a long breath and shook her head. "Want to hear something ironic? If you hadn't taken my NourishCubes and tossed them into the port-o-let, I might not have fallen in love with Jack. I really do wonder about that. Those NCs were designed to suppress sexual attraction until the right time in my life, what we called the 'Reproduction Cycle'. And I've long suspected they kept my emotions on an even keel, too. Not in a sinister way, just *supportive*." Sarah blinked. "I love Jack Warren with every bit of my being and I always will. But I think I might have missed the experience we shared at Woodstock if I'd continued my NCs. I might not have been so irresistibly drawn to him. They likely would have ruined it."

Kelly stared at Sarah for a moment and then turned away, directing her speech upward to the mountain peak in front of them. "Well, that's devastating to hear, Sarah, I won't lie to you. I was so damned bitter when I found out you went to Canada with him. It took me a long time to get over that."

Sarah waited a moment and then reached to swivel Kelly's face to her own with a fingertip. "There's more than what you know, Kelly. I did that because in the original version of events in 1969, Jack missed his ride at Woodstock and ended up being drafted into the army after returning to Boston. He died in an explosion six weeks after he arrived in Vietnam in June, 1970. His armored personnel carrier ran over something and blew up."

Kelly blinked at her. "Oh, God. I…" she managed to eke out through her tears. "I never…I loved him back then, you know."

Sarah nodded. "I know. I grew to love him, too. So much I couldn't let that happen." She bit her lower lip, a gesture familiar to Kelly from herself and both her girls. "The way history had recorded it, you were emotionally devastated when Jack died. You went on to marry Giles, but the pain of Jack's death haunted you for years. I read journals you'd written." She grasped Kelly's hand. "And he has no idea, Kelly. I never wanted to see the effect that knowledge would have on Jack. I married him without telling him. I've lived with him for *fifty years* without telling him. If he started contemplating the impact of what we did…" Sarah paused and added, "It all worked out for the best, Kelly. You've had a wonderful life with Giles, with your family, as it was always meant to be. And you really *do* have twenty-one more years of time to treasure them."

Sarah's voice trailed off as Kelly put her face into her hands, unable to react with words. When Kelly recovered herself, she focused on the bracelet, desperate to avoid any more revelations.

She said, "This is lovely, but I really can't keep it."

"Of course you can," Sarah said. "It's a reverse family heirloom." She reached for Kelly's hand. "I promise, that's all the difficult stuff I had to tell you. Now come on, I want to show you something." She pulled Kelly to her feet and both women wiped the last traces of tears from their cheeks. They walked back into the hotel, feeling Jack and Allie's eyes tracking their path along the way through the windows above.

Instead of going toward the restaurant, Sarah turned down a hall lined with framed art, huge showy pieces of local scenes on display. She stopped in front of an oil painting that looked like the most colorful Aurora Borealis ever seen, with translucent swaths of pink and purple and yellow and green in the sky among brilliant white stars that seemed to glow on the canvas.

"This is what I do," Sarah said, pointing out her signature at the bottom right of the painting. "I've been an artist for many years. My favorite subject is Kelly's Sky, which everyone believes is a particularly wild and vivid version of the Northern Lights we see here. But it's not. Thanks for the inspiration."

Kelly laughed. "I don't believe this. How dare you?"

"I'm your great-great-great granddaughter," Sarah answered. "The idea's my inherited intellectual property, I believe. And I'll get that bracelet back when we visit you in Huntsville, Kelly. We want to visit. I want you to show me what the city was like."

Kelly felt her legs weaken and sat down opposite the painting on a velvet bench. "Is it awful? What happens? What changes everything?"

Sarah settled next to her. "Not awful at all. No one loses their lives. It's a change for the better, assisted by exponential progress in artificial intelligence and strides in genetic manipulation. There's so much talk about the evils of AI now, but people are wrong to worry. Humans can and will steward it into improving all our lives. I loved my home; I loved my life there. The only bad thing that ever happened to me in Unity was being punished for altering Jack's timeline and, of course, the way the geneticists used Jackson. But they had their reasons. I understood that."

"Do you miss it?" Kelly asked.

"There are a lot of conveniences I miss. But mostly, I miss my mom. Every minute of every day, I miss my mom. I've tried to keep a record of Jackson for her to see in Facebook archives, one that doesn't disclose anything about his whereabouts. Keeping him safe is everything to me," Sarah said.

"It is to any mother, isn't it?" Kelly answered. "*Like mothers since the beginning of time, she broke her own heart and used the pieces to fix mine.* I love that quote."

"Thank you. I thought of that and had to show my mom," Sarah said. "Anantha is an incredibly special woman and she deserves all the credit for saving Jackson and me. She'll be thrilled to know we've reconnected. I'll post something about that tonight."

"How old is your mother now, anyway?" Kelly asked.

Sarah offered her a bright smile. "She will have just celebrated her one-hundred-and-fifth birthday. But bear in mind, people in her time have a life expectancy of a hundred and fifty years. I put all these things on social media for her to see, but she has no way to safely communicate back to me. And what she's viewing all happened well over a century before her time. She'll know about things I haven't experienced yet; it's an archive."

Kelly looked at Sarah. "Do you have a life expectancy of a hundred and fifty? Does Jackson?"

Sarah raised her brows. "I'm pretty sure traveling back here destroyed that. It has to do with more than genetics. For one thing, those NourishCubes are perfect nutrition, as opposed to the fifty years of pizza and chocolate I've grown to love." Her mouth twitched into a smile. "And that's fine by me."

"I don't even know what to say to that," Kelly replied. She took one last look at the painting, cocking her head to one side. "How many of these have you done, anyway?"

"About eighty," Sarah said. "They sell really well. Maybe because I've never acknowledged they're based on my great-great-great grandmother's hallucinations."

"I won't tell if you won't. There are some secrets worth keeping." Kelly reached for Sarah's hand and they walked to find Allie and Jack. *Forgiveness as a reset, a new start.* Kelly's mind danced with the idea as she looked over at Sarah. Together, they entered a future that was both familiar and foreign, certainty and uncertainty lost to anywhen in time.

THE END

Author's Notes

I have taken minor liberties with the geography of the Woodstock festival site, perhaps ushering my characters from Point A to Point B(indy) a little faster than possible. There really was a cornfield down the road for Kelly to trip in, though.

I also present my artistic license about the time at which Joan Baez took the small Free Stage near the Hog Farm kitchen. No one, not even Joan, seems sure when that was. There is one account placing her appearance there around three p.m. Saturday, and that worked beautifully for me. It's unlikely she had to stand in line to sing, but I could easily imagine her doing so. In addition, I believe Country Joe McDonald initially appeared without his Fish, but the iconic "I Feel Like I'm Fixing to Die Rag" is so associated with the band, I chose to include it that way.

Steven Tyler, then Tallarico, was a Woodstock attendee the year before the formation of Aerosmith (Joe Perry was there, too). I sincerely hope Mr. Tyler, one of my musical heroes, won't be offended at the insinuation that he may have smoked marijuana.

Did a helicopter drop daisies, or flower petals, on the crowd at Woodstock? There are many who claim to have witnessed it. I absolutely love the imagery, so it's a part of *Anywhen*.

The food shortages at Woodstock are well-documented. The local folks who made and sent sandwiches, the U.S. government's assistance, and the sharing of food among strangers are, too. I doubt any attendees came with a VW bus full of groceries gathered by a hungry pregnant woman who loved to bake—a veritable Mary Poppins' bag of goodies in a relatively small vehicle—but bear with me on that. I didn't want my people spending too much time foraging.

The Vietnam War was a highly controversial subject in 1969, and I've tried to accurately represent the typical pro-peace attitudes of those who attended Woodstock.

However, one of the people I love most in this world fought bravely in that war, my uncle Lt. Colonel Maurice Holder. Reese is among my heroes and I both respect and honor his service and that of his family. The same is true of many others I hold dear who are proud Vietnam veterans.

David Boyd served in the war after Woodstock was held in 1969, but graciously allowed me to place him there for a conversation with Jack. David is a good friend and I will always be grateful to him for enhancing their dialogue with his words and ideas. He added credibility and a lot of texture to his namesake. You should know he actually made and wore those leather-insert bell bottom jeans and cool shirt! As a proud fifth-generation Floridian, he still sports that alligator belt buckle, too.

I used names of some others I know (who are mostly nothing like their characters). There has been a good-luck Kristin in all my books since *It All Comes Back to You* to honor my friend Kris Gause. To the best of my knowledge, she's never eaten pineapple upside-down cake with her hands.

Lillian and Tony Pizzo are beloved friends who let me use their names for some Woodstock attendees Jack helped. In real life, Tony would have CARRIED an ankle-injured Lil to see Joan Baez. Lillian does possess a New York accent, and it was she who suggested "awwf" for off, "cawwl" for call and "lawng" for long. Lillian's sweet sister's name really is Nancy, so she's in this novel, too.

Dr. Jacquie Tessen is one of my favorite people and the world's best gynecologist, much better than the one who attended Baezy in 2102. She's also a writer and when she releases her debut novel, I'll be first in line to buy it.

Kelly Adams has wanted me to use her name for a character for years. I don't know if she shares *Anywhen* Kelly's mathematical brilliance, but she's a devoted reader. The real Kelly is warm and kind and not at all prickly like the one in this book—but they *do* share those pretty green eyes.

These folks are too young to have attended Woodstock, by the way. They'll be mad if I don't tell you that.

I thank them all for allowing my name-drops.

Finally, after this manuscript was completed, I received an email from Dr. Neal Hitch, Senior Curator of The Museum at Bethel Woods. He'd just unearthed a quote to share with me:

"While you were playing, you could feel the presence of invisible time travelers from the future who had come back to see Woodstock."

Jerry Garcia, co-founder of The Grateful Dead

Mind, blown. That's a great idea for a book.

Acknowledgments

The book you're holding would have been impossible without my engaging the hearts and minds of seven very special people. They offered invaluable insights, chapter by chapter. My early reader team is filled with avid bibliophiles I love and appreciate, and they are listed in alphabetical order so I don't lose my mind trying to arrange their names fittingly:

Marianne Barnebey

David Boyd

Kninah Bradley

Savannah Fish

Lillian Pizzo

Patricia Poucher

Debbie Tuckerman

I am forever grateful to two Woodstock attendees, Jill Schneidman Cohen and Linda Whelan, for sharing their extremely contrasting experiences there. The heart of the two accounts is the same, though: both emphasized over and over how the atmosphere at Woodstock '69 was one of sharing and taking care of one another. That's a theme I've heard and read countless times, the essence of the festival.

I had the most wonderful weekend with gracious hosts Deneen and Neal Hitch when I visited Bethel, New York to research The Woodstock Music and Art Fair of 1969. They were exceedingly kind and a lot of fun. Dr. Neal Hitch is the perfect person to serve as Senior Curator of The Museum at Bethel Woods. He has an exhaustive knowledge of music (I'm pretty sure he mentioned curating some of his playlists by guitar chords and drumbeats), a master's degree in American history as well as a doctorate in philosophy…and those are just a couple of highlights. He and Deneen allowed me to stand where my characters stood, to see what they'd seen. Neal showed me artifacts from the site: a makeup brush, a bread wrapper, dented metal camping cups, each still whispering their stories after fifty-five years.

Perhaps the best summary of Dr. Hitch's devotion to Woodstock is this, which he said to me as he and Deneen rushed to get me to my departing train to the airport: "Working within the Woodstock Nation is a lot like working in a church. You're working with people that have core beliefs and personal experiences who want to be in fellowship with one another, who feel like they've had an experience they want to tell others about, and a deep belief in peace and love."

I thoroughly enjoyed my tour of The Museum at Bethel Woods, which is a beautiful and thoughtful assemblage of historical displays that go back to the formative years that impacted the tastes and attitudes of attendees, the 1950s, and continue through a fascinating look at all things Woodstock. I came to understand what shaped the Woodstock Nation through the brilliant insights of my tour guide, Jim Shelley. Jim was an attendee, a working class kid without anything particular in common with the stereotypical image of hippies. He made me feel like a 19-year-old boy in 1969, completely immersed in the times and the experience of those who were there. This book is better for the museum tour, and I am better for having met Jim.

My editors, Jodi Warshaw and Alison Jack, brought their unique talents to both the story as a whole and each line as a vital component. I thank them very much.

Anywhen is beautiful inside and out because of Rachael Gartman and Rachel Lawston, respectively. I'm not sure I can ever have a new novel without each of those wonderful, kind, spectacularly gifted ladies.

Many thanks to one of my favorite authors, Karen Emilson, for reading an advance copy of this book and offering a delightful quote for its cover. Karen also served as my Canadian Sensitivity Reader. If you haven't read her books, make them your next (my personal choice is *Be Still the Water*).

I thank my husband Jay for having the patience of a saint whilst enduring the writing of yet *another* hundred thousand words by his wife, whose brain was often bouncing between the years 2101 and 1969, occasionally visiting 2024 to say hi and act normal. He, Jason, Savannah, Matt, and my mom Patricia are my world.

Finally, it's always about you, Reader, and I hope you loved this one. *Anywhen* is my novel especially intended for book clubs. As the dedication says, you've given me so much and I designed this one to be a lot of fun for your meetings. If you want, I'll be there with bells (bell bottoms) on, if at all possible. Email beth@bethduke.com to schedule.

Beth Duke
September 2024

Book Club Discussion Guide

Gather around a pineapple upside down cake
and talk about these and other aspects of ANYWHEN:

1. What do you think about G-HOP, the Genetic Homogenization and Optimization Project, that essentially eliminated distinct racial characteristics in Baezy's society?

2. The "Reproduction Cycle" in Unity guarantees a perfectly compatible mate, "falling in love", and joy for the participants. Would you appreciate the opportunity to experience this designed union, rather than search for it?

3. In addition, Unity has eliminated hunger and prolonged human lifespans significantly via the replacement of traditional foods with NourishCubes specifically designed for each person and their health support. Can you imagine this? Would you be willing to accept it to completely eliminate hunger?

4. What would your AI glitch animal be?

5. In Baezy's utopian society, artificial intelligence has been harnessed to improve the lives of its citizens rather than presenting the threat many have predicted for our futures. Do you think that's possible, or likely?

6. Baezy's world is fully climate controlled. What impact would the elimination of weather have on human behavior? Would the end of global warming, natural disasters like hurricanes and tornadoes, and gloomy days be a positive change, or could this affect people in a negative way?

7. Given a chance to learn anything within an extremely short period with no effort (like Baezy did with the Lakota Sioux language), what one topic would you select?

8. If you were presented the opportunity to time travel, what and when would be your destination?

9. Sixties counterculture was the product of more than opposition to the Vietnam War; it was preceded by a decade of prosperity and conservatism in the United States, and represented a quantum shift in attitude. In what ways did this happen?

10. "There's no need to be vulgar or start all that women's lib crap with me, Kelly," Dr. Lawton says in 1969. Do women of later generations understand the struggle for female equality in that time? Have we achieved it?

11. What is your favorite Woodstock music? Would you have enjoyed the festival?

12. Baezy's society has no currency; money is of no use. Does this represent the realization of the ideals of the hippie movement?

13. If you had the opportunity to meet your great-great-great grandmother in her time, how do you think she'd receive you as a person? Would she be proud? Would she see herself in you?

14. What do you think of Jack's decision to avoid the draft by going to Canada?

15. "I think I'm falling on you" is one of Baezy/Sarah's many mangled metaphors, idioms, and bits of slang. If a person's understanding of a language is strictly literal, what other common phrases might cause them problems?

16. The *Boston Globe* reported, "The Woodstock Music and Art Festival will surely go down in history as a mass event of great and positive significance in the life of the country…that this many young people could assemble so peaceably and with such good humor in a mile-square area…speaks volumes about their dedication to the ideal of respect for the dignity of the individual. In a nation beset with a crescendo of violence, this is a vibrantly hopeful sign. If violence is infectious, so, happily, is nonviolence." Does this capture what actually happened in 1969? Do you feel the festival was truly a seminal moment in history?

17. Were you surprised by Sarah's decision to accompany Jack to Canada, and her previously unrevealed reason why? Was the punishment for her actions she received in Unity fair? Should it have been more harsh?

18. *Chocolate. Cake. Pizza.* These are things Baezy misses desperately when she's returned to the future. What would you miss desperately if transported to Unity?

19. "Like mothers since the beginning of time, she broke her own heart and used the pieces to fix mine," Sarah/Baezy wrote of Anantha's sacrifice. Does this reflect your knowledge and experience of mothers and their children?

20. "Forgiveness takes us back to the people we were and lets us start over. It's kind of like time-travel. We can change our lives this way," Sarah tells Kelly. Do you think this is true?

Also by Beth Duke

Delaney's People

Don't Shoot Your Mule

It All Comes Back to You

Tapestry

Dark Enough to See the Stars

BETH DUKE is an Amazon #1 Best Selling Author and the recipient of numerous awards and honors for her fiction on two continents. She is eyeing the other five.

Beth lives in the mountains of her native Alabama with her husband Jay and an assortment of dogs—including a recently-rescued coonhound named Daisy who has stolen her heart. Beth is the adoring and proud mother of Jason, Savannah, and her new son-in-law, Matt. She is a constant reader, travel aficionado, and likes to pretend she's in baking competitions.

Her brain is absolutely stuffed with trivia and she wins every round of *Jeopardy* from her living room sofa. However, she would be a combination of a deer, a rabbit, and a Rhode Island Red quaking in the headlights of the studio.

Beth finds great joy in joining book clubs for discussion (usually via Zoom). If your group would like to schedule a date, please email beth@bethduke.com.

Her books DELANEY'S PEOPLE, DON'T SHOOT YOUR MULE, IT ALL COMES BACK TO YOU, TAPESTRY, DARK ENOUGH TO SEE THE STARS and yes, ANYWHEN, are all love letters to her home state.

Huntsville, Alabama is one of her favorite cities for many reasons.

For more information and lots of photos, including the most beautiful readers in the world, please visit **www.bethduke.com**.

The Museum at Bethel Woods, Bethel, New York
Site of the historic Woodstock Music and Art Fair of 1969
June 8, 2024

www.ingramcontent.com/pod-product-compliance
Lightning Source LLC
Chambersburg PA
CBHW030145310726
48970CB00005B/1600